THE WOVEN RING

Sol's Harvest: Book I

by

M. D. PRESLEY

ISBN:
ISBN- 9781520615103

DEDICATION

To my wonderful wife, both the beauty and the brains behind the crime-fighting duo Baby and Baby.

Table of Contents

Maps

For more in-depth maps and info on the culture of Ayr, please visit mdpresley.com.

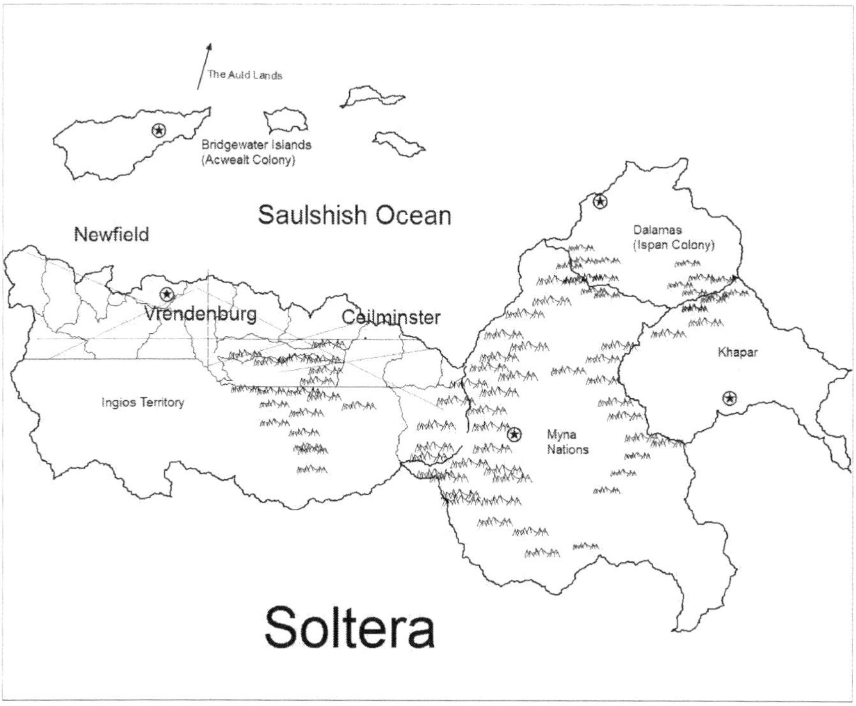

The West

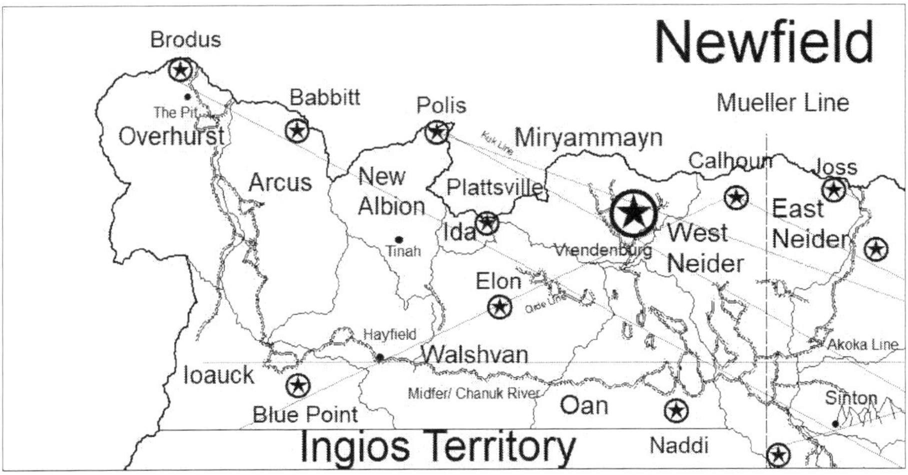

The East

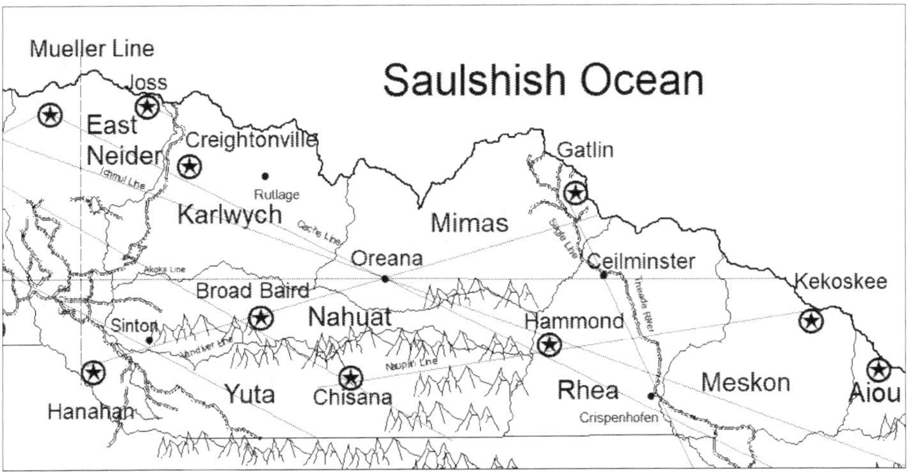

Lacus and Mynan Nations

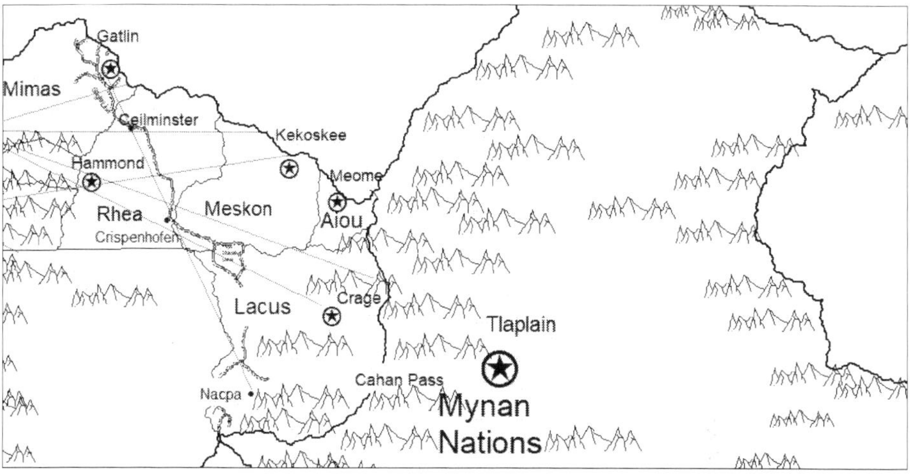

Seasons of Ayr

Spring	Marz
	Avril
	Maia
Summer	Iunius
	Iulius
	Weodmonad
Autumn	Septembris
	Winterfylled
	Blotmonad
Winter	Decembris
	Jenvier
	Solmonad

Prologue

Solmonad 9, 561 (Six Years Ago)

In the beginning there was Sol.

Ed Oldham cared little for the scriptures, but he could not escape them. In his eight and twenty years, he had not found a use for a single line in the Biba Sacara, yet the words followed him everywhere and refused to leave him be.

His hands tightened on the grip of his musket, a weapon Ed never expected to handle. The steel was cold to the touch, the wooden stock not much warmer. Only the spark box gave off any heat, and Ed refused to touch it, lest he misalign the mechanism. The situation was dire enough that he dared not taunt fate further by even chancing to render his weapon inert.

Ed pulled his planters hat lower against the winter chill. Compared to his other compatriots, Ed was well-prepared. His wife had made sure he was outfitted with thick mittens and woolen long johns before stuffing his work boots with scraps of cotton cloth. Despite her forethought, his sack coat proved insufficient against the elements.

And Sol wandered the void, the black spaces between the stars, until His wanderings led Him to the empty Ayr. And upon finding Ayr Sol was pleased and marveled at its beauty.

Ed did not believe a single word of the scriptures, but the hardbound Biba Sacara was the crown jewel in his father's little library of three books. So it was the one his mother taught him and his siblings to read from, Ed forced to recite the scriptures each day before breakfast. The words were therefore indelibly linked with food and comfort in Ed's mind, the man unconsciously reciting them to invoke better times when he was worried.

And he certainly had reason to worry now that the nation of Newfield teetered at the brink of civil war.

No, he was no longer a citizen of Newfield. *Not any longer*, Ed reminded himself. Two weeks past his home state of Karlwych seceded from Newfield, the states Meskon, Rhea, and Mimas soon joining Karlwych to form their own country: the Covenant. With their defection the nation of Newfield fell into disarray, the newspapers declaring that the states of Yuta and Nahuat would soon join these rebels in their insurrection.

Their secession made sense to Ed. In a way it was a natural progression, the religious Weavers of the East demanding their own government separate from the Render dominion far to the West. The Eastern Weavers now just wanted from the Renders what the Renders desired in the first place when they fled religious persecution in the Auld Lands, and Ed saw no reason why they should not be allowed to worship however they saw fit. Not that Ed did much worshiping himself. Renders were known to hold solemn services in their kirks in the West, whereas the Weavers preferred to search for Sol in nature in the East. Ed did neither, and until this day had not met either a Render or a Weaver before. Yet he still found himself swept up in the eternal enmity of these two Blessed orders. Because they could not agree on the will of Sol, the nation of Newfield had split in two, Ed now awaiting the arrival of invaders that would have been his countrymen two weeks ago.

The Karlwych militia, of which Ed was now a member, numbered no more than forty men spread out on the edges of the main road into Karlwych, which was five miles from the border with the state of Neider. Some of the men were interspersed within the tree line, but the majority took up posts behind the Johnson's stone wall with their recently issued muskets. General Loree instructed them to hold this position and swear not to advance under any circumstance. Their purpose was to defend their new nation, he told them, not spark a war.

Ed should be among his fellow militia men, mostly farmers and toilers of the soil like him. He too should be hidden safely behind that sturdy stone wall. Instead he had been selected to wait far ahead of their defensive line in a gully off to the side of the road. Though concealed from sight by the earthen indentation, they would be in the middle of the battle. That alone was bad enough, but then Loree added insult to Ed's potential injury with the inclusion of his three Weaver companions. The four of them were the linchpin to Loree's strategy, the score of luz jars at their feet brimming with Breath and sure to turn the tide in their favor if called upon.

For eons Sol wandered the empty Ayr, enraptured at the land and waters so unlike the void He had known before. And so Sol knew He had found His home.

Ed did not adhere to either the Render or Weaver way, but were he forced to choose between them, he would certainly side with the more dignified Renders over the capricious Weavers. All three of the Weavers sharing his space in the gully were decked out in bright mismatched clothing. It was garish as Dobra garb and nothing any self-respecting man would wear. The woman was the worst. Disdaining a bonnet, she did not even bother to dress in a skirt like a proper lady would instead wearing woolen trousers similar to Ed's.

He must have stared too long at the woman, the Weaver gracing him with a grin. It was probably a friendly gesture, but Ed felt there was a willful edge to it as he turned to gaze back to the militia men. Again he wished he was with his fellow patriots behind the stone wall, but Loree had picked Ed personally because of his skill with the musket.

Most of the militia volunteers were woefully inaccurate, Ed barely above average himself. But Ed's fingers were dexterous, his hands steady, and for that reason he was fastest at reloading during their meager training. Though the process was new to him, it made sense to Ed. He found the tamping of the powder and wadding followed by the musket ball prior to setting the spark box to be a rhythmic activity somewhat similar to shucking corn. There on the training field, it was almost calming in its repetitive nature, but now that he found himself on the battlefield, he worried his hands might stray for his sword.

Ed felt far more comfortable with a saber, a real gentleman's weapon. Like all Eastern children, he grew up practicing swordplay with sticks, the boys imagining themselves knights, like in the tales of the Auld Lands. Ten years ago when Ed struck out to claim his own homestead, his father had gifted him with a saber to defend his property. That same saber sat in its scabbard beside him now, Ed tempted to set his musket down and claim it.

But nothing breathed upon the land or waters, nothing with life to share Ayr with Him. And so Sol despaired.

Again Ed mentally bemoaned the situation, one he should not even be a part of. Tensions between the Renders and the Weavers had been building for years, mostly over the treatment of Sol's Breath in the form of the festations that worked the plantations in the East. Only aristocrats were wealthy enough to commission a Weaver to create a festation, a mindless servant that would slavishly obey its owners until their death. The Renders swore this act of taking Breath out of Sol's flow for years at a time was blasphemy. For that reason each of the Western states made the owning of a festation illegal, but the practice remained common in the East, where the majority of the Weavers resided. The festation issue proved so thorny that eventually the high court was forced to declare the Weaver constructions to be a matter decided state by state.

President Ruhl did his best to ensure the matter was settled as he preached his peace between the two factions. They were all the Children of Sol, Ruhl reminded them, all made up of Sol's Breath be they followers of the Render or Weaver way. The Biba Sacara declared as much in the first book, stating:

The Children of Sol awoke to behold the beauty of Ayr and thanked Sol for His sacrifice. And they knew they were Sol's chosen because they reflected their creator and took dominion over the plants and animals, over all that swam in the sea, flew through the sky, or walked upon the land.

Ruhl was quick to quote the scriptures, always with another verse close at hand: *And it came to pass that the children of Sol multiplied across the face of Ayr, daughters and sons born unto them, each according to type. And the children of Sol became numerous, living together in peace in one great tribe that covered the land.*

Ed did not care much for Ruhl, had voted against him during the election, in fact, but he could not question the man's knowledge of the scriptures or his ability to lessen the tensions between the two factions. Because of Ruhl's tireless work crisscrossing the nation on the train network so the Newfield citizens could hear his pleas for peace personally, the uneasy truce over the festations held for nearly a year.

But then that damn Render Aloysius Pulley ruined it all. As brazen as a crow among carrion, Pulley marched right up to the emet in the city of Creightonville, the state capital of Karlwych, and severed its Breath with his glass blade.

For the life of him, Ed could not understand why Pulley would do such a thing. He had visited Creightonville several times to purchase supplies and had seen the emet there with his own eyes. It was benevolent, an engel if ever there was one, and so Pulley was arrested for its slaughter. Within a matter of days, the Karlwych court declared that because the emet contained a Soul Breath like a man, the Render's act was tantamount to murder. And so

Pulley was sentenced to death.

It should have been settled then and there: Pulley tried and sentenced in the state he committed his crime in; however, then President Ruhl overstepped himself, ceding to the demands of the Renders by giving a presidential pardon to Pulley. Such an affront to justice was something the Easterners could not abide, and so the state of Karlwych seceded from Newfield. They were the first, but the other Eastern states soon joined them in forming their own Covenant nation. Backed into a corner by these breakaway states, Ruhl faltered again by sending federal troops to reclaim Pulley.

Ed racked his mind for another scripture, but all the words fled his head as soon as he heard the tattoo of the snare drums. The rhythm was that of a march and it approached beat by steady beat. He strained his ears, but Ed could not catch the trod of boots hidden beneath the drums, though he was sure they were there. Even the feckless Weavers in the gully with him seemed more somber as they ceased their chatter to listen. Finally, the stamp of feet reached them, Ed chancing another glance over the edge of the indentation to spy the Western soldiers.

There must have been a hundred of the Western troops, a sea of blue uniforms flowing slowly down the road behind their blue flag with its six white vertical bars divided by the single star. The sabermen came first, two rows of them with their long swords slung at their waists. But it was the squads behind them, six men in each, which stole Ed's breath. Every soldier carried a rifle, at least sixty of them and more muskets than the Karlwych militia possessed by at least twofold. Ed was sure the fear he felt was also flicking through the rest of the Eastern militia as they laid eyes on their enemies.

General Loree showed no fear as he rode out to meet them. Alone, he trotted down the road, all the Western forces coming to a sudden halt at his appearance. Their drums falling silent, forty sabers scraped against their scabbards, and all the muskets set to awaiting shoulders.

"At ease, boys," Loree called out in a clear voice. And some of the Western soldiers obeyed their former commander's words, lowering their weapons only to realize their mistake and returning them to the ready.

In his gully Ed was close enough to see the amused expression on Loree's face. "Send out your commander and hopefully we can have everyone home for supper," Loree quipped. "Should be hominy and hardtack tonight if I'm not mistaken. Personally, I'd rather chew my boot than those teeth-dullers, but I'll not keep you from your meals. So save your shoulders the effort while we hash this out."

Ed could see the indecision among the Western ranks, as could Loree as he smirked. "If it will allay your fears, I personally promise I won't hurt you boys. See for yourselves," he said, opening his suit coat to prove he was unarmed.

Loree's bravado in the face of such a superior force received its desired effect, as guffaws sounded from both sides of the Johnson's stone wall. Many of the Western soldiers had previously served under Loree, and he was well-liked among the men, as their squads split to allow their current commander to ride forth.

Ed recognized General Davis Underhill from his picture in the papers and could not hide his shock at seeing the head of the entire Western armies here in Karlwych. Underhill was every bit the preening peacock in his freshly pressed uniform with his insignia flashing in the sun. Shining brightest was the silver pistol at his waist, the ceremonial gift given a Newfield general when bestowing the rank upon him.

General Loree carried neither a silver pistol nor even a uniform to call his own. Having left his Newfield uniform behind when he fled the West, Loree instead wore his best Solday suit. Yet he seemed much more regal than the gussied Underhill as they came face to face.

"Davis," Loree nodded to his guest.

"Clyde," Underhill answered with far less warmth. "You disgrace yourself out of uniform."

Even at this distance, Ed could see Loree flinch, though his voice remained civil. "It's less a disgrace than seeing your grubby hands sully that pistol. Did you know they offered it to me first?"

From the look on Underhill's face, this was news to him as Loree continued, "A waster is a wastrel they say, so that might even be the same pistol. If you'd care to be sure, you can check inside the barrel. I carved my initials there before I decided I couldn't keep it."

"Before you deserted, you mean."

Loree was taken aback by Underhill's words, and Ed swore the man looked chastened when he spoke again. "You're here for the Render, eh?"

"As the vested agent of the government of Newfield—"

"Pulley was tried by the Covenant and found guilty. He committed his crime in our nation and—"

"He is a citizen of Newfield and I will return him home!" Underhill bellowed. "President Ruhl gave me this order personally!"

"Well, I'd hate to disappoint your president," Loree curtly replied before raising his voice. "Bring him out, boys."

Four men stepped forth from behind the stone wall and approached the two generals. Between them the Easterners carried the wooden box by its rope handles. It was not until they unceremoniously dropped it at the feet of Underhill's horse and scampered back for their cover that Underhill recognized the coffin for what it was. At the realization Underhill's mouth opened, though it was Loree who spoke first.

"Aloysius Pulley was executed today at dawn, hung by the neck until his Breath left him in accordance to the laws of the Covenant. But as we are not unkind men, we now return his body for a proper burial. So do as your president ordered and take Pulley home. But you best hurry because, as of five miles ago, you've encroached upon sovereign Covenant ground. If you do not retreat immediately, I will be forced to remove you."

Ed could not help but feel Eastern pride at the righteousness of Loree's words, said loud enough that all the men on both sides could hear them. Underhill's face flushed as Loree finished, his jowls blazing purple as he sputtered. Before he could speak, Loree leaned in close, his voice so soft Ed could barely catch it as he said, "Choose your next words very carefully, Davis. You don't and it will be war."

Underhill considered, his face finally returning to its usual pallor. He opened his mouth, but Ed never heard the words because the musket shot cut them off.

It was a single report that shattered the silence, Loree and Underhill staring stupidly at the other a moment. Then the second shot sounded, followed by another almost immediately. The first few were like single drops of rain heralding the thunderstorm, joined seconds later as both sides added their musket balls to the deluge and chaos commenced.

Both Loree and Underhill raced back to their respective side through the gunfire. Underhill's distance was significantly shorter, the ranks of his sabermen opening to allow him entrance before snapping shut behind his galloping horse.

Loree's journey back to the stone wall was much farther and cut short when his horse was shot out from under him. The sight of it caught Ed's breath, but Loree miraculously kept to his feet, instantly shifting course to head straight for their gully. Crashing into the earthen indentation, Loree slumped beside Ed to watch the battle.

Not that it would be much of a battle. As soon as their general was safely behind them, the Western onslaught began in earnest. They were already advancing, each rifleman firing his single shot and falling back to the last of their line to reload as a fresh rifleman took his place. The motion made the Newfield army look like a slowly churning wave with no intention of breaking upon the stone wall. True, some of the Western troops were cut down by Eastern shots, small holes opening in their ranks, but they did not falter in their advance. The trained soldiers' number of shots dwarfed that of the militia, and already Ed could see many of his fellow Easterners slumped over the stone wall they swore to hold. They had planned this defense for many days, but now that the battle was unfolding, they would be routed in a matter of minutes.

Loree came to the same conclusion as he turned to the eager Weavers in the gully with him. "Ply your trade. Defend your homeland, and may Sol have mercy upon us."

Loree looked distraught, but not so much the gleeful Weavers as they began smashing the luz jars at their feet. Each glass jar contained at least eight Breaths, all invisible in the daylight. It was only once all the jars were crushed and the Weavers began gesturing that the Breath came alive to glow with ethereal light.

Ed had very little poetry in his soul, but he inherently knew each Breath shone with colors a man was never meant to behold. They were like the strange shades left on the underside of his eyelids, an afterimage from staring at a bright light too long. They were the colors no one was meant to see straight-on, something eerie and breathtaking that was to be marveled after. But the Weavers did not pause to marvel as they did as Loree bid. Each of the three Weavers' fingers flitted through the air, as if working an invisible loom, and with each gesture a separate Breath flared and obeyed. Silently the Weavers spun their selected Breaths into groups of three, entangling them into knots that would not come undone for a full day. With another flutter of the Weavers' fingers, each new knot of Breath inflated, doubling in size, and then again as they made their manifestations.

The manifestations quickly took shape as four limbs sprouted from their trunks, pairs of luminous arms and legs materializing in seconds. Although each manifestation had the primitive outline of a human, the limbs were too thin and no more than rough approximations aping a man. Each new manifestation was no larger than a child, the tallest of them scarcely reaching Ed's chest were he standing. But the child-like forms did not remain benign for long, as the Weavers added atrocious touches to their creations, including claws and fangs.

As soon as their first few were finished, the Weavers set their monstrous manifestations upon the Newfield army. The first wave only contained nine manifestations rolling over the edge of the gully to tear towards the Western ranks. Some of the riflemen spotted the manifestations immediately, instinctively firing their muskets at them. Their volleys proved futile though, the musket balls passing through the insubstantial manifestations as if the creatures were no more than smoke.

The manifestations were not insubstantial when they reached the Western soldiers though, their claws cleaving flesh from bone, their fangs silencing the screams of their victims. Like a scythe through wheat, those nine manifestations alone hewed through the Western rank, cutting down every living thing in their path. To these nine the Weavers added another nine, then a dozen joining the slaughter in a matter of moments. The Western dead soon littered the ground, and though he could not see their dying Breaths in the daylight, Ed knew their Breath must be filling the air, three for each man who fell.

The Western army was in disarray, the rallying Eastern musket shots winnowing their numbers further. Ed did not hear the Western cry to retreat, but the army suddenly broke apart, all semblance of order gone as they took to their heels. The manifestations did not pause in their relentless attack, pursuing the fleeing soldiers until Loree spoke.

"Call them off. Now!"

"Why?" the female Weaver asked. "We can end all those Render puppets here and now."

"They're not Renders and they're not puppets. They're men, good soldiers. Let them return home to tell everyone about this rout and perhaps Ruhl won't make this mistake again."

The Weaver's face displayed her disagreement, but the manifestations on the road immediately halted their inhuman hunt. Her hands balling into fists, she then snapped both hands open and all her manifestations disappeared, dissipated back into the three separate Breaths that made them up. No longer under the Weavers' influence, the Breath of the manifestations began to fade in the daylight, mingling with the already invisible Breath of the men they had killed.

Only then did Ed recognize that the battle was at an end, the bloodshed barely lasting as long as the two generals' discussion preceding it. Looking at his hands, Ed realized he had not reached for his saber, as he had feared, but held his musket the whole time. Yet his finger had not touched the trigger, his musket remaining silent throughout the ordeal. Shame invaded Ed, but Loree granted him a sad smile.

"Not to worry, son. You'll have other chances to prove yourself."

Ed was not pleased to hear fear tingeing his voice as he responded, "You think they'll come back?"

"Not if they're wise."

Loree's smile faded as he gazed back at the fallen. The coffin containing Pulley's body remained not far off from the first of the Western dead, the purpose of the battle forgotten about during its din. When Loree spoke again, it was in a quiet voice. "I shouldn't have used the Weavers, not yet."

"Why not?" the Weaver woman inquired incredulously. "Our order handed you your victory today. Don't tell me the great General Loree is afraid of the West."

"Of the West, no, it's just a direction. What I fear is the nation of Newfield. Their armies, their factories, and their Tinkers. Their supply of munitions and men. But most of all I fear the rage of the Renders."

"If the Renders are fools enough to challenge us on the field, it will indeed be a grand war," she answered with fervor in her eyes. It was this zealous fervor, so contrary to her careless words, that caused Ed's anxiety to bubble up again. He knew he should not feel it, not after having witnessed only three Weavers collapsing an entire company of trained soldiers in a matter of minutes. With the Weavers at their vanguard, it was entirely inconceivable that the Covenant could taste defeat. Yet Loree's concern was contagious, fear soon consuming Ed like a fever.

And the children of Sol knew life rolls on so long as Sol's Breath flows freely on Ayr. And so it will continue until each fragment of Sol has fastened with every other and Sol is again whole to return for the Harvest.

"May Sol hold off the Harvest," Loree answered, Ed chagrinned to realize he had muttered the scriptures aloud. "I fear that if Sol returned to judge us now, He would find us entirely unworthy."

Loree rose as cheers filled the air. The militia finally broke rank, emerging from behind their stone wall to surround their victorious general and carry him off in celebration. Watching them depart back for camp, Ed stood alone among the forgotten dead on the battlefield, his hands still clutching his unfired musket.

***

In the years that followed, both sides of the ensuing conflict would swear it was the other that fired the shot that started the Grand War. Ed Oldham was there at the very beginning, but until his dying day he remained unsure which side fired that fateful first shot.

All he knew for certain was he was not to blame for the bloodshed that came.

Chapter 1

Iulius 7, 548 (Nineteen Years Ago)

Marta was mad. Carmichael had lied to her. Again.

Her older brother's lies were nothing new, Marta expecting them now whenever he spoke. But this time he had gone too far, had Whispered upon her, and for that he would pay.

Her mother had saved Marta that morning by removing Carmichael's mental hold over her, but Cecelia Childress also knew her middle child's tendencies well, ordering Marta to catch four Breaths from the nearby Coak ley. It was a mission of diversion, one meant to keep Marta occupied until her father returned. During daylight the ley was entirely invisible, the flowing Breaths that made it up almost impossible to capture. The task should have kept the six-year-old Marta busy all afternoon, but after two hours her head began to ache, each throb reminding her of Carmichael's lie. Finally she had enough, flinging her luz jar to the ground hard enough to shatter the glass.

Cutting through the fields, the cotton crop loomed high above Marta's head, but she navigated the rows easily towards the sprawling manor in the center of the plantation. Up ahead she heard a rustle, most likely a festation toiling away. Unlike the manifestations, their Weaver relatives, festations did not fade away after a single day, instead existing until their creator dismissed them. Needing neither food nor rest, festations made perfect workers, and the Childress family owned hundreds to tend to their crop of cotton and tobacco. There was no chance the mindless festation would alert her mother to her disobedience, but Marta shifted her course nonetheless. The lifeless eyes of the festations disturbed her, so she dodged through the stalks furtively from row to row until she reached home.

Once inside, she stormed up the first of the three sweeping staircases of Hillbrook Manor, the steps too steep to accommodate her stride. But Marta reminded herself she was growing every day, and soon she would outgrow the childish frills her mother loved dressing her in and receive her own gowns, girdles, and bustles. Soon she would be old enough to do something that mattered to the clan.

Carmichael was not in his bedroom and Marta gave the door a satisfying slam as she marched on down the hallway. If not in his room, then he was probably with their tutor, Mr. Mitchell. Mitchell was only required to stay for lessons until three bells but could linger for additional instruction if requested by one of the children. Although Marta's shadow never remained in the classroom after the third bell's final note died, Carmichael, to Mitchell and her parents' delight, often took on additional studies.

Marta did not feel delight when she burst into the classroom to find Carmichael hunkered over his textbooks with Mitchell. Her brother always gave the appearance of the perfect oldest child, at least in the presence of others. Marta knew the truth, as her little sister, Oleander, would discover soon enough herself.

Carmichael stood at her sudden intrusion, decorum dictating he rise at the entrance of a lady, even if the lady was now plowing straight for him with no intention of stopping. Three years older, he towered over Marta, so she jumped as she aimed her fist straight at his face.

She missed by inches, Carmichael laughing at her attempt even as Mitchell scolded her. The laughter, more than the reprimand, enraged Marta further. Carmichael's hands latched to her wrists before she could react, Marta struggling against her stronger sibling to no avail.

"Whatever is wrong with you?" Carmichael's voice was amused, each word another twist of his knife.

"Rosealee," Marta spat back.

To her surprise Carmichael blinked uncomprehendingly at the name. It had been rattling around Marta's head like a Breath in a bottle for the last three months, but to him it seemed meaningless. Then the corners of his mouth curled up, Carmichael finally remembering.

"This is about our older sister? I forgot about her entirely."

His dismissal of her months of misery infuriated Marta all the more, the girl fighting harder against his grip. Her helplessness stoked her anger further, fanning it into blazing rage.

And with the rage came clarity, Marta suddenly aware of each Breath within her body. There were the usual three all humans were born with, one in the center of the chest representing the Body, the second in the middle of the forehead for the Mind, and the third at the crown of the head signifying the Soul. But in that moment of clarity, Marta could feel a fourth Breath nestled deep in her chest next to the Body. Were she not so angry, she might have been surprised to find it, to feel it thrumming with its own frequency. It had a resonance, a musical identity all its own that only she could hear.

So she inhaled, filling that Breath with both her air and anger.

The fourth Breath stirred, summoned by Marta's will and obeying on her exhale. Though its base remained firmly in her chest, she felt it elongate as it stretched through her throat and out towards her mouth. The appendage was entirely new to her, but it felt natural as she experienced each sensation through this fresh limb: the light scrape as it edged over her teeth, the sudden coolness of the air outside her body; the crunch of her brother's bones as it collided with his nose.

Carmichael released her as he fell, his face spurting blood as he sputtered for air. Mitchell was speaking again, almost yelling, but Marta paid him no mind as she stared in awe at her new appendage. It looked like a strange tongue, a tentacle thin as a ribbon and made up of her iridescent Breath. It was a marvel, one that entirely belonged to her and made her special; one that utterly disappeared as her anger dissipated. One moment the Blessed Breath was there, ethereal and unreal, but upon her inhale it retreated back within Marta to nest again in her chest.

Marta tried desperately to bring it back, but her clarity was gone, the fourth Breath again a mystery as Mitchell's voice finally penetrated her mind. Though Carmichael was still calling for aid on the floor, Mitchell's attention was turned solely upon the Childress' middle child.

"Congratulations, my girl, you are one of Sol's Blessed. And a Shaper, no less. Your parents will be very proud."

But looking down on her brother dripping blood upon the carpet, Marta was not so sure.

***

Marta remained in her room for the rest of the evening, forgoing dinner, though her belly soon cursed her for it. Her father was still away at his kennels, and her mother, having married into the Cildra clan, did not make decisions on important matters. The discovery that she was a Shaper would certainly be considered an important matter, so Marta determined it was best to remain hidden until her father's return. Only her little sister dared to disturb her, Oleander too young to realize the gravity of the situation and wanting to play as if this were any other day. Marta sent her away rudely, Oleander's sobs haunting as they disappeared down the long hallway of the children's wing. Though she felt a pang of regret for Oleander's tears, Marta realized she would be lucky if those were the only ones spilled after her father returned home.

"I'm Blessed," Marta whispered. "A Shaper."

It was true and today's events proved it. She was Blessed and touched by Sol Himself.

The tale was taught to all children as soon as they were old enough to understand: In the beginning the divine Sol had wandered the black void between the stars until He found Ayr. And there their deity had fallen in love with the beautiful, but lifeless world. Saddened that there were no living beings like Himself to take pleasure there, Sol performed the ultimate sacrifice in surrendering His own life, shattering His essence into an untold number of fragments. It was those fragments, known as Breath, which gave life to Ayr.

All living things therefore had an aspect of Sol within them, a piece of His divine essence a part of them from the moment of their birth. Plants, as the lowest form of life, had only the one, consisting of the Body. Animals, being imbued with intelligence, had two: the Body and the Mind. And humans, as Sol's greatest creations, were superior with their three aspects of the divine: the Body, Mind and Soul. It was this third Breath, the Soul inherent in all humans, that made them Sol's chosen children and the inheritors of His beloved Ayr.

And some humans were made sacred by a fourth Breath of Sol, marking them as Blessed. Their abilities depended upon where the fourth Breath resided. Those with it within the Body were called Shapers and were capable of constructing solid, spindly Armor around their bodies to give them inhuman strength. If it inhabited the Mind, then the Blessed were known as either Listeners or Whisperers depending on how their powers manifested. The Listeners were capable of hearing stray thoughts of those around them, whereas Whisperers, like Marta's mother and Carmichael, were able to implant ideas into the minds of others. If the fourth Breath was within the Soul, the Blessed was able to influence the flow of Breath and became either a Render or Weaver depending if they lived in the West or the East.

Overall, the Blessed were quite rare and no one knew exactly how they were chosen since a child of two Blessed parents was no guarantee their progeny would share their abilities. Some, like the Dobra, increased their chances in the lottery of birth by only breeding within their tribes, but even then their numbers were almost laughably low, only two in ten Blessed and the majority of them simply Listeners. Only Marta's own Cildra clan had any real understanding of Sol's secrets, the proof being that many more of their clan were Blessed than not.

And she was finally fully one of them.

Singing the ode "Joy and Ease" with abandon, Marta heard her father's approach before she caught sight of him. His kennels were located a half-mile from the house to save them from the hounds' constant baying. Only a few miles outside the Mimas' state capital of Gatlin, buyers often traveled hundreds of miles to purchase her father's famed hounds. The kennel and the hounds were all pretense though, expected of an aristocratic man of leisure, as her father pretended to be. Although the plantations around them and the sale of his hounds explained away their affluence, the family's true purpose always belonged to the Cildra clan.

The ode meant he was in a good mood, one cut abruptly short as Marta's mother met him at the front steps. After a few quiet words, her father looked up at her window, Marta slinking for cover behind the curtains. His Cildra training ensured Norwood Childress saw her movements, which meant he knew she was watching. Her hiding was pointless, but Marta was not ready to face her father quite yet.

A servant summoned her to his study minutes later, Marta trudging down to finally receive her punishment. Her father's study was the one place her mother still allowed him to smoke his pipe indoors, and the smell of his fragrant mixture permeated the hallway like a stain upon the air. It was a pleasant scent to most, but to Marta it was sour since it meant she was about to receive yet another entirely undeserved punishment.

To her surprise she found Carmichael waiting outside the door as well. As far as she could recall, this was the first time he had to enter Father's study, though she had been within so many times she had lost count. Carmichael's nose had been set, but a bruise bloomed around his eyes, making him resemble a raccoon. He refused to look at her directly, but upon her appearance Carmichael turned the handle and strode inside their father's study. Marta had no choice but to follow or be considered a coward.

Father was seated at his desk, and though Marta expected him to be angry, he looked them both over gently. He held his pipe in one hand, the tobacco packed and ready, yet the matches remained forgotten on the desk as he spoke in a calm voice.

"Let me see if I have this correct. Carmichael, you told Marta you have an older sister named Rosealee, but she never met this sister because

Rosealee was not Blessed like the rest of us and your mother and I sold her to a traveling tribe of Dobra Wanderers. I have that right?"

"It was a test to see if she could spot-the-lie."

Her father chuckled at Carmichael's response, Marta's cheeks burning as her brother joined in. Spot-the-lie was a common game among Cildra children, one Carmichael loved tormenting Marta with. Yet her brother's laughter died instantly as her father's voice turned hard.

"And if that was the all of it, I would congratulate you, but it wasn't. You Whispered at your sister, kept her from searching for the truth. You locked her mind in a cage with a lie, and if your mother had not noticed and undone your deceit, the damage would have been terrible. You used your abilities upon your sister, Carmichael, something forbidden to the Cildra clan. We do not use our blessings to harm each other, something you must keep in mind as well, Marta."

Her father's gaze flicked from one child to the next, neither willing to acknowledge the other. For a moment he looked crestfallen as he regarded them both. "Hate is easy. Love hard."

"And indifference the most difficult," Carmichael chimed in. The saying was old as time, most people only recollecting the first half. But Carmichael was a good student, always reciting his lessons proudly.

"That it is," her father responded, waving Marta forward.

Marta remained planted firmly in place, her words spilling out in an attempt to lessen her impending punishment. "I let my anger get the better of me again. Instead of acting, I should have stepped back and thought first. I'm sorry. Again."

Her father smiled, her apology not fooling him for an instant. "I think you can be forgiven so long as you both learn a lesson today. Marta, my precious little girl, you must remember to never use your Blessed abilities in front of someone outside the clan. For the rest of the world, the Blessed are a tiny minority, only one in twenty gifted by Sol. But we of the Cildra clan are special, nearly eight out of ten of us touched by Sol. And this is our secret, only to be shared within the family. So though it is law that all Whisperers and Listeners wear pins to announce their abilities, neither I, your mother, nor your brother do so. This is our secret to be used to our benefit and none others. Even though it was your first time, it is no excuse for showing your Shaper nature in front of an outsider. Mitchell is not one of the clan, yet he now knows you for what you are. We must ensure his knowledge remains hidden, which means we must keep him under our employment until he dies to keep our secret."

"He could die early, then."

Shock took hold of Marta at her brother's casual suggestion, only to be replaced by horror as her father seemed to be genuinely considering the idea.

"Mother could just Whisper at him and make him forget! She can make it better!"

"Your mother is strong, Marta, but she couldn't make him forget. That type of power is the stuff of fables. A Whisperer can impart impulses in someone not paying attention, but to make him forget entirely is impossible."

"No! Mr. Mitchell's a good man. He was happy for me today. You can't kill him!"

Hot tears ran down Marta's cheeks as she screamed. Real tears were a sign of weakness, something a Cildra child, lest of all a Childress, should be embarrassed by, but Marta did not care as she defiantly stared her father down.

"He will not be harmed," he replied without emotion. "Not because he is a good man, but because his death might raise suspicions. It's more risk than he's worth, especially when he already enjoys taking our money. Greed is easy to use, whereas those with principles significantly more difficult. You must remember that every action you take has repercussions, not just upon you, but upon the clan as a whole. Remember that, Marta. Remember it well."

Again her father waved with his pipe for her to approach and Marta trudged forward. Though she expected her long-awaited punishment, her father set his pipe aside to pick up a small inlaid box. Carefully lifting the lid, he revealed the ring.

Marta's tears instantly disappeared, her breath catching as she beheld the thing: three silver strands intricately woven together with a fourth golden one.

"Your mother has one just like it, one I gave her when I asked her to marry me and join the clan. But this one is yours, to commemorate the moment you became Blessed. This was a special moment, Marta, one I am sorry I missed. And though that moment must remain a secret, when you look upon this, you can remember the secret is yours to treasure. I'm very proud of you, Marta, very pleased that you are Blessed. You are a single gleaming gold strand in a world of dull silver."

Her father suddenly scooped her up, planting a kiss upon Marta's forehead. "But I would have loved you no matter if you were Blessed or not. You are my daughter, Marta."

With another kiss he deposited her back upon the ground, Marta snatching her ring away. Too large to fit upon any of her fingers, Marta slid it over her thumb and held it up to see how her new treasure glinted in the light.

Waving them both away, their father finally remembered his pipe, setting it to light and bathing the room in the sweetest scent Marta had ever known. Never taking her eyes off the ring, Marta dutifully shuffled towards the door, though Carmichael remained in place. Snorting derisively at Marta and her gift, his bloody nose turned the noise into more of a gurgle.

"And what is my lesson in all this?" Carmichael said.

Their father did not even look at his son, instead blowing a smoke ring into the air. "Never antagonize someone more powerful than yourself."

Too entranced by her prize, Marta did not see her brother taken off guard. It was an entirely new look for Carmichael, one she entirely missed. By the time she glanced back at him, his indifferent façade was firmly back in place.

"I will remember it well, Father."

Chapter 2

Winterfylled 16, 567

Her stomach gurgled, Marta unsure if it was the liquor taking effect or her meal attempting escape on out her throat. The boardinghouse she resided in provided her dinner for the evening. The potatoes were mealy and the meat gone to gray, but she wolfed down the offering without hesitation before retreating to her room. It was a sagging place, the wallpaper peeling back to expose the warped wood underneath, the scent of mildew eternally tickling her nostrils. Marta initially hoped that the haze of the liquor would help her ignore the odor, but it instead only made the cloying scent more pronounced as she took another pull off the bottle.

Upon their first introduction, the acrid sting of the bust-head liquor nearly made Marta wretch as she fought to keep it down. In her youth Marta loved the taste of sweet things, but there was no more sweetness left in Ayr, not since the Grand War. So she forced herself to take a second sip, the liquor going down smoother and smoother as the months mutated into years. Sleep was still a few more fingers off, so she looked around the room for diversion, her eyes alighting on the covered mirror. No longer caring how she appeared, the mirror usually only served Marta as a hook to hang her greatcoat, but she tossed it to the bed beside her slouch hat to appraise herself in the cracked glass.

Marta never made eye contact anymore, instinctively avoiding it even from her own reflection. So she started at her boots, gathering courage with another pull from the diminishing bottle. Her boots were covered in the pale rock dust from the quarry, the last time they were polished a distant memory. Her jeans had held up well enough, but they too were faded and bleached by a layer of dust. The shirt was cut for a man, but Marta made do with suspenders holding up her ill-fitting pants.

Had she any care left in her appearance, the state of her hair would have horrified her. As a child she brushed it a hundred strokes a night, but now it was a tangled mess, the auburn tresses that had inspired countless suitors in her stint in the Auld Lands faded to the brown of mud. Pulling her hair back with her free hand, Marta intended to examine her face, but her eyes flicked to the ruin of her right ear. The bottom half was lost at the battle of Bergen Creek, but it was not the worst scar she bore.

She was currently in the state of Walshvan, working by day at the Hoback Quarry. It was hard, backbreaking bullwork, even inside her childish Armor. The foreman had spotted her for what she was instantly since she did not remove her hat when she came asking after employment. For that he claimed a third of her wages, calling them taxes for keeping mum. Marta was not particularly bothered by this loss of the lucre, the remainder sufficient to keep a roof over her head and enough liquor to lull her to sleep each night. Compared to the Grand War, this was indeed a life of joy and ease.

But for the last week, the townspeople had been giving her hard stares on the streets, and Marta suspected her foreman had not proven true to his word. Perhaps it was time to move on again, though the where of it eluded her. Abner would have dutifully followed to wherever she chose, Reid with a clever quip and mocking salute as they bid another town farewell. Gonzalo would then chime in with one of his dire warnings gleaned from the stars as Tollie meekly kept step. But they were all gone now, all scattered to the winds or interred in the dirt.

The knock at the door disturbed her reverie, Marta releasing her hair and turning from the mirror before she met her lifeless eyes. In the last two months, she had neither expected nor received a visitor, and the sudden caller only cemented her suspicion that the townspeople had arrived to encourage her to move on. There was the possibility she would have to hurt a few as she made her exit, but if they were polite enough to knock, then perhaps they were not out for blood.

It still paid to be prepared for the possibility though.

Marta pulled her haversack out from under the bed, all her worldly possessions within. The only two missing were her greatcoat and the slouch hat waiting where she had left them on the bed. She considered leaving the hat there as she answered the door. If her caller was there because of what she was, then there was no reason to hide the fact any longer, but then her fingers rose reluctantly to her forehead and she felt the hard, scarred skin there.

Her fingers retreating as if touching a burning brand, Marta grabbed her hat and pulled it low over her brow. Another swig off the bottle and her head swam as she answered the door.

The man waiting for her was entirely nondescript, his suit a few years old, eyes and hair a burnished brown that matched his well-trimmed mustache. He would have blended in with any crowd, just another anonymous face, but the crook in his nose gave Carmichael away. It had been two years since Marta last beheld her brother, but she recognized him instantly despite his disguise.

Her anger immediately roiled to a boil, burning away the effects of the alcohol as the perfect clarity of rage roared within her. Her fourth Breath also flared to life, begging to be released. Straightaway, Armor plans filled her head: a club to stave his skull in, claws to tear out his throat, or even the serpentine tongue that had shattered his nose all those years ago. Some part of Marta's mind clinically noted there would be a certain symmetry to that act as her Breath again implored her to be released to wreak havoc.

The Blessed Breath remained in her chest though, Marta incapable of releasing it now. Carmichael had seen to that when last they met.

"Are you going to continue to gawp like a provincial on her first trip to town or can we conduct our business inside?"

His voice was familiar, always soft, but demanding attention. Yet there was something new to it, a further depth to his indifference Marta had not encountered before as she stepped aside to allow him entrance. If she did not acquiesce willingly, he would be forced to force her.

Carmichael's eyes did not even flick about the ruin of the room, but she knew he had instantly taken in her squalid surroundings. The always fastidious Carmichael she had grown up beside would have made sure to verbally eviscerate the inhabitant of such a hovel, but now he politely held his tongue, his politeness making his condescension all the more difficult to digest.

"Propst said he encountered you on the street recently, and I hoped I might still catch you before you disappeared again." Marta remained silent, refusing to be baited by him. Not appearing to notice, Carmichael continued, "I dined with Richard just three nights ago. He's doing well, expecting his second child in a matter of weeks."

Marta could not help but wince as his second verbal blow found its mark. If he enjoyed her discomfort, Carmichael's face gave no sign as he produced a bottle from his coat for his final insult. "I considered bringing a Karlwych vintage, perhaps a red. You always had a fondness for those if I remember correctly, but then I decided this might be better received."

The liquor bottle's label matched the one forgotten in her hand, and

Marta was not too proud to refuse it. "A waster is a wastrel," her father had been fond of saying, and Marta had no intention of wasting this moment as she swung her arm down. The nearly emptied bottle in her hand smashed against the wall, leaving only the neck with its jagged teeth that pleaded to be slid across her brother's throat.

Despite her desire for blood, again Marta did not take action, Carmichael not even flinching at her outburst. He was too sure of his own Whisperer abilities as he spoke again, "Now that the pleasantries are behind us, I have a job for you."

Though she had sworn she would not deign to even answer him, a laugh escaped Marta. Carmichael continued on as if he did not notice, "Orthoel Hendrix has gone missing and we believe the Covenant Sons have him."

Marta knew the name of Orthoel Hendrix well, as did every citizen in Newfield. The damned airships were his brainchild, his named pronounced in the East as if it were the vilest of curses. Back home the only person more hated than Marta and her ilk was Hendrix.

Dropping the broken bottle, Marta licked her fingers clean as she examined the new bounty Carmichael had provided. She considered herself many things, but a wastrel was not one of them as she spoke. "Then he's dead."

Remnants of the original Covenant rebellion, the Covenant Sons were fanatics that refused to accept that the East lost the Grand War. With no formal army, the Sons did not engage the Newfield forces directly, rather waging a war from the shadows. Compared to the victorious Newfield armies, the Covenant Sons were little more than flies buzzing around the head of a bear. But flies were known to bring pestilence with them, and so the Home Guard defended the nation of Newfield by rooting out these rebels whenever they could.

"No, I assure you, he is quite alive and well, working with the Sons, in fact. Or, they for him, if I am to be entirely accurate."

Marta could not have been more surprised if her brother had announced he was Sol himself returned for the Harvest as Carmichael continued, "Hendrix's Tinker talents are far too valuable to remain in the hands of collaborators. As such, we need you to find him for us. It seems he departed Vrendenburg in quite a hurry, so much so he left his daughter, Caddie, behind in his haste. But he wants her back now, agents of the Covenant Sons already searching for her. That is why you are going to escort her to Ceilminster for a family reunion. And when you find him there, you will end him."

Carmichael's offer was tempting, Hendrix a man Marta hated with all her withered heart. He was a fiend, one that deserved death—hopefully by her hand. But if Carmichael wanted someone dead, his deputies in the Home Guard could handle it for him. There must be more to the story, though Carmichael seemed finished and content to wait for her reply. It was a battle of wills, a game they had played many times as children to see who would break the silence first. Carmichael always won, as he did again when she finally replied.

"I wouldn't make it ten feet across the Mueller Line before someone slipped a knife in my back. Whatever you promise, whatever you threaten, it won't be done. At least not by me. Not for you."

"You misunderstand, Marta. This order does not come from me, but from Father."

Carmichael idly produced a letter from the folds of his jacket, Marta snatching it away. She recognized her father's elegant handwriting immediately, and despite the fact it was addressed to her brother, she searched its contents for her message. The words in the letter themselves were of no matter, an absolutely mundane missive recounting his days. At least to the uninitiated since the letter was composed in the Cildra codex. Each child in the clan had a separate cipher, one only shared between parent and child. Carmichael's current marching orders were undoubtedly contained in this same text, as were the ones Marta was meant to follow, hidden in the code only she could read. It had been nearly six years since she had last received any contact from her father, and Marta's head again swam as she finished reading.

Carmichael plucked the letter from her hand to make it disappear back within his coat while she pondered her father's words. When his hand reappeared he kept it closed as his soft voice floated through the room.

"As we are again reunited, I thought it fitting to return this to you." His fingers unclenched, revealing her woven ring. "This took no small bit of effort to find, but I assure you, it is no facsimile."

Marta seized it instantly, the familiar weight revealing that her brother told the truth, this time at least. Slipping it over her finger, Marta suddenly felt whole again. For a moment her misery melted away, happier memories she thought long dead gurgling to the surface. But the memories quickly faded, replaced by ones not nearly as friendly as she found her voice.

"I met Hendrix at a gathering the first year of the war. He was an odd man, but even then I knew he was dangerous and said he should be eliminated. If Father had heeded my suggestion, then the Covenant would have won, and Oleander..."

Carmichael's carefully crafted indifference cracked at the invocation of their sister's name, a look Marta believed to be entirely false and something he practiced in the mirror for when he had an audience. Still, his voice was somber when he spoke again.

"The past is a mirror, to gaze at it too long simply vanity. I too wish Hendrix had been removed then, and we could have all been spared his solution to the war. But you and I are both simply marionettes in Father's show. He's the one who pulls our strings and makes us dance."

His indifferent façade again in place, Carmichael tossed a large bundle of banknotes upon Marta's bed rather than handing them to her. As always, he had refused to touch her.

"All the information you need is within, and I hope I do not need to remind you to destroy the note once you've committed it to memory. There's also a ticket for the train to Miryammayn. It departs within the hour."

At the door, he paused, looking his sister over again and finding her lacking. "News of Hendrix's daughter's disappearance will soon reach the Covenant Sons, and to keep up appearances, my agents in the Home Guard will be searching for her and her rescuer. I will keep their search hamstrung, but I strongly suggest you do not allow them to catch you."

He obviously expected her to accept his mission, departing despite the fact she had refused him. His certainty again irked her as she examined the cash, more than she had earned in the two years since the Grand War, yet discarded by Carmichael as if tossing away a used match. He was now the public safety secretary and lived the life of luxury they had both been raised to expect. His influence rose with each passing day, whereas Marta's star had waned until it flickered at the edge of oblivion. Yet as she pocketed the money, Marta could not hide her smile, the motion an unfamiliar sensation.

But grin she did until her face hurt.

Carmichael had said they were both Father's puppets, each one controlled by one hand and playing its assigned part in the performance without having seen the script. Sometimes the puppet in the right hand would take on the role of the hero and slay the villain in the left. Other times their roles were reversed, the only constant in the equation being that they did not know the part they played until the show was over.

But this time her father intended her to be the hero, Carmichael surely unaware he was going to be the one to fall. Hidden within her codex Marta found her instructions, ones Carmichael could not hope to decipher.

Her father's message began oddly enough: *Families belong together.*

Norwood Childress was not one for sentimentality, and the sudden emotion took Marta aback as she had continued reading: *Take your brother's mission, but do not kill the target. Reunited with his daughter, he will give us our victory. The East will rise again. Do this and you will be forgiven. Families belong together.*

Her father had somehow found it within him to forgive Hendrix for what he had done to the East. And if Marta could find it within her to return his daughter and not kill him, she too would be forgiven. She would be allowed to return to Gatlin to again be embraced by her family.

Marta did not know if she had any forgiveness left within her, all her kindness burned away by the Grand War. Killing Hendrix would be a supremely satisfying act, possibly the last in her life if she disobeyed her father. Carmichael would surely seek revenge as well if she were to deviate from his plan, his unyielding cruelty something Marta knew firsthand.

Families belong together.

The sentence still mystified Marta as she chewed it over. The reappearance of her woven ring certainly made it appear her father's overdue overture was legitimate, though Carmichael claimed he was the one to find it. It was possible he did this at their father's behest, but it was equally possible this was simply another of her brother's machinations meant to confuse her.

Unable to tear her eyes off her returned ring, Marta claimed her greatcoat. Once a deep navy blue, it too had faded over the years. All Western soldiers were issued such a coat as part of their uniforms. Marta had removed the insignia long ago and considered burning the coat then as she had the emblem of Newfield. The coat marked her as a former Western soldier, told anyone who looked at her where her loyalties resided during the Grand War. It had been a hateful thing to wear and part of Marta wanted to be done with it for good. But it was warm and there was no way to ever hide what she had been during the war, coat or no. Carmichael had seen to that.

Hefting her haversack, Marta departed into the deepening night to find the train station. She was still unsure whose mission she would complete, her brother or her father's, but for the first time in a long time, the decision was hers alone to make.

The fate of Newfield again depended upon her.

Chapter 3

Avril 23, 554 (Thirteen Years Ago)

Marta meant to surprise her sister as she silently slid Oleander's bedroom door open, though not out of tenderness. Part of their Cildra training focused on mastering the art of stealth, and competitions between siblings were always encouraged. Sneaking up on the other was a point, as was noticing the instigator before she succeeded. Like the games of spot-the-lie she had begrudgingly played at her brother's behest, Marta now initiated the games of stealth with Oleander.

Too entranced by her latest attempt at Refrain, Oleander never stood a chance as Marta jammed her fingers into her sister's sides. At Oleander's squeal she gave up another point, Marta now ahead by sixteen. Though it might seem like quite an advantage, Oleander still held her own despite the two-year difference in their ages. Carmichael's advantage over Marta was surely in the hundreds when he finally stopped toying with her. He had never played with Oleander though, saying she was far too young to be any competition. Not that Marta had been much herself.

But Oleander was not concerned about their ongoing contest, and although she tried to put on a pleasant face, Marta could tell she was worried. The source was obvious: Refrain was one of the most difficult Cildra lessons, Marta having only mastered it a few months ago herself.

"Try it again," Marta said as cheerful as she could.

Reluctantly Oleander obeyed, extending her pointer finger on each hand. She began with her left, tapping a steady beat upon the table. A few measures of that tempo established, her right began tapping an entirely different one beside it.

Refrain was a requirement for being sent out on a mission for the clan. Listeners were the Cildra's inherent enemy, even though they included many Listeners among their ranks as spies. A stray thought caught by one of these mind readers could lead to their capture and jeopardize the clan as a whole. Though anyone could intentionally hide their thoughts from a Listener when aware of his or her presence, hence the pins all Listeners were required by law to wear to allow everyone this chance, the Cildra found a way to feed an eavesdropping Listener false information. It was not an easy thing to do, partitioning off a piece of the mind with a continuing loop of a repeating thought, like a refrain of a song, while still thinking true thoughts in another mental partition. The hardest part was learning to simultaneously think two dissimilar notions at once, something the exercise of Refrain was meant to instill.

Though she held them for several measures, soon the beats from Oleander's hands began to converge, the left speeding up while the right slowed down, until they mirrored the other entirely in striking the same faint staccato, Oleander finally throwing her hands up.

Despite her defeat, Oleander smiled pleasantly. "How was Cyrus today?"

Marta liked Cyrus more and more each day, and today was no exception. Though his last name was Livermore, not Childress, he was still a member of the clan and therefore family. His own manor, nestled deep in the mountains of Nahuat, was called Sable Hill, Cyrus commanding all the Cildra clan residing in the state from there. Although older than her father by at least ten years, Cyrus had come without question when her father called since Norwood Childress was the head of the clan in Newfield. And just as the Cildra within the nation all bowed to her father's decrees, her father followed the instructions that came across the Saulshish Ocean from the clan elders in the Auld Lands.

Cyrus was an accomplished Shaper, the best on the continent of Soltera to hear him tell it, and he would teach Marta all of the Cildra secrets to Shaping. Most Shapers spent years perfecting their mental plans to their Armor, but Cyrus swore she would be a master in a matter of months. If she listened to all his lessons and took them to heart, that was.

The vast majority of Shapers developed one single plan for their Armor: a suit that looked nothing like knights of old from which its name derived. Her father had hired several Shapers when he last expanded his kennels, Marta watching them easily erect the building with their abilities. Their Blessed Breath was stretched thin as a hair's breadth as they labored, tracing the outlines of their limbs and leaving vast swaths of their body exposed. The largest collections of their Breath were around the hinges that hovered over their joints, these moving parts said to be quite difficult to construct.

When surrounded by his or her Armor, the Shaper was strong as twenty men, but by spending all their mental energies in maintaining such a large and complex set of moving parts, the Shaper was therefore slow and plodding, both things the Cildra disdained. So instead of the single complex plan for Armor, Cyrus taught Marta several simple ones: the club for either hand, gauntlets for crushing strength, the cold torch that provided light without heat, a sword she was still mastering, and legs like a rabbit's for astounding leaps. And if she were very studious, he promised to teach her the empty palm, a maneuver capable of springing locks without a pick. Her crowning achievement would be the phantom blade though, a weapon capable of killing a man without severing a single thread on his clothing.

It was not what Cyrus taught her that made Marta like him, but instead the how of it. Her first lessons were easy enough, Marta able to exude her Breath whenever she wished without effort. Mastering the club took only a matter of hours, but Marta hit her first impediment when she attempted to hone her club into a blade. Though she followed Cyrus' instructions perfectly, after four days it still refused to obey her. Cyrus scarcely paid her any mind as Marta wrestled with the infuriating puzzle, instead availing himself to her father's library. After the first day he did not even bother to look up from his book as he simply told her "again" after each failure.

It was midway through the fourth day when Marta could not take his inattention anymore, her frustration boiling over until it turned to rage. So she gave her rage voice, screaming at her instructor until her lungs hurt. It was that moment Cyrus threw the book at her, the tome sailing through the air like a missile. Unable to take her rage out upon her tutor due to the edict against harming members of the clan, Marta instead took it out on the book by bringing her club to bear and cleaving it clean through.

Cyrus' chuckle infuriated her all the more, and it took Marta a moment to realize her club now sported a sheer edge. Examining it intently, Marta did not notice Cyrus until he was beside her, his hand resting upon her shoulder.

"There's more ways than one to top the mountain."

Cyrus' words became Marta's mantra, deviating from Cyrus' prescribed methods whenever she was stymied. It was this act alone, more than his instructions in her Blessed nature, which made her love him. Whereas her father always insisted on tamping down her anger, the genial Cyrus allowed Marta to harness her emotions and let them design her Breath's shape.

And Cyrus loved her in turn, dubbing Marta his youngest daughter and assuring her she could come and visit him and her distant cousins in Sable Hill. Marta suspected her father would not object since traveling to other places and learning from as many cultures as possible was the Cildra way. The Cildra were born spies after all: thieves and collectors of information they continually funneled to the clan elders before receiving new orders in return. Learning in any form was encouraged, the most important lesson being that of obedience to the elders, something Carmichael would soon study firsthand in the Auld Lands. Marta could not wait for her own journey across the Saulshish Ocean, and could already speak three of the Auld Lands languages in preparation for her opportunity.

Marta wanted nothing more than to share all this with Oleander, but she held her tongue. Though Oleander's smile never faltered, Marta knew she did not want to hear about her older sister's special Blessed training. So Marta extended her own index fingers.

"Let's try it again."

"It's too hard."

"Maybe for a runt," Marta challenged. Never one to back down to a dare, Oleander's hands remained balled into fists. "If you give it another shot, I won't count that point for sneak-and-see."

Reluctantly Oleander extended her fingers. Marta began the beat with her left hand, Oleander soon matching it with her own. Then Marta started her second rhythm, Oleander's right hand thumping along. As she did, Oleander's brow furrowed, the concentration of keeping the two beats, even with her grinning sister's assistance, taxing her abilities.

"I don't think you'll be a Whisperer or Listener like Mother or Father," Marta said. The wrinkle in Oleander's forehead deepened as her sister continued. "I was Blessed in the Body, so it stands to reason you'll be something new too. I think your fourth Breath is in your Soul. You will be a Weaver. Just imagine how wonderful it will be to conjure a manifestation to obey you."

Oleander's furrow evolved into an outright scowl, her words terse. "I'm not going to be a Weaver, or a Render. Or anything else. I'm not Blessed, Marta. I'm a fruitless branch on the Cildra tree."

"Cildra tree?"

"The map Father has in his study. It resembles a tree."

Marta had been summoned to their father's study more times than Oleander and Carmichael combined, probably twice over, but she had never seen the map her sister referred to. Her father's door remained locked whenever he was not home, and Marta never dared to venture into the lion's den, even after she had learned to use her lock picks.

"You sprung the lock into his study?"

A proud smile curled upon the corners of Oleander's mouth only to quickly disappear as she struggled to mirror Marta's beats. "And I found his family tree for the clan. He has everyone marked, just like he does with his dogs in the kennels. I don't know what all the marks mean, but he had Anice's marriage listed months before they made the announcement. He picks everyone's mates, Marta. That's why we have so many Blessed in the clan. Father breeds us like his dogs."

Marta almost lost track of her own beats as her mind puzzled over Oleander's implications. The Cildra of the Auld Lands and their descendants in Newfield prized their pale complexions, avoiding the sun and the tans it brought as a sign of prestige. They looked down upon the duskier tones of the Solterian natives, the Ingios and Mynians. Marta's own skin was ruddier than her cousins' though, as were both her siblings.

She had heard that it was quite the scandal when Father had chosen their mother to be his bride, a woman of Mynian descent and of little standing in her home state of Lacus. The Childress family was of old stock, one of the first to cross the ocean and stake a claim on the land that would one day be called the state of Mimas. Her father always told his children it was because once he saw their mother's dark-skinned beauty, he was instantly smitten, but perhaps it was because she was already a well-known and powerful Whisperer. Or perhaps it was not his choice at all, but insisted on by the elders of the clan. Marta shivered as she realized perhaps it was not love that had produced her and her siblings.

"At least as a fruitless branch I'll be able to choose my own husband," Oleander snorted. "If he doesn't sell me to a Wandering Dobra tribe first."

"Father can still use you," Marta countered. "Many of the best in the clan weren't Blessed either."

"Name one."

"Floyd Seelmire."

Oleander had to nod her agreement at that. Seelmire had singlehandedly been responsible for the invasion of Bance upon Acweald, this act of war having divided the Acwealt forces after Newfield declared its independence from the empire. It was this division of forces that allowed the Newfield rebellion to succeed and establish their nation. Though he was barely mentioned in the history books, Seelmire was a hero to the Cildra in Newfield, a man who had fulfilled his mission, even though he never agreed with it.

"Plus Theo Fitch. And Theresa Mallory," Marta continued.

"And the only reason we remember their names is because of what they weren't!" Oleander worked herself into a lather, tears threatening. "If another Blessed had done those deeds, no one would have even noticed. And they were at least sent out on missions, something I'll never be allowed."

"Unless you master Refrain."

"Exactly!"

Marta held her hands up in defeat and Oleander allowed herself a sad smile of triumph. It only lasted a moment before she then realized she was now tapping along alone. Oleander's eyes went wide as her two different beats continued, neither changing in tempo. They both beat on the table as ceaseless as the tides until Marta finally encircled her sister in a tight hug.

"That was a dirty trick," Oleander whispered, tears still brimming. But at least they were tears of victory now.

"You think that was good, you should see my second."

Oleander was instantly suspicious. Another of the games the sisters played was smuggling something into the other's pocket without being noticed. It was one of Oleander's specialties, and so Marta took great joy in upstaging her sister as Oleander batted at her dress until she found what she had been slipped.

Opening her hand, Oleander revealed the woven ring and a sound akin to a cough escaped her. "I... I can't keep this."

"Of course not, it's mine. But you can keep a hold of it for me until you earn your own. And every time you look at it, know you're my sweet sister. You'll do that for me, won't you?"

Oleander suddenly engulfed her in a hug, the dam holding her tears back finally burst, spilling them upon the frills of Marta's dress.

Chapter 4

Winterfylled 17, 567

She had the eyes of a dead man. At least that was what Reid joked when he was feeling particularly reckless in taunting his commander. They were disturbing, he said, eyes that belonged to a corpse. He was not wrong though. Marta hated meeting her own gaze and kept her dead eyes aimed at the floorboards to avoid the other occupants of the train car. The man beside her attempted to strike up a conversation, but Marta ignored him. With an offended grunt he returned to his newspaper as they departed the Walshvan station. Obviously he was not Blessed, as he quickly fell asleep, lulled by the quiet hum of the train.

Marta was not so lucky, her headache thundering for the last few hours. The pain was nothing new, Marta having traveled along the ley hundreds of times before, but it had been years since she had felt the gnaw of a ley headache firsthand, the pain crawling along her nerves until it invaded even her teeth. The only relief was in grinding them, but she refrained from this reprieve as she instead chewed on her pipe. Its lip had been assaulted in this manner thousands of times before, proudly displaying the indented teeth marks, not all of which belonged to her. An ugly thing, Marta felt a certain kinship for it, the pipe an emblem of when she had been considered someone of importance.

Someone had cracked a window, the Winterfylled wind cutting through the train car's stuffy air. It was a warm autumn thus far, nearly stifling: an Ingios summer that promised a brutal winter. Looking out the window, Marta begrudgingly marveled at the wonder of the train hurtling on above the line of ley. When the first floating trains had been introduced, there were, of course, naysayers, those that believed that if Sol had wanted them to fly, he would have created humans with wings. Marta was far too young to remember those days, but the benefit of the trains was obvious. As her old instructor Mitchell was fond of pointing out, Sol's consent was always demonstrated by humanity's ability. If capable of doing something, then humans were obviously expected to do so.

They were Sol's greatest creations after all. They were Sol's children.

Though all living things possessed a Breath of Sol, not all of his fragments were contained within the living, the majority of it flowing over the land in the form of ley, like the line supporting the train. When a living thing died, its Breath was released to float again along the land. Individually they were tiny, no larger than a fingertip, and weightless. Nearly transparent in daylight, at night they each glowed with their own ethereal light.

In a sense each fragment of Breath was like a raindrop flowing freely along the land until it coalesced with more of its kind and formed a running stream. These streams would in turn meet up into rivers known as lines of ley. And so the ley flowed, at night molten rivers made up of millions of raindrops of Breath, the lifeblood of Sol and Ayr alike.

These loose fragments could pass through any object, living or inanimate, the only substance capable of containing Breath being glass. As such, children were often equipped with their small glass luz jars and sent out at dusk to collect Breath to light their homes. But Sol's Breath must constantly flow, so these same children were also scrupulously taught to release the Breath from their luz jars before dawn lest they be punished by the Renders.

The Renders ardently believed all Sol's Breaths should remain in a state of constant flow, each fragment of Breath meant to adhere with every other, Sol finally returning for the Harvest after all his fragments had experienced life with all the others in some living form. It was therefore a Render's sworn duty to ensure the flow continued unimpeded, using their glass blades to separate any fragments that stayed bound together unnaturally. This obligation usually entailed destroying gasts, which were the remains occasionally lingering behind when a human died and their Breath did not separate. Marta had never witnessed a gast firsthand and had no desire to. Gasts retained the memories of the deceased yet were unaware they were dead. They therefore still attempted to interact with the living, torturing their loved ones with the constant reminder of what they had lost. Though Marta had no love for the Renders, the service the Blessed order provided in ridding the living of these gasts could not be denied.

But even the non-Blessed could benefit from the ley. The train on which Marta traveled was proof enough of this as its propellers churned the air above the train, a massive lodestone in the nose of the engine keeping it on course along the magnetic ley. Another obvious benefit of the ley was spark boxes like the three stowed in her haversack. Some ancient Tinker, those non-Blessed that worked with the ley through technology, learned long ago that by funneling a fragment of Breath through a filament, he could make a small electronic charge. Though the charges were minute individually, leaving the filament on a line of ley for only a few minutes would create a battery. Soon everyone carried several spark boxes with them to work Tinker devices. These spark boxes then quickly grew in size, now powering entire cities with the free flow of the ley provided by Sol's sacrifice millennia ago.

Yet another inventive Tinker had realized that since Breath could not flow through glass, if they were to cover their trains with glass bottoms, they would float upon the larger lines of ley and overcome the need for tracks. The generators were then built into the engines to fuel the trains without the need to burn coal like their ancestors in the Auld Lands had. The citizens of Newfield were suddenly unfettered from having to lay tracks, and what had once been a journey of months from one corner of Newfield to the other was reduced to a matter of days, again thanks to Sol's sacrifice and the flow of ley. The abundant energy was then harnessed to power the huge ships that crossed the Saulshish Ocean, and even Hendrix's damned airships.

Ahead, Marta could see the glow of the upcoming nodus, a spot where two or more ley converged. The train was still probably ten miles away, but the nodus shone on the horizon like a setting sun. Yet whereas the setting sun gave off only a handful of colors, the nodus swam with a multitude of hues, a maelstrom of flowing Breath eddying in place like a furious whirlpool.

The most famous nodus on the continent of Soltera was Brimstone, some saying it was the biggest on the planet of Ayr. Brimstone resided hundreds of miles to the southeast in her home state of Mimas, the city Oreana beside it the capital of the Covenant's rebellion during the Grand War. Many believed that Sol's Breath traveled into the center of Ayr at the nodi, only exiting again when they floated up through the soil to attach themselves to a new living body at birth. And so the ceaseless cycle of life continued, Sol's Breath eternal, though the bodies they inhabited came and went like waves in a vast ocean.

As a child Marta had thought nothing more beautiful than a nodus, the colors illuminating the night for miles around like a flame that gave off no heat. Now she could only feel her headache intensifying at its approach and wished for nothing more than a moment of relief. The general non-Blessed populous could spend nearly eight hours in the ley before feeling the effects of the headaches, but the Blessed only a few hours before the pain became nearly unbearable. Though favored by Sol by birth, they were not blessed in every respect.

Fortunately, the train began to slow, finally alighting at the Gungersburg station to silently hover at the wooden platform. Such stops were commonplace and allowed the train to trade cargo and passengers. At smaller stations there was only one platform, but Gungersburg was a large town, complete with a nodus. Like the track-bound trains of old, this made the town a hub for the trains to be set upon new lines. The Shaper roustabouts in their Armor waited at the gate that held the train in place, ready to haul the train on to its proper line of ley for the next leg of its journey.

But before the roustabouts could get to work, the passengers had to depart. Her haversack slung over her shoulder, Marta waited her turn as she watched the engineer beeline to the first-class lounge along with the rest of the important patrons. Less cherished passengers were only provided rough benches outside the nodus' reach on which to rest.

Stepping off the train, she was surprised to see Carmichael making his way to the first-class lounge as well. Clean-shaven and no longer sporting his silly disguise, her brother never looked her direction. Both children of Norwood Childress passed each other like strangers, he to his affluence, she to the crowded benches. His indifference suited Marta fine and was a far step better than his hatred two years prior. Marta's headache now seemed a living thing, a hatchling bird pecking its way out of the shell of her skull as she gazed at the benches. There were a few spots left among the weary passengers, but Marta expected no solace in sitting. Instead she trudged on, hoping the exertion would dull her pain.

Though a woman wandering alone at midnight in a strange city, Marta was not worried. Between her men's clothes and slouch hat hiding her face, she could easily pass as male in the dark. And if anyone did attempt to harm her, she felt reasonably safe unless they were carrying a musket. Those weapons were made illegal for civilians in the aftermath of the Grand War by decree of the president though. Even before their proliferation during the war, muskets were relatively rare, the expense of black powder keeping them out of reach except for the affluent. Her father possessed one, of course, locked within a glass case above the fireplace. The thing was just for show though, a family heirloom that was probably long gone. Marta was still pondering the fate of her father's prized musket when she turned the corner to behold the beast.

Its body resembled that of a massive bull reared back, an eagle's head atop it with a bladed beak open in a fierce screech. The thing shone with an unnatural light, its maw open and promising to devour her, but it was the creature's forelegs that made Marta recoil, the appendages strangely human and reaching stubby hands towards the sky. The gesture was that of an offering, and the incongruous human posture mingled among the brute's animal form caused revulsion in Marta.

It was an abomination, one that needed to be destroyed.

The plans to her phantom blade were immediately in mind, her Blessed Breath ready to extend the weapon when Marta realized her mistake. Though she had flinched, the creature remained motionless because it was simply a statue. The strange sheen of its skin was no more than the flickering light of the nearby luz jars reflecting off its bronze body.

Glad no one was around to witness her mistake, Marta approached the effigy. The word "Gunger" was carefully carved into the base and suddenly the statue made sense. The town of Gungersburg resided next to a nodus, which meant it was home to an emet.

Although all living beings had at least one fragment of Sol's Breath within them, not all living beings made up of Breath were contained in corporeal bodies. The emets were such creatures: created, like humans, of three Breaths, though they were entirely inhuman. Despite the intangibility of Breath in its natural state, the emets were able to give their essence substance, similar to the Shapers and their Armor or Weavers when fashioning their manifestations.

Though some modeled their bodies after humans, the majority of emets appeared as animals, oftentimes mixing and matching the body parts of different beasts. The why and how of their construction eluded most, the emets only capable of communicating with Renders and Weavers. Generally, emets ignored humanity, but a small minority took notice: the malevolent ghuls caused suffering whenever they were encountered and were hunted mercilessly by the Renders. Those that behaved benevolently towards humans were known as engels.

The emet Gunger must have been included in their benevolent number and resided at this nodus for decades if the citizens had named their town after it. Emets needed neither sleep nor sustenance to maintain them. As such, they wandered nearby the nodus of their birth until they finally disappeared back into Sol's flow. Some existed only a matter of hours, others for centuries; the only similarity between the emets being their inscrutable nature.

Some said a few emets were manifested of four Breaths, exhibiting the abilities of the Blessed like Waer, the progenitor of their kind. Through her abilities to draw like the Renders and Weavers, Waer was said to have created this species, using them to torment humanity throughout the centuries until the engels rebelled against their maker.

Though the Renders spoke of Waer as if a living entity, Marta knew she was just an excuse: a means to explain humans turning away from the will of Sol. Like the stories of the ancient Shaper Gerjet who always fought for good beside her faithful dog Baas, Waer was simply a story meant to entertain children. Marta had little time for stories since she had grown up and currently had more important things on her mind, such as whose mission she would complete, her brother or father's.

Though she despised her brother, Marta hated Orthoel Hendrix more and dreamed of putting an end to him. She had also given up on ever seeing her family again, so her father's promise of forgiveness was extremely tempting. But Marta was also aware that if she were to encounter Hendrix this night, her decision would be made for her. Between the lingering ley headache and her embarrassing reaction to the statue, she wanted an outlet for her ire to spread the shame and pain she felt to another.

She saw the silent flash before she heard the collective gasp. Just around the corner of the deserted street, Marta became aware of the murmur of dozens of voices. Though she could not make out individual words, the emotions behind them curled up her spine like sudden frost. There was fear, anger, and hatred hanging heavy in the air. Yet it was the three Breaths rising into the night sky to begin their inevitable journey back toward the nodus which drew Marta's undivided attention.

Something had just died, and if the nearby murmurs were any indication, it was not a kind death.

Marta was in motion before she realized it, her haversack slid off her back and onto a shoulder to be quickly discarded if she needed her hands free. The murmurs became more distinct as she rounded the corner, finally catching the words "Gunger" and "Render" too late to stop her advance.

Coming to a halt, Marta spotted a crowd of townspeople surrounding the wounded Render, the presence of the two Home Guardsmen at his flank the only thing keeping the crowd from devolving into a murderous mob. The townspeople's hatred was so intense that the air around them seemed to shimmer, and was aimed entirely at the Render in their center. He held a saber in his right hand, its blade fashioned of glass, not steel.

He had served in the Grand War, of that Marta was certain, though he wore no insignia. The Renders never did so, instead favoring their plain black cloaks and tri-cornered hats shared by the Home Guardsmen. This Render had a rangy look to him, his skin sallow and pulled taught across his bones. All those that had served during the Grand War had the same bearing about them, marking them as survivors rather than civilians.

The Render might not survive the night by the look of him though. An open gash stood red on his chest in stark contrast to his black clothes. It did not look like a life-threatening wound, but if the crowd had its way, he would not live long enough to seek out a sawbones.

Yet no body lay before him, and as the cries of "Gunger" continued to spatter the night, Marta realized whose death it was she witnessed at a distance: the Render had severed the strands of the emet Gunger and had killed the creature the townspeople named their city in honor of.

Someone hidden in the crowd cried, "Remember Creightonville," and Marta winced. She had heard those words hundreds of times before, and each occurrence ended in bloodshed. The Render Aloysius Pulley's execution of an emet had been the spark that set Newfield afire with war, and Marta found herself wondering if the same scenario would play itself out again here in Gungersburg.

Marta did not see where the stone came from as it flew through the air to connect with the Render's head. The man staggered but did not fall. He kept to his feet out of obstinance, and this defiance of the crowd seemed to spur them further as more fists reared back with awaiting rocks. The two Home Guardsmen stepped forward to protect him, but it was the Render's voice that stayed their hands.

"The next to raise arms will be named a conspirator and be dealt with accordingly."

The crowd paused as the tip of the Render's fragile glass blade rose. His eyes searched the crowd, Marta noticing each person his gaze fell upon step back as if pushed. For a moment Marta thought the Render's threat might be enough, but then the old man stepped forth. He could barely hold his brick aloft, yet the old man strode unafraid through the crowd. Even from her distance, Marta could see their eyes lock, the elder man at first hesitating then halting entirely. The old man seemed to diminish before her, Marta sure he would wisely drop the brick and disappear back into the throng. But then his arm reared back and the old man sealed his fate.

He was not strong enough, the brick not even clearing half the distance between them before it cracked into two hunks upon hitting the ground. The larger of the two pieces had not even finished rolling by the time the old man joined it there.

The Render struck soon as the brick left the old man's grasp, his hand rising like a conductor's, his fingers bared and open towards the sky. Almost too fast for the eye to track, his fist closed, his arm swinging back as he drew the old man's Breath with his Blessed ability.

The old man staggered, his mouth gasping as his Breath poured through his pores, stretching itself like taffy to cover the distance between him and the Render. No thicker than a finger's width, it almost reached the Blessed man when it finally could not be elongated any farther.

It was still inches out of the Render's grasp, so he drew again. He wrenched the old man's Breath harder, sending him stumbling several steps forward as his life-force finally cleared the gap to set itself weightlessly into the Render's free hand. Then the glass blade descended, the downward arc sailing through the stretched Breath as a strangled hiccup issued from its owner. The Render released the old man's Breath, and it returned inside its owner instantly.

The man crumpled as his life left him, his body now no more than a cooling husk as his three Breaths separated and escaped his gaping mouth to drift along invisible currents back towards the nodus. The brick he had thrown finally stopped rolling, the two of them motionless in the silent street.

If there would be any further bloodshed, Marta knew it would be decided in the next moment. The Render had demonstrated his power to the crowd, but they still outnumbered him and his protectors ten to one. Many would die, but the Render and his two guards would surely be among their number if the crowd rushed at them as one.

The Render remained calm as he speared each individual in the crowd with his gaze again. He silently dared each and every one of them to take the first step, to single themselves out among the crowd and become his second victim. When his eyes alighted on Marta, they lingered, or his right one did at least. Marta was not shocked to see his left eye was white and without an iris. Only a powerful Render would be capable of what she had just witnessed, so it was no surprise that his left eye was made of glass. He was clearly revered among his Blessed order.

His gaze remained upon her, probing Marta's face and posture. Her haversack still slung over her shoulder, she appeared poised to take action against him. Or perhaps the Render recognized her gauntness, marking her as another survivor of the war. Marta realized then that though she might be able to disguise her presence as a man in the dark, she still stuck out among the soft and well-fed townspeople of Gungersburg to a fellow former soldier.

As not to startle him, Marta's hand slowly caught the strap of her haversack and gently lifted it over her head to slip it across her back. The

Render did not twitch, his living eye still fixed upon her. So she tipped her hat to the man before departing the way she came. Though she did not look back, Marta could hear the crowd dispersing behind her. As she again approached the statue of their precious emet, Marta absently wondered if she was the catalyst for the crowd's breaking up without further bloodshed. It was possible they followed her lead without being aware of it, saving the lives of both the Render and dozens of townspeople.

Marta did not care for the lives of either the Render or the citizens of Gungersburg; it was her own survival she was ensuring. The Render had proved he was not to be trifled with, certainly not for a town she cared nothing for or its dead emet. What she had stumbled upon was clearly a message, a reminder of who held sway.

The presence of the Home Guardsmen proved that at least. Dedicated to the protection of the nation of Newfield, the Home Guard took their orders from the Department of Public Safety, to which Carmichael was acting as secretary. Both her and her brother's arrival in Gungersburg on the same night that the government of Newfield allowed a Render to destroy a beloved emet was no coincidence. Carmichael had meant for her to see the Render at work so she would remember who it was she served.

Or perhaps it was her father who ordered this display as a reminder of the cruelty the Western Renders were capable of. His coded message promised that if she delivered Hendrix his daughter, the East would rise again to throw off the Renders' rule. She just needed to complete her mission and return the nation of Newfield to a war he seemed sure they would win a second time around.

***

They arrived in the nation's capital, Vrendenburg, as the horizon was still shaking off the last lingering strands of dawn. Built like a wagon wheel with the senate and president's offices at the center of the hub, it was the heart of Newfield, a governing cog the whole nation revolved around. A thin mist hung over the city, making the cobbled streets slick and treacherous as the shrouded electric lampposts gave off a ghastly glow. The city was erected upon a swamp, an engineering achievement even modern Tinkers marveled at. Despite draining the land of the fetid water, the mists still lingered each morning as a reminder of when the landscape belonged to the swamps. In the beginning Vrendenburg had been a dangerous place full of sinkholes and disease, and though it hardly resembled its original state now, Marta suspected little had changed.

She had spent nearly two years here during the beginning of the Grand War in the highest echelons of society, but if any of her old companions saw her again, she hoped they would not recognize her now. Her encounter with Propst back in Walshvan had been awkward to the point of pain. Propst was always a well-meaning man, each of his hearty hails to Marta a stab at her heart as she tried to shuffle past him unseen. He remained oblivious throughout the ordeal though, first offering her a meal, then a job when he learned how she was employed at the quarry. Marta flatly turned both down and was glad he was bright enough to finally realize she had no desire to become reacquainted and allow her to depart.

As she disembarked the train, she spied Carmichael entering an awaiting carriage with Home Guardsmen making up his retinue. No one waited on Marta as she slipped through the crowd and into the awakening street as unnoticed as a shadow. Though tired beyond measure, the ley headache having kept her from sleep the entirety of the trip, Marta trudged along until she found the tram line to take her north to the outskirts of the city where the Lindaire Sanitarium and Hendrix's daughter awaited her.

It was nearly noon when she found the place, the high wrought iron walls imposing but doing little to obstruct Marta's view. A tavern across the street would provide a sufficient vantage point, Marta's mouth watering at the promise of sustenance, but upon stepping into the fancy foyer, she realized she stuck out like a pig in a Solday dress in her shabby clothing. She retreated back to the street, finally finding a vendor who sold her strong black tea she took in the tin cup she produced from her haversack. She spent even more money on the single cube of sugar, allowing herself little nibbles between slugs of the bitter drink. Usually she could not afford such luxuries, but flush with Carmichael's cash, she allowed herself the indulgence.

Her minor extravagance consumed, Marta slipped into an alley. Sure she was alone, she summoned the plans for her Cildra Armor and chose her rabbit legs. Her Breath instantly stirred at her bidding, swallowing her legs in the formation. The nickname of rabbit legs was not by accident, the Armor extending the length of her feet nearly threefold. These strands of Breath then connected back up to the forms over her calves, the fulcrum at her ankle allowing for the powerful leaps that gave the plans their name. The roof of the two-story building she chose for her new vantage point was about twenty feet up and the upper limit of the ability, but Marta made the leap without hesitation.

Landing lightly atop the building, she listened, scanning the sounds of the street for any alarm at her display. Hearing none, she slunk to the edge of the roof, lying prone and watching the comings and goings of the sanitarium. The habits worn by the sororal women attending the patients meant it was affiliated with the Dacist religious tradition. Such a place that followed the teachings of the Daci back in the Auld Lands was an anomaly. Most citizens of Newfield had readily chosen either the Render and Weaver way, little middle ground between the two. The Daci instead preached peaceful coexistence between the orders, referring to the Weavers as his right hand, the Renders his left. Dacist enclaves such as these were certainly few and far between, making it the perfect place to hide Hendrix's daughter. Despite her smoldering hatred towards her brother, Marta was still impressed by Carmichael's foresight in choosing it.

Her stomach gurgled, Marta slipping some hardtack from her haversack to stave off hunger as she waited. Her patience paid off finally as a flaxen-haired girl was led to a bench by a sororal wearing a Listener's pin. At this distance her age was difficult to determine, Carmichael's description putting Marta's target at twelve, but small for her age. This girl could be Hendrix's daughter, but Marta needed confirmation before she could act.

Her confirmation came when she saw the girl's eyes, bright blue and clearer than an untroubled summer sky. Between them and her hair, there could be no mistake as to the girl's identity. Not fifty yards away, Marta beheld Caddie Hendrix, daughter to the destroyer of the East.

The sororal woman stayed at the girl's side only a moment before leaving her to soak up the sun's rays alone. There the girl remained, motionless as a sculpture for the next several hours. Only once was the girl disturbed, a male patient hobbling over to shoo the child from her seat. But Caddie Hendrix remained absolutely stationary, and eventually her fellow patient departed. The girl did not turn her head at any point of their interaction, Marta unsure if she was even blinking from this distance as the hours rolled on. Finally, the sororal with the Listener pin returned, ushering the girl back inside as dusk descended.

Marta waited until the sororal with the Listener pin departed the sanitarium, dropping back into the alley and silently shadowing the woman down the street. The sororal's home turned out to be an unassuming boardinghouse, Marta waiting outside until she saw the light in her mark's room come on. Memorizing its location, she waited another few minutes before taking a room herself. When the clerk behind the counter asked for a name, Marta, on a whim, gave that of Steff Heitsch.

Her lodging secure, Marta fell into the awaiting bed, her exhaustion nearly all consuming. She set her spark box to the awaiting lamp out of habit, its harsh electric light revealing this boardinghouse to be head and shoulders above Marta's last in Walshvan. Her spark box contained enough electricity to keep the lights on throughout the night, but she pulled it free of its housing a moment later. Light in any form was unnatural to Marta, whereas darkness felt far more familiar.

Sluggishly she remembered the bottle of o-be-joyful Carmichael had so kindly provided her, finally deciding she would let it remain within her haversack. She needed a clear head for the next day when she would again prove her worth to her family as she returned to Cildra work.

Chapter 5

Maia 15, 558 (Nine Years Ago)

Marta carefully folded her favorite Solday dress, adding a pine sachet to the bundle before packing it in her trunk. Oleander looked on, perched atop one of the other five trunks that would outfit Marta in the Auld Lands. Their family would depart for the port of Chateaugay on the morrow, where Marta would sail off across the Saulshish Ocean for her new home alone.

The years spent in the Auld Lands among their Cildra kin was a rite of passage for the Childress children, one that Carmichael had recently returned from. Marta teased Oleander about her departure, stating at least Carmichael would again be here to keep her company. Though her sister smiled sweetly as she reminded Marta that their brother was meant to soon go into the field to do his Cildra work, Marta knew Oleander was relieved he would not share the manor with her. Even her parents' composed consideration, the servants' polite deference, or the mindless festations silently toiling away in the fields was preferable to Carmichael's presence.

Carmichael spent little time with their sister, never tormenting her like he had Marta. Instead he treated Oleander with absolute apathy, like an ugly piece of furniture that could not be disposed of, only endured. He scarcely even looked at her, certainly less so now since the family had accepted that Oleander was not born Blessed like the rest of them.

Yet Carmichael had also changed during his sojourn in the Auld Lands, now more aloof than ever. He had been absent a long time, even before he left to complete his training across the ocean. Since Marta had broken his nose, he had become distant. Although he had been antagonistic before the incident, she had always felt some form of affection in his taunts, yet since that moment, they had become like strangers forced to interact every day. They were both perfectly polite about it, but there was no love passing between them any longer.

Father was certainly not pleased when Carmichael returned wearing a Listener's pin with its two silver bulbs. Whisperer pins only sported one orb symbolizing the single mouth a person possessed, whereas the two heads of the Listener pins resembled the two ears. The Cildra eschewed both sets of pins though. Throughout their long and hidden history, no one in the clan had ever advertised their Blessed abilities, least of all abilities they did not possess. Though their father's face did not display his displeasure, he was quite irate that he had not been consulted before Carmichael made such a drastic decision in donning the Listener pin.

Carmichael remained equally impassive as he calmly explained his choice was in fact to make his Whisperer abilities more effective through misdirection. If his marks were spending their attention trying to keep their thoughts hidden from the apparent Listener, they would not notice him subtly placing new impulses into their minds as a Whisperer. This ploy would open up new avenues of mental ingress hitherto unavailable to him.

Mother came to his aid, of course, Carmichael always Cecelia Childress' favorite child. She flatly stated Carmichael's logic was sound, his heart strong and willing to make a daring decision. Father was not pleased by his wife taking their son's side in front of the entire family, but ultimately there was nothing he could do. The glass cap had already been removed, the Breath released from the luz jar, and nothing was capable of putting the escaped Breath back in.

Marta was excited to see her kin in the Auld Lands and to complete her Cildra training in the nations in which their clan was born. She had spent a similar stint of six months with Cyrus in Sable Hill to master the phantom blade and open palm a year past. There, she had been the darling of her more rural cousins. The older girls took to her instantly, each as genial and accommodating as their father, Cyrus, by ensuring there was not a single inch of the neighboring city of Broad Baird Marta was not familiar with by the time she departed. Marta played her part well, her manners and lovely dresses endearing her to the local aristocrats. This trip was more than just learning her Shaper abilities with Cyrus though; it was also a test to see if Marta could swim well in unfamiliar waters by blending with an entirely different set of high society. And Marta passed with high marks if one counted the inundation of requests that she soon return.

The city of Broad Baird was certainly lovely, if a bit quaint when compared to the more cosmopolitan Gatlin. Broad Baird fit her more provincial cousins perfectly, they soon to marry into the local gentry and guide their decisions from the shadows. The city and district would be in good hands, but Marta was meant for greater things. As oldest daughter of Norwood Childress, head of the Cildra clan in Newfield, Marta would not be wasted on a single forgotten county. No, whole states would one day be under her influence, perhaps even the fate of the entire nation.

Despite her desire to finally see the Auld Lands she had read about firsthand, she was still apprehensive. This trip was meant to last two years, an entire ocean between her and her family. In Sable Hill she had begun to miss the lingering smell of pipe from her father's study and her mother's tales of her home in Lacus and the war they had fought against the glassmen of Myna to claim it as part of Newfield. She would not miss Carmichael one iota, but the idea of being separated from Oleander for years was almost more than she could bear.

Marta shut the last of her trunks and, for a moment, she felt the impulse to reopen it, to leave the possibility for one last item to be crammed within. But she was fully packed and to leave the lid open simply on a whim would be childish. Marta would turn 16 in two months, and it was time to put childishness behind her as she clicked the latch into place.

The sound of the latch had an effect upon Oleander as well, her face going ashen. The look of apprehension vanished as quickly as it appeared though, replaced by a mischievous glint in her little sister's eyes.

"One last game of luz jars before you leave me?"

The offer of the game was a ruse, same as any of the Cildra games she had played with Oleander. Along with their Blessed abilities, the Cildra were expected to be the ideal model of aristocracy: well read, cultured, and as courteous as they were duplicitous. Marta had never been one for the strict manners demanded of her, something both her siblings took to naturally. But whereas Carmichael's polite words were a thin veneer for his continual disdain, with Oleander they always seemed genuine, even as she taunted Marta yet again.

Having never been forced to divide her time with Blessed training, Oleander instead maintained the prescribed Cildra physical and mental regiments of adolescence, her body now a coiled contraption and her mind honed sharper than any blade. Though two years younger, Oleander had overtaken Marta in their games and was now up by four points in their tally. Catching the flowing Breath within the luz jars was one of Oleander's specialties, Marta never able to match, let alone surpass, her at the game.

It was obviously a trap, but Marta fell into it willingly, both girls scrambling over each other to collect their jars and reach the ley.

In most households collecting Breath in the luz jars was a nightly chore for children, and in the wealthy Childress home, it was the duty of the human servants. But Norwood Childress' youngest children appropriated the chore and made it their private game, a point for each Breath they collected.

The lithe Oleander reached the Coak line of ley first and caught two Breaths before Marta even arrived. Oleander in action was truly a wonder to behold, with none of the awkwardness displayed by other girls her age as she darted among the flowing Breath. She had already claimed another three, sealing and discarding that jar before Marta even captured her second.

Marta had no chance of beating her sibling in this last chance before the continents divided them. No matter how much she treasured Oleander, it would never do to allow her younger sister to defeat her so soundly.

So Marta cheated.

Summoning her gauntlet to grasp the glass jar, Marta thinned her Blessed Breath and extended the appendage enough to catch a Breath beyond her normal reach.

"Blackguard!"

Oleander trilled the word, her smirk glinting like a dagger in the dark. There was no judgment to her pronouncement though. This was simply another challenge, one she was sure to overcome as she redoubled her efforts.

With her extended reach Marta soon closed the gap despite Oleander whirling through the air like an acrobat. But by watching her sister, Marta's attention was diverted, missing her lunge at one Breath. Unwilling to let it escape, Marta dismissed the gauntlet and summoned her rabbit legs, leaping after it and seizing it in her jar.

Oleander ignored the spectacular catch, her awareness solely focused on capturing the fragments of Sol. If Marta intended to prove herself Oleander's equal, she too could not allow her focus to be sidetracked, pushing her sister from her mind as she concentrated at the task at hand.

And so the daughters of Norwood Childress spent the evening playing together at their private game. It ended without a word, both girls finally collapsing upon the earth with just enough air left in their lungs to cackle at the absurdity of it all. A home needed just one or perhaps two luz jars per room, no more than six required to keep a house well-lit. Even with all the sprawling rooms of Hillbrook Manor, they needed no more than forty Breaths. Yet as they counted out their catch, they had reached eighty-six in total, a truly ludicrous number.

As Marta rechecked her math, she realized her haul was forty-five, exactly four more than her sister and tying them up in their total scores. For the first time in over a year, they were equals. The number was too perfect, Marta regarding her sibling with suspicion. Though no Listener, Oleander shook her head with mock severity.

"Don't think for a second I don't intend on still winning."

Oleander dissolved into giggles, prying opening the lid of one of her overstuffed luz jars and watching the released Breaths flee into the night. Marta responded in kind, her laughter twining with Oleander's as their former captives mingled in the flow of the ley.

Marta did not know where the impulse came from as the opening stanza to the song "The Sun Rises in the East" filled her head. She released the song along with a second luz jar, the first strain rising in the night air to join the escaped Breaths.

Oleander joined in instantly, adding her voice to her sister's with a haunting harmony. They sung well together, both said to have voices of mudbirds. Marta never cared for the comparison since mudbirds' stunning songs were equaled only by their infamous ugliness. Beautiful mudbirds were said to be myths, a metaphor for the unattainable and an ideal of perfection that could never be reached. Yet lying upon the grass, the sky resplendent with countless stars gazing down upon them, Marta thought such perfection was more than just possible; it was an actuality, a moment the two sisters shared, one that only disappeared when the last strains of the song finally faded and Marta's Blessed ley headache threatened.

***

The entire Childress family reached the port of Chateaugay by noon, over four hours for Marta's trunks to be stowed before the ship departed for Hydford across the sea in Acweald. Much of their dwindling time together was depleted by having an image taken, the photographer forcing the family to remain stock still for an interminable amount of time as he fiddled with his Tinker contraption. Their parents and Carmichael stood stiff as sculptures, but at the last second, Oleander's hand snaked out to give Marta a stinging pinch. The point she craved was denied her though, Marta's smile remaining as statuesque as the others when the bulb finally flashed.

Spying the ship Sanct Rosario for the first time, Marta was surprised by how huge it seemed with its three decks and dual propellers. Lines of ley existed within the oceans as well, ancient sailors using them as landmarks as they made their way. Within her parents' lifetimes Newfield Tinkers had figured out how to harness this energy to fuel their mechanical ships. Gazing at the mechanical marvel, Marta found it hard to believe those ancient sailors had braved the seas without these modern machines.

Carmichael was the first to give his farewell, perfunctorily pulling Marta to him in a dry hug. His words were cryptic and probably cribbed from one of the philosophical tomes he had been absorbed with lately as he whispered, "To dig through the dirt, one cannot expect to come out completely clean."

Her mother's hug held more tenderness, though just barely as she implored Marta not to lose the lilt of her Mimas accent while abroad. Her father's words were more foreboding, reminding her even though he would not be there physically with her, everything she did would reflect upon him as if he were. Then, placing his hands solemnly upon her shoulders, he instructed Marta to make him proud.

Oleander's embrace felt like home, a place Marta was forced to part with as she finally broke the hold. Oleander's hands shot out to catch her own, clinging to them with a desperation Marta had not expected. Marta tried to commit the moment to memory, to capture every detail in its entirety sure as the tintype they had taken had. Then the ship's horn sounded the final boarding call and Marta was forced to extricate herself.

"Have yourself a grand adventure," Oleander called as Marta strode towards the awaiting ship. "And don't forget for one moment that we're not equal."

Climbing up the plank to the vessel, Marta looked down to see the Shaper stevedores resting in the shade of the ship. The summer heat had not yet even begun in earnest, but they sweated with abandon after having hauled all the cargo aboard. A few swears wafted up to reach her, the rough men and women that made up her fellow Shapers with no idea at how high she walked above them. Taking swigs off of a flask passed among them, they preferred hard drink befitting the hard work they did, and Marta again thanked Sol that she had been born into the Cildra clan where her Blessed abilities could be put to better use.

Looking down from the deck, the ship suddenly seemed much smaller, the ocean that much more vast. She waved to her family as the Sanct Rosario broke away and it was then that Marta noticed the additional weight upon her hand. Glinting upon her finger a familiar ring resided, one gold strand woven in among the three silver.

The ring had not adorned her finger for years, but it felt inherently a part of her again as Marta realized Oleander had slipped it upon her finger during their goodbyes. In the distance she could not make out Oleander's face, but Marta knew her sister was grinning. Oleander had indeed intended on winning their game, now up by a single point and Marta with no chance to catch up for another two years.

Though not Blessed, Oleander truly was the best aspects of her other siblings, with Carmichael's cunning and Marta's physicality. With time and the proper opportunity, Marta was sure Oleander would prove herself one of the greatest of the Cildra clan.

Marta grinned as she examined the ring. Oleander had been amazing as always, but she had also made a mistake in showing her up so theatrically. Such a challenge could not go unanswered, and Marta now had two years to plan how to defeat her dear sister.

Chapter 6

Winterfylled 18, 567

Marta awoke with a clear head, her mind alive and running through her plan as she stretched her body. Though her stony face did not show it, her hands itched to get to work. The plan itself was simple: taking only minutes to formulate, a few hours to acquire the proper supplies, and hopefully less than an hour to execute. The problem with plans though, Marta knew, was they never entirely resembled the initial idea in the actual execution.

The first supply she obtained was the basket, a wide one meant for collecting washings. To complement it she chose several white sheets, tossing them within with barely a glance. Next came the can of resin, a thick and viscous liquid she poured upon the basket and sheets back in the boardinghouse. Leaving them to soak, she trudged towards the stop she had wanted to put off as long as possible.

Stepping into the dress shop gave Marta a strange sense of double vision, her memories of hunting in similar stores with her mother surfacing as she breathed the air of the place in. It was nothing compared to the fancy stores of Gatlin, but the smell remained the same: cloth, strong spices to perfume them, and the expectation she would leave prettier than she had entered.

Her mother always gave the girl free rein to wander, allowing Marta to search through the store to her heart's content. And when her heart was filled to bursting with the store's wares, she was forced to use her head by explaining in detail why the dress she had chosen would be the best decision. If her argument hinged upon the dress being the prettiest, Marta would leave with one of her mother's uninspired selections. But if she could form a sound argument her mother approved of, Marta would depart with her prize. As with all interactions with her family, this too was training by teaching the girl to hide her real intentions as she swayed others.

Marta found herself analyzing the dresses by rote, finding not the prettiest, but those with the strongest stitching, the ones that would disappear into a crowd best. She tried one on for herself, the soft fabric feeling unfamiliar and clinging against her skin. The smaller dress she simply slung under her arm, hoping it would be the right size by her rough estimations. The child's coat she bought on a whim, unsure if the girl would need it on their journey since it would conclude long before winter arrived. Marta would be playing the role of mother for the next few days though, and she reckoned a mother should care if her child was cold.

Depositing her collection of clothes back in the boarding house, Marta examined her spark box next. Sure its charge was full, she contented herself with a cold meal before making her final acquisition.

Slipping silently down the hallway, she checked the sororal's door to find it locked. Such precautions from the woman were no matter to Marta as she touched her fingertip to the lock and brought forth her mental plans for the open palm. Her fourth Breath responded straightaway, exuding out her fingertip and sliding into the lock to expand until it fit the cylinders perfectly. With a twist of her finger, the lock gave way, accepting Marta's false key as surely as the real thing.

Shutting the door behind her, Marta was rewarded by the woman's dirty linens. As she had hoped, a second sororal habit awaited her, close enough in size that it could pass cursory inspection. More importantly, the wimple would cover Marta's forehead and hide her most distinguishing feature. Folding the garment up, she departed, relocking the door behind her.

Hidden back in her room, Marta dressed herself in the stolen habit. It certainly lacked a studied hand, but it would have to do since her time was running out. Gathering up her washer basket, Marta left the boardinghouse as dusk deepened into night. The sororal she had stolen from would return soon, and Marta had no desire to encounter her while wearing the pilfered clothes.

Keeping her head down as if examining the full basket, Marta returned to the Lindaire Sanitarium, walking, not to the front gates, but around the back. There, Marta studied the imposing wall. She had cleared a higher jump just yesterday, but now anxiety nibbled at her stomach. Something felt wrong as she inspected her surroundings again, finding nothing there to account for her unease.

It was only when her gaze returned to the spiked iron of the wall that Marta realized she alone was the cause of her anxiety. Though her face usually remained stoic, Marta sneered as she chided herself for the stupidity of her sudden fear. During the Grand War she had performed much more dangerous missions than breaking into some Dacist asylum. In those instances she had felt no fear, no anxiety as to the outcome. In those battles her life hung by the thinnest of threads, but she had performed her duties without a trace of disquiet. These sororal sisters were no threat to her, Marta capable of taking the girl from the women by force if she was willing to spill some of their blood. It was true that the sororal sisters were all innocents, but Marta had no qualms spilling blood, innocent or not, so she could not comprehend why she still felt so anxious.

The seconds melting away, Marta turned her attention to her fear. It felt familiar, and it took a moment for her to realize where the familiarity hailed from. It was not from the Grand War as she would have expected, but from her childhood and the games of sneak-and-see she played with Oleander. In those instances there was no threat of physical pain, only the anxiety of being caught, and Marta found herself wondering why this fear of discovery trumped that of death. She also found herself idly wondering why it was the image of her sister that came to mind on her mission to extricate Caddie Hendrix.

But these reveries would never do, Marta's Cildra training returning to tamp down both the anxiety and image of Oleander. Her mind made up, she summoned her rabbit legs, hopping over the fence with several feet to spare lest she snag her stolen sororal garb.

Alighting on the ground, Marta found the yard devoid of patients, who were probably stowed safely within their rooms. The only question was finding the right room now. And not being caught as she made her attempt would not hurt either.

Marta learned long ago the best antidote to being noticed was to appear as if she belonged. She belonged nowhere now since the war, but Marta kept up the pretence by lowering her head behind the camouflaging sheets as she marched up to the door. It was a back door meant for the serving staff to use and possibly requiring a key. Marta had no fear of the lock and only hoped no one would spy her as she sprung it.

She need not have worried though, as a smiling sororal sister swung the door wide.

"I did not see you go out, Sister."

The accent was foreign, probably Ossain from the sound of it. That would make sense, the Daci's seat within the Auld Lands nation of Ossan.

"Just needed to return the washing, Sister," Marta answered while keeping her head down and refraining from making eye contact.

Marta did not remain long enough to ascertain if the Ossain sororal was suspicious of her sudden appearance in the yard as she pushed through the kitchen and into the building proper. Keeping her steps steady and unhurried was the hardest part as Marta made her way, taking a turn around the corner to pause and listen closely. There were no cries of alarm, no hurried steps behind her, so she decided her disguise held up. The only question was for how long.

It took Marta no time to find the basement and disappear into the dark below. Dropping the basket, she removed her spark box and set the filament to the resin-soaked sheets. For a moment she worried they were still too wet to sustain fire, but finally the spark caught, Marta blowing upon it until it bloomed into living flame. Soon the whole basket was smoldering, the first trails of pungent smoke wafting up to the ceiling. The resin would ensure it would be a slow burn. The smoke was tremendous, though there would be little chance of it spreading along the stone floor.

Leaving her burning basket behind and the door to the basement ajar, Marta set out down the halls until she found the wing containing the patients. Heavy sleeping breaths emanated from their rooms, the whole hallway seeming to inhale and exhale in unison. Marta unlocked each door with her open palm, checking to see if the girl resided within. Each door she then left unlocked, her unsought sleeping occupant undisturbed as she continued her search.

At last Marta found her prize, the girl's nearly white stock of hair conspicuous even in the dim light. Mentally marking the room, Marta moved on, unlocking one door after the other as she waited for her trap to spring. The smell of smoke was already obvious to her, but so far the sororal sisters remained oblivious. She considered giving out the call of alarm herself, but drawing any more attention might be more than her disguise could endure. So Marta decided on a hundred-count before she gave the alarm.

She was over halfway through her count before the frightened cry of "fire" finally sounded from the kitchen. Soon as she heard it, Marta began throwing open the doors, yelling at the patients to hurry outside. The first one stared at her in shock, but soon other cries of distress joined hers, the patients roused and hurrying along.

Suddenly another sororal rushed into the hallway, keys jingling in her hands and confusion evident upon seeing all the open doors and fleeing patients. Marta again felt the familiar twinge of fear of discovery, but she pushed the disquiet down as she followed her plan.

"The patients! Get the patients outside before they burn!"

There was honed authority to Marta's command and the sororal woman instantly obeyed, Marta secretly thanking the order's strictness and sense of obedience.

The girl had not yet emerged from her room, Marta more than happy to collect her in person. Returning to the door, Marta stepped inside and was surprised to find the girl still tucked into bed.

"Caddie, your father sent me. I'm here to take you to him. I'm here to take you home."

The child did not move, and when she arrived at her bedside, Marta found her blue eyes open and staring, her breathing calm and unhurried. For a moment she worried the girl might be deaf, but a second look into those blue orbs and Marta realized she was not so lucky. The eyes of Orthoel Hendrix's daughter aimed straight at the ceiling, her gaze blank and unfocused. Waving her hand before the girl's face, Marta received no response as her fear was confirmed.

During the Grand War Marta had seen similar cases of combat fugue, the soldiers unable to retreat from the bloodshed physically and instead recoiling within their own minds to sit still as the dead. The men and women Marta encountered like this before had waded through blood so thick it had turned the dirt to mud, and suddenly she found herself wondering what this girl had seen that had left her in this state.

The cries for escape from the frightened sororals had reached a fever pitch, Marta with no more time to reflect on the child. So she summoned her most comforting voice.

"Caddie? Can you hear me, Caddie?"

Still the girl did not stir, her eyes never leaving the ceiling. Marta's anxiety fluttered its wings again, but its existence did not last long as her anger flared up to quash it. Carmichael and his network of informants would have known the girl was comatose, but he had not included this information in her mission. That meant he intended for her to fail, to be caught, and Marta's anger roared. But there was no clarity in it this time, her rage hitting an immovable impediment as she picked over the problem.

Marta had seen Caddie move before, had watched her take a seat outside under her own power. The only question was how to make her, the girl unfortunately a lock her open palm could not pick. Her anger without an obvious outlet, Marta shook Hendrix's daughter roughly.

The girl never stirred during her outburst. Marta finally let go, the girl's head lolling to the side like a damaged doll. Her open eyes still stared straight ahead, Marta considering carrying her from the room when the sororal burst in, her Listener pin glinting.

It was the same woman whose clothes she wore, Marta unable to miss the recognition in the sororal's face as she beheld the thief. She was caught, had finally been discovered as she had feared. Marta's fear was long gone though, only her anger remaining. She also now had a target to take her frustration out on as Marta considered killing the woman to save herself the trouble of fashioning an excuse as to her presence.

The sororal's eyes went wide, and in that moment Marta's clarity descended to give her anger purpose. The sororal was a Listener, and so Marta set a mental refrain, her cover story tinged with the truth: she was sent from the Covenant Sons to retrieve Orthoel Hendrix's daughter.

The woman's eyes widened farther, Marta sure her lie had taken root even as she lunged at the sororal. Pressing her up against the wall, Marta's voice was cold as an Overhurst winter wind.

"Tell me how to make her move."

The sororal's teeth clacked shut, the woman apparently devoted to her charge. So Marta prodded the woman's eye with her thumb, not quite enough to puncture it, but enough so the woman would not see properly on the morrow. On top of the pain, Marta altered her refrain, adding how she had killed many men who had not acquiesced to her demands.

Again, it was a lie tainted with truth.

The sororal broke, her words tumbling over each other, "You have to touch her. Skin to skin. A woman, it has to be a woman. Just touch her and she'll obey."

Suddenly it made sense as to why Marta's father and brother had chosen her for this mission. Even though Marta had hoped the ultimate reason was her chance to prove herself again to the clan, the truth was refreshing in its uniqueness. They needed a woman, a woman they would not mind losing if the mission proved too difficult, and she fit the bill.

Though she had all she needed to complete her set task, she still wanted more as she pressed her thumb into the woman's uninjured eye. "How did she end up this way? What happened to her?"

"I don't know. No one does. She just appeared on our doorstep. We could not turn her away."

It was the truth, that much being obvious from the way the sororal's mouth contorted in fear. The woman no longer any use to Marta, she considered killing the sororal again in the deeper part of her mind where the Listener could not plumb. Yet the woman's abilities still had their use, even if it was only misdirection. So Marta set a new refrain, how she would take Caddie straight to Oreana to meet up with her contacts in the Covenant Sons.

The only question was if the woman would remember this as Marta dug both her palms into her victim's neck, pressing against the arteries with all her might. Within moments the sororal's eyes fluttered, unconsciousness overcoming her as she went limp in Marta's arms. She allowed the woman to slump down against the wall as Marta again turned her attention to the girl staring at the ceiling. Her fingers encircled the child's wrist, the girl's skin so thin Marta could feel each and every steady beat of blood in her veins.

"Look at me."

The blue eyes turned to bore into Marta, the woman unsure if the girl actually saw her or was just following the sound of the voice. It was still progress though, and her time to safely remain within Lindaire Sanitarium was quickly winding down.

"Stand up."

The girl rose to stand beside Marta without hesitation. Her movements were smooth, but once she reached the requested stance, the girl went slack, as if awaiting other orders. It reminded Marta somewhat of the festations growing up on Hillbrook Manor, the creatures with basic intelligence but no will of their own, no spark stemming from their Soul to give them desires. Marta also remembered when she had first met the girl's father years ago, how his demeanor too had reminded her of festations and their lack of emotion. But if he had only echoed this similarity, his daughter resounded with it, the girl mechanical and even less useful than a festation since Marta had to remain in contact with her to give her orders.

"Come with me."

Caddie complied readily enough, falling into step with Marta as she hurried down the hallway. The initial plan was to take the girl out the back, over the wall and into the maze of alleyways of Vrendenburg. But like all plans, this one too had broken down at the unexpected appearance of the sororal, and so Marta modified it as she went.

She led the girl straight out the front door, through the confusion of the other milling sororals with their patients, and out into the streets. Glancing over her shoulder, Marta saw no one noticed as the two made their escape. They fled through the alleys and then the streets until she found her boardinghouse. Spiriting the girl upstairs to her room, Marta rid herself of the sororal garb, Caddie waiting exactly where she had been left without complaint.

Getting the girl dressed proved no issue. Like festations, the girl proved capable of simple tasks such as putting on her dress and coat without having to be walked through the steps individually. Holding the girl's wrist, Marta noticed the marks crawling up her arm, tiny scars no larger than pinpricks swarming over her flesh. They were evenly spaced, less than a thumb's width between them as they spiraled up both arms. Though hardly noticeable against the girl's pale skin, Marta noted them nonetheless, hoping if they were considered identifying marks they would be covered by the coat she had fortunately bought.

Fastening a bonnet over the child's forehead and then her own, Marta then turned her greatcoat inside out. The Grand War had left a surplus of such coats to match the sudden surplus of widows. A woman wearing one turned out was a sign she had lost a husband in the war, a silent announcement of her bereavement, and Marta hoped this would give an obvious answer to anyone wondering why a mother and daughter were traveling alone at night. Slinging the haversack over her shoulder, Marta took the girl's soft hand in her own rough one.

"Let's go see your father."

The trip to the tramline took no time at all, the car not quite empty even at this late hour. It dropped them at the train station without incident, Marta hurrying with the girl to the ticket counter. She knew she was not yet too late to purchase a ticket, but Marta was ready to put Vrendenburg far behind her.

True to the refrain she had set for the unlucky sororal woman, Marta purchased a ticket for Oreana, though she had no intention of ever reaching that destination. The man behind the counter was happy enough to issue their tickets, smiling sleepily at Caddie as he told Marta she certainly had a well-behaved daughter. Marta bestowed a thin smile upon him in response, not because she cared for the girl, but because it was what her cover story required.

***

The first leg of their journey went smoothly, Marta almost believing they could make their way to Ceilminster entirely unmolested in the silence of the sleeping car. But a straight shot to their goal would be exactly what any pursuers would be expecting, messages along the Dobra networks traveling faster than the trains. Marta therefore had no intention of plotting such a simpleminded course.

She hauled Caddie off the train at the second rest stop to purchase another ticket on a new route to Keysville. The girl followed her promptly and seemed willing to obey any order she was given. The girl never shut her eyes though, and she never attempted to sleep as the car's gentle rocking lulled Marta to drowsiness despite the promise of the oncoming ley headache. Though Marta never spoke unless issuing instructions to the girl, she found Caddie's silence disquieting.

Splurging on another sleeper car, with any luck Marta could fall asleep before the ley headache could take hold to then disembark in the forgotten city of Naddi. Bordering Ingios territory and far away from the main train lines, this tiny train hub was the last place anyone would think to look for them. If this new direction proved successful, Marta would then buy a new ticket for Ceilminster in the hope they would arrive there without incident to make contact with the Covenant Sons, at which point she would find herself beside Orthoel Hendrix.

But her mission would only be complete as she drove her Shaper claws into his chest and watch while his eyes turned dead as his daughter's. Marta's father might be able to forgive the man, but she realized she was now too far gone to be capable of such humanity herself.

***

His rear firmly planted in the earth, his hands occupied by furiously whittling with his straight-bladed knife, Luca Dolphus kept his bare foot within the Cienegas line of ley. His headache raged beyond the point of distraction, Luca barely able to maintain his attention on the ill-formed block of wood.

He would have preferred an instrument, a fiddle maybe, or better yet a mandolin. Playing music apparently alone along the ley would draw attention though, so he contented himself with the whittling. A few more slivers removed from the outer edge of the block, he still puzzled after what it would be. He had learned long ago that to carve with intention was a fool's errand, the wood resisting any attempt at giving it form opposed to its own internal will. No, the wood wanted to provide its own shape independent of the person doing the whittling, revealing itself only when it was good and ready. So far he was still clueless as to the final form, but it was only a matter of time before it made itself known.

These were all foolish thoughts, Luca knew, wood with no consciousness except what he bestowed upon it in his distress. His headache had continued unabated for two weeks now, the exact amount of time he had kept his foot within the ley, and it was influencing his thoughts.

Frustrated again at the inscrutable piece of wood, Luca looked for Isabelle. She was probably close, but not making her presence known. Usually the woman refused to shut up, chattering so much about her dreams the night before it made his head swim. But since they received their latest, and hopefully last, mission together, Isabelle avoided him as much as possible, content to let him suffer alone in silence.

The headache had grown past the space of Luca's head, making him want to get up and shake himself free of it. Yet Luca remained, his right hand reaching down to feel the comforting weight of his lockblade in his right pocket. Just the touch of it made the pain retreat somewhat as Luca's concentration again coalesced on the block of wood. Unless he found some new inspiration, it would be an ugly thing discarded to join the dozen others littering the ground around him. He wanted this one to be beautiful, just as he had wanted the others to be, but again inspiration eluded him. His hands kept moving ceaselessly though, chipping away at the wood as if it would help.

Suddenly a message came through the line, Luca sitting up and reaching his hand into the ley as if more contact would actually help decipher the Dobra transmission. It was the usual drivel, mostly an outpouring of the nation of Newfield's bureaucracy. There were also the usual personal messages, far-flung families sending their love to their relatives, but buried deep within the transmissions was a message to Luca himself.

Simza had finally spoken, had finally given purpose to his suffering along the ley.

Replacing the forgotten boot upon his foot, Luca stood, blood rushing to his head and making him dizzy. Or perhaps it was the mission, finally a chance to be reunited with Jaelle that made his head spin. Either way, Luca returned his straight-blade knife to its sheath at his waist.

Isabelle appeared beside him, quiet as a thought as her hazel eyes gazed into his brown.

"Time we were off," he said.

Isabelle cocked her head, her face remaining slack. Her lips did not even tremble as he tucked the unfinished block of wood into his belt.

"No, no need to hurry. They won't arrive in Naddi until morning."

Chapter 7

Solmonad 20, 559 (Eight Years Ago)

It had not even been a year yet Marta had come to the conclusion that the Auld Lands were tranquil, beautiful, and utterly boring. Opportunities for intrigue certainly abounded in the balls, salons, and banquets she attended, Marta whirled from one to the other so fast they were but a blur of finery. Whispers and snippets of information filled every corner, the lands abuzz with plots.

All the intrigues felt tired to her though, the plots perfunctory, as if everyone was simply going through the motions of a game that had gone on for far too long. There was no passion to it, all the discussed territories already having been claimed for centuries, their borders secure and the residents of the Auld Lands simply politely arguing over scraps.

The continent had run its course. The Daci had seen to that as he preached his peace, not just between the Renders and Weavers, but for all of Sol's children. There were no more wars; no more sense of discovery. Everything had already been established and agreed to by all, their roles already assigned and readily accepted. All in all it was a far cry from the constant excitement provided her in her hectic home of Newfield.

The Auld Lands were certainly more cultured though; Marta could not deny them that. The people here were also much more refined in their affluence. To hear them tell it, civilization sprung up on their shores thousands of years ago, and they had the heirlooms to prove it. The mansions her Cildra relatives lived in here each had dozens of beautiful tapestries and portraits that would surely reside in a museum back home. But here no one even noticed them. They were too commonplace and faded into the background beneath all the senseless chatter.

There was more minutia to their maneuverings as well, an almost indecipherable maze to penetrate. Marta made her first mistake the night of her arrival by kissing her host's cheeks twice, not the three times as demanded by high society here. Her host had been kind in his response to her gaff by deviating from decorum to return the same flawed gesture to her, but as she realized her mistake, Marta saw the reaction on her cousins' faces. The fact they looked down upon her was obvious, they considering her the provincial girl who would not last a week when faced with all their cosmopolitan glamour.

What was worse, she soon realized her hairstyle was long out of fashion here, her dresses two seasons out of date. If Marta wanted to be considered one of their numbers as her Cildra training demanded, she would have to make some drastic changes.

Marta made the requisite alterations immediately, throwing out all of the dresses filling her trunks and availing herself of the shops and boutiques her cousins frequented. In a matter of days, Marta was the height of fashion, her corsets cinched so tight she could scarcely breathe in dresses that were as alluring as they were low-cut. To these she added jewelry to accentuate her choices with a surprisingly adept eye.

But in regards to her hair, Marta decided to establish herself as separate from everyone else. Instead of mirroring her Auld Land hosts, Marta chose to plait her hair in the style of her cousins' back in the state of Nahuat, staying up late to perfect the intricate braids they favored in Sable Hill.

In so doing Marta stuck out from the crowd, her aberrant hairstyles and darker skin drawing all eyes to her, especially from the boys desperate for something new to turn their attentions upon. Marta found them all genteel, erudite, and utterly undeserving of her interest. She still smiled sweetly at their entreaties though, laughing coquettishly as each one took the uniqueness of her braids as an opportunity to approach her. The most difficult part was making sure her female cousins were nearby to witness her hoarding of the boys' undivided attention.

Soon her female cousins sought her out, first one or two at a time, and then finally whole flocks anxious to learn the secrets of her plaits. Within a matter of weeks, the whole coterie sported the same style, Marta smirking internally each time she doled out her knowledge. Back home these braids were considered provincial, but here in the Auld Lands they suddenly became the height of fashion.

Although the fickleness of fashion was amusing, the idea of her identity now perplexed her. If anyone back home had asked her where she hailed from, she would have answered Mimas immediately. Back home being from Mimas meant something, yet here in the Auld Lands, Mimas was simply a small spot on a vast map, just as Acweald or Bance were to her before she stood upon their shores. So now when the people of the Auld Lands asked her where she was from, Marta found herself answering Newfield rather than Mimas.

This realization disturbed her, a sense of loss there, though she could not put her finger on the why of it. Back home she would have had an instant dislike of anyone from the Western state of New Albion, arguments over the necessity of festations sure to factor into their heated conversation. Back home they would be at each other's throats, only decorum keeping them within the barest semblance of civility. But here in the Auld Lands, she and this imagined citizen of New Albion would become fast friends, the two of them bonding over their similarities of being from Newfield as opposed to these inscrutable denizens of the Auld Lands. Here their differences would be forgotten in favor of the fact that they were both foreigners.

Identity, it seemed, was a matter of difference and distance: the farther she traveled from it, the larger her home became, now encompassing states that she had considered her enemies not a year ago. Following that line of thought to its conclusion, Marta found herself wondering if the entire world would feel like home if she traveled far enough.

Her journey took her first through Acweald for several months, then to the neighboring nation of Bance. There, she tested out the language of Bancel with natives for the first time, discovering that her years of instruction in the language from Mitchell were significantly less than adequate. Although her diction was technically correct, she found the native speakers constantly asked her to repeat herself. Not only was her accent atrocious, she quickly learned her phrases were terribly formal and not at all reflecting how the real people of Bance spoke. Though she redoubled her efforts, Marta often found when she spoke to them in Bancel, they answered her in Acwealt. Marta knew they were being considerate to her in these instances, but more than anything, it made her wish she had been more attentive in her studies back home.

From Bance she moved on to the nation of Anamahn, where she stayed with the family of Steff Heitsch. Marta could not stand the girl, Steff focused entirely on the trappings of an aristocratic life rather than gathering information and influencing events as was required by their Cildra upbringing. At first Marta thought Steff's affectations were only an act similar to Carmichael and his false Listener pin: a guise she wore so no one would expect more from her. But after a month in her presence, Marta realized Steff was simply shallow.

So Marta fashioned a new test for herself by becoming Steff's closest friend and confidant, the task made more difficult because Steff was a Listener able to hear her unguarded thoughts. She hated every moment she spent by Steff's side, each one of her fawning refrains a misery to Marta. It was like putting her hand above a candle's flame to see how long she could stand the pain: the experience was entirely unpleasant, but the proof of her willpower more than made up for the misery. So when Steff burst into her room with her retinue of friends, Marta put on a pleasant face, soon giggling along with practiced abandon.

"He's written you again," Steff nearly sang, "and included a poem this time."

Steff produced another letter from the boy still smitten with Marta after her sojourn in Acweald. To hear him tell it, he was destined to be a count, but Marta knew he was a baron at best, his family's influence on the wane and his name the only valuable thing he possessed now. So of course he would be fixated upon this enthralling Newfield girl, her family's fortune calling to him all the way from Mimas. His letter was written in Acwealt and included a sonnet he composed extolling Marta's beauty.

"... as soft as the moon's embrace on the summer seas," Steff translated into Mahnen for her friends.

"As the moon's kiss," Marta interjected, correcting her cousin's translation. Though she would never be mistaken for a native speaker, Marta took pride in that she understood Mahnen better than Steff did Acwealt.

Marta earned a quick glower from her cousin, Marta suspecting Steff had finally grown wise to the fact she was being manipulated. So she sought to diffuse the situation, Marta dissolving into laughter that all the girls soon echoed while Steff droned on in her inadequate translation. The boy's sonnet was as absurd as his professions of love were, the idea that some forgotten barony in Acweald would be enough to claim the oldest daughter of Norwood Childress fueling Marta's sniggers further.

Marta had hoped for another letter from her father, or perhaps Oleander, the written word their only means of communication now. Through their private codex her father still kept her apprised of life back in Newfield as best he could. Tensions were coming to a head between the East and West, war a real possibility that might extend Marta's stay in the Auld Lands.

Oleander's letters were much more enjoyable, deviously hinting at her further training in the code shared among the sisters. She was excelling at every test they gave her now that there was nothing else to focus upon in Marta's absence. Oleander hoped their father would send her into the field soon, the brimming hostilities between the states curtailing any chance she would have of visiting the Auld Lands herself. There was an immediate need for a Cildra spy with Oleander's skills, and the possibility of her being deployed became more of an actuality with the passing of each day.

Reluctantly Marta returned to the clucking of the Auld Land girls who were desirous of dining out in some stylish restaurant in town. Listening to their inane chatter, Marta was exceedingly bored with their silly affluence. Suddenly she wanted to do something new, something daring and unexpected.

"Why don't we visit the Wanderers?"

The other girls' voices were instantly silenced at the very idea. They were horrified at the proposal, but beneath their looks Marta could see something more: real intrigue and interest at her plan. Steff could see it too, instantly putting her foot down.

"Impossible. To visit the Dobra without chaperones? What would our parents think if they found out?"

Marta's father would find out as soon as theirs, but Marta dismissed their doubts with a flare of her shoulders. "I guess I'll have to go alone then."

Her defiant declaration cinched it, all the girls agreeing to accompany the intrepid explorer lest they be labeled craven. Within moments they were all of one accord, Steff with no choice but to accompany them or lose her tenuous status as their leader.

***

They arrived in one carriage at a restaurant at the edge of town, waiting within the building long enough for the driver to depart before hurrying on into the woods to find the Dobra encampment. The sounds of the celebration plotted their course, leading them through the trees as sure as any map. Out of the manors and mansions she had been staying within these long months, Marta felt alive again, the smell of the dirt and night air giving her new vigor. It was not home by any stretch of the imagination, but it was better than the stifling society that had caged her until now.

Though the night was still young, many townspeople gathered at the encampment, the Wandering Dobra bringing a carnival-like atmosphere wherever the wind blew them. The camp exuded elation everywhere, but Steff was still simmering at the insult of being forced to attend. Her friends had chosen Marta over her, and for that Steff intended on making Marta pay.

"We should find secrets while we're here," Steff offered slyly.

"Whoever discovers the best one will be the winner."

It was a Cildra game, old as the clan itself and the plaything of children. Steff's friends were not members though, and so the idea was novel to them. Only Marta knew this was really a test for the leadership of the coterie, a silent battle between the two Cildra for dominance.

Despite Steff's declaration, the other girls remained unsure as to the game. So Marta sealed the deal by adding her assent, all the girls instantly agreeing to Steff's chagrins.

Their new mission decided, the gaggle of girls linked arms as they broke into groups of two to explore the Dobra encampment. The pairings quickly determined, Marta discovered Steff was the only other odd one out. The Dobra were said to steal more than kisses from young girls, but Marta made her way alone unafraid, forcing Steff to do the same.

The Dobra certainly took notice of the well-dressed solitary girl as they called out from their wagons in a mix of languages, all entreating her to approach and sample their exotic wares. From one wagon Marta was offered glimpses into her destiny via their mysterious bix sticks, differently colored twigs they tossed down and purported to divine the future from. Other wagons tempted her with ancient tales, whereas more promised the latest news fresh from the Dobra networks. Still others offered her the chance to communicate with her relatives through the lines of ley. One particularly persistent old woman swore she would part with an imbued locket, though Marta knew only the cursed Ikus tribe dealt with these profane objects. Despite this well-known fact, all Dobra tribes hawked these goods and were always sure to find an ignorant taker among the towns they visited.

Marta kept walking since she was well aware offered objects had no value, simply trash the Dobra wished to unload upon the unsuspecting. No, things of real value had to be earned.

They had to be taken.

Marta spotted her mark just as he spied her, the boy giving the unaccompanied girl a wolfish whistle. He was a handsome lad, dark of hair and with sharp eyes. Only a few years older than Marta, he was attractive and well aware of it. Instead of approaching her, he kept his distance, only his whistle and wandering eye any indication of his interest. He was clearly used to fawning girls; only having to invite them over before they willingly came running.

Marta was also skilled in such flirtatious games from her time in the Auld Lands high societies. She knew she should match him step for step in the dance of attraction, actively ignoring his advances and looking away so as to become more inviting. Instead she brazenly caught his gaze, a sudden fire in her stomach as she saw the obvious hunger there in his eyes.

Like the Cildra clan, the Dobra controlled their breeding, only marrying within their own tribes. This ensured their higher concentration of Blessed, mostly Listeners who had learned how to send messages along the lines of ley. Through this the Dobra had shortened the distance of the world, had found a way to pass information from one corner of the continents to the others in a matter of minutes. This was accomplished by the divisions of the Dobra: the Wanderer tribes, like the ones Marta encountered this night, rambling along the ley and setting up temporary camps near smaller towns. Through the ley they could contact their Cousins, the tribes which set up permanent settlements in the larger cities.

The Dobra Cousins were their own enclaves, a society entirely separate from the cities they inhabited. And via these enclaves they created hubs through which they could reach any corner of the continents by their Wandering brethren. Through them and the ley, the whole world was now connected, the Dobra considered neutral messengers. Their neutrality was never in question, both sides of warring nations availing themselves of their services without fear. For a Dobra to pass a message not meant for its intended recipient was an instant death sentence, the tribes meting out their punishments lest their entire enterprise be put in jeopardy.

In their own way the Dobra were like the Cildra in that they dealt in information. The mundane populous seldom strayed more than a few miles from where they were born, making both groups outsiders in that regard. Few but the Cildra spies and Dobra Wanderers knew the world at large, their Dobra Cousins keeping abreast through their network in the same way the Cildra passed messages to their elders through their codices. The Dobra tribes were just caretakers though, passing news to whom it was intended, whereas the Cildra kept all their information to themselves. Both groups dealt in secrets, Marta realized as she approached the handsome boy. The only difference was that Marta knew this, whereas he was entirely ignorant.

Both were also predators in their own way, Marta deciding to test her mettle against him in single amorous combat. Flashing her most coquettish smile, she twirled a ringlet of her auburn hair and made sure the golden glint of her woven ring caught his eye.

The older Dobra boy never stood a chance.

***

Back in the carriage to be returned to their parents, the girls breathlessly shared their acquired secrets. One claimed that the Dobra Wanderers stole children from the towns they visited. It was a rumor as old as the dirt, but one that plagued the tribes wherever they went. Another girl declared the Dobra secretly shared the messages passed along their network, selling the secrets to the highest bidder. Still another girl asserted that she had purchased an imbued pocket watch. She happily dangled the cheap thing before them as she swore it would identify the man she was meant to marry if it glowed when she caught his reflection in its face. Marta had the strong suspicion the girl would lead a long, lonely life if she adhered to this belief.

Steff went next, vowing this tribe dealt in the Dead Breath, a practice in which the Dobra caught the Breath of the recently deceased in great glass globes to answer the questions of the living. Steff swore on her mother's life she had witnessed such a summoning that very night, but Marta knew that such displays were simply parlor tricks meant for fools since the act would damn the entire tribe to death by any Render who learned they had taken Sol's Breath out of the flow. But Marta held her tongue since she was sure her secret would trump them all and ensure her place as the winner.

The girls gazed expectantly at Marta, their new ringleader if the night worked out as she intended. Marta milked their silence until the anticipation was almost more than their fragile forms could contain. When they could not possibly hold their excitement a moment more, she finally announced her secret.

"Ix culla."

The girls stared at her first in shock then confusion as they attempted to parse her words. Marta expected as much, explaining to them in the same calm tone her tutor Mitchell used when Marta could not comprehend a concept he found obvious.

"It's a Dobra swear, the vilest of their curses. To call another Dobra that is to invite them into a vendetta, nothing but blood able to wash the insult away."

Their confusion deepened into skepticism, Steff riding the cresting wave to announce, "That's not a real secret. It's not even a part of the Dobra language. It's nothing but gibberish. You're too easily taken in, Marta."

It was the truth though, Marta having wrung the words from the Dobra boy's lips with her kisses. It was the truth; it had to be: there was no way a simple Dobra boy could fool someone from the Cildra clan, least of all the daughter of Norwood Childress.

Steff's ensuing laughter was shrill with cruelty, the other girls soon joining her cackles. At the sound of it, Marta's anger boiled as she imagined her Shaper gauntlet smashing into Steff's pretty face, all her cousin's pristine beauty crushed by Marta's real power.

Marta kept her rage and Breath contained though, her clarity that came with her anger allowing her to see that Steff was not worth her father's punishment. In the moment the violence would be intensely gratifying, but there would be repercussions, a lesson her father always had trouble teaching Marta. Far from her father's grasp, Marta finally took his lesson to heart as she forced a thin smile Steff's direction.

Marta must not have been minding her thoughts around her Listener cousin though, as Steff's laughter suddenly cut off like she had swallowed a bug. Having just brushed Marta's mind, Steff was abruptly given a glimpse of the fate that almost awaited her.

Dignity dictated that Marta be gracious in defeat, even if the loss was unjust. So her laughter at her own misfortune replaced Steff's to the bewilderment of the other girls.

Marta would make sure to include this incident in her weekly letter to her father through their codex. Both it and the secret swear of ix culla would prove to him she was learning her lessons in the Auld Lands well, lessons she would put to good use when she finally returned home to Newfield.

Chapter 8

Winterfylled 18, 567

The sun had barely begun its ascent when the train arrived at the edge of civilization in Oan. Carved out of what had previously been Ingios territory a few years before the Grand War, towns were few and far between in Oan, the only major city being its capital, Naddi, in which Marta found herself. Her headache had grown so pronounced that she could not help but constantly grimace as the train came to a stop. The girl did not appear to be in any pain, even when Marta roughly grabbed her by the wrist to haul the mindless child outside with her to escape the ley headache.

They descended the platform, Marta taking a short constitutional around the shops bordering the station as the city awoke. Outside the range of the ley, her head began to clear, her exhaustion sweeping in to occupy the space the pain so recently resided. She again considered the liquor she carried with her as a reprieve, but suddenly the thought of the sharp taste on her tongue disgusted her. The bust-head was a necessity born of poverty, and Marta was by no means poor anymore. Though the day was still new, she had no doubt she could find an establishment with something with a better bouquet.

The only question was what to do with Caddie.

It was only a half hour until the train departed again, and the child slowed her down significantly with her small steps. It would be impossible to hurry in her search for relief, so she decided Caddie would be safe on the train while she performed her hunt. With a swig of something sweet in her, Marta would be able to think clearer and then make up her mind if they would remain on this route or take the next scheduled train, perhaps aimed directly at their real destination of Ceilminster.

They were nearing their return to the platform when Marta noticed the Home Guardsmen, their Listener pins tipped with the head of a bear rather than the simple dual spheres all Listeners wore. The bear was extinct in the Auld Lands, now unique to the continent of Soltera, and therefore chosen as the national symbol of Newfield.

The Home Guardsmen too were unique products of Newfield, sworn to personally protect the president. But after an Eastern assassination attempt on President Ruhl near the start of the Grand War, they reinterpreted their mandate to protect the nation as a whole and keep all its citizens safe. Their ranks swelling with Listeners eager to avoid the draft, the definition of safety was reinterpreted too, threatening it now meaning sowing discord through either deeds or thoughts. The Home Guard zealously sought out any seeds of dissent, and any citizen they questioned was required to open his or her mind to the Listener's mental probes. To refuse access of one's thoughts was an instant sign of guilt warranting a trip to a cell for further, more invasive, inquiries.

Stationed at different ends of the train, the two Home Guardsmen were not questioning any of the milling passengers. Instead they scanned the crowd, their eyes never remaining on anyone for long. Marta's breath caught upon spying them. Finding a single Home Guardsman riding the trains that tied the nation together was not an uncommon occurrence, but Marta personally knew that when they worked in groups, they were out hunting.

Clutching Caddie's hand tighter, Marta turned them around and fled the platform as quickly as she dared. She wanted more than anything to turn and check, to see if they now had two new shadows sporting bear pins, but she kept her head facing straight forward, eyes down and bonnet pulled low. To do otherwise would be a dead giveaway.

Their trip only took a few minutes, each second dragging by and allowing Marta's imagination to conjure numerous scenarios as to their capture. Every moment she expected a hand to descend upon her shoulder, a man brandishing a pistol as he commanded her to halt.

But the hand never clamped down upon her, Marta hauling them off the main street to find a hotel. When the proprietor requested her name, Marta gave them the name May Oles, a woman she had served with; the girl her daughter, Donna. Requesting a breakfast be sent up, she retreated to their room, drawing the curtains and wondering how much time they had left.

Carmichael said he was going to put on a good show for his superiors, the Home Guardsmen his minions who would be sent out to find the apparent agent of the Covenant Sons who had rescued Orthoel Hendrix's daughter. Her brother had also said he would hamstring their search, so it made little sense they would be waiting for Marta here in Naddi. It could just be that Carmichael did not expect her to take such a circuitous route to Ceilminster and had sent his agents to the farthest-flung cities to clear a straight path for her. It could just be chance that put the Home Guardsmen here, but Marta did not believe in chance any longer—not in regards to her brother, at least.

Flopping onto the bed, Marta rubbed her eyes. She needed a clear head if she was to make sense of her situation, and the night would provide a better chance of escaping the noose. The girl still stood stupidly beside the bed, Marta finally catching her wrist and telling her to lie down beside her. She had not seen the child sleep since she had been taken, and Marta briefly wondered if she had to be ordered to sleep as well before slipping into slumber herself.

***

Her body resisted as Marta awoke. Hours had flown by with dusk now not far off, yet her body cried out for more sleep. Marta resisted the request, pushing upright to behold the prone girl beside her. Again Caddie's eyes remained upon the ceiling, her gaze unfocused. They were blank eyes, only daring to match Marta's dead ones because there was nothing behind them.

Many commanders did not believe in combat fugue, thinking their men were simply playing old-soldier and nothing more than hospital rats faking their conditions when no injuries were evident. Marta believed in the fugue though, the mind only able to withstand so much horror before it finally said no more. She understood both those soldiers' and the girl's retreat from the world rather than confronting its awfulness. She also knew she was stronger than that, that she was willing to stare straight at the wretchedness of the world without blinking. It was this willingness alone that made her better than those who succumbed to the fugue.

Picking at the remains of their cold meal, Marta bade the girl to eat, Caddie complying once Marta told her again when holding her hand. Night was oncoming, the darkness providing a bit more cover for Marta to purchase horses to make their escape. Traversing Oan off the main roads would be a risk, the state too far south for Marta to know the territory firsthand, but the risk was a far step better than being brought down by the Home Guard again.

Leaving Caddie and the haversack within the room, Marta set out upon the street. There, she was chagrined to find the city was sophisticated enough to have lampposts, each topped with electrical bulbs rather than the luz jars used in smaller towns. The lights were steady and without the flicker of the contained Breath she preferred, Marta pulling her bonnet lower to keep her face hidden as she made her way in the uncomfortable dress. The populous of Naddi was diverse enough, Marta spotting a Mynian woman across the street, her dusky skin darker than Marta's own and ensuring Marta would not stick out too much. The only question was if she could find a livery stable still open and willing to part with two horses before it closed for the night.

The stables would most likely be on the outskirts of the town, Marta nearer the center after having hurried to a hotel close to the train station. Staying within the shadows of the street, she set her course for the edge of town. As Marta passed a general store, she realized they would also need supplies for their journey on horseback, foodstuffs to last them the weeks it might take. Perhaps she would need to acquire three horses, one acting as a pack animal. Two women alone on the trails would also be a hazard, the seldom traveled paths to the East said to be plagued by harriers who took what they wanted from travelers and left nothing but corpses in their wake.

Marta took another turn down a street when she realized she was being followed. Her Cildra training had drilled awareness into her until it became almost an instinct, Marta stopping to examine her reflection in a storefront window, though her eyes never trailed to her own image. Her shadower stopped too, only a few feet behind her as he suddenly seemed quite interested in something in the nearest store.

Continuing on after a moment, Marta could only catch a glimpse of him. He sported neither the uniform nor the bear-headed pin of the Home Guard, but she also knew from experience they often worked undercover, leaving their identifying marks behind on their hunts.

Still, the Home Guardsmen were known for their training in deception, not quite that of a Cildra, but at least better at tailing an unaware mark than this man was. Perhaps he was a ne'er-do-well picking Marta for easy prey. Or perhaps he was an admirer seeking an opportunity to strike up a conversation. It had been years since Marta had last been sought out as the object of a man's affections, far more recently that she had last been assaulted. Both occasions had ended badly for the men in question.

Wishing to ascertain his intentions, Marta made her way into the nearest tavern, stopping a few steps past the door and waiting to see if her pursuer would follow her inside.

He did not, ambling easily along and scarcely giving the saloon a glance. When he did his eyes connected with hers, no sign of recognition there from either of them. Through the window she could spy him in better detail. He was dark of hair and without a beard, his duds fashionable and meant for the city, but well-worn. His face was comely enough, the grin he bestowed upon her effortless and sure to have melted the heart of many a woman.

Marta's heart remained quite frozen as he wandered on, happy only that he passed without incident. It was only when she was sure he was gone and not to return that Marta realized that all eyes in the saloon were fixed upon her. The reason was obvious: While leading her pursuer on, Marta had sought out a rougher section of town so no one would notice if she had to deal with him roughly. But now he had moved on, and Marta found herself the victim of the trap she had set herself, her pristine clothing in contrast to the coarse workmen's garments populating the bar. Not a week past Marta had frequented an establishment similar to this one, drinking with abandon and no one raising an eyebrow. She had not been wearing a dress last week though, now feeling their eyes trace her form under the folds of her outfit.

She knew she could simply step back out into the night and the men would return to their drinks. No one would follow her, and if they did, they would soon realize their mistake. Marta almost slunk out, but then she spied a bottle of wine behind the counter. It was a Karlwych vintage, and Marta hungrily remembered the bold flavors. It had been too long since last they were acquainted, so Marta strode to the bar to throw down her money and demand a taste. The glass the bartender provided was clean, the wine deep red and inviting. Marta's mouth salivated, her tongue eager to test the bouquet against her memory.

The wine tasted of disappointment: sour, sharp, and entirely unlike her reminiscence. In her heart she knew it was not the fault of the establishment or the wine, but rather her own for having even attempted it. It had been too long, her palette having wasted away until it was now good for nothing more than the harsh taste of red-eye. The years had stolen it from her as surely as the woven ring again residing upon her finger. Although the ring had been returned, she realized there was no going back to those untroubled days of her youth. She was a marked woman now, one who no longer cared for the taste of alcohol, only its effects. Not wanting to be a wastrel, she intended on draining the remains of the glass before she departed.

Unfortunately, the uniformed Home Guardsman and the Render entered before she had a chance.

Marta's face belied no trace of her fear as she kept her façade in place even as she instinctively set her mental refrain. Her dress marking her as different from the other patrons, her cover was obvious: she was May Oles, her husband, Richard, having stepped out on her nearly a week ago, so she was searching for him, seeking out the rough taverns he frequented.

The Render in tow, the Home Guardsman took the lead, stopping at each man and quietly asking him to open his mind. All complied, their faces frightened and strained. The guardsman moved on from each, finally reaching her at the bar. Marta put on the proper mask, emoting anxiety at being questioned by someone with such terrible authority. Upon his request she opened her refrain to him, the guardsman touching her thoughts and gracing her with a sympathetic look before moving on.

The Render remained though, gazing intently at her. His thumb casually traced the hilt of his saber, the blade surely made of glass. It was a practiced motion, born not on the battlefield, but out of boredom. He fashioned himself a hard case, but his hands were far too soft to have swung the blade during the Grand War. His face was too pink and unlined, not having suffered the scourge of hunger as real soldiers had. His swagger marked him as a pretender, making Marta hate him all the more.

The Render's voice was polite enough as he called her, "Madam," and doffed his cap. Marta nodded civilly, biting her tongue to keep from emitting any obscenities. He seemed to sense her disdain, his smile widening with a sour tint to it.

"That's a lovely bonnet you have there. Not to overstep the confines of courtesy, but I've been courting a girl of late. She's been hankering for a fine bonnet, and I believe yours might fit the bill. Do you mind if I take a gander of yours?"

On its surface it was a question, but there was a demand to his voice, Marta suddenly sure her charade was up. Dipping her head, she untied the bonnet's ribbons, removing it roughly and ensuring her frazzled hair fell over her forehead before handing it over. The boy took the offered hat, his other hand still tracing the saber at his belt. Instead of inspecting the claimed bonnet, his hand that held it reached for her forehead to brush back the hair hiding Marta's scar.

At its revelation Marta felt the burning brand again as if it were the first time, the phantom smell of roasted meat searing her nostrils. His eyes upon it were like a slap to the face causing her physical pain. Though she had never seen it straight with her own eyes, Marta knew what he saw: two sets of three vertical lines with a star in their center—the symbol of the nation of Newfield forever etched into the center of her forehead.

"Traitors Brigade."

Though his utterance was soft, suddenly everyone in the room stared at Marta instead of the fearsome Render. The guardsman was already on his way back to them, Marta's jaw setting, her voice barely able to escape her lips.

"Furies. We were Bumgarden's Furies. I served under Bumgarden directly."

The Render's smile dripped with disdain, his words hurled as if they offended his tongue. "How many of your countrymen did you cut down? Ten? Twenty? A half-hundred, Traitor?"

He was trying to bait her, Marta knew, a Shaper no match for a Render by any stretch of the imagination. His desire was obvious, she nothing but a first notch on his belt, the death of one of the fabled Furies a fine pelt to launch a legend with.

"You're all traitors. More than just the name, your stain of cowardice goes all the way down to your Soul. You have no spine, not the will Sol even gave bugs."

It was all Marta could do to remain at the bar and not to take the step that would give him cause to do her harm as the guardsman closed the gap. Not quite there yet, he called out to the Render, "Hold your tongue."

Turning his gaze to Marta, the guardsman tipped his cap. "Please pardon my comrade, his mouth spits poison. There's been a bit of a misunderstanding, and I would like you to come with us for a few moments so we can clear it up. If you'd be so kind, ma'am."

He was polite, at least, and for that Marta decided he would live. The Render might not be as lucky as Marta reached for her bonnet, which was still in his grasp.

As her hand was about to take it, he let it drop to the ground, a sneer on his lips. Though her face remained lifeless, Marta oscillated as to his fate again, finally deciding the slight was not enough to earn him his death.

But then he spit upon her face.

Her rage came instantly, the perfect clarity there and familiar as a lost love. And with its return came the violence. She could see each person there in the room in perfect detail, the moment frozen in time even as her fist hurtled into his sneering mouth.

Blood spurted as she connected, Marta's free hand already closing around his wrist, her Breath doing her bidding as her gauntlet appeared around her hand. Through her summoned Armor she felt his wrist snap at her compression, the bones giving way to her superior strength.

Well aware he needed to gesture to draw her Breath, she took his opportunity away by brutally wresting his shattered wrist up to his neck. There, she extended her gauntlet's reach, wrapping it around his neck and pinning his arm to his throat.

His other hand still remained on his glass saber, trying futilely to draw it. She had no intention of allowing him this symbol of his station, so Marta drew his blade herself, the weapon he was meant to surrender only upon death. For that insult alone she took it from him, the sacred blade brandished in her hand before the guardsman even took his second step.

He stopped instantly, Marta not needing to be a Listener to know he was considering the pistol holstered at his hip. So she extended her Armor again, the gauntlet growing to encase her arm. It was a rough design, stretching her Breath nearly to the breaking point, but she did not hesitate as she flung the Render at the guardsman.

The force of the throw hurled them both to the ground, Marta upon them instantly and cracking the guardsman with her gauntlet. His eyes rolled back as he collapsed, the man shuddering once and then going still as Marta turned her attention back to his companion.

The Render stirred, enough fight left in him to try and regain his feet. He found his glass saber awaiting him when he did though, the tip pressed into his throat and pushing him back to the ground. Her rage consuming her, Marta took a step forward, forcing the boy to slide backwards, his shattered wrist making him cry out as it bore his weight. So she took another step, a stiff smile frozen upon her lips.

"All Renders worth their salt have a glass eye, yet yours are still flesh. How about I help you along your path? Which one will it be, the right or left?"

"Please, please, no!"

"Death, then? Time to stand up for your ideals against this Traitor? Time to die for the righteous cause?"

"No!" His voice took a plaintive tone, pitiful and without any traces of the arrogance that had landed him here. "I don't want to die, not like this, not for some—"

Marta did not let him finish as she smashed his sacred saber upon the ground. The outer edges of glass gave way instantly, but a jagged heart of the blade still remained close to the steel core that gave the weapon its heft. With that sharp remainder Marta stabbed, slashing first his right check and then the left. She struck six times, three slices divided upon each cheek.

The cuts were not life-threatening, but the scars would remain, deep and obvious to anyone who looked upon his formerly soft and unlined face. The boy would survive, she decided, but her action was by no means a mercy.

He would forever bear his scars, surely as she carried her own, but he would be unable to hide them as she did with her slouch hat.

She did not allow the Render to consider her cruelty as she cracked him upon the chin with the hilt of his saber. The boy was separated from his consciousness before she could even drop the remains of the hateful glass blade.

Her rage finally sated by the ruination of the Render, Marta turned her attention to the unconscious guardsman, then to the frozen patrons that gawked at her with respect and the proper amount of fear she deserved. Marta knew she should run, her fate sealed by her actions against the Newfield agents and demanding death. Instead she bellied back to the bar.

She found her wine awaiting her and downed the glass in a single slug. It still did not match her memory—no sweetness there—but it was hers and she refused to let anyone take from her ever again. Retrieving her forgotten bonnet, she gave the patrons a milk-curdling glare, a thin smile flitting across her lips quick as a summer storm.

"First man I see step out that door dies—and not kindly."

With that she departed, silence enveloping her on the street. Her first goal was again covering her scar with the bonnet. That secured, her next move would be to claim Caddie and then hurry out of town before the whole city started looking for a former Fury. She only hoped she still had enough time before one of the saloon patrons realized she would be insane to remain in the street long enough to carry through on her threat.

Back at the hotel Marta shed the womanly clothes, the rough-woven men's shirt again welcomingly scratching her skin. Her slouch hat felt freeing, just as the greatcoat turned right side out and the haversack she tossed over her shoulder did. The girl had not stirred from the bed where she had been left, Marta grabbing her hand and hauling her outside. They left, not by the front door, but by the back, stalking through the servants' hallways until they found an exit.

In the alley Marta felt his presence in the shadows before she saw him, lashing out with her gauntlet to grab his throat. Pressing him against the wall, she recognized the man with the sly smile that had followed her outside the saloon. Despite the gauntlet wrapped around his neck with the force to crush rocks, he gave the same grin now.

"Why I do believe I would not mind going blind now that I've seen your face up close."

It was a well-practiced line, one Marta knew was meant to distract her from his right hand thrust into his pocket. So she tightened her grip, cutting off his air.

"Show me what you have there. Slowly."

The man complied, his right hand slipping out to reveal a large lockblade with a dark sheen. In capable hands a lockblade was a dangerous weapon, the blade released with a simple flick of the wrist. But why a man would need one when he had a straight-blade knife at his waist eluded Marta.

"Drop it."

To her surprise he hesitated, unwilling to part with the lockblade. His air running out, he finally did as he was bid. Not entirely releasing him, Marta slackened her grip enough to allow him his breath again. It still took him several moments before he spoke, his voice coming in huffs.

"Here to help. We're here to help you."

"We?"

At his knowing nod the woman materialized from the shadows to Marta's left, a wicked steel hatchet in her hand. After years of sneak-and-see, both with her brother and little sister, Marta was horrified that the Mynian woman had gotten the drop on her. She still kept the fear from her face as she regarded the grinning man.

"And you are?"

But he kept smiling, one hand pointing idly at her gauntlet wrapped around his neck. She would have to release it before he offered more, and Marta was in no mood for a game of wait-and-see as she dropped him to the ground.

The man instantly snatched up the lockblade, inspecting it for damage and finally deciding it remained unscathed before returning it to his pocket. Then he grinned again.

"The Covenant Sons, of course. Come, we have horses waiting."

Chapter 9

Weodmonad 14, 561 (Six Years Ago)

Marta had been back in Newfield for almost a year, but still had not seen her home. Although she suspected she would miss Gatlin, she never supposed the pang would be so pronounced. The sights she had seen in the Auld Lands, then grand Western cities of Newfield, were amazing, but they did not compare to the scent of honeysuckle in her mother's gardens, the yelps of a new litter of her father's puppies, or simply walking along the long canals snaking through Gatlin.

Most of all she missed Oleander, wondering again how much her little sister had grown. Oleander sent no more letters, her father only obliquely referring to her in his own messages. Her sister must already be doing her Cildra work, Marta decided, serving the clan as Marta now was.

It was nice to be back in Newfield, even if it was not quite her home. She had disembarked from her sojourn in the Auld Lands in the New Albion city of Polis to be welcomed by Cildra relatives so far removed Marta initially could not recall all their names. They were happy enough to show her the sights of her new abode though. In the Auld Lands, they measured the history of their cities in centuries, and though Polis was scarcely over a hundred years old, it dwarfed anything she had seen across the ocean. Polis was a paragon of progress, constantly adding to its visage. The city was now so massive that it had entirely devoured the peninsula with its sprawl and had begun to build upwards. One of the tallest buildings nearly scraped the sky, her cousins taking her to the top of its eight stories so she could behold the city in its entirety. Marta had to hide her amazement of such an engineering accomplishment lest she appear an unrefined yokel, not the daughter of Norwood Childress.

Marta never spoke of her mission with her cousins any more than they would to her of theirs. Each child of the Cildra was simply an extension of their parents, doing their duty and reporting back, all decisions made by the heads of the clan. Fortunately, her father had decided to throw his support behind the East in what had become known as the Grand War, and Marta was glad he had not sided with the Western Renders over his own countrymen. If her Cildra relatives in Polis were bothered by being instructed to turn against the West, they gave no sign. Nor should they, the Cildra's loyalty to the clan superseding that to the nation. Still, Marta was glad she had not been ordered to help the Renders to victory.

Marta did not stay in Polis long, departing for the national capital of Vrendenburg barely five months after she arrived. This city seemed more familiar, no building more than four stories tall. It was still a far cry from the winding beauty of Gatlin though. Like all Western cities, Vrendenburg was laid out in an unimaginative grid pattern, all the streets straight, the buildings square and lacking personality. It was the Render influence, their religious beliefs invading their architecture and demanding function over form. There was little splendor here as there was in the East. The Weavers back home knew how to enjoy life, creating their festations for tedious or backbreaking work to allow their masters time for leisure. The fact the Weavers could enjoy life was proof they were superior to the Renders in Marta's mind, proof that they would eventually win the war. They deserved to by being inherently smarter than their austere enemies.

Thankfully, Vrendenburg was a hotbed of intrigue with all the couriers, senators, politicians, ambassadors, and aides running about. As Gatlin was the state capital of Mimas, her father had once taken her, Carmichael, and Oleander to the statehouse to watch the politicians fashion their laws. Marta was impressed at the men and women as they argued and harangued until they finally reached their compromise, but then her father disabused her of her illusion.

"They're all fools," he announced. "The politicians and statesmen, they all believe themselves leaders, but they're simply slaves to their desire for power in the public eye. Once we learn what these so-called leaders covet, the Cildra gain power over the politicians. This is what makes us able to manipulate them, knowledge of what they want. In this way the clan controls all of Ayr, influencing the course of nations without having to even take one step inside a statehouse. This is what makes the Cildra great."

From the corner of her eye, Marta caught Carmichael nodding shrewdly, as if this were simply another recitation of one of Mitchell's lessons. Oleander nodded in turn, and so Marta did as well so as not to be left out, but she stayed up until nearly dawn tossing and turning in bed as she chewed over her father's lesson.

It was Marta's task to infiltrate the upper Western echelons of Vrendenburg society and report all she found. Initially she thought that being an outsider in the West would make her information collection more difficult, especially being the daughter of a displaced Eastern aristocrat in the capital of the enemy. Instead, her distinction as an oddity made it all the easier, everyone taking pity upon the unfortunate Covenant girl unable to return home. All the Westerners seemed to be in competition to befriend her, each wanting to demonstrate how reasonable they were, whereas it was her countrymen that were the zealots. And so Marta soaked up every secret they spilled, influencing the events on the battlefields while far removed in the lap of luxury.

For the most part Vrendenburg was untouched by the bloodshed of the Grand War. The only sign there was even a war was the comings and goings of the messengers rushing straight from the Kuk line of ley to President Ruhl. All the fighting was taking place in the bordering states surrounding the Mueller Line separating the East from the West. Unable to pick a side, the state of Neider had split in two, what was now called East Neider having sided with the Covenant against their former countrymen.

Everyone knew that the war would have ended long ago in the West's favor were it not for the brilliant tactics of the Eastern General Clyde Loree. The Western general Davis Underhill shared equal blame in prolonging the bloodshed, his blunders so egregious that some of the papers dubbed him "Dunderhill" and demanded his resignation. But Marta knew the truth: many of Loree's brilliant feints and charges were the results of already knowing Underhill's plans through the information she passed to her father. She was personally helping to make a hero of Loree and a ham-fisted villain out of Underhill.

Despite the public calls for Underhill's dismissal, President Ruhl stuck by his general, devoted to the man, even if none knew quite why. Marta met Underhill once, courtesy of her beau, Richard, and found him a man full of conviction, but utterly lacking in ability.

She was much more impressed by meeting the president himself, again courtesy of Richard's expanding influence. Despite the fact he was the epitome of the enemy, Marta found herself almost overcome by the president in spite of herself. Though no Dacist by any stretch of the imagination, Ruhl believed in peace between the Renders and Weavers and frequently called for a cessation to the bloodshed. Though she fervently hoped for the East's utter victory over the Renders, when in Ruhl's company,

Marta found herself hoping for peace instead. He had such a powerful presence, a sorrow emanating from him while somehow still giving a sense of hope. Though her father said all politicians were simply fools, after meeting Ruhl, she was not so sure. Perhaps not all politicians were out for personal gain.

Perhaps some, like Ruhl, were called to serve.

Marta met other Western war celebrities as well, Richard more than happy to provide an invitation to any upper-class gathering she took a fancy to. A Tinker by the name of Hendrix was the most fascinating, and Marta believed it was the will of Sol that put her beside him.

It had been a rather uneventful soirée, Marta mingling with her usual crowd and finding nothing of interest. Then she noticed the man in his rumpled suit, which was several seasons out of date, remaining alone by the punchbowl for nearly an hour, Marta sliding up beside him the third time she refilled her cup. He was new and, as such, should be investigated.

"Will you be attending the Blalock gala next week?" she inquired in a casual tone. It was a neutral question, but Marta made it a point to appear as approachable to this wallflower.

Although he had surely heard her, the man did not look up from his drink. Marta considered asking him again when he finally caught her eyes with his pale blue ones.

"No. I will be working then. Should be working now."

His words were so quick and clipped that Marta could barely catch them in as he fidgeted with his cup. The motion drew Marta's attention, noticing the smudges of chalk on the blades of his hands and the residue of grease under his nails.

"Could I possibly be fortunate enough to be in the presence of Orthoel Hendrix?"

No matter his answer, she was sure she was. Between his blue eyes and receding hair so thin it was almost undetectable, his identity was easy to ascertain. Marta had heard whispers of the man rising quickly in the Western Tinker ranks, but had not had the chance to make his acquaintance quite yet. So she smiled all the brighter to invite his attention.

But the man's gaze returned to his cup, his words spilling out all over each other. "Working. Should be working. War is an opportunity, one that will not last forever. But perhaps a year more... if I'm lucky. Technology doesn't have a lifespan like man, you see. It must therefore be nurtured in times of crisis. War is the real opportunity every Tinker must take advantage of." He glanced up then back down, his flitting gaze not quite making contact as he continued at an even faster rate.

"During warfare it jumps forward at an unprecedented rate. We only realize the applications after the fact. Muskets. Did you know muskets were first called harkbuts? Terribly primitive contraptions. They were too slow to fire, so a Drolant general set several men in a line. The first would fire, the second behind him passing him a new harkbut, the third loading a new one while the fourth cleaned the spent weapon. Each man had a set task, one he performed individually to make a process between them. Years later we applied what he learned from warfare to the factories, giving each man a small task that allows us to build machines in a matter of months. Don't you see? It's the technology that's important, not the war itself."

Marta could barely keep track of his argument, but he was opening up at least. "But the loss of human life," she said. "Surely that's not worth the price we pay for this technology."

Hendrix sucked air through his teeth several times, Marta unsure if he was tisking her or laughing. "The bloodshed is incidental. The loss of life means little, the dead's Breath simply retreating to Sol's flow to return anew. That is what makes technology unique. It is the only creation that is not of Sol, the only thing outside his flow. It remains when its inventor dies, waiting for another Tinker to pick it up and give it life again. That is why this Grand War is an opportunity that should not be wasted. That is why I should not be here. I should be working. I should take advantage of the destruction while I can to create."

As he rushed on with his words, Marta found her cheeks tingling. The idea that something good could come from being outside of Sol's flow and that anyone could think human life was worth less than inanimate technology was horrifying to her. It was monstrous, and though she tried to keep her face pleasant, she quickly found her façade flagging.

"You don't understand either." He looked away, shuffling off with his cup of punch still grasped in his hands. "Should be working," Marta caught him mumbling as he made his retreat.

The odd man reminded Marta of the festations she grew up beside. Despite what she had been assured was a powerful mind, the man seemed almost mechanical in his manic interactions. Like the festations, he seemed to have no Soul, and it was this Tinker's lack of humanity that disturbed Marta most of all. As she knew that Newfield was much further ahead in the technological race against the Covenant, Marta suggested to her father that Hendrix should be removed before he widened the gap further. But her father did not respond to this point, instead telling her to keep close to Richard.

Richard Torbee was the whole reason she remained in Vrendenburg, Marta reflecting on him again as she brushed her hair. She had met him a week prior to the start of the war by chance, running into him again a few days later entirely on purpose. The boy was instantly smitten, and so the girl used all her charms to the Covenant's advantage. As an aide to the Secretary of War, Richard was close to the flame of leadership and wanted to impress Marta by demonstrating his burgeoning influence. Through Richard she learned about Underhill's Chilwist Basin offensive a week before it launched, Loree easily outflanking his foe after she informed her father.

Marta's eyes alighted on the dried rose beside her mirror, a gift from Richard at their first outing alone together. Time had sapped the rose's color from bright red to a muddy brown, but Marta still treasured the thing. They had become quite close over the last few months, Richard considering him her confidant in her time of need. And although all his attention and offerings were quite flattering, the greatest gift was the knowledge she had him wrapped around her finger as surely as her woven ring. Absently her thumb scratched at it, waiting for the day she would slip it to Oleander and again be equal.

There was much to like about Richard, the boy handsome, clever, and above all ambitious. He was a rising star in Ruhl's government, perhaps holding office himself someday. For that position he would need a wife, and on a whim Marta imagined what it would be like to occupy that space. It was a silly impulse, the idea of affection towards her mark laughable. Although the attraction she felt for him was indeed genuine, she could never allow herself to let her emotions get the better of her. Cildra children were taught at a young age any sentiment towards others should be a show only—a sham. Any actual affection towards their targets was a weakness.

But Marta liked feeling weak in Richard's presence. Having climbed so high in society, she had the sudden overwhelming urge to fall. The impulse was like a cliff that called to her, leaning over the edge to see what mysteries resided in its depths. Teetering on the tip, the longing to allow gravity to ply its trade and plummet her to whatever awaited below would suddenly fill her heart. Each time she steeled herself, had turned back from the emotional abyss. Yet each time she found herself climbing further out, waiting along the edge longer. If she kept at it much longer, she was afraid her fall would be a foregone conclusion.

A knock came from the door of the hotel room that had recently become her home, a servant announcing Richard's arrival in the hall below. Giving her cheeks a good pinch, Marta hoped it would be enough to mimic the blush that was expected upon seeing her suitor.

Her bustle bouncing behind her as she swept down the stairs, Marta pushed past the servant and spied Richard among the thronging crowd. Decorum dictated she remain modest at his arrival, but Marta made it a point to publically fall into his arms, this perfectly expected by a girl besotted by her beau. But his arms suddenly surrounding her, she realized her blush might now be genuine.

***

Dinner was a wonderful affair, the war's food shortages not yet reaching the finer restaurants of Vrendenburg. Richard was his usual conversational self, several state secrets slipping out as he bragged about his day with abandon. Marta gobbled these morsels down while picking delicately at her food as a lady should, but as she tried to cut her steak into dainty bites, Richard suddenly trailed off. Looking up, she found him staring with abject adoration.

"You're beautiful."

His words were barely above a whisper, but rung about Marta's head, she now at a loss at such an outpouring of emotion. It was raw, unfiltered, and without any of the guile she was taught to expect in high society.

More than that, it was unlike being a part of the Cildra clan. Though Marta had learned her Cildra lessons well, there was another moral underneath it all she had accidently ascertained: she must act adequately to earn her love. Her parents cared for her, of that Marta was certain, but to be given any sign of their affection, she had to perform, had to excel. When she stumbled at her lessons, her parents were quite willing to withhold their attention. As a child Marta had thought they loved her the same way as she had seen in her non-Cildra acquaintances. But now as an adult at nineteen, she recognized they certainly showed more affection with her and Carmichael than they ever had to Oleander. Her sister had never received a woven ring except from Marta. The conditional love in her household was completely different from what she received from Richard.

Looking into his eyes, Marta realized he believed he saw her for what she really was: a scared girl far removed from home. And embraced in his gaze, Marta certainly felt that way, her mission and her family's expectations entirely forgotten as she soaked his stare in. Caught in that moment, Marta wondered if she could give it all up and forsake her family to fully fall for him.

Chapter 10

Winterfylled 18, 567

Marta hated horses and had a strong suspicion they felt the same about her. Perhaps it was because she had eaten some of their kind, the beasts still able to smell their fallen kin on her skin. More likely it was because they could sense how much she distrusted them.

As of late, children avoided her as well, but not this girl. Caddie seated on the horse before her, Marta could feel the child's steady breathing in the dark. It felt strange to have her arms around someone again, the posture one of comfort. Marta could not give herself fully to the pose though. Soon she would kill the girl's father, probably before her very eyes, so it made little sense to get attached. But detachment was suddenly hard while holding the girl so.

Marta chewed her pipe as she followed the form of the silent Mynian woman in the dark ahead of her. The woman certainly knew her way through the scrub of squat trees, then the grasslands that overtook them. Having ridden out of Naddi by the back roads with the man in the lead, the woman then took over, picking through the terrain with a practiced eye. A few miles out they made their first turn, then another a few miles farther. Then they doubled back, riding over their tracks before heading out in yet another direction. Even with her Cildra training to notice minor details, Marta was impressed at how the woman could pick out the barest hint of a trail in only the moonlight.

The man rode behind her, Marta giving him another backwards glance. He favored her with another grin as he had done the other dozen times before. He remained as mum as the woman though, shutting up entirely after leading her and Caddie to the awaiting horses. Many miles from Naddi now, they were more than likely safe to speak again, but if her new companions chose to hold their tongues, Marta would as well. Although she had seldom won against Carmichael in these waiting games, she felt she had better odds against these Covenant Sons. Her goal was to wait out her time in silence until she and the girl could escape. The two had proven themselves useful in the moment, but the moment had passed, and her cover as a Covenant Sons sympathizer might not stand the additional scrutiny from two actual members.

Marta slowed to a stop as the woman ahead reined her horse in. There, she listened to the night, finally turning back to approach the man behind Marta. For the first time since the city, Marta was not boxed in by their horses, her opportunity to flee suddenly very real. She had no idea where they were though, the landscape utterly foreign to her, so Marta gigged her horse and moved closer to the two to hear their conversation.

No words passed between them, the woman instead making several quick gestures with her hands. The man looked up at Marta with another smile as she drew near. Closer to them, she examined the two with more scrutiny. The man wore no hat, his shirt thin and jacket more suited for the city, as was the kerchief bound round his neck. He was older than Marta's 25 years, though probably not by much. His dark hair had a bit of a curl to it, and if he wore it much longer, it would probably turn to locks.

The woman was several years younger than Marta, the white voluminous skirts of the Mynian dress she wore having proved to be a lie. Once they reached the horses, the woman pulled her bottoms into two halves to reveal that the skirt was split up the middle. The two halves she tied around her legs, making two puffy leggings that allowed her to ride like a man. Her dark hair was straight and now pulled back into a long plait. The braid was a simple thing, without any of the intricate patterns favored by those in Nahuat and now the Auld Lands. The style did not match what Marta gleaned from her mother of Mynian fashions, the women there preferring stark layers to their black hair. And though the woman's skin was deeper in hue than those of Newfield, upon closer inspection it did not seem dark enough to deem her Mynian. Her hazel eyes were also a giveaway, Marta deciding she was of mixed stock, like herself. With the hatchet and small, but heavy bag at her belt, Marta had a good idea as to where she hailed from.

The man nodded at Marta, his voice cheery despite the news. "Think someone's following us. Isabelle's going back to check."

Isabelle gave Marta one last look, her eyes narrowing a bit before departing, the soft clomps of her horse's hooves disappearing into the dark.

The man took the lead, heading straight along their previous path. Although he rode well, Marta suspected the outdoors were not his domain, but Isabelle's. Perhaps he too had been playing the waiting game with her, because now that their silence was broken, he called out over his shoulder.

"What should I call you?"

He had been waiting outside her hotel, so Marta decided it was best to give the name she used on the ledger. Caddie's identity proved thornier, however, Marta having signed her in as her daughter, Donna. But if he was from the Covenant Sons, he was sure to know the girl's real name.

"May Oles. And this is Caddie Hendrix."

"Luca Dolphus," he responded, nodding as if this had been the answer he expected all along. "Been waiting for you since we heard about the break out. You do that all yourself or you have help?"

"Why Naddi? How did you know we'd be there?"

Luca laughed at her lack of an answer. "We didn't. There're dozens of groups waiting at all the train stops. We were just the lucky ones. Well, and you. Not so much that Render bug."

He continued rambling on, the sound of his voice apparently pleasing to him. Marta paid his words no mind though, considering his companion instead.

"Isabelle's Ingios, isn't she?"

If he was annoyed at being interrupted, Luca showed no sign as he switched topics without a moment's hesitation. "Half. Father was a Newfield citizen."

It made sense, the stones in the pouch at her belt surely for the sling that the Ingios favored. Their tribes were already on the Soltera continent when the first colonists from Acweald arrived, watching the settlers from a distance as their cities sprung up. Though they had their own Blessed, the Ingios did not possess the technology of the Auld Lands, had not harnessed the ley and had no Tinkers among their number. In fact, they avoided the ley, and as such had little interactions with the new colonists that soon founded the nation of Newfield. As the nation expanded the Ingios retreated south, deeper into the interior of the continent and inhabiting the grasslands there to graze their herds of sheep and goats.

Oan had belonged to them until nine years ago when it became the latest state in the nation. The Ingios were welcomed, so the Newfield government said, but they preferred to keep their herds far away from these invaders. Finding an Ingios in the states was said to be as rare as discovering a beautiful mudbird, though Marta did not know the odds of finding a half-Ingios.

"She doesn't speak Acwealt?"

"Feel free to ask yourself. I've never gotten a word out of her personally."

More than his companion, Marta wondered after Luca's accent. It lacked all the lilt she expected from Eastern sympathizers in the Covenant Sons. It sounded a bit like those she had heard in the Auld Lands, though she could not quite place it. He was not a fellow Easterner though, of that Marta was sure.

"You're not a part of the Covenant Sons. You're a freebooter."

She expected some reaction from the vile term for his profession, but Luca turned in his saddle to grin at her again. "And what do you call your line of work, May Oles? A job's a job, and Eastern lucre is good as any others. So long as they pay in hard Newfield cash."

Marta heard the approach of Isabelle's horse, but her mind remained on Luca. Though he had readily owned up to his initial lie, Marta trusted him even less at his new truth. Freebooters were no better than harriers, taking what they wanted from those weaker than they. In fact, they were worse, many harriers former farmers and Eastern soldiers whose homes had been destroyed by the war and therefore taking to the sword to survive. Freebooters instead chose their lots and enjoyed the bloodshed. Not for the first time, Marta considered staving Luca's head in, taking his horse and departing before his companion reached them.

As if sensing her unease, Luca nodded towards the approaching Isabelle. "Might want to wait on letting out until you hear what she has to say."

With her arrival, Isabelle again boxed Marta between them. She feared the woman more than the man, so Marta turned her horse towards Isabelle. The dark-haired woman remained mute though, Luca joining her silence until Marta could not stand it any longer.

"What is it?"

Isabelle's eyes flicked to Luca at Marta's inquiry, the man still not saying a word as Marta's anger flared. "Go on! Spit it out!"

Isabelle opened her mouth, Marta expecting her to indeed spit. Instead she held her mouth agape, Marta noticing the void within. Where the woman's tongue should be only a stump remained to wriggle like a worm torn in two.

Marta had seen worse wounds during the Grand War, but having the mutilated stump brandished before her caused her to flinch. At the motion Isabelle barked, her eyes sparkling at the utterance. Another bark followed it to be joined by Luca's own laughter.

"That's the best you're going to get, I'm afraid. Won't get a word out of her now, not since the glassman."

Marta's mother would have touched her forehead with two fingers to ward off the invocation of a glassman. No better than ghuls, and far more dangerous since they were not bound by the ley, glassmen had been eradicated in both the Auld Lands and Newfield. But the city-states of Myna to the east had been ruled by these monsters for centuries, going to war with Newfield not twenty years ago over the territory that became the state of Lacus. Though the single pass between the Bone Ridge Mountains separating the two countries was now held by Newfield, the Home Guard scanning the minds of any who tried to pass through to weed out glassmen, there were said to be secret pathways still. Tales of terror by glassmen insurgents were common in her mother's home of Lacus, Marta wondering if Isabelle appreciated the irony of disguising herself as Mynian when it was a Mynian glassman that had maimed her.

Neither Luca nor Isabelle seemed to care about the irony as Luca inquired, "Posse?"

Isabelle shook her head side to side.

"Dragoons?"

Isabelle sneered, revealing her front teeth. One was slightly askew, giving her a momentary rat-like appearance as Luca exhaled heavily.

"Posse would have been better. Probably the sixth regiment, they're stationed out of Naddi. They won't be on our trail, not yet. Breaking into squads to see if they chance across us. Means they're spread thin. Might be able to slip on through in the night, but come daylight they'll be riding us down."

At his announcement Isabelle again rode to their head, picking up the pace as she led them through the grass and scrub. Luca's horse fell into step behind her, Marta left alone in the night. Her chance to bolt again presented itself, but Marta pressed her heels into the horse's sides, coaxing a short gallop as she caught up to the two.

***

Fatigue set in as the night wore on. Marta was sure she felt it more keenly than the others, both Luca and Isabelle continuing on without complaint. Caddie never complained either, her hand now covering the woman's finger and resting lightly on her woven ring. Her arms still around the girl, Marta could feel each inhale and exhale through her thin body, realizing that the girl still had not yet slept. Letting one of Caddie's fingers slip between her own to ensure physical contact, Marta whispered.

"Go to sleep."

The girl did not, her eyes wide and breathing even as ever. As the hours rolled on, Marta noticed the girl's rhythm was in time to her own, as if this was an unconscious game of Refrain as she had played with her sister all those years ago. Her face soured as Marta realized the girl was about the same age as Oleander had been when she saw her last. So she shifted her own breathing pattern, the girl falling into synch after a few inhales. Marta considered changing it again, but decided against the effort as her exhaustion deepened.

Suddenly a bugle cried out behind them, distant and haunting. It was soon answered by another, far to the north, and Marta suspected there were more blaring in the night she was unable to hear. The sound reminded her of when her father took her and her siblings hunting with a pack of his famous hounds to run down rabbits. If they were out for sport, he would only release one dog to allow the hare a chance. But if he had a hankering for rabbit meat, he would release all the dogs and the hare would not stand a chance against the pack working in unison.

Isabelle instantly shifted their course perpendicular to the sound of the horns as Luca called out, "They haven't found our trail, not yet. Still just whistling in the dark."

The dragoons would discover the trail soon enough though, dawn not a long way off by the look of the horizon. Marta blinked her tired eyes again to realize the glow up ahead was not the threatening sun, rather the flickering of a nodus. Isabelle's path aimed them right for it.

Again, Marta's suspicions of the pair were raised. A nodus meant strong lines of ley in the area, a city sure to be abutting it and offering additional reinforcements for the Newfield troops.

"Not to worry, they won't follow us there. Tolmen."

Marta was now sure they deserved to be in the Lindaire Sanitarium more than Caddie had. Tolmens were blighted areas where the nodi spewed forth ghuls by the dozens, the evil emets destroying all life within. No one in their right mind would enter one, save a powerful Render, probably aided by several Weavers. Only when destroying a tolmen would those Blessed sects stoop to working together, the only other exception being battling a glassman.

There was another more glaring issue with Luca's obvious lie though: all the tolmen in Newfield had been destroyed long ago to make the land habitable.

"It's a new one," Luca said as if sensing her doubts, "not even a year old. Been five of them sprung up since the end of the war, Sol's punishment for all the bloodshed. Or perhaps Waer working her mischief again. So far they've all been in Ingios territory, so no one's been too bothered clearing them out."

Marta still doubted their sanity, but the hunting horns bellowed again, much closer than before. Luca and Isabelle spurred their horses at the blare, Marta with no choice but to do the same as she followed them towards the cursed tolmen.

Chapter 11

Marz 11, 562 (Five Years Ago)

Marta swirled the wine in her glass, afraid to take another sip lest she become tipsy. The bottle she opened for dinner deserved to be savored since it cost more than what a common citizen made in a week, and she wanted to remember this evening perfectly without the alcohol's added haze. Richard still had not arrived at the restaurant, had been acting strangely all week, and Marta had a good idea as to why. Five days ago, he asked to examine her woven ring, gently teasing her about her attachment to the tarnished thing on her third finger. Although he thought he was being surreptitious, Marta easily spied him slipping it over his own finger to mentally mark how far it slid.

He was appraising her ring size, marriage on his mind.

Richard had every right to be considering this eventuality. They had certainly been courting long enough to have raised the specter of matrimony, a fact Marta desperately reported to her father in her nightly letters with the hope he would send a speedy reply. He did not though, Marta maintaining her contact with Richard as normally as she could despite her trepidation. For the hundredth time that day, the thousandth time that week, she wondered if she could be happy as Richard's wife.

It was a pointless consideration though. Richard was not Blessed and her father zealously guarded the bloodline of the Childress. There was no way he would allow their superior stock to be sullied by Richard's inferior one.

Her mind still on the absent Richard, Marta noticed the entrance of the Home Guardsman, his bear-headed pin polished and shining far from the rigors of war. Since the conflict began, their numbers had swelled in the nation's capital as they ferreted out potential traitors and Eastern sympathizers. Though he took the table next to Marta, she was not worried as she put her refrain into place. She played the part of the young girl expectantly waiting her potential fiancé, and fortunately there was a spoonful of truth to make the lie easier to swallow.

The deeper part of her mind also returned to Richard. He had proven to be an overflowing fount of information, so it seemed a waste to shut this resource off. Perhaps her father was also still considering this fact, allowing Marta to wed him to ensure their source remained secure. Not for the first time, Marta wondered if her father would demand that she marry Richard, if she would be expected to bear his children to maintain her cover.

More importantly, she wondered if she would obey.

The host led another guardsman inside, this agent believing himself undercover due to his civilian attire. Marta instantly recognized him for what he was though, his rubber-soled boots a dead giveaway. They were the pride of the Home Guard, allowing them to move quickly and silently, and few but the guardsmen wore them. Honestly, it was an amateurish effort at disguise, Marta's Cildra training teaching her how to seamlessly infiltrate—

Marta's refrain almost crumbled as it occurred to her the Home Guard could be there for her. The most recent one headed her way, the host leading him to a table that had just opened up. Between him and the one in his cloak, Marta was cut off, both of them between her and the exit.

Her face belying her fear, Marta dropped her napkin to the floor. Bending down to claim it, she glanced at the patrons' shoes closer, finding two more sets of tell-tale boots.

Marta's head spun as she returned upright. *Stupid, complacent… and stupid most of all*, she chided herself. It was only a matter of time before her information leaks were traced back to Richard. She had remained in Vrendenburg for far too long.

Or perhaps they were there to vet her before Richard proposed, Marta soothed herself. His position keeping him close to the president, of course the Home Guard would need to test the loyalties of a girl of Eastern origins. Or maybe they were simply here by chance, this restaurant favored by those in Ruhl's government. The guardsmen were not even considering her after all, paying more attention to their meals than anything else.

The only way to know for sure was to act though. Feigning the wine having gone to her head, Marta rose from her table before the most recent guardsman seated himself and headed towards the women's washroom. He thankfully sat down rather than following, and Marta allowed herself a sigh of relief, one that caught in her throat as she opened the door to find the woman with the silver, bear-headed pin waiting.

"Marta Childress?"

Marta did not miss a beat, her face contorting in fear. "Sweet Sol, it's not Richard, is it? He's not hurt, is he? Please tell me he's safe!"

Though not her best role, Marta could play the part of the hysterical waif well enough. The façade firmly in place, Marta took a step towards the guardswoman as if seeking comfort from a fellow female's embrace. But the woman took a step back at Marta's advance, her hand reaching for the pistol at her waist.

Marta never hesitated, her blow catching the guardswoman in the gullet. The woman sputtered pitifully, a look of utter surprise aimed at the girl in her extravagant gown. The gown was the last thing she saw as Marta grabbed her head and slammed it into the marble counter.

The guardswoman slumping to the floor, Marta wasted no time locking the door before considering the window. It was far too small for her gown, and so the bustle would have to go. Fortunately, the guardswoman was unconscious, Marta safe to summon her Shaper gauntlet to tear through the bustle's joints and discard the thing on the ground like a savaged skeleton.

The fit was tight, but Marta pushed her way through to the alley. Although she could still blend on the street in her diminished dress, she instead chose to climb. It was not easy, her hem tangling her feet as she tried to gain purchase, and after a few attempts at ascent without the sound of alarm from the guardsmen, Marta used her gauntlets to make the rest of the way.

Once on the roof she did not dawdle, hiking up her skirts and summoning her rabbit legs to make the leap to the next building and then the next, landing as gently as she could manage in the fluttering dress. It was then that the alarm was raised, the Home Guardsmen's whistles cutting through the chatter on the ground. They came from the street outside the restaurant, and Marta suspected there had been more Home Guardsmen than the five she had seen inside. If they were lying in wait, it was surely for her, and Marta felt vindicated in fleeing when she did.

They were certainly not prepared for a Cildra Shaper as she made her way along the rooftops away from the shrills of their whistles. Blocks from the restaurant, Marta paused to listen. Their whistles headed back towards the hotel that had been her home for the last year, and Marta knew she could not return to collect her belongings now.

She had prepared for this eventuality though, months ago having stashed a gunny sack with all she needed high on a Render kirk tower ledge, somewhere no one but a Cildra Shaper would be able to climb. In it was money, a new change of clothes, and a pair of sheers: all she needed to become a new person. It was not far, but the kirk resided in the midst of a vast garden, the rooftops not giving her the proper route. So Marta dropped to the ground, stepping out to join the night's milling crowd.

She only made it two blocks before the pair spotted her, another guardsman with a constable in tow. They immediately gave chase, Marta darting into an alley seconds ahead of them. Considered the safety of the rooftops again, Marta feared her pursuers might see her performing her Cildra Shaper abilities if she attempted it. Luckily, she spied the side door to a bakery. It was locked, Marta using her open palm to spring it and close the door behind her. Her right ear pressed to the door, she exhaled relief at hearing her pursuers rush past.

The appearance of this guardsman between her and her bag concerned Marta. It meant there were several groups of Home Guardsmen throughout the city searching for her. The fact they were so close to her hidden kirk was more worrisome though. The only other person who knew its location was her father. Had he somehow been caught? Was that why he had not responded to her missives about Richard?

No, that possibility was impossible. Surely some other Cildra relative would have alerted her already if this was the case. Perhaps the Home Guard knew she was a spy for the East, but during the Grand War between the Covenant and Newfield, her actions would not be considered surprising. They may have discovered her, but her family was still safe. They had to be.

Marta pressed back into the night, choosing the rooftops again over the streets. She would also forgo her gunny sack, the possibility of it being watched making the risk not worth her attempt. Instead she headed for the docks of the Pico River, Cildra relatives across its banks in the city of East Junction that would help her escape this mess.

As she made another leap, Marta found herself thinking about Richard again. He had not been there that night, though the Home Guard had. Was he the one who had informed on her?

More likely it was the Home Guard who had made the discovery, keeping Richard away as they sprung their trap. She wondered how he had reacted to the news and if he had believed them. In her mind's eye Marta could imagine Richard bellowing that they were wrong, that there was no way his sweet Marta could be a Covenant spy. Though he was supposed to be no more than a mark, Marta hoped he would not be too devastated and that his career would not be derailed by his mistake in loving her. Even though he fought for the wrong side, deep down Richard was a good man, and she hoped that he would go on to lead a good life despite meeting her.

Chancing a glance over the side of the building, Marta saw motion in the streets, constables and guardsmen rushing through the crowds. None of them thought to look up though, this one misstep providing the only opportunity for her to escape. Despite herself, Marta felt exhilaration in being a part of the chase. It reminded her of when Father would take them out hunting rabbits. Though she cheered along with her father and brother for the hounds, Marta always secretly hoped the hares would escape their bloody fate.

Finally, she reached the riverside docks, far removed from the crowds and hunting Home Guard. A good distance from the center of the city, there was no way they could have expected her to have made it this far this swiftly. A large ferry connected Vrendenburg with East Junction, carrying swarms of passengers across the Pico River for a pittance. One was just now arriving, sure to depart within the next half hour. Marta's best chance of flight resided in one of the smaller boats though, ferrymen always ready to accept private passengers for the right price. She was already halfway home.

Despite the benign scene, Marta scanned her surroundings and spotted the Home Guardsman hidden in the shadows. It was a sloppy effort and no match for her training, so Marta felt a slight twinge of sympathy for the man. Making sure he was alone and no one watching, Marta dropped down upon him, his chosen shadows suddenly becoming a liability as she pounded him in the skull. Never having seen his attacker, he fell, a drop of his blood splattering her dress. Marta stared at it in disgust, scratching at it with her nail to remove the offending speck.

The best spies were the ones who spilled no blood themselves. The Cildra were not above bloodshed, but it had to serve a purpose. It had to have intent, and Marta had no intention of soiling her dress any further this night. Though she had harmed another this evening, two if she considered Richard, Marta had not broken this Cildra tenant until now. His offending blood was evidence she had made a mistake, Marta kicking the downed guardsman for his transgression.

Her anger at the man spent, Marta hiked her dress up to keep the hem from the mud as she made her way towards the shore. The ferry had released its passengers, providing a flood of people for her to get lost in. Pressing her way through the crowd, Marta spotted a Render. She was powerful, judging by her glass eye, and Marta made sure to watch her carefully as she changed pace to avoid her as casually as she could manage.

So intent was she on the Render that Marta did not see the other guardsman until he was beside her, his hand clamping tight to her wrist and twisting it behind her back.

Surrounded by the crowd and with the Render close by, two incongruous Cildra lessons simultaneously sprang to Marta's mind: not to reveal her Shaper abilities to those outside the clan and to never be caught. In that moment the two lessons clashed and she knew she would have to choose between them.

Marta's anger at having even been touched by this guardsman made the decision for her. His presumption was more than she could bear, and so Marta exuded her gauntlet from under his hand to break his grip. A second gauntlet joined its twin on her free hand, slamming it into his nose. The crunch of his bones was satisfying, though he sullied her dress further with blood.

Marta did not consider the blood as she wheeled towards the shore, plans for her rabbit legs filling her mind. With any luck she could leap into the river, far from the reach of the Render.

Her luck finally ran out though, the Render drawing the Breath of Marta's gauntlet with a gesture. Despite Marta's control over her Blessed Breath, the Render easily commanded it as if she owned it, strands of it covering the few feet between them in an instant and holding Marta in the woman's thrall.

The Render unsheathed her glass blade, a saber as favored by the Renders serving in the Grand War. The edge of it hovered over Marta's violated Breath, a simple flick of the Render's wrist capable of cutting away Marta's Blessed abilities, if not her life.

Marta's anger appeared at the Render's touch, begging her to run, to at least make an attempt at freedom, even if it meant her death. But it was the clarity that came with the rage that knew Marta would not stand a chance. So she went slack, dropping her hem into the mud.

"His belt," the Render said. "Get the ekesh and drink it down."

Ekesh was an awful drug, stealing a Blessed's abilities while leaving them weak as a newborn. Every guardsman carried a dose for dealing with Sol's chosen children, and Marta found the vial filled with the viscous liquid easily. To imbibe it would mean defeat, to be a captive of the West and a failure to the Cildra clan, but she would keep both her life and her Blessed Breath.

Marta slugged the liquid down, the effects far faster and headier than any draught she drunk before. Instantly her notions scattered like pheasants at a musket shot, cogent thought a fleeting memory.

As Marta collapsed into the mud, she was surprised to find in her last thought was that she still felt safe. Though she had been caught, her father would find a way to release her. He had agents in every major city throughout the nation. Politicians and statesmen were his plaything, no better than his puppets. He would secure her escape.

Surely, as the head of the Cildra clan in Newfield, he was capable of that.

Chapter 12

Winterfylled 19, 567

He rode into Lemoor at dusk along the Chacoog line of ley. Although indistinguishable from any other of the dusty travelers bundled up against the autumn winds, the townspeople of Lemoor found themselves lingering where they stood until he passed. Though the air felt more oppressive in his presence, none could find their tongues to give voice to the sudden sensation. He plodded past them all without a glance, arriving at the message station to dismount gracelessly and head inside with heavy and careless steps. The Dobra Listener looked up from his desk at the disturbance, hoping for his replacement to relieve him. Instead he saw the stranger in the worn Western bummers cap, a bullet hole straight through the center.

The man did not look at the Dobra though, instead gazing up at the four corners of the room as if they contained more wonders than anything he had encountered in his lifetime. For a moment the Listener believed the interloper must be lost, coming into this building simply because it was on the outskirts of town. Reaching out with his mind to hear the stranger's thoughts, the Listener suddenly leapt to attention. The man had no authority over him, as he was simply an agent of the government that paid for his services. But from having just barely brushed the man's mind, the Listener also knew he was not to be kept waiting.

Without a word the Listener opened his log to reveal all of the transmissions he had recorded throughout the day. Those that could possibly pertain to the man he quickly translated with a shaking hand, the stranger never looking his direction.

When the translated pages were pressed to him, the stranger finally looked down absently, the Listener suddenly afraid he was unable to read. He had such an unfocused air about him, his face that of a simpleton; his mouth never closing completely and exposing his front teeth. Finally the stranger pointed to the paper, his voice oddly tremulous despite his substantial girth.

"This one, the kidnapped girl. Tell him the Traitor will be dead soon."

"And the girl? What should I say about the girl?"

But the stranger was already away, the Listener left to mentally compose the man's message. Although the man in the bummers cap had not stated who the "him" he wished the message addressed to was, the Listener knew. When he had brushed the man's mind, he caught the name Philo Frost, and those who dealt with him were best avoided. The heavy clomps of the stranger's boots died as he mounted his horse, aiming it back out into the Ingios territory. And so he departed the same way he had come, blown by the ceaseless wind along the ley.

***

At the edge of the tolmen, Marta watched Luca and Isabelle remove their saddlebags. Horses, like all living things worth their salt, feared tolmen and would be less than useless getting them through. Marta offered no assistance to the two since all she needed remained within her haversack, which had not left her back since she mounted up. She hoped they would hurry though, dawn not waiting on them and its light making the tolmen ghuls harder to spy by each passing moment.

Their supplies stowed, Isabelle led the skittish beasts away from the tolmen to release them. Caddie standing beside her, Marta considered the girl again, wondering how quickly she could run or if she was even capable of it. It would be unfortunate if she had spent so much time and effort for the girl just to die in some unnamed tolmen.

"Won't take more than two hours," Luca said. "No worries, we've been through this one a half dozen times."

If she believed a single word that came out of his mouth, Marta might be reassured. It might indeed be possible to sneak through a tolmen without the ghuls finding them, but if they were discovered, the battle would be pitched. Like their more intelligent emet brethren, the animal-like ghuls of the tolmen were intangible, weapons passing right through them; however, the weapons of the ghuls were deadly. Her Shaper abilities would give them some hope though, her Breath capable of cutting through theirs as easily as they could pierce her skin.

She was but one of the four invaders entering the tolmen though, and she would be hobbled by having to keep one hand on Caddie to ensure her movement. She could let the girl go, perhaps entrusting her to Isabelle to allow her use of both hands, but to do so would give Luca and his partner control of Caddie, cutting Marta out of the loop and possibly making her unnecessary in their equation.

Marta realized she was lucky. Caddie only obeyed the instructions of other women, and Isabelle was unable to speak. This fact gave her an edge, one that Luca needed to understand as she caught his eye.

"The girl suffers from combat fugue. And she's locked up tight, the only key a woman who tells her what to do. I will bring her with us, but if I fall, you can't tell her to eat, can't keep her alive long enough to reach Ceilminster. But while I'm looking after her, I'll only have one hand, not enough Breath to fight against the ghuls. Understand?"

"What happened to her to make her this way?"

Marta offered him a shrug, praying it was sufficient as the man considered. With regret she remembered the Render's glass saber she had recklessly shattered earlier that evening. Although possessing it would mean an instant death sentence if caught by the Newfield dragoons, in Isabelle's hands it now might tip the balance in their favor.

Isabelle's hands were not empty though. Having tossed her saddlebag over her shoulder, she produced a handmade knife, its glittering blade chipped from black stone. The weapon was ludicrous in the tolmen, Marta unable to hide the derision from her face. Luca's smile was equally derisive, but Marta suspected it was aimed at her rather than his companion.

"You've never spent any time with the Ingios, have you?" Not waiting for Marta's answer, Luca's lockblade emerged from his pocket. A casual flick of his wrist triggered the blade, which measured longer than Marta would have expected. It was a murderer's weapon, no other possible use for it other than sinking it through human skin. As he examined his reflection in its edge, Luca's beam broadened.

"Don't worry about the little beasties, I'll protect you. So long as I have this open, I can't be defeated."

"I defeated you pretty easily."

"Isabelle might disagree with you in that regard," he shot back.

As if summoned by her name, Isabelle appeared behind them, Marta again unable to hear her approach. Turning towards the tolmen, the nodus glowing in its center, Luca's grin faltered. The motion lasted only a second, replaced almost instantly by his ceaseless smile, but Marta had spotted it and decided it did not bode well.

Isabelle took the lead, slipping through the scrub that inundated the tolmen. Marta fell into step behind her, Caddie's hand in hers, Luca and his lockblade again in the rear. Though no one said it, Marta knew no more words would be spoken within the tolmen's borders.

The shrubs grew taller the farther in they went, Marta suspecting the source of the growth was the creek she heard gurgling not far away. They never spotted the running water though, staying on a path parallel as they pushed deeper in. The nodus glowed its eerie gleam nearby, flickering like a massive candle upon the horizon, but Marta was more worried about the smaller glow she spotted to their left.

This one was moving.

Isabelle spotted it as well, shifting their course away from the unaware ghul. But not fifteen paces farther, a new glow appeared before them. Again Isabelle changed direction, navigating the increasing undergrowth seamlessly. The chase reminded Marta of the games of killer-in-the-dark she played with her Cildra cousins at gatherings. The lot of them would be let loose on the grounds at night, one of them designating the killer, whereas the rest were victims. No one but the killer was aware of his or her identity, but upon the killer's touch, they would be dead and forced to remain motionless on the ground until all the other players joined them or the adults grew bored and called the children in for bed. Like all Cildra games, it was a lesson in stealth and deceit, but what Marta remembered most was the fear intermingled with the elation of the chase. Like that childhood game, this chase was a matter of remaining invisible, of moving silently long enough to elude their pursuers. But here in the tolmen, the elation was gone, only the fear remaining as they shifted course yet again.

Despite Isabelle's expertise, soon a half dozen of the glows surrounded them, silent as the mute woman darting among them. It felt to Marta that they were trying to steer their way through a maze where the walls shifted continually around them. Isabelle's course changes became more rapid, sometimes taking only a few steps before being forced to jag another direction.

The smaller moving glows now entirely encircled them. They had made it this far based upon their guide's ability and a bit of good fortune, but fortune finally failed them when Isabelle stopped to let a wandering glow ahead cut across their path. So focused was she on the glimmering ahead, she did not notice the one to their right until the ghul emerged through the trees, the branches not even shaking as it passed right through them.

Like all the emets Marta had encountered, it was entirely inflated with Breath, a full animal form rather than the thin angular lines the Shapers used in making their Armor or the Weavers their manifestations. Though made of three tiny Breaths, they were stretched to the breaking point like a bubble puffed up and ready to burst. The ghul was still spindly as a spider though, and reminded her of a monstrous harvestman. In the West they called these tiny arachnids granddaddy longlegs, a fitting name for the little ones with their gangly legs that occurred naturally.

There was nothing natural about this beast though, its body the size of a large dog, its legs spanning nearly six feet of unnatural light. But the body was not entirely arachnid: two tentacles replacing its pincers, the odd appendages swishing back and forth like a serpent's tongue tasting the air. The ghul paused in their presence, its tentacles increasing in their oscillations as if considering their appearance.

Marta never hesitated, releasing the girl's hand while summoning her rabbit legs to launch herself at the beast. The moment she left the ground, she recalled the legs, shifting her Breath to her claws and driving them into the insubstantial body of the monster.

The ghul made no noise as it died, the three Breaths making it up instantly returning to the size of candle flames and floating off in different directions. Marta herself made more noise as she alighted in the copse of trees behind the dissipated being. It was not much noise, simply a rustling of leaves, but it shattered the still night as surely as a clarion bell. The sound echoed throughout the tolmen, but Marta did not linger upon it as she charged back to reclaim Caddie.

Isabelle did not pause to gawp at Marta's display, instead plotting a new course. Though the smaller glows surrounding them made no noise, their motions were swifter now. They grew closer, encircling them sure as the hunters' horns outside the tolmen had. Only Isabelle's quick darts allowed them to escape the noose once more as Marta again wished for the shattered glass saber.

Suddenly three more ghuls passed through the trees to their left, each similar to the one they had already encountered but with slight differences. They reminded Marta of musical notation, the melody established early on in the piece and each of these monsters a variation upon the theme. All were made up of the same basic body consisting of spindly legs and waving tentacles. Yet there was no order to their pairings, each ghul seemingly assembled at random from these parts. Marta found herself wishing they had been caught by the dragoons instead. She understood how to make humans bleed and die. These ghuls were alien things though, not meant to exist upon Ayr, and their strangeness inspiring revulsion within Marta.

Slipping her haversack off her shoulder, Marta set it upon the girl's. "Keep this for me."

Not waiting for the answer that would never come, Marta hurled herself at the monsters, forgoing the rabbit legs and covering the ground between them on foot. Her Breath she divided up, forming claws upon her left hand, a blade in her right. It was a strain on her abilities, her Breath pushed until almost the breaking point between the two weapons, but Marta had no time to worry as her clarifying rage plotted her attack.

The first ghul never stood a chance, rearing back to keep its body out of her range. Marta sliced through its front two legs before whirling upon the second beast. Her back upon it as she dealt with the first ghul, it had closed in, extending its tentacles towards her. Marta chopped through each, not waiting for them to retract back into its body before she swung her spectral sword deep into the core of its carapace, the three Breaths shooting off into the night with its death.

Again she returned to the wounded ghul, removing another two limbs before turning her rage upon the third creature. It too raised high to meet her advance, Marta ducking at the last moment to slide underneath and drive her blade's point into the beast's belly.

Its Breath still lingered in the air as she regarded the injured ghul. It had turned its back upon her, skittering away into the scrub on its diminished appendages. The almost piteous retreat would not save it though, Marta well aware a wounded enemy could still prove fatal. But she never had a chance to dispatch the beast, Luca leaping forward with his lockblade and driving the point into its body.

It was a brave maneuver, one that Marta was certain would cost Luca his life, his attack doing nothing but drawing him within range of its flailing tentacles. Marta would not mourn his loss, the woman Isabelle much more useful overall. The only question would be if she would still assist Marta once her partner died.

But to Marta's surprise his blade cleaved cleanly through the creature, the three Breaths shrinking and returning to their natural form as they disappeared into the night. Despite all the wonders and horrors Marta had seen, she could not help but stare at the grinning man and his lockblade that cut like glass.

"I told you I could not be defeated."

Luca tossed a wink her direction before returning to Isabelle. Shaken back to the moment by his movement, Marta hurried over herself, waiting on the half-Ingios woman for their next direction. Isabelle glanced over the woods, assessing the glows skittering among the trees like stirred-up hornets.

Suddenly Isabelle was off, Luca falling in after her, Marta grabbing Caddie's wrist and hauling her along. All sense of stealth was discarded, Isabelle crashing through the trees with an abandon born of fear. The glows coalesced behind them, now a solid wall of movement at their rear while scattered clumps grouped ahead and to their sides. Though the ghuls still made no sound, the air around them rushed about as if the woods surrounding them were breathing.

Several times, Isabelle tried to head south, the clusters of ghuls forcing her to instead cut north, back towards the poisoned nodus. Their way finally cut off entirely, they splashed through the creek. Coming up a small hill, they spotted the nodus and the hairs on the back of Marta's neck stood on end. Although the cold fires of the Breath swarmed around the nodus, there seemed to be a blank spot at its center, a black core that allowed no light to escape. More puzzling was the crater underneath, the earth indented for dozens of yards around and devoid of life.

Marta had no time to piece the tableau together further as the ghuls emerged through the trees and Isabelle darted another direction. Each creature bore the spidery theme, tentacles mixed in with their limbs, no sense of order in the beasts. Singularly they were a dangerous nuisance, a pest with poison, but collectively they would be the death of them.

Isabelle seemed to sense this, pressing towards the lightest group of glows surrounding them, Marta much slower in her pace than the fleet-footed woman due to the dragged girl. So slow was she that Luca had to deal with the next ghul, dodging between its tentacles and legs to stab his lockblade into its body. Isabelle waited for him to finish the beast, allowing Marta and Caddie to catch up. She was about to depart again when Marta called out.

"Wait."

Isabelle paused, her eyes trailing to Luca for direction as Marta finally reached her. The woman was useful, could very well lead them through the tolmen if their luck held just a bit longer. Still, she was also a liability in that she could not harm the ghuls. Marta could, but not while she had to keep hold of Caddie. Grabbing Isabelle's hand, Marta set it upon Caddie's wrist and looked into the girl's blue eyes.

"You follow her now. Do what she does and move where she does."

Caddie's eyes shown as blankly as before, but for a moment Marta believed she saw something deep within them. It was only a twinge, and quite possibly just imagined, but for a moment Marta swore the girl looked hurt.

Marta had no time to dwell though, as she removed her hand, nodding to Isabelle to move on. And move Isabelle did, Marta holding her breath until Caddie fell into step beside her. The decision to put the girl in the lead with Isabelle and leave Marta unencumbered by her haversack proved the right one as they ran into the next knot of ghuls.

Marta flung herself into the fray with the five creatures, her claws and phantom blade streaming light as they swung through the air. To her surprise Luca was right there beside her, his lockblade glinting the ghuls' light back at them as he lunged. Next to him Marta felt like a blunt instrument, her weapons an onslaught of unfocused fury while he darted in and out, his strikes surgical. She hacked away at any target available, slicing through legs, tentacles and carapaces with equal vigor, whereas he aimed only for the kill-shot of the bodies.

The first three were easy, the monsters with no sense of collaboration. Marta and Luca worked as a team, she cutting a swath through the limbs while he swam in her wake and finished off the beasts with his blade. She cut the legs out of the first, Luca driving his knife home even as she was turning her attention to the second. It split apart to rejoin the flow a moment later, Marta already engaged with the third as Luca circled, catching the creature by surprise.

Then another ghul dropped down upon Marta from the trees. It weighed nothing, its legs passing through her body, as if no more substantial than fog. But when its tentacles touched her skin, the pain burned, the attack not aimed at her body, but rather her Breath. The ache was enormous, so great that the shock of it almost shattered her consciousness. It felt as if her Soul was being torn apart, its pieces scattered along the winds.

Marta fell to her knees, her body rebelling against her mind and control of her limbs a futility. Its legs still passing through her, its body cohabitating the same space as she, the ghul's tentacles reared back to descend upon its prey.

Having pressed forward to engage another ghul, Luca would be no help, and the monster within her certainly would have spelled Marta's doom had she not spied Isabelle and Caddie cornered by another arriving ghul. Isabelle kept herself between the girl and the creature, her stone knife brandished. It was a useless gesture, the weapon sure to pass through the ghul as certainly as the monster would pass through her and attack the child. Of this Marta was sure.

The sight sparked the rage within her, her Breath flaring in response.

Marta's blade leapt into her hand, her formerly sluggish arm again with momentum, as if animated by the Breath exuding through it. She stabbed it into the ghul still invading her body, its Breath disappearing into the night. The pain did not disappear with it, but for the moment Marta did not feel it as she hurled herself at the ghul attacking the girls.

The monster never saw her coming, Marta's assault blindsiding it as she sunk her blade through its body. Its Breath departed, floating off on the wind even as Luca dispatched his own target. And with the dissipating Breath, Marta's rage disappeared, leaving her with only the protracted pain from the ghul's poisonous touch. Blackness nearly enveloped her as she collapsed, her vision down to a pin-prick and fading further still.

"Move," Luca's voice bellowed in Marta's ears, the sound enough to draw her back to the moment and realize her legs were made of lead. He held her upright as she tried to move the dead limbs, but they refused to respond, just as her lips and tongue betrayed her as she tried to explain this to him.

"You move now," he told her, giving her a good shake for emphasis. "You move or we leave you here, no grave to mark where you fell."

The idea of earning a grave was laughable, a grunt all Marta could manage in response. Traitors gained no grave, were simply left where they fell. She had never expected more than that, and the idea this freebooter would try and use this to motivate her was more than ludicrous.

"Useless."

She did not see his hand, but she felt its sting as his slap snapped her head to the side.

"Less than useless."

Marta was many things: a spy, a soldier, a Childress of the Cildra clan, and a traitor above all, but of all of her myriad identities, uselessness was not one. And to be called such by this freebooter was enough to set her rage off again, Marta's world growing in scope from the pin-prick. It was enough to remember the plans for the full Armor she had used in the Grand War, her Breath emerging to give it form. It was a childish thing, something any capable Shaper would look down upon with disdain. But it was enough to sculpt her Breath into the basic outline around her body, the woefully thin ribbons enveloping her legs. It was the Breath of the Armor Marta moved, not her legs. The Armor proved to be enough, its form holding her erect and allowing Luca to leave her as he dealt with the approaching ghuls.

Isabelle thrust on with Caddie in tow, Marta's haversack bouncing upon the girl's back with each step. It was on her haversack Marta focused. Aimed only on it, she forced one Armored foot forward, following it laboriously with the other. She heard cries from Luca behind her, unintelligible and composed entirely of emotion that superseded language. He was afraid, she realized, the thought gurgling to the top of her consciousness long enough to recognize that Luca was also defiant, and that was good—it meant they still stood a chance.

Isabelle suddenly stopped as they passed the cluster of rocks, six stacked one atop the other. It was no natural formation, its strangeness made more pronounced by the white dot painted upon its apex. There, Marta halted as well, the plans to her Armor a tenuous thread she clung to desperately as they waited.

Finally, Luca burst through the scrub, the glow of the dozen ghuls fierce at his back. The monsters did not follow him past the outcropping of stones though, the man stopping on the other side to catch his ragged breath. He grinned again at Marta, the woman turning away from his gaze to force her Armor forward farther still.

Reaching Isabelle and Caddie, she dispersed her Breath, her poisoned body teetering as she grasped the girl's thin wrist. Caddie turned to face her at the touch, her eyes dull as a cow's. Marta had a moment at most before her body finally betrayed her entirely.

"Don't let them near me," she ordered, her voice more a vague assortment of utterances than words. Marta only hoped that the girl would understand and obey as the blackness swallowed her whole.

Chapter 13

Blotmonad 13, 562 (Five Years Ago)

Marta had been in Overhurst for nearly seven months and could not conceive of a more wretched place in all of Ayr. The official name of her prison was the Calderon Quarry, but everyone referred to it as "the Pit." It was an apt name, nothing but a wide hole carved into the granite by Western Shapers and now housing the Eastern Shapers captured in the Grand War.

Shapers, by their Blessed natures, were difficult to imprison, their Armor allowing them to smash through stone walls easily. Ekesh made them docile, but the drug was costly and kept in reserve for the war effort. Execution was a far less expensive alternative, but by killing their captives, the Newfield government would give the rebellious Covenant another incident to rally behind. So the captured Eastern Shapers were shipped to the northernmost state in Newfield and tossed into the Pit.

The solution was almost elegant in its simplicity, the walls of their hole too tall to scale and sharpshooters poised at the lip with muskets to bring down any Shaper caught using their abilities. This situation was not explained to Marta as they lowered her down the winch, her head still swimming with ekesh, but it was easy enough to surmise when she came to enough to survey her surroundings. There were over 400 of her fellow prisoners here, all Covenant volunteers who now found themselves hauled to the farthest point from their homes. Like most Shapers, they were heavy laborers and farmers, professions where their strength was an asset. Just looking them over, Marta was sure not two in ten were able to read, she probably the only one who could recite the multiplication tables.

Once ensconced in the hole, the Eastern Shapers were left to their own devices, food and necessities lowered down once a day by the same winch that deposited Marta. Their leader was a man by the name of Joel Kearney, who Marta found beside her as the ekesh worked its way out of her system. Kearney might have been a paunchy man once, but the months in the Pit had filched the fat from his body. Somehow he had fashioned an ugly pipe for himself, and though there was no tobacco in their prison, he chewed on it with authority as he looked Marta over.

"You done been cast out, girl. Been cast into the Pit, and even Sol can't find you here. He has no will here, the only rule that of me and my men. I'm the big bug here, the food comes directly to me each day. The first week you get for free. The next depends on how well we like you. And I like you well enough, girl."

Kearney chomped down harder on his pipe, his smile obscured by the bowl's edges. His smile might have been intended as benevolent, but Marta found it oily.

"We men-folk take in women on occasion. For the lady's protection, of course, so everyone knows they belong to someone. There's safety in that. Got one here already. May's a good woman, but she's not as pert as you, girl. Perhaps you'd like to take her place. It would mean double rations for you if you did."

His eyes roamed over Marta, appraising her in the remains of her mud-soaked gown. Unable to move more than her face under the influence of the ekesh, Marta hoped it properly displayed her revulsion to his offer. It was all she could manage, but it was enough.

"Soon as you can stand, I'll take you to your tent."

It was Kearney who put them to work building their hovels and latrines. For a few weeks it had kept the prisoners of the Pit occupied, but now the rudimentary buildings were all fashioned, nothing for the Eastern Shapers to do now but wait out their time in the cold.

Though she shivered constantly, Marta hoped the cold would soon come in earnest and freeze the ground. Kearney had the latrines dug as deep as he could without the use of either tools or their Shaper abilities, but the Pit was a former quarry, and rainwater collected at the bottom. Eventually the latrines overflowed, the fetid liquid covering the ground in a cesspool of rank. With any luck the frigid Overhurst winter would come and put an end to the stench and sickness that galloped with it.

It was already colder than anything Marta had ever experienced, even in the Auld Lands. There, she had been outfitted with thick coats lined with marten fur. Here she only had the remains of her formerly fancy dress, her ring taken from her after her capture and sure to have been pawned to finance the war effort against the Covenant. Huddled in her hovel, Marta occasionally missed the ring when she was warm enough to remember it.

Given the chance, she would happily part with it again were it enough to trade for something warmer to wear. But gold and jewels would be useless here, clothing and shelter the only form of currency.

There was, unfortunately, one other thing the men in the Pit were interested in. Newfield law was quite clear that all Blessed were considered equal despite their genders, their abilities granting women the same rights as Blessed men. As such, Blessed women were welcomed into the Covenant and Newfield armies. Yet fewer Shaper women were willing to risk their lives in warfare, making the female prisoners probably only one for ten of the captured men. Stripped of their abilities by the sharpshooters on the walls, the men took charge, their fists deciding any disagreement. So the few women here sought safety in the arms of the most powerful men, Marta subjected to a dozen proposals for protection in addition to Kearney's own before he had even shown her to her tent.

He extended his offer again the next two times he passed out Marta's rations personally. It would have been a wise decision to take him up of his offer, Kearney the most powerful male in the Pit. But Marta was the daughter of Norwood Childress and turned him down with another withering glance. Her derisive looks were enough for the next three rude suitors when she left her tent to collect her meager rations.

The fourth tried to take her by force, Marta leaving him crippled for his troubles. Using Armor the grounds for death from the sharpshooters, Marta retreated to her tent, feigning fear as he advanced upon her. Once protected from prying eyes in the folds of her tent, Marta's anger raged, her clarity and training barely stopping her from killing the man outright as she pounded her gauntlet into him again and again. Dead, he might cause the guards to look into it, but alive he would provide an object lesson to the others. So Marta tossed his broken body to soak in the waste water outside her tent. His moans finally summoned Kearney's lackeys, who hauled the wounded man away without a word.

Word soon spread of Marta's deed, and she hoped it would be enough to keep the rest of them away for good. If others came seeking revenge for their fallen friend, she assumed it would be in the next few days, and that they would come in force. She was not worried if they did though. If anything, she was hoping for it, her anger her constant companion and screaming for a violent outlet to purge her pique. Two days later, the flap to her tent slid back, Marta turning upon the invader with a smile on her face and the promise of violence in her eyes.

Instead, Marta made an ally in Abner Schlater.

He was not much to look at, a small, dark-skinned man with a plain face and white tipping his temples and beard. Abner gave every impression of a middling farmhand, his speech equally slow and with an Aiouan twang.

"How'd you break that man? How'd you turn him out?"

Her teeth clenched to keep from clattering from the cold, Marta hissed like a serpent. "Take another step and you'll find out firsthand."

The man wisely remained at the threshold, perhaps not as simple as he seemed. He looked her over again as if assessing the yearly yield of corn.

"I want to tie to you," he finally drawled.

Other men had wanted the same of Marta, all more odious in their phrasing. This one was at least polite, and for that she would not break any bones. As she took her first step towards him, Abner held up his hands in surrender, his words coming quickly for a change.

"I ain't here offering my protection. Well, I reckon I am, but in exchange for yours."

His seeming sincerity took Marta aback, she expecting a trap as he went on. "Got a daughter about your age back home. A wife too, one I love dearly. One I fear more than you if ever I strayed, little thing."

Marta studied him, still unconvinced as he broke into a grin. "In exchange for your protection, I'll offer you my eyes, my mouth. Two sets of eyes see enemies in the night better than one, two chances to call out an alarm if they come. Plus, I make friends easier than you, little thing. Got a group already, good folk who watch out for each other, not beasts like some of them here. We pool our food, our eyes, and our voices. Only way we're going to survive is as a group. We keep each other human. Otherwise we're no better than animals caught in a cage."

Her eyes narrowed as Marta considered his offer. It was true: another set of eyes would allow her to sleep again instead of keeping watch alone in the night from the attack she was sure would eventually arrive. Others watching her back might well ensure her survival.

Marta was not there to make friends though. She had expected her father to use his incredible influence to have her ransomed and released from this prison within a matter of days, but she had been here nearly two weeks and her nerves were worn nearly threadbare. A good night's sleep would do her good, but the idea of tying herself to such common Shaper stock irked Marta to no end, at least until Abner cleared his throat.

"Thought you might want to know the full extent of what I'm offering. The man you put through the mill, Benny Doyle, he died today. Pneumonia, the sawbones said, but the state you left him probably came into play. He's got a cousin in here, a man I wouldn't want to make enemies of. Unless, of course, I had you by my side."

Abner's last pronouncement had its desired effect, Marta moving into his tent that night, not as his prison wife, but with her own bedroll. Their new partnership did not stop Marta from staying awake throughout the night though, even with one of Abner's friends keeping watch outside the tent. Part of it was to ensure Abner did not go back on his word and try and creep upon her in the dark. But Abner slept soundly, turning his back to her and his gentle snores soon filling the frigid air. Long after she was sure he was not faking, Marta could still not fall asleep, the fate of Benny Doyle rolling around her mind. He was dead and she was the cause.

Surely other men had died because of her. Marta's transmission of Newfield secrets to the Covenant guaranteed that hundreds, if not thousands, died because of her actions. But these men and women were just numbers, lists of names of those who might or might not have fallen just as easily had she not taken action. Benny Doyle, on the other hand, had died because of her directly. It might have been pneumonia that finally finished him off, but it was the violence she did him that sparked the process. Part of her was glad: he was a bad man that deserved his fate, her anger threatening to roll to a boil when she remembered the look of glee on his face in response to her feigned fear.

But another part of her remembered that he had family, and not just the cousin who might seek revenge in the Pit. He had parents and siblings, perhaps children of his own that would mourn his death in spite of his horrid nature. He had a face, one Marta remembered quite well. He had a mouth that would never again speak, eyes that would never see.

And all because of her.

***

To her surprise Abner was good to his word and proved to be as loyal as he was plain. In the morning he introduced her to his gang, including the quick-witted Reid Paxton. His hair as pale as a shock of corn silk, Reid was certainly easy on the eyes, even in his shabby state. More importantly, he was the son of a successful merchant from Meskon who had insisted on bettering the family name through his son. She took to Reid instantly, the man educated enough to trade snippets of poetry when the mood struck him. Within a matter of two weeks, they exhausted all the poetry in their collective memories, Reid instantly turning to riddles he produced each day.

"I have far too many teeth," he called to her as they passed one morning, "but you let me kiss your head each day. If you're pretty, that is."

It took Marta a few hours until she discerned the answer, the mental diversion ingratiating Reid to her all the more.

Abner's gang also included Tollie Pryor and Rupert Kelly. Hailing from Rhea, Marta could not imagine the soft-spoken farmer Tollie in battle, the man seemingly incapable of maintaining eye contact with anyone more than a fleeting glance. It was Rupert that proved invaluable though, the man's skinny frame swelled by a black beard so bristling he appeared like a chimney brush. A former woodsman and master forager, Rupert swore that until the Grand War he had more fingers than he did nights spent indoors, and it was his knowledge that proved invaluable. Though their five rations were of equal size to the other prisoners, Rupert mixed them with boiled water to make the stew that sustained them. Although it was a far cry from the fine food Marta was accustomed to, they fared much better than their fellow prisoners. Each night they set guard around their tents, always on the lookout for Benny's cousin. But if the man was seeking revenge upon Marta, she saw no sign.

Soon their success drew others, including the star-gazer Gonzalo Talreja, who would consult the heavens each night and make dire predictions as to their fate. Another woman, Ida Rombach, also joined their number, soon sharing Reid's tent and sly looks between them during the day. In all they were a good group, people Marta could trust, even if she would not have chosen them as comrades. But it was only Abner that Marta taught her Cildra Shaping skills to.

She resisted at first, but Marta finally succumbed out of boredom. The winter winds raging around them, no one leaving their tents except to collect food and use the frozen latrines, they had to find a way to pass the endless hours somehow. It was the only way to stay warm and sane as the winds wailed.

Abner was a slow learner, which suited her fine since it killed more time. Although he had no gift for his Shaping talent, Abner was dogged and as unyielding as the Armor he favored. Marta's first mistake in his education was to try and teach him the snake tongue she was introduced to her Blessed abilities by. They spent weeks at it, Abner unable to conceive of the fluid motion of the appendage. It was only a single element of Breath, requiring a minimum of mental plans to operate, but it seemed beyond Abner.

"There's more ways than one to top the mountain," she told him, trying her best to mimic Cyrus' indifference when Abner again encountered an impasse. But she was no teacher, and Abner scarcely a student. Only when they had finally given up in frustration did Marta try to instruct him in constructing a blade.

Abner mastered it in a matter of hours.

She soon learned he preferred static forms, his mind unable to comprehend change, but latching onto dogmatic mental plans. Though the Cildra gauntlets required seven moving parts, Abner understood that complexity easier than the single mobile stalk of the snake tongue. He explained this paradox away by pointing out that his personal Armor had nearly a hundred joints, but Marta never truly understood his aversion to simplicity, which was the Cildra way. He learned the rabbit legs soon enough, never able to test the form properly in the confines of their tent, but the tongue forever eluded him, as did the flickering phantom blade.

He offered to show her his Armor, perhaps teaching her a thing about the full form that the Cildra disdained. Marta turned him down as politely as she could, sure there was nothing of any value she could glean in his lumbering Armor. To his credit, Abner took her snub well, instead focusing on his new Shaper forms.

Abner asked again and again after where she had learned this understanding of Shaper abilities, Marta evading his questions with all of her available social guile. Finally, frustrated by his constant questions, she told him it came from her mother's Mynian upbringing.

The lie seemed to satisfy him, Marta happy she was keeping the clan's secrets, even if she revealed some of her own heritage. It was but a bit of truth to flavor her lies, her dedication to hiding her clan's existence proving her loyalty. But as the months rolled on, she waited for her family to prove their loyalty to her, for someone to come and rescue her from the frigid wastes of the Pit. It had already been eight months, yet they were nowhere to be seen, and she was growing colder by the day.

Chapter 14

Winterfylled 20, 567

Marta was warm as she swam in her dark delirium.

The pain has been too much for her body, her mind recoiling into the recesses of her skull. The pain chased her through the darkness, persistent as a hound driven mad by the scent of blood. Marta retreated further, but still the pain came. So Marta summoned her will as if it were her Breath, solidifying it into a wall the pain crashed into. The pain broke like a wave upon a rock, but some spilled around the edges of Marta's makeshift barrier to torture her further. So she encircled herself, the barrier of her will enveloping her and allowing the pain no hole to slither through. She imagined herself as a bird inside its egg, floating motionlessly in the fluid. Outside her protective shell something was shaking her body, but the fluid around her absorbed the shock, allowing Marta to rest for the first time in what seemed like ages. Outside her cocoon the pain seethed, but inside her shell Marta was safe and warm.

The warmth was intoxicating and Marta felt drunk on the stuff. As she drank the warmth in deeper, her body became less distinct and faded incrementally. At first it was the definition of her fingers and toes, their edges blending and becoming indistinct until they melded together like fleshy mittens. But then these new appendages faded, Marta vaguely aware she could no longer feel anything below her elbows or knees. She was diminishing, but she did not care as another shake came through her protective shell, Marta barely able to feel the outside world any longer.

Utter oblivion would be a welcome respite, but Marta held off giving herself to it fully. Hazily she became aware her protective shell was not thin and fragile like the egg she initially imagined, but thick as stone. This stony cocoon dragged her deeper down, Marta becoming more indistinct as it digested her. Through her diminished appendages she was scarcely able to note the next round of shaking outside her protective world.

Aboard the Sanct Rosario on her trip across the Saulshish Ocean, Marta overheard a sailor claim that there was a peace that came in drowning. To fight against the inevitability of death was a futility, he said, and true freedom only came when one let go and succumbed to the enveloping waves. She had wondered then how it was he came upon this knowledge if he were still living, but now she knew the truth to his words. She certainly felt at peace as she drowned within herself, the totality of it only slightly disturbed by another shake to her body.

Something was summoning Marta back to the cold and vicious world, and Marta petulantly retreated further into the warmth. Growing fainter and fainter, the shaking still persisted, and Marta realized her life was at stake. She knew that she could die then and there, swaddled in her warm shell, or survive a bit longer in the harsh reality of Ayr.

She chose the latter, clawing her way through the stony shell then out of unconsciousness like a grave. The real world brought pain instead of peace, but Marta chose pain over the oblivion of death. Survival was not her choice, rather a compulsion she could not refuse.

Marta's eyes fluttered open to spy Luca and Isabelle approaching, Caddie shaking her for all she was worth. Neither of the freebooters held weapons in their hands, and for that Marta was thankful as she sluggishly stirred.

Surprise flitted across Luca's face before being replaced by his wry grin. "You've come back to us. Sol be praised, but we need to get moving soon as you can stand."

Despite his desire for speed, Luca had taken the time to shave that morning. Most men Marta had known on the trail were happy to let their beards grow. In Marta's opinion those that meticulously cared of their appearance had either too much time on their hands or a strong sense of vanity, and Luca certainly sounded rushed.

Isabelle took another step towards them, and Caddie shook Marta all the harder at her approach. The half-Ingios woman barked a clipped laugh as she produced a bundle of leaves.

"Put those under your tongue, but don't chew them," Luca said. "Swallow down your spit though, that'll clear your head."

Marta ignored the leaves, instead gazing at Isabelle. Though dressed the same as before, the woman now had several different-colored strings pushed through her earlobes, the strands braided together in an elaborate pattern. Marta had read that the Ingios used different braids to communicate between the tribes, but had never seen anything like this.

"It's to state our intentions," Luca answered, following her gaze. "Ingios weave them through their ears to tell other tribes they come across their purpose. Like a ship at sea flying its banner for identification, except their weavings can't be taken down quick and replaced. So when they go into somewhere new, their intention is set ahead of time."

"And what is her intention?"

Luca's blithe shrug was her only answer, Marta accepting the offered bundle of leaves and placing them under her tongue. The taste was intensely bitter, Marta forcing herself to swallow it. Caddie still shaking her made it even more difficult, Marta finally setting her hand over the girl's.

"No more of that," she said, adding, "You did good," almost as an afterthought. Caddie ceased at once, her blue eyes gazing blankly into Marta's. Although she had obeyed Marta's command, if there was any thought behind those eyes, Marta could find no evidence.

Still too weak to stand, Marta pressed herself up to an elbow to survey their surroundings. It was near midday, the nearby tolmen's glow faded in the daylight. The ghuls still surely prowled the cursed place, but at least had not passed the odd outcropping of rocks they stopped beside.

The two horses took Marta entirely by surprise, both bearing the brands and saddles of the Newfield dragoons. Their riders were nowhere to be seen though, Luca's grin widening as Marta made her discovery.

"Not to worry, they're still alive."

"Punishment for horse thieving and murder's the same. You should put them down to be safe."

"When you're the one dealing with them, you can decide if they live or not. Until then, I'm the one calling the shots."

Freebooters were known to take chances, but Marta had never heard of one who left his victims alive when he could silence the witnesses. The man vexed her, and so she studied him closer as he continued.

"Should probably thank you for your help, though. If they hadn't seen you laid out there, we never would have gotten close. But we best hie out quick before the rest starts wondering where they got off to."

Isabelle approached with a horse and hefted Caddie to the saddle. The girl situated, Isabelle extended her hand to assist Marta as well. Marta refused the gesture and climbed atop the horse by will alone. Isabelle's eyes glittered again as she gave her bark, hopping on the other horse while Luca took the spot behind her. It was Isabelle who claimed the reins, though, gigging the horse and leading them deeper into Ingios territory.

***

Encumbered by two riders each, the horses did not keep a quick enough pace for Marta's liking, Isabelle's choice to continue to double back on their tracks every so often reducing their progress further. With each step Marta's head cleared, the agonizing pain she first felt fading into only a nagging soreness, Isabelle's herbs doing their job well.

Isabelle shifted their course yet again, sticking to the thickets of trees that populated the Ingios territory. The open ground surrounding them would have made for a faster route, but Marta silently agreed with her decision to remain obscured by the foliage. The land around them was vast and without any signs of the civilization Marta preferred. They were far away from the strong lines of ley that carried the trains connecting the nation of Newfield.

Ley was weak in the Ingios territories, no one sure if they chose these realms because of it or if the ley remained low because of the Ingios' small population. Her former tutor Mitchell once proffered a popular theory that it was civilization that strengthened the ley. By building a city its inhabitants razed the ground of plants, releasing their Breath to join the flow. The city's large population also demanded an equally large amount of food, the plants and animals they consumed releasing even more Breath to join the ley. Mitchell said this was a good thing, sure to make Sol happy when he returned for the Harvest to see how the humans had reshaped Ayr, just as their deity intended when he created them.

Marta had given up on her belief in both Sol and the Harvest long ago, but if he ever did return, Marta was sure he would be entirely unimpressed by their accomplishments. If Sol was capable of creating life from nothing, what would he care about the erecting of inanimate cities? If anything, he would probably consider them the same way a child would a colony of ants digging their intricate maze of tunnels inside a glass jar. Their struggles to build and survive were, of course, amusing, but in the end they were no more than bugs.

***

By afternoon Isabelle gave up on obscuring their trail, Luca starting to speak as soon as their course was set due south. The man could talk about anything, everything: the cities he had seen, men he had known, differences in dishes in the states, why the mandolin was a superior instrument to the fiddle. Though

Marta listened for the first half hour, she soon took to actively ignoring him. She decided he never said anything of import, just eternally battling against the silence with his voice. Several times he asked Marta her opinion, waiting for her to turn his soliloquy into a discussion. Each time she refused to take the bait, her face stony and focused only on the terrain. She had no story to tell, not one she wished to share with his kind, at any rate. Luca never seemed to mind her silence and answered his own questions. Marta reckoned he was used to a mute companion, content to carry on a one-sided conversation all on his own.

Only briefly pausing to rest their mounts, they arrived at the outskirts of the township a bit before dusk. Though a stray line of ley ran through it, it appeared too weak to support a train, making the town small enough that Marta did not think any Dobra Cousins would be in residence. This meant their crimes would still be unknown here, giving them the chance to restock their supplies.

The horses were her greatest concern, their brands and tack marking them as property of the Newfield dragoons. This made the horses useless in trade, and each moment they sat upon them put them in further jeopardy. So they pulled their mounts off the trail and into a thickly wooded area as Marta decided how to proceed. Luca would have to purchase the new horses, of that she was certain. Isabelle could not haggle, and Marta had no intention of doing so while leaving Caddie with them unattended.

The real question was how much money to give him. The cost of three horses and gear would not even deplete the cash Carmichael had given her by a quarter, but to reveal to these freebooters how flush she was would also invite them to take the remainder by force.

Movement on the trail diverted her companions' attention as a singular rider passed by. Marta prayed the handful of bills she pried off while they were watching would be sufficient, hoping Luca was half as gifted at haggling as he was a gabbing. She was ready to turn the money over when she glanced at the rider and noticed the bummers cap with the single bullet hole through it perched on his head.

Marta went rigid, the air driven from her lungs as he rode by not twenty yards away. Though his back was to them, she knew they were in danger of discovery. They would not be safe until he was miles away, the entire continent preferably between them—and perhaps not even then.

Luca and Isabelle noticed her reaction, their hands alighting on their weapons as they watched the solitary rider reach the edge of town. Once he had dismounted and entered a building, they relaxed, looking to Marta for an explanation.

Marta mounted up behind Caddie, not risking words as she turned their shared horse due east. The other two caught up quickly on their own tired beast, Luca's mouth opening for a question, but upon meeting Marta's eyes, his teeth clacked shut, the three racing the setting sun in silence.

They rode hard over the next hour, giving the township and the man with the perforated bummers cap a wide berth. Finally Luca spurred his weary ride alongside Marta to whisper, "We push the horses much harder, they'll likely die under us."

Marta ignored him, Luca finally catching her horse's bridle to yank them both to a stop. It took all of her self-control not to attack this infuriating freebooter for slowing their flight by even an instant as Luca looked back toward the distant town.

"Who's this bug that's got you so cowed?"

"Graff." The word felt risky in Marta's mouth, as if even invoking his name might draw his attention their direction. "A Render."

"Just a Render? I saw you take one apart not two nights back."

"Graff's no mere Render. He's Blessed even among the Blessed. He's never been hurt, not even during the war. The only blood he ever lost was by his own hand when he cut out his eye, which means he can track us from anywhere if he has our scent. And if he's already this close, then he must have scented us."

"He's still just one man," Luca countered.

"Yes," Marta snarled. "The man who held the line at Stone Cleaver."

Marta took a perverse pleasure in the fear that flitted across Luca's face. She was more pleased when he released her reins, Isabelle kicking their horse's flanks hard to try and coax a bit more muster as they resumed their flight. Perhaps it was still possible to escape Graff's gaze, Marta thought.

It was possible, but more than likely already too late.

Chapter 15

Decembris 18, 562 (Five Years Ago)

The year was drawing to a close and Marta was cold to the core. She woke up cold and shivered throughout the day, only to return to bed, where she received no relief. The frost had become ever-present, had wormed its way into her bones, her being. Abner proposed bringing the others of their cadre inside to share the tent with them, sleeping in a pile like puppies to pool their warmth. Marta flatly refused. There would simply be too many to take with them, and she planned on escape.

Abner at first believed the winter had driven her insane, but after an hour of hushed discussion, he began to entertain the idea. His consideration of Marta's plan was originally patronizing, Abner indulgently letting her speak her fill with the intention of shattering her strategy as kindly as he could. What he was not prepared for was Marta's silver tongue and powers of persuasion honed by her Cildra training. At the half hour mark, Marta knew she had him hooked, and before the hour was out, Abner was fully a part of the plan.

During the next snowstorm, after the sharpshooters retreated to their lean-tos atop the Pit's lip, they intended to use their gauntlets to scale the walls and slip away into the night. A guard had recently let slip that the Tea Spring River was not a few miles east of the Pit and they could use the cover of the blizzard to follow the river to the Overhurst capital of Broadus. There, Marta had Cildra relatives that would surely smuggle them home.

Ultimately, it was a foolish plan, as daring as it was dumb. But they had no choice and both knew they could not survive in the Pit much longer. Working with Rupert, Reid and the others kept them alive while those like Kearney wasted away to almost nothing. There was a conceivable chance they could wait out the rest of the winter and survive, but the recent rumors had become too much to bear.

Rumors always ran rampant in the prison, the guards constantly hurling down updates on the war and assuring their captive audience that the West was winning every battle. By no means a novice in matters of misinformation, Marta paid these tidbits little mind, but the last few weeks new reports had sprung up about the Whisperer prison. Like Shapers, Whisperers were notoriously difficult to inter due to their ability to manipulate guards caught unaware. So the Renders found a simple solution in cutting away the Whisperers' Blessed Breath to render them powerless. Now nearly done with the Whisperers, the Renders would soon turn their attention to the captured Eastern Shapers, so the rumors went. Such a fate would be worse than death as far as Marta was concerned.

Death was one thing, but what she could not abide would be to be mutilated, to have her Blessed Breath stolen from her. She refused to be reduced to average and then be forced to live out the rest of her life a shadow of her former self. It was this fear of being castrated like some unruly bull that needed to be broken which stoked the flames of her rage and finally led to the formulation of their escape plan.

The sky had gone still the last few days, brimming with black clouds and promising a blizzard. In preparation, Marta and Abner only gave half their rations to Rupert and his stew for the last week, hoarding their remains for once they escaped. With any luck the snows would start that night, giving them the cover they needed. Abner was ready to tear a square of cloth from their tent to carry their foodstuffs when one of Kearney's lackeys appeared at their flap.

His appearance caused Marta's hair to stand on end. Not half an hour earlier she heard the creak of the winch being lowered. This was a deviation from the routine, as was being summoned to Kearney, and at this late date any deviation was worrisome. Only she and Abner were privy to their plan, or so they thought. Perhaps one of their friends had reported their strange behavior with their rations. In her heart Marta hoped she could depend on these fellow castaways, but her head still chewed over the problem as she followed the lackey through the frigid wind to Kearney's tent. There, she found her brother waiting.

Standing beside Kearney, Carmichael was in disguise with spectacles and a beard, but she recognized him instantly from the slight crook in his nose. Despite decorum and her Cildra training, Marta was so overcome she almost threw herself into his arms, but before she had the chance, Carmichael extended his hand and formally introduced himself as "Philo Frost."

Marta fell into her assigned role by rote. Her brother was using a cover identity, and she would not be the one to destroy his guise while they had witnesses, like Kearney, with them. So she took Carmichael's offered hand, the proper amount of confusion displayed on her face for their audience as she gave her brother her own name in turn. This preamble out of the way, Kearney excused himself from his own tent.

Alone together for the first time in years, Carmichael still stood stiffly, his eyes appraising her. And for the first time in months, Marta felt embarrassed by the ruin of her dress, all her affluence hanging off her in tatters. Her first impulse was to cover herself, to hide from her brother's gaze. Instead she held her head up higher, defiantly staring back at him in all his finery. Though it had been nearly ten years since they last played one of their waiting games, both fell into the role again and waited for the other to break the silence first.

Finally, Carmichael spoke, his voice as calm as she remembered yet containing a hint of awe. "You remind me of a beautiful mudbird."

The comparison was ludicrous, Marta with nothing approaching beauty in her currently shabby state. As if sensing her thoughts, Carmichael smiled wanly. "Your song will prove all the more lovely now that all the shine has been scrubbed from your feathers. And the clan has need of your voice."

Some small part of her mind noted that this was the first time Marta had bested her brother at their waiting game, but the majority of her mind had more important questions to consider.

"Why have you waited so long to rescue me?"

"The moment was not right. Even this meeting was difficult to make. The tide of the war is turning, the Covenant now on the offensive and making Ruhl's government nervous of anyone visiting captured Shapers. But we have not forgotten you." Carmichael produced a small cake from the pocket of his coat. "An early Yuletide present."

All sense of self-control gone, Marta snatched the sweet away, wolfing it down in a single bite. The taste was divine, the sugar dissolving upon her tongue a welcomed reminiscence. Her gift devoured, Marta's composure returned as she examined her brother.

"Is it true what they say? Are the Renders mutilating Whisperers and cutting away their Blessed Breath? Are the Shapers next?"

Carmichael laughed dryly, an altogether unpleasant sound. "That's just silly scuttlebutt. Both sides in this unfortunate war treasure the Blessed, your Shaper abilities still of some use to the West. They are desperate now, and their desperation will lead them to make a dangerous offer to your kind here. You are to take them up on their offer, to insinuate yourself into a position of use. This is important, Marta. The whole war could hinge upon this ploy."

Marta's anger awakened at his instruction, the clan demanding even more from her after abandoning her for the last eight months, but she bit back her displeasure, keeping her voice even. "Father orders this?"

Carmichael's face fell slightly at the invocation of their sire. "We are both servants of the clan in all things. They ask much, but above all obedience. But it is all for a reason. Even your suffering has a purpose." Without another word Carmichael pressed through the tent's flaps and into the night.

Her father still demanded more of her, and Marta was unsure what else she had left to give. It was not until Kearney reentered that her reverie broke and she realized that she had not thanked Carmichael for his sugary gift, the taste still lingering in her mouth.

She returned to Abner straightaway, unsure if she should inform him of her brother's instructions. Though he was still free to attempt to escape on his own, she was bound by her duty to the clan to stay. There was little chance he would survive the Overhurst wilderness, even if he did somehow scale the walls alone, and finally Marta informed him of the upcoming Western offer. If they accepted, they might be able to win the war for the East.

Abner did not believe her at first, but she reminded him she was stuck in this hole for being a spy, and his demeanor changed instantly. The potential of winning the war for the East was a disease worming its way through his veins until it reached his brain, his eyes burning again with Covenant fervor. He wanted to tell Reid, Rupert, and the others in their troop, but Marta was unsure. Then she remembered Carmichael's cryptic comparison of her to a mudbird. He had told her the clan needed her to use her voice, and so she decided to sing a lovely tune.

That night they all huddled in their tent, Rupert, Gonzalo, Tollie, Reid, and Ida sharing Abner and Marta's paltry store of rations like an early Yuletide feast. As they split the meager meal, Marta put her voice to use, convincing them to accept the Western deal so as to assist the East. The grim Gonzalo was the most difficult to convince, peeling back the flap of the tent to ascertain his choice from the stars.

But the blizzard had finally begun, obscuring any view of the skies. Gonzalo declared this an ill omen, though he too finally fell under Marta's sway. And as the winter wind buffeted their tiny tent, they were at least happy, the knowledge that they had the chance to still be of use to their distant homeland warming them against the cold.

***

Yuletide came and went with the blizzard, the New Year looming when Marta was again called to Kearney's tent. She was not the first one summoned, all those that refused returning to say that the Renders were offering a deal: if the Eastern Shapers would fight for the West, they would be released, their sentences commuted after the war was won. Many refused the chance, but Kearney was wholeheartedly for it and promised of a full meal to any takers. Those who accepted the food never returned, the prisoners' ranks winnowed significantly by the time Marta was finally brought before him. She readily accepted the deal before Kearney even offered it, her suffering stomach awakened and restive by the promise of food. But the first sustenance they offered was another vial of ekesh. Marta swallowed it down, intent on doing her duty to the East as well as her clan.

The daughter of Norwood Childress, Marta tried to comport herself with dignity under the drug's influence as they winched her up the wall. Even here her behavior reflected upon her father and she had no intention of disappointing him as they hauled her to the wooden mess hall with the delicious smells issuing from within. When they threw open the door, she was so hungry her stomach openly revolted against her senses, the scent of roasting meat so strong it was all Marta could do to not break away and hobble towards the glorious smell. Her mouth watered to such a shameful degree she could not help the drool dribbling down her chin.

They roughly heaved her into the room, shoving her into the chair and binding her wrists. Marta's eyes affixed on the smoking stove, craving the beef they would soon produce. For a moment the small part of her mind wondered how she would be able to eat with her hands tied, but such thoughts as dignity were exiled, Marta happy to lap food like a dog from a bowl so long as she was fed.

It was only when they removed the glowing branding iron from the stove that Marta realized where the smell of searing meat was coming from. With the realization came her rage as she desperately tried to summon her Breath. But she was too weak from hunger, too inebriated on ekesh to do more than feebly turn her head. So they grasped her about the ears, holding her face steady as they pressed the red iron hard into her forehead.

The pain was blinding, the agony all-encompassing as the smoke of her seared flesh scorched her nostrils. But despite the pain and her horror,

Marta's mouth watered all the more at the scent. She smelled like meat.

She smelled delicious.

Chapter 16

Winterfylled 21, 567

Meat would be all the horses would be good for if they kept their pace up much longer, Marta finally relenting and allowing a rest around midnight. After caring for the horses, Luca and Isabelle sought solace in their bedrolls. Marta retired to her own, Caddie in tow. The girl still refused to sleep despite Marta's numerous orders to do so, so Marta again grasped the girl's wrist and instructed her to shake her awake if either of their traveling companions approached.

In spite of the weariness seeped down all the way into her bones, Marta still could not succumb to sleep as she chewed on her pipe. Although the girl confounded her and the presence of Graff flat out terrified her, Marta's mind kept returning to Luca and the lockblade he carried. It actually cut the ghuls, separating their Breath to rejoin the flow. That was something only glass was able to do, and Marta suspected there was more to his weapon other than the claim he could not be defeated so long as he held it. Though he should have proven his intentions true by saving her life, Marta found herself wishing she could test his claim firsthand. Even if he was right and it cost Marta her life, at least she would finally be free of him.

The night passed slowly, Marta peering after each sound in the dark. Caddie remained stolidly beside her, staring either at something only her eyes could perceive or perhaps nothing at all. Dawn was just awakening when Marta saw Luca stir, she feigning sleep as he slunk off alone. It stood to reason he was out only to relieve himself, but Marta slipped after him nonetheless.

Luca never looked back as he crested a small ridge bathed in the sun's first tentative rays. Reaching into his coat, he removed a small cloth roll, unfurling it to reveal several dozen small sticks. These Luca touched to his forehead before scattering them upon the ground. Without any sense of pride, he lay down in the dirt beside them and puzzled over their formation.

Marta knew bix sticks when she saw them and had seen enough. Between them and his mysterious lockblade, her suspicions were confirmed. She was ready to confront him when she felt the presence behind her, whirling to find Isabelle there, hatchet in hand.

Luca's head snapped up from his sticks, Marta ready to summon her Breath and put the woman down before turning her wrath to Luca. But Isabelle simply pointed with her weapon. Marta's eyes followed its arc to spot the Breath hovering there in the air above them.

The slight twinge of amethyst was still evident, even though it was fading in the morning light. It did not move, did not aimlessly follow the magnetic flow of Breath towards the ley. Instead it waited.

"He's found us?" Luca asked.

Graff had, surely this being his Breath he kept contained in his glass eye. Like all powerful Renders, he was able to unweave his second Soul Breath and send it to search for prey at speeds no horse or even Tinker train could match.

"Not yet," Marta answered. "It has to return to him before he knows what it's seen. Get the horses. Quick, before it departs."

Marta was surprised how rapidly the two she had been ready to kill obeyed, Luca gathering up his scattered bix sticks before hurrying to their horses. The exhausted animals were more sluggish, Marta leading hers on foot, her other hand grasping Caddie's. They had been traveling east, and she had every intention of continuing that direction again. But while Graff's Breath watched them, Marta headed south.

The Render's Breath followed a good half hour, the sunlight fading it until it seemed nothing more than a simmering smudge on the air. Then suddenly it was gone, Marta not sure if it had departed or she simply lost sight of it. She was still considering this when Luca mounted up.

"It's gone. Isabelle saw it go."

Marta trusted the woman's eyes over her companion's, even more than her own in her haggard state. Setting Caddie upon their horse, Marta joined her.

"We look for settlements now. Fresh horses, even if we have to take them by force. Graff works alone, does not share his prey with others. He may have discovered us, but we may be able to outrun him if we're lucky."

Turning her horse east again, Marta urged it forward as fast as she dared. She cared little for the spent beast, but if it died under her, she would be forced to claim Luca and Isabelle's mount, and she simply did not have the time to waste killing them for it.

***

Luca and Isabelle again took the lead as they followed the flow of Sol. It was Luca who spotted the ley despite it being nearly invisible during the day. Under normal circumstances Marta believed she would have seen it first, but her sleepless nights had taken their toll. The people of Newfield instinctively stayed close to the ley, and this line's presence greatly increased their chances of finding a settlement. It also made spotting Graff's Render Breath more difficult, but in her current condition, spotting his Breath was the least of Marta's troubles. What she needed more than anything was a fresh horse, preferably two, and a good night's sleep. For those she would gladly give the entirety of her cash, would kill without hesitation. Their only chance now was to outrun the man, to travel faster than Graff could manage alone.

Marta spied the homestead peeking out among the woods as midday approached, her ley headache now the only thing keeping her awake. It relented somewhat as they turned away from the line to approach the settlement. She was glad to see the two buildings in the clearing, one the home and the other a barn. She was nearly overjoyed at the small stockade though, handing some of her cash to Luca with instructions to procure new mounts as she and Isabelle led their spent horses to the trough near the well. As the horses drank, Marta splashed the water on her face, her senses reviving somewhat.

She was about to wash the girl's dusty face when she heard Luca's yell from the house.

"Murder!"

Grabbing Caddie's hand, Marta hurried to the homestead, Isabelle beside her with hatchet at the ready. The air was warm inside, an iron stove still emitting heat as Luca led them to a small bedroom. In her haste Marta almost pulled Caddie inside with her, but Luca stopped her at the door.

"The girl doesn't need to see this."

Marta left the motionless girl in the hallway and stepped inside. The man in the bed was stout, bearded, and probably quite strong if the size of his arms were any indication. But his strength had not availed him in the least, his head twisted at an unnatural angle and his neck clearly snapped. From the position of his body, Marta did not believe he had been asleep during his attack. No, he fought valiantly and had died for his troubles.

"Where's his wife?" Marta asked, her eyes on the mirrored brush on the nightstand.

Luca shrugged his reply, unable to take his eyes off the dead man. "Who could have done that? The strength it must take to twist his neck like that, Isabelle and I probably don't have it between us."

"It's easier than it looks," Marta offered in reply.

Reclaiming Caddie in the hallway, they made their way to the kitchen, the pantry wide and yawning. Marta was not fast enough to turn Caddie's head and keep her from seeing the dead boy. He was probably not more than six, his head twisted the same unnatural angle as his father's.

Caddie stared straight at him, her countenance not changing to show any apparent interest in the body. At this Isabelle softly tapped her fist to her chest three times then touched it to her forehead in a gesture that reminded Marta of her mother's motion to ward off evil.

"To kill a child," Luca whispered as he shut the boy's dead eyes. "What kind of monster could kill a child?"

Marta knew many from the war, had readily served beside more than one, her voice flat as Caddie's affect. "Gather any supplies we can carry. I'll see if they have any horses." She considered the dead boy again, making mental measurements before examining Caddie's dress. "And see if they had any clothes that might fit her. It would be better if we traveled with a boy instead of a girl."

Marta hauled Caddie after her and away before Luca could respond, happy that there were no more questions from the man.

When they reached the barn, Marta released Caddie, the girl falling still as a rundown wind-up toy. Plans for her phantom blade at the ready, Marta threw the door open to hear the snort of a horse. There was only the one, but he looked to be of good breeding, Marta scanning the room for anywhere an attacker could lie in wait. Finally sure she was alone, she grabbed the saddle from the wall.

The others would be on their own now, she and Caddie hopefully far from the homestead when Luca and Isabelle discovered their flight. She would be forgoing any found supplies and the possibility of any boy's clothes to disguise the girl, but Marta knew it was the right decision. She would at least be able to sleep again and not worry about one of the freebooters slitting her throat.

The horse saddled and following her, she joined Caddie outside. Marta was reaching for her hand when she heard the girl faintly say, "Help."

It was an odd voice, somehow resonant despite the child's slight frame. Marta pondered the implications of the girl's first word when the cry for help came again. Caddie's lips did not move during the utterance, because the voice came from the nearby well.

Marta knew she should follow her plan, should collect Caddie and gallop away while she still had the chance. Instead she looked down the hole to see the woman floating in the water, her lips blue from the cold.

To save her would steal more of Marta's dwindling time, would ensure Graff would be even closer, and would mean she might not be able to quit Luca and Isabelle as easily as she could moments before. The woman's fate was surely already sealed from the cold water. And even if she did survive, she would discover her whole family murdered. To let her remain in the well would soon provide her sweet oblivion, a salve against the pain of existence. To let her die would be a mercy.

Marta grabbed the bucket beside the well though, its rope firmly suspended by the crossbeam, and dropped it down to her. That was all the time Marta would allow herself to squander, again grabbing Caddie's hand. She had just hoisted the girl up when Marta heard the piteous voice again.

"Please... not strong enough to... please..."

Marta wanted to ignore the plea, to let the freebooters discover the woman and slow their pursuit of her and Caddie further. But they might not hear the woman, and Marta found herself staring into Caddie's blue eyes. She had failed from keeping the girl from seeing the dead boy, and now she was going to show her how she intended to leave his mother to her sodden fate. Even though the child was a simpleton, this was still too much to foist upon her.

Cursing the girl who made her doubt her first instinct, Marta returned to the well, turning the crank and hauling the bucket back up. The woman clung to it, rising into the air until she had almost reached the well's lip. Holding tight to the bucket with one hand, she reached for Marta, water cascading down her arm to return to the depths below. Setting her shoulder to the crank, Marta reached out for the woman, about to make contact when she heard Luca's bellow.

"Glassman!"

At his pronouncement the woman dropped the guise of victim, her face twisting into a malevolent sneer. Marta leapt away, the bucket released and plummeting back into the well.

The glassman was faster yet, her hand catching the lip and hauling herself over the side in one fluid motion. She was close, too close, as she hissed at the retreating Marta. One lunge and Marta would be dead, but Luca called out before the glassman had the chance.

"We don't want any trouble, and you want none of the trouble we've brought here with us today. You've already fed, no reason for you to get hurt."

Marta could not believe the gall it took to threaten a glassman as Luca strode toward the monster with his open lockblade. But Luca's ever-present grin was on full display as he spoke. "If this turns to blood, it will be your Breath that rejoins the flow today."

The malevolent woman did not seem to know what to make of his confidence either, confusion evident on her face as he reached them. Too late did Luca realize this too was a ploy as she lunged for him.

Isabelle was not taken off guard though, the metal bearing launched from her sling striking the glassman's skull with a sickening crack. Such a blow would cripple a normal person, if not outright kill, but the woman hardly stumbled as she again aimed at Luca. She moved impossibly fast, a speed Marta had only seen in striking snakes.

Somehow Luca evaded the serpent's strike, sidestepping and delivering a slice to her attacking arm. His blade bit deep, the glassman recoiling even as Luca launched a new series of strikes. Seeing him in action, Marta recognized both training and experience there as he mixed in feints as he sliced with his lockblade. He caught her again with a superficial wound on the other arm, an act that was extraordinary considering his adversary.

The glassman must have thought so as well as she stepped outside his range to examine her wounds. With a quick flick of his wrist, Luca slung her blood from his blade to water the grass. "It's come to blood after all. Still intent on joining the flow or will you now run?"

Only now did the glassman notice Isabelle circling to her rear, her hatchet in hand. In the mute woman's eyes, Marta saw a burning hatred she recognized well.

Marta knew she should add her strength to theirs, the three of them able to offer an offence even an elder glassman would not withstand. Instead she leapt atop the horse to join Caddie, turning its head and kicking it hard. She was leaving them to their messy fates, but Marta did not care. They were just freebooters after all, and she was a traitor.

But the glassman was faster than Marta's horse, faster than either Luca or Isabelle as she snatched a stone the size of her skull from the well. Its bonding gave way like paper as she sent it sailing at Marta's horse.

The bones of the horse's legs snapped with brittle cracks as it fell. Marta put her arms around Caddie, cocooning the child and hoping to shield the girl as they were thrown. They hit hard enough to rattle Marta's teeth and make her senses swim. Her haversack took much of the blow, but the tin cup inside was driven painfully into her spine. It hurt badly, Marta barely opening her eyes in time to see the glassman racing in their direction.

The sight awakened Marta's anger, the milieu slowing as her mind raced. She knew glassmen to be innate Listeners, and so set a refrain that she was terrified. Though she had both the plans for her phantom blade and gauntlet at the ready, Marta kept her hands empty, hoping her apparent helplessness would lure the woman close enough to be taken by surprise.

The glassman stopped just out of range though. Ignoring Marta, something approaching awe spread across her face as she beheld Caddie. "What treasure is this?" Her eyes turned to Marta's, no hint of humanity there. "You can live so long as you tell me what she is."

The glassman was still too far to reach, too fast for Marta to lunge for. She needed to draw her closer, and so Marta feigned fear again.

"Don't hurt my daughter!"

Even with the clarity her rage afforded her, Marta did not know why she chose those words, but they had the desired effect as the glassman strode forward to claim her victim. Marta's Breath instantly appeared into her hand, her phantom blade thrusting into her attacker. Her aim proved true, Marta's blade burying itself into the glassman's gut until her fist slapped to a stop as it impacted on the monster's stomach.

To Marta's dismay the glassman was not felled as she leapt back again. She was wounded, but not mortally, and now the glassman knew all their tricks. The only chance now was to overwhelm her entirely and put an end to her evil.

Luca and Isabelle rejoined the fray, fanning out to encircle the woman. Marta joined their number this time, her blade in her right hand and gauntlet covering her left. So long as they held formation and struck together, Marta believed they would be victorious.

But then Isabelle launched herself at the glassman with an inarticulate cry more terrifying than her hatchet before Marta was ready. The woman turned to meet the assault, Luca slipping in even as she dodged Isabelle's swings. Her attention now on his flashing lockblade, the glassman did not see the hatchet descend as it buried itself in her back. Lashing out, she sent Isabelle sprawling, wrenching the weapon free and letting it fall even as Luca attacked again.

The glassman never saw Marta coming, the gauntlet slamming into the back of her head with the force that could kill a cow.

The glassman collapsed on the ground to roll onto her back. Her hands flailing through the air, her eyes were awry and unfocused. She had been blinded by the blow, and ready to finish the job, Marta raised her blade.

"It's a trick! She's trying to lure you in!"

At Luca's words the glassman dropped the act, looking up to see the circling Luca and Marta, Isabelle hurrying to rejoin their rank with her crude knife. She could still surely kill these three, but the tide of battle had turned; the initiative now theirs. Bernice Mauch was many things, a murderer and monster among them, but she was no fool. So she ran.

Not a one of her enemies were ready for her retreat, the glassman reaching the woods before Isabelle could even set one of the steel balls into her sling. She slipped between the trees silent as a shadow, quickly out of sight and range. They had fared well, Marta and Isabelle only absorbing cuts and scrapes, whereas the glassman had been wounded gravely. Victory had eluded them though, and they knew it. The only true victory over glassmen was killing them outright. Anything less was to court misery.

The whines of the dying horse brought them back to the moment, the animal piteously trying to stand on its destroyed legs. Luca shot Marta a harsh look as he slid his blade across its neck and silenced it. It was a small mercy, one the glassman would not afford them.

Their horses were not fit to ride, but Marta set Caddie on the back of theirs, forgoing the collection of any new supplies in favor of haste as she led the animal away on foot. Luca and Isabelle walked alongside theirs as well, their weapons at the ready. They were not ten minutes into the woods when Isabelle's hands fluttered with another message to her partner and Luca shattered the silence.

"She's still following us. Hunting us."

"You expected otherwise?" Marta seethed through clenched teeth. "To wound a glassman is to spit in the eyes of death."

"You don't have to tell us what meeting a glassman means," Luca hissed back. "They're able to Whisper as well as Listen, stronger and faster than the humans they were before they sold their Souls to Waer. You'd have a better chance killing a bear with your bare hands than one of them. But more than that, they heal in a day what a human would in a year. She'll be hale and hearty by dusk."

"I doubt we'll have to wait more than an hour before she comes to claim her vengeance." Pulling her horse to a halt, Marta scanned the woods for the ley they had followed earlier.

"You intend on just waiting for her?"

"No, I intend on using what she is against her."

Luca came to a stop as well, Isabelle questioning them both with her hazel eyes. Some part of Marta wanted to let them stew further, but the wounded glassman did not allow her the luxury of time.

"Despite all their strengths—or, more accurately, because of them—glassmen have their weaknesses too. They earn their eternal lives by feeding off their victims, absorbing the Breath of the dead. They hold it inside them, sure as a glass luz jar, for years at a time."

"You said we don't even have until dusk, let alone years."

"No, but she's fed today. We saw two bodies, and I'm betting we'd find a third if we searched much longer. That means she has at least six or, more likely, nine Breaths inside her now. That makes her more Blessed than any of the naturally Blessed, which means the ley headache will hurt her all the more. If she follows us on the ley, she won't even be able to see straight."

If her rough laughter was any indication, Isabelle understood first. Despite herself, Marta was heartened as Luca's grin returned. "You're a good woman to know, May Oles."

***

They found the ley soon enough, following it for several hours without catching sight of the glassman. When the ley headache came, Marta welcomed it, aware their pursuer would be suffering all the more. She noticed a slight strain to Luca's grin around the time her own pain set in and was not surprised. He might play the part of the boisterous fool, but his fighting skills and imbued lockblade meant there was something more to the man.

Only Isabelle and Caddie showed no signs of the headache as the hours rolled on towards dusk. The line of ley grew stronger as they followed it, now tracing the edge of a rocky ridge, and Marta suspected a nodus nearby. Even this far from the more civilized states, a nodus would mean a town of some size, enough people there willing to finish the abhorrent glassman off.

Soon the ley was shining quite brightly, another shimmer leaking over the nearby ridge beside them. Marta was certain it would intersect the line they followed and deliver them there. Gritting her teeth against the pain, Marta reminded herself she only needed to endure, to make it around the bend where safety was awaiting them. She could already hear movement ahead, the town brimming with life.

But when they rounded the bend, no township awaited, the ley instead disappearing into an imposing crag. Staring in shock, Marta realized the noise she heard was not from civilization, but from the cascade of water spilling out of the crag to form a dark pool at its base. There was absolutely no life, no ley, no salvation here.

Too late Marta recognized that the nodus she had expected must be within the rocky ridge, no one willing to settle here due to its inaccessibility. They were alone in the dark, the cliff blocking the glow of the ley and boxing them in even as it relieved them of their headaches. The three could only gape at their mistake, struck dumb by their misfortune.

Turning their backs upon the crag, they spied the glassman slipping out of the darkness. Her time in the ley had its desired effect, the inhuman woman's face quivering with pain, but it gave her an even more malicious appearance as she approached. Gazing into the eyes of their enemy, Marta saw only a wounded animal, one more desperate and therefore more dangerous. The three had no chance of escape and would only be able to earn their lives through bloodshed. No quarter would be offered, and Marta hoped at least one of them would survive.

But Marta knew if she was the last living defender and the glassman sure of victory, her dying act would be to kill Caddie cleanly. Killing a child would be a terrible act, sure to stain her Breath before it was released by death to feed the glassman. Yet it would be a mercy to spare the girl the horribly short life she would surely endure at the hands of a willing devourer of children.

Isabelle's sling whistled through the air, the blade of her hatchet tucked under her left arm and exposing the handle to claim quickly. Luca held his lockblade in his right hand, his straight blade in his left as he shifted his weight back and forth. Marta dropped her haversack, her anger and clarity calling forth her mental plans for her Cildra weapons. Pushing Caddie behind her, she stood between the girl and glassman.

No one expected the savage battle to last long, the horrid glassman crouching and ready to pounce when the pool of water behind them exploded outward and the emet made its presence known.

Chapter 17

Jenvier 17, 563 (Four Years Ago)

Marta did not know enough anatomy and feared this ignorance would cost her her life.

For the last month the Western army had trained her and the other former Eastern prisoners for their spots on the newly formed 1st Shaper Company, and Marta was sure she would not make the cut. Not two days since her branding, her wound still raw and weeping, they were forced aboard a train. Strung out on ekesh, they were shipped south until they arrived at the island of Mitkof, which would serve as their training ground. Although it was an island and not a hole, it was a prison nonetheless, with no chance of swimming the Arrowhead Lake that surrounded them. The land had been cleared of trees, Marta realizing the Western strategy as soon as she saw the hundreds of huge steel shields, each nearly ten feet tall, a half foot thick, and sloped slightly inwards.

They were at least fed again, their sustenance nothing more than boiled barely for breakfast, potatoes, and perhaps some dubious meat for dinner. Marta wolfed it down without a care as to the taste, needing all her strength for her training.

Stood in formation, they were introduced to their new commander, one Colonel Absalom Bumgarden. Marta never met the man in Vrendenburg, but she knew he earned his rank through the daring deployment of a single Render to win the battle of Brandywine. He was said to be a master tactician, reworking outdated strategies for modern warfare.

The idea of a force consisting entirely of Shapers was nothing new, the ancient lords of the Auld Lands assembling units of Shapers to fight beside their knights. A trained knight was a match for any Shaper, his sword slipping through the swaths of the open space within their Armor with deadly results. But knights were expensive to train and maintain, whereas Shapers could be conscripted from their fields. Given pikes three times the length of a man, Shapers were a deadly force so long as they were protected by men carrying shields ahead of them. A squad of Shapers on the march was a sound strategy: as unstoppable as rolling a boulder down a hill, the ancient Shapers serving as shock troops for their feudal lords.

Then muskets were developed, their projectiles picking the Shapers off from a distance sure as any sword thrust. Muskets changed the face of warfare, rendering the slogging Shapers and knights equally obsolete. New armies were then built around speed, charging the musketeers with nimble sabermen to cut them to ribbons while they reloaded their slow contraptions. Shapers were still useful to the armies though, again relegated to the role of heavy laborers. Traditionally, they stayed close to the supply trains, but now Bumgarden intended to change the game entirely by making the Shapers the shield bearers.

Staring at him from across the formation, Marta did not think he looked like much, only a thin man with dark skin. His green eyes surveyed them passionlessly, reminding her of a coiled snake watching its surroundings as it waited for its next meal to approach. There was no emotion in his stare, neither affection nor aggression there. He looked like the foreman at an abattoir examining the ignorant sheep being led to slaughter. To a certain extent Bumgarden's gaze reminded her of her brother's stare, making Marta hate the man all the more.

Kearney seemed blissfully unaware of how Bumgarden regarded them, constantly at his superior's side and groveling at the colonel's every word. He had tobacco for his pipe now, smoking it with relish before the other Eastern Shapers as if it made him better than they despite his forehead bearing the same scar as theirs. It was only a matter of time before Bumgarden discarded the sycophant, Marta was sure. She was also sure Kearney would not live out the night, many of the Shapers blaming him for convincing them to accept the Newfield deal and to be branded like cattle. Marta would have considered killing Kearney herself, but had more pressing matters on her mind, like anatomy.

Abner had been assigned to another platoon, his team's tent on the far side of the field from Marta's, the Shapers not allowed to fraternize with anyone outside their tents after dark. Marta was sure he must hate her now as the other Shapers hated Kearney. She had only seen Abner once in passing, wincing in expectation of his fury. Though he went stiff when he spied her, he held his tongue, moving away quickly like she was something sickening.

Gonzalo shared her platoon's tent and still deigned to speak to her despite what she had convinced him to do. He was kind enough not to point out that his final prediction had proven correct, that Marta's plan had been worse than their time in the Pit. Reid still called out to her whenever they passed too. Despite their doleful situation he still found his amusements. In days Reid had mastered the scornful salute, his homage to his superiors mocking and full of derision, though it appeared to be within regulation. His last riddle had been: "Poor people have it while the rich need it not. If you eat it, you die." Had anatomy not been taking up all of Marta's mental efforts, she might have sought the answer to Reid's riddle.

She had seen Ida and Rupert as well, the always resourceful forager having somehow scrounged a shard of a mirror. The fragment was constantly passed around the camp, each Shaper examining the scars that marred their faces.

When it came to Marta, she passed it on without a glance. She already knew the two sets of three vertical lines with a star between them well—the symbol of Newfield. She saw the same scar everywhere on foreheads of her fellow soldiers, so there was no reason to gaze upon her ruined beauty with her own eyes. She was sure she must appear a shadow of her former self, all her splendor scraped away by her time in the Pit and her scar. She was sure she must look monstrous.

Making matters worse, Marta was also the least adept of the Eastern recruits, the position of bottom pull an entirely new experience for her. Most Shapers spent years designing their full Armors, perfecting their mental plans before clearing their teens. Marta was capable of many unique Cildra techniques these simple Shapers would have no chance of mastering, but the Western army wanted only one thing from her, the one thing she could not give: a full Armor.

Gonzalo tried to coach her in the Armor's basic plans at night, but his instructions were less than useless. The full Armor form was a native language to him, all the joints and moving components a foreign tongue to Marta. A full Armor had nearly a hundred moving parts in a dozen different locations, all the joints following the same basic layout as the human body. Marta could not keep track of them all and constantly mixed up the joints as she tried to form the Armor Gonzalo described. It was simple, he said, just following the human form, but the only lesson Marta took away was that she did not know nearly enough about human anatomy.

The other Shapers looked down on her for her lack of knowledge, Marta recognizing the disdain in their eyes as they must have recognized it in hers in the Pit. She in turn had newfound respect for these Shapers and their sluggish constructs. And she would have to learn their plans if she was to fulfill her father's mission, Marta reminded herself as she finally fell asleep after another day of failing at her training.

The next morning, Kearney again ran them through their drills, each Shaper easily hefting one of the colossal shields. Instead of carrying each shield individually, they were meant to move as a group, the convex shields matching up one to another so they formed the shape of a boat turned upside down when held together. This hull wholly encased the Shapers while providing enough space in the center for more troops to be ferried through the deadly hail of musket fire. These mobile bunkers made the Shapers like the shield bearers of old, forming a phalanx to protect their comrades. And like the phalanxes of old, the loss of a single shield would open their flanks and expose the entire rank to attack.

Kearney watched them from the sidelines, puffing away on his pipe in between curses aimed at Marta when she failed to lift her shield. He approached, falling short by a good ten feet when she turned her gaze upon him. He sounded brave enough when he called out though.

"You're no good. Useless."

"More useful than ten of you, you damned bug. You're no more than the bottom pull, a poxy sack of flux."

Marta's mother would have slapped her had she heard her daughter's words, but the months spent with the Shapers in the Pit had left its mark on Marta sure as the brand she bore, but had never seen. Her outburst garnered a few guffaws from the ranks, but Kearney's face went a livid red.

"Off my field, Childress. Back to the Pit with you."

He was serious about returning her to the prison, Marta could tell. With that realization her rage roared, Kearney taking a step back as she made one towards him. But as he retreated he summoned his Armor to surround him.

"Another step and I'll make you bleed, girl."

His Armor was meant to intimidate Marta, to make her reconsider her threat. Instead she grinned as her own Breath begged to be released. She was still contemplating between her phantom blade to drive into his belly or her gauntlets to rip out his tongue when the shot sounded.

All eyes turned upon the composed Bumgarden, the pistol spent and smoking in his hand. "You Shapers forget yourselves. You are not people, you are the property of Newfield. And anyone caught defacing property of the state will be hanged immediately."

He spoke calmly, as if discussing the weather, but Kearney dropped his Armor soon as Bumgarden's green eyes alighted upon him. The tone of Bumgarden's voice did not alter, but Marta could feel the smack of reproach there. "You required your Armor to deal with a girl who cannot even summon her own? Perhaps I have chosen the wrong commander for this detail."

Marta puffed up at Kearney's dressing down until Bumgarden turned his gaze to her. "He is a simpleton, but he is not wrong. You are defective equipment that will be sent back to the Calderon Quarry on the morrow."

"That's not fair! If I bear the mark, I at least deserve the same chance to fight!"

Bumgarden's head tilted at Marta's outburst as if considering laughter, though his voice maintained the same lethargic tone. "There is no fairness, not anymore. This is the start of a new age, the old rules thrown out at the start of this war. Many may believe this war will decide the answer to the Render and Weaver conflict, but that is ultimately nothing. What this campaign will be remembered for is a new form of warfare. Make no mistake, Childress, you are only a cog in this machine, one that must play its proper role if it is to be of use."

Bumgarden paused as the full weight of his words crashed down on Marta.

"But I am not devoid of mercy. You will be given one more chance in the morning. If you fail, I will personally offer you my pistol if you choose not to return to the Pit."

Marta could not miss the implications of his offered pistol, she expected to swallow the shot rather than face her fate in the Pit. But if it came to that, Marta intended to make sure Bumgarden feasted on the bullet before she was hanged for defacing Newfield property.

***

Abner came to her that night, Marta with no idea how he slipped out of his tent and made it across the field unseen. Though she was ecstatic to see him, Abner remained stiff as he refused her embrace. Looking her over now, he reminded Marta of her former tutor Mitchell.

"You've been going about this all wrong. You may be an adult, but you're still a child when it comes to understanding Armor. So I'm going to teach you a child's Armor, one I mastered before I even had hair on my chin. But know this, Marta, there is only one way to top this mountain."

Marta could not hide her gratitude, either at his appearance or his instruction. Yet one question still nagged her as she beheld his brand up close:

"Why? Why look after me when I dragged you into this?"

Despite his previous deflection of her affection, Abner forced a smile. "Because the past is a mirror, and I will not gaze at it overlong. And I still intend on escaping with you at my side when we're deployed. By grace or grave, we will be quit of this army. But to do that you must earn your spot in the 1st Shaper Company. Are you ready to learn?"

Marta was, though she proved to be a terrible student, only able to summon the childish Armor Abner taught her one time in three by the end of the night. Her failures ringing about her head, Abner gave her a grim grin.

"Just make sure you fail twice before you make your attempt today."

Setting his hand to her shoulder, he then slipped out the tent and left Marta alone among her sleeping comrades. Though his last words were meant to be rousing, Marta thought just two failures seemed far too few for her current state.

***

Marta took the field alone the next morning, the entire 1st Shaper Company watching along with implacable Bumgarden flanked by Kearney puffing away at his pipe. Before her ordeal began, Marta tried to summon Abner's childish Armor a dozen times, only halting when she hit upon two failures in a row. She was due a success now, she assured herself as she trudged to the heavy shield. But as she took her place behind it, Marta realized all of Abner's training was for naught. She was going to fail him as she had failed her father. She had done nothing but fail for the last year, and the idea of only two failures earning her a success was entirely laughable. Defeat was still sinking its fangs into her, its slow poison of doubt swimming in Marta's mind when she looked up at the shield's handle to behold Abner's final gift.

Rupert's shard of a mirror awaited her on the handle, tilted up so Marta received a full look at her ruined visage. For the first time she saw her new face and the scar she would forever be forced to bear. Her former beauty was broken, shattered and scattered to the winds. Seeing her loss in its entirety, Marta's anger bloomed, her clarity there as she considered Abner's Armor. It was suddenly such a simple thing, something made for a child, not the woman she was.

Her Breath came effortlessly, forming the Armor as she claimed the shield, the shard knocked away as she grasped the handle to strain against its weight. The shields were said to weigh one ton, lifting it a simple task for the rest of the Shapers. But Marta struggled under its burden, barely able to hoist it up. It was rage alone that allowed her to take the first step.

Willpower carried her through the following three, Marta unaware how she made the next dozen. She finally set the tottering shield down before it crushed her. Her entire body was spent, promising aches to last weeks as she released her Breath, but there was exhilaration there as well as she heard Abner cheer for her. The rest of the Shapers joined in, their voices in defiance to Bumgarden. Better yet, Kearney looked like he could spit nails as Marta basked in her victory.

Bumgarden waited until their cheers died down before he spoke. "It's not enough. The formation will break down if you cannot even make ten strides on command."

In spite of her weariness, Marta's rage returned, she suddenly aware she could clear the distance on her rabbit legs to rip out his and Kearney's throats before Bumgarden could even level his pistol, but Bumgarden's next announcement saved his life before she had the chance.

"Yet you can still be of use as a flag-bearer."

He said it as if it was a boon, but Marta knew it to be a death sentence. Standard bearers were tempting targets for enemy sharpshooters, their shots seeking out the leaders of charges. But more than the dread of death, she was afraid that she would fall still clutching the symbol of Newfield, the nation that had scarred her. She would be felled by her former allies, all of them unaware of the price she had paid for them and none the wiser of why she bore her mark.

Marta had no plans to ever be a flag-bearer or see battle in the first place though. Soon as they were able, she and Abner would slip away to join their Eastern brethren and continue the struggle against the West. She would ultimately escape her current state.

After she killed Bumgarden and Kearney, that was.

Chapter 18

Winterfylled 22, 567

The emet was entirely unlike the mindless ghuls they encountered within the tolmen, but far more terrifying. Its body was that of a massive bear, but its front two legs ended in human hands with wraithlike claws far too long to occur in nature. Its head was ursine too, its glowing eyes those of an animal. Yet strange pins protruded from its neck and back, reminding Marta somewhat of a creature called a porcupine she had seen in one of Mitchell's books years ago.

Marta had little time to ponder its form as the beast barreled past them to lift its head and give a silent roar in the face of their pursuer. The glassman stepped back at the emet's emergence, considering the creature as she stalked back and forth like an animal herself. She seemed hesitant, perhaps afraid, until her face split into a wicked smile.

"I've never feasted on one of your kind so old before."

The final syllable had scarcely left her mouth before the glassman sped at the emet. Though her hands were flesh, and therefore should pass through the emet as if air, each of the glassman's blows connected, the inflated Breath that made up the beast compacting under each onslaught. The woman was noticeably faster, each attack so rapid the eye could scarcely track, but the emet absorbed her blows as if only water lapping lazily at the hull of a boat. Its maw snapped silently in the night, huge human hands tipped with claws swinging through the air. The glassman was faster, but the emet had three weapons to her two while her crushing blows had no effect on the creature.

Isabelle took a step towards the fray, Luca's hand snaking out to hold her back. This fight was no place for humans, the two titans crashing against each other with the force of wayward continents.

The emet finally connected with its massive paw, rending the glassman's flesh and sending her skittering across the ground like a ragdoll. The creature charged after her, covering the ground before she could get to her feet. It had the chance to finish her off, to end her evil once and for all, but it stopped not two feet from the woman.

The emet had reached the end of its invisible leash, unable to escape the confines of the nodus that had borne it. The glassman seemed to understand this as she slowly regained her feet, turning her attention from the emet to the three of them.

"You still have to leave eventually."

With that she disappeared into the dark outside the confines of their temporary asylum.

But Marta's mind was not on the glassman as the emet turned upon them. She again wished she had not shattered the arrogant Render's glass blade. Even a glass shard might be useful as the emet swayed back and forth, its pupil-less eyes aimed right at them.

It was a roll of the dice each time an emet came into existence: either benevolent, malevolent, or indifferent to the presence of people. This emet might have saved them out of kindness, but there were equal odds that it had just been attacking another predator wandering heedlessly into its territory. Now that the invader had been dispatched, it might be again regarding at them as prey.

Aware how trapped they were within the confines of the rocky ridge, Marta reached behind her until her hand connected with Caddie, taking a step back and readying herself. Luca and Isabelle between her and the beast, she might be able to pull the girl to safety while it took them to pieces. She mentally marked the spot the glassman had fallen, estimating the invisible line the emet was unable to cross and hoping she could close the distance in time with the girl in tow. If not, she could still perhaps throw the girl that distance, though the waiting glassman made this strategy untenable.

The emet dropped to all fours, rolling its head several times like the animal it mimicked might. Isabelle's black stone knife appeared in her hand as it approached, though Luca pointed the tip of his blade towards the ground.

"You don't mean us any harm," he said with his usual amount of charm. "No more than we meant you. We thank you for saving us and will be on our way if you'll allow us."

Only Renders and Weavers could communicate with emets, and Marta knew Luca was neither of those. Yet he kept speaking to the creature, his voice calm and confident. The emet paid him no mind though, heading straight for Marta even as she took another backwards step towards the pool.

It was only when the beast stopped a few feet away, now shifting its path perpendicular and circling them, that Marta realized it was Caddie, not her, the creature aimed at. She held her ground, her plans for her blade ready in case it attacked.

Instead the emet kneeled, finally flopping to its side and rolling to reveal its ethereal belly. It was exposing its softest parts to them, an act Marta had seen before in the hounds in her father's kennels. There, the beasts had sensed her inherent human superiority bestowed by her Soul Breath, showing their submission the only way their limited minds knew how. Marta had never heard of such behavior among emets though, suddenly wishing they had a Weaver or Render with them to make it make sense.

Finally, the emet rolled back to its rump and scooted the remaining distance between them. Even seated, its head towered high above theirs, its cranium the size of the child's torso. Its arm came slowly up, the ursine appendage with a strangely human hand. Marta noticed its claws had disappeared as it reached for the girl. Her Breath flared at this, a useless gesture to the creature that had easily defeated the glassman that had put them on their heels, but she was still willing to stand her ground, still willing to go down fighting rather than submit like a dog.

"For Sol's sake!" Luca shouted, his voice cutting through Marta's mind. "It's an engel, it doesn't mean any harm. Just step aside and let it give its blessing!"

Luca might be right. The emet had saved their lives, had submitted to them, its gestures benign and without threat. Marta still kept her Armor plans well in mind as she cautiously stepped aside to expose Caddie to the creature.

The emet leaned slowly towards the girl, its paw alighting gently on her skull and its human fingertips wreathing her forehead like points of a strange crown. The emet's eyes seemed to close, though Marta suspected it did not need eyes to see. It was an unnatural act, something about seeing the eerie emet connecting with the human girl kindling revulsion in Marta. It was all she could do to keep from attacking and let its uncanny hand continue to touch the child.

Its hand remained a long while, Caddie staring at the creature or, more likely, through it with her blank gaze. Finally, the emet rose to its full height, its hand remaining on the girl. It then took a step forward as Caddie took a step back, the two of them moving together towards the pool of water.

Marta's intangible blade extended in her hand. She would have surely swung, but she did not get the chance, as she spied something she had never seen before.

Caddie blinked.

The motion was not unusual in any other human, but from the girl it felt momentous, the mental plans for Marta's weapon suddenly forgotten at the sight.

The emet released the girl, Caddie turning on her own to face the pool. Then, untouched and unbidden by another, she took a halting step. Then another followed by more still, each step more certain as she approached the pool.

She reached the edge of the water before Marta caught her, grabbing the girl's wrist and yanking her to a stop. Though Caddie halted her progress, Marta could still feel her straining as if urged on by invisible forces, like those that directed Breath along the lines of ley.

Marta chanced a glance back to see that the emet had not stirred from its spot and was still silently watching the two of them. Luca and Isabelle were rooted where they stood too, having only pivoted to face the pool. They shared a look, Luca finally nodding and closing his lockblade.

"Let her go. She can't possibly lead us anywhere worse."

He strode towards the water, Isabelle collecting Marta's forgotten haversack and the saddlebags before joining him. With a look back towards the emet, Isabelle again tapped her chest three times with her fist and then touched the knuckles to her forehead.

Marta did not believe they were right for a moment, the suddenly mobile Caddie sure to lead them nowhere except another dead end. But she also wanted to be quit of the eerie emet, to keep it between them and the vengeful glassman. So she let the girl go.

Caddie's feet splashed as she entered the pool, which soon came to her knees, the hem of her dress floating around her. Marta kept step with the girl, ready to snatch her up if the pool proved too deep, but the water barely kissed Marta's waist by the time they reached the falls.

The girl continued on at the same insistent pace, never hesitating as she passed through the cascading falls. Marta had to catch her slouch hat as she passed through, amazed when she found a gaping cave, not a rocky wall, on the other side. She could only see a few feet into it in the dark, but Caddie's path led them ceaselessly towards it.

Marta summoned her cold torch by focusing all her fourth Breath into one hand, its flickering light providing them enough illumination to continue deeper into the cave. Outcroppings of stones worn smooth by centuries of water flow awaited them, their slickness proving treacherous as they attempted to scale them. Marta's headache soon returned, and she looked back to see Luca wincing as well. They were close to the nodus that had birthed the emet, and even hidden underground, they could still feel the effects of the ley. Caddie never paused though, steering them through the branching caverns. When they reached the first fork, she took a turn without any indecision. She did not hesitate at the second either, drawing them deeper into the dark.

It was slow going, the water at times reaching Caddie's neck, other times the path dwindling down to a narrow passage they were forced to crawl through on hands and knees. Now far beyond the nodus and the reach of the ley, Marta's headache faded as the hours wore on. A thought kept nagging her though, Marta poking at it like a loose tooth. If the emet had shown Caddie this path, was it not bound by the leash of its nodus? It was impossible for the beast to have traveled this far from the ley, meaning Caddie's sudden knowledge came not from the emet, but from somewhere else.

Marta fixated on this thought with her whole mind as she looked back at Luca. The man's grin still gleamed in the flicker of her cold torch, Luca reaching back to Isabelle to help her over a rock hidden under the flow of water. Isabelle refused his aid, her crooked tooth exposed in a snarl. And in that moment Luca's grin faltered. It could have been that Luca was overexerted, but Marta suspected his slipped grin meant something more.

Silently they followed the girl nearly an hour more, Marta sure they could have made better time by scaling the ridge instead. But the catatonic Caddie would have been a liability in the climb while making her way on her own through the tunnels. Her new mobility was a gift, one Marta did want to become a wastrel by wasting.

Suddenly the path widened, rising above the waterline to reveal a vast cavern. Their footfalls echoed in the expanding dark as they breached the water, crystals covering the walls in huge formations that refracted the light of Marta's cold torch. Their heavy breaths filled the cavern, but Marta focused on the gems rather than the noise. Next to the crystals Marta spotted marks, catching hold of Caddie and halting their progress to examine them.

The marks were old and faded, barely more than faint smears on the wall, but they were definitely laid there by human hands, their patterns geometric and unnatural. One was a tight spiral, its end trailing off into several short, straight lines in a circle that reminded Marta of a starburst. The other appeared the approximation of a human, the body and limbs made up only of lines. The head of the drawing resembled that of a beast, the marks too faded to say for sure, though Marta suspected it was a bear.

Underneath the marks a half-dozen clay pots resided, their sides bearing the same illustrations as the wall. Remains of plants, perhaps flowers, littered the space around them. Marta looked to Isabelle for explanation as to their meaning, but the half-Ingios woman simply shrugged, not bothering to tap her chest and forehead at the sight.

Caddie never looked at either the paintings or the pots, her eyes aimed only at the continuing maze of caverns. Marta released her hand, the girl leading them farther into the dark.

***

It was not light that signaled their journey's end, rather a slight shift in the rich scent of water. The air suddenly smelled sweeter as they stumbled out the mouth of the cave, the twinkle of fading stars awaiting them. Waterlogged and weary beyond measure, they exited, Caddie suddenly falling still as a statue soon as they passed the threshold into the shallow pond.

Isabelle pushed pass them, Luca at her side as they slogged their way for the bank. The woman instantly flopped down upon the dry earth, extending her arms and legs to let the fresh air wash over her. Though he looked as tired as she, Luca opened his lockblade and shook it free of any lingering water. Producing a small case from his pocket, he removed a soft cloth and vial of oil before sitting down beside Isabelle to clean the knife.

He cared for this weapon, much more so than the straight blade at his hip. It was the one he had cut through the ghuls with, the one he swore ensured he could not be defeated so long as he held it open in his hand. Such imbued objects were rare, more tall tale than truth, but they did exist. And they only came from one source.

Marta was tired, but she still set a new refrain. Her false thoughts focused on killing Isabelle, of driving her Shaper blade deep into the woman's chest. Intent on this idea, Marta left Caddie where she stood and edged nearer to the unaware woman.

Luca leapt up at once, his lockblade brandished. His action proved what Marta had long believed: He was a Listener who wore no pin. But there was more to his story, and she suspected she knew the plot quite well.

"Ix culla."

She took Luca entirely aback by the vile and secretive swear. His face first showed he recognized the words then that he realized he had fallen into Marta's trap. His grin bloomed, reflecting her own grim one, the honed edge of his lockblade shining from the glow of the phantom blade Marta summoned into her hand.

Chapter 19

Marz 13, 563 (Four Years Ago)

Marta and Abner never got their chance to escape, and now she suspected they never would. When they were finally deployed, it was far behind the front line, an entire regiment between them and the freedom of the Eastern armies. There, they were told many things, the most salient being that deserters were killed on sight, and everyone watched the 1st Shaper Company with particular scrutiny.

So far hunger had been their greatest adversary. They were outfitted the same as any Newfield soldier with uniform, greatcoat, and haversack. Weapons they were not allowed, only a dull knife accompanying their mess kit, but when they received their equipment, they were gleefully told by the quartermasters they would not be fed. All their meals they would have to forage since food was reserved for the true soldiers.

Back behind the line of fighting, the land had already been picked over, only the scraps of scraps remaining. Rupert again proved invaluable, showing them where to look and how a bone discarded by another soldier could still provide sustenance in their stew. Somehow he was always able to scrounge some foodstuffs, plopping them in the communal pot the companions from the Pit contributed to and shared. They still went from two meals a day to none, and this lack was slowly killing the 1st Shaper Company.

Kearney ate well though, sharing his meals with Bumgarden in the commander's tent. He avoided them all now except in the presence of Bumgarden, only leaving the man's company to retreat to his own tent to sleep. He still had his tobacco though, Marta could smell it on him when he passed, but he wisely did not smoke it before the starving Shapers. Instead he chewed on the pipe when issuing orders they grudgingly obeyed.

Bumgarden might not have discarded Kearney yet, but the Shaper had discarded his former prison wife in May Oles. He had convinced her to join the Western ranks, same as he had with the other prisoners, but now free of his prison, Kearney no longer desired her. Because of her former association with the man, few in the Shaper Company cared for her either. So May was forced to find a new consort to protect her from the other former prisoners, the woman falling into the same role she played in the Pit, though she was now outside its walls. Her time in the prison had marked the woman though, sure as the brand she bore, May unable to shake off its influence any more than the scar.

Finally, Kearney announced the 1st Shapers would face their Covenant kin the next day at Stone Cleaver. The company had been broken into fourteen platoons, each one with a full mobile fortress made up of their shields between them. These Bumgarden divided into two groups of seven, setting one group at each flank of the front line. Marta was glad Abner's was one of the platoons paired with hers. Though they had not given voice to their plan, both knew once the fighting started they would break rank and escape to the sanctuary of the Covenant forces. And she was also sure the two of them were not the only Eastern Shapers considering this possibility.

The battle was already raging before they were finally called to duty, the barks of musket shots and boom of the cannons surrounding them as they formed up. Holding her hated Newfield flag in the bow of their upturned metal boat, Marta looked back at the Western troops among them. The Shapers and their shields provided protection for the 23rd Saber Company, each man equipped with his eponymous saber. Marta could not hide her disdain at their chosen weapons, the Covenant army preferring to fight in the gauche style with a dagger clasped in their off-hand rather than the single heavier saber favored in the West. Marta knew the Eastern sabermen were more than their match with two weapons to the Westerners' one. Just like the Weaver over the Render way, the East again proved superior in terms of tactics.

The swordsmen of both sides were still easy targets for the muskets though, their numbers frequently cut down to nothing before they could reach their targets. So she and the rest of the Shapers would supply them safe passage through the hail of musket fire, opening their phalanx and releasing the sabermen only when in the midst of the Covenant ranks.

The strategy was sound and would surely break the Eastern line, especially when coupled with the release of another thirteen Western saber squads farther down the line. Bumgarden had already employed this tactic earlier in the morning to great success, and it stood to reason it would work again. But sweating inside the bunker with the Shapers and nearly fifty sabermen cramped together, Marta felt suddenly apprehensive at the upcoming push.

Finally, Kearney's voice rang out from far in the rear, signaling the charge. Marta waved her flag, the massive phalanx lurching forward, six more fortresses slowly trudging towards the Eastern musketeers beside them. Her duty was done for now, Gonzalo now leading in the front of the fortress and guiding their path through the vision-slits cut in his shield. She was rendered useless until it was time to give the signal to open the phalanx and release their passengers, just another set of boots treading the muddy ground. Once they were away, Marta had no intention of giving the signal to reform the phalanx, instead dropping the Newfield flag and slipping through a gap for safety as soon as the opportunity arose.

Their march was slow and torturous, cascades of musket fire pounding their shields in a downpour of ruinous rain punctuated occasionally by the thunder of crashing cannonballs. But their shields held, the Shapers keeping their steady and well-trained march, the sabermen within quite safe. Gonzalo called out and Marta knew they had arrived. Waving her flag, she signaled the phalanx to open its sides into the midst of the musketeers.

"Remember Creightonville," one of the saberman cried as he pushed through the breach. The phrase was a rallying cry for the West to remind them of the Render who had been executed to spark the Grand War. Marta heard that those in the East cried the same words, remembering the emet that the overzealous Render cut down to start the war. Neither side seemed to mind they invoked the same incident.

The sabermen streamed out the openings, their swords flashing as they engaged their Eastern enemies. Armed only with knives and swinging their muskets as clubs, the musketeers should not have stood a chance against the charge. But no one in the Western command had taken the pride or savagery of the Easterners into account. Though ill-equipped against these close-quarter fighters, the musketeers did not retreat, instead hurling themselves against them with a bravery Marta had not witnessed before. Though they fell left and right, they held the line, Marta both awed and inspired by their valor.

Huddled behind their shields and catching glimpses through the slits, she was not the only Easterner to feel the twinge of pride. Some Shaper near the front began singing "The Sun Rises in the East" slightly off key. Soon all the other Eastern Shapers joined in, delight in their undefeated kinsmen shining in their eyes.

Somehow the musketeers held the line long enough for gauche

reinforcements to arrive to engage the Newfield sabermen on equal terms. Except the bravery of the Eastern soldiers could not be equaled by the Westerners, and soon the sabermen's ranks dwindled. Marta did not even need to race for safety. Sanctuary was coming in their direction, sure to eliminate the last of their captors in moments.

Suddenly several squads of the gauche swordsmen broke off from the fray and aimed at each of the open phalanxes. The refrain of "The Sun Rises in the East" still reverberating in their bunkers, the 1st Shaper Company hailed their liberators as they opened their shields wider.

Four of the Covenant swordsmen pushed into her phalanx to be welcomed with open arms. Only one shield away from her, the first gauche swordsman then hurled a word that would haunt Marta for the rest of her life.

"Traitors!"

His sword flashed, slitting the throat out of one of the singing Shapers and silencing his voice forever. His Covenant companions hesitated no more than he had, slashing and hacking their way through those in the mobile fortress.

Cutting down the man next to her, the first gauche fighter turned his sights upon Marta, who held the Newfield flag. His sword arm rose, but never had a chance to swing, Marta driving her phantom blade into his chest by instinct.

It was the second time she had killed, both times Easterners, but Marta did not pause to ponder as she turned her fury on the next gauche invader. He tried to use his dagger to deflect her blow, but Marta made her blade intangible to pass through his parry, returning its substance in time to cleave his skull.

The other Shapers in her platoon rallied, turning against those they had thought would liberate them. But they carried no weapons, their slow Armor open to sword and dagger thrusts. They finally overwhelmed the Eastern invaders by their numbers alone. The attack by the four Covenant swordsmen only lasted a moment, but by the time they were finally dispatched, the Shaper ranks were reduced by a third.

They would stand no chance out on the battlefield without weapons, Marta realized. Hoisting her flag, she swung it high and cried out at the top of her lungs.

"Retreat!"

Having been drilled for months, the Shapers should have snapped to action, but now horror galloped rampant among their ranks. Confusion and betrayal accompanied the horror as they realized their countrymen had turned against them. Some Shapers dutifully grasped their shields, but too late Marta noted their numbers were too depleted to create the full fortress. There would be too many holes, more gauche fighters able to sluice through once they finished with the diminishing Newfield sabermen.

Looking out the sight-hole at the nearest phalanx, Marta saw they too had been decimated and were frozen in place from the loss of men. There were not enough Shapers to mobilize either fortress, but perhaps between them there might be. Marta swung the flag again, drawing everyone's attention.

"Leave the shields! We run for the other platoon! Now!"

The flag unfurling behind her, Marta raced through the nearest opening, unsure if any of her platoon would follow. And perhaps they would not have, but Gonzalo followed her charge, the first pebble that began an avalanche of bodies.

The run across the battlefield without weapon or any defense took only a few moments, but to Marta it lasted two lifetimes. She heard each snap of the flag fluttering above her like a musket shot, sure each one would send her Breath out into the flow.

She crashed into the other phalanx to see they had fared no better than hers, but Abner awaited her there, stumbling over a dead Covenant fighter as he threw his arms around her. No word passed between them, but each understood there would be no salvation in the East. Their only chance resided in retreating to the West.

"Take hold a shield, boys!" Abner called. Members of Marta's platoon replaced those that had fallen in Abner's, all ready to close rank and make the slow march back to their captors.

But then the Weavers arrived.

It was only a squad numbering not more than five of the Eastern Blessed. Yet between them, they summoned two dozen manifestations to cut a swath through the last of the Western resistance. The Weavers then caught the Breaths of the dying men and fashioned them even more manifestations to swell their ranks. These they aimed straight for the remains of the 1st Shapers.

"By grace or by grave?" Marta whispered to Abner, her hand seeking his.

"Only wish I was on Eastern soil when I joined the flow," he replied. Then the opening strains of "The Sun Rises in the East" escaped his lips. Marta joined in as the manifestations swarmed their way, their song infused with defiance and defeat equally.

The manifestations never reached them though, a solitary man stepping to intercept them with a bummers cap upon his head and a glass dagger brandished in his hand.

Marta had never truly seen a Render in action before and did not know how deadly their drawing could be when coupled with a glass blade. She had heard tales, but they were as insufficient in capturing the reality of the actual event as a description of the cold would have been to those who had survived the Overhurst winter in the Pit. The Render was constantly in motion, drawing the Breath of the manifestations to him long before they covered the ground, his glass blade cutting them apart as it flashed. The manifestations were reduced by half even before they reached him.

She was sure he would be overwhelmed then, but miraculously the Render remained untouched, whirling through their ranks and slicing them apart. It was as if Sol Himself laid His hand upon the Render to declare no harm should befall him. He was truly Blessed among the Blessed.

The Eastern Weavers summoned even more manifestations to hurl them against the Render. But they fell faster than they were fashioned—not a one a match for the man as they crashed against him like waves against rocks.

The humans of the Covenant armies thought their swords might fare better, his glass dagger sure to shatter when it clashed against their steel. None reached him, the Render drawing their Breath and cutting them down from a distance. So severe was his slaughter that the gauche ranks broke before they met him, whole squads now fleeing from the single man.

Then, to Marta's amazement, the Render advanced, slaying the stragglers as he marched straight for the knot of Weavers. Perhaps they remained to cover their fellow troops' retreat, or perhaps they did so because they were filled with arrogance and sure their Blessed abilities were more than a match against this man with the opposite understanding of the will of Sol. Their motivation would never be known though, the Render falling upon them and massacring them to the man.

Suddenly a cheer sounded from behind the pinned Shapers, Marta looking back to see the Western forces charging forward to pursue the shattered Eastern army. They flowed through the now immobile fortress like water, flooding the remains of the Eastern line and washing it away in a cleansing tide. Marta found herself caught up in the wave, only breaking free when she found herself beside the Render who had held the line alone.

He was a big man and ill-proportioned, his neck flopping out the unfastened collar of his cloak. This close to the stout Render, Marta could not believe he was capable of the quick and agile motions she had witnessed moments before. His eyes were mismatched, Marta realizing it was because one was glass, the Render powerful enough to fashion one already, though he could not be much older than she. Such a feat was unheard of among one so young, her confusion confounded further by his dull stare. He seemed nothing but a simpleton.

But he had saved their lives, a fact Marta was grateful for.

"Thank you."

She thought perhaps he had not heard her as he continued to gaze at the horizon. Then he shook his head, turning towards Marta, as if he had not realized she was there. But once he saw her scar, his look of scorn was so severe Marta recoiled, as if she had been branded again.

"You were lucky they were Weavers, traitor."

***

The name stuck, soon both the Newfield and Covenant forces calling the remains of the 1st Shaper Company the Traitors Brigade. The fact their numbers had been reduced by nearly a quarter in a single engagement, now not enough men to even fill a proper company, let alone a brigade, did not matter in the least. Whenever anyone saw them, all they saw was the traitor.

Upon returning to the Western line, they counted their casualties. Marta's squad of twenty-five had lost seven, men she had known from training and their time in the Pit. Abner's platoon had lost nine, but the other five phalanxes had fared much worse with over half of their members dead on the field and one platoon gone entirely. They had no weapons during the attack, were unable to defend themselves against the Easterners they had, until that moment, considered their allies. Regrouping to lick their wounds, Marta felt that her fellow Shapers viewed her differently.

That night she met with the rest of her Pit cadre, dutifully dropping what little she had scrounged into the pot. When she did, she found Reid, Gonzalo, Ida, and Abner's eyes upon her.

"Time to teach the rest of them," Abner said soberly.

Instructing even Abner had been a mistake, Marta forbidden to teach the Cildra techniques to anyone outside the clan. Her answer was preordained before she even inhaled.

"No."

So Rupert set the lid back on the pot, refusing to serve her. She could, of course, take it by force, but Bumgarden had already made clear that to hurt another member of the company would earn her a date at the end of a rope. Marta knew she would die someday, but she had no intention of doing so while still wearing the Newfield uniform.

"Tonight after dinner, we'll begin training then."

***

She told only those five she would teach them, but it was eight Shapers who arrived for the first session. The next night, there were fourteen, and by the end of the week nearly all of the 223 remaining soldiers of the 1st Shaper Company were in attendance. They were not promising students, but neither had Marta been when she had tried to learn their Armor. And they worked hard at it, sure that her Cildra techniques would mean their survival.

The next night, Kearney arrived in a right froth, commanding them to stop at once. The training ground fell silent, all turning upon him as one. Crushed under their collective gaze, Kearney quickly scampered away before he was divorced from his Breath.

Marta was sure she would be summoned to Bumgarden's tent at any moment to be told to cease her nightly lessons. Some of the Shapers had learned enough to form basic clubs, at least, and Marta hoped it would be enough with their instruction halted.

But Bumgarden's call never came, and the Traitors Brigade continued their training.

Chapter 20

Winterfylled 23, 567

"Which is worse," Luca inquired, his eyes and blade gleaming with a hateful glint, "a Dobra or a freebooter?"

Both were equally horrid to Marta, the combination of the two exponentially worse. She watched Isabelle out of the corner of her eye, the woman up with hatchet in hand. Marta was happy she had chosen the hatchet since it did not have the range of her sling. Isabelle wanted to attack, her posture said as much, and Marta readied herself for the sudden press.

"Isabelle intends on feinting, of drawing you off."

Isabelle seemed almost as surprised by Luca's offhand admission as Marta was. Their confusion must have amused the man, his grin widening. But his next action mystified Marta all the more as his left hand slowly closed the exposed lockblade.

"Don't put that away," Marta sneered. "I want to test the claim of your imbued blade."

"Because I cannot be beaten with it is exactly why I'm putting it away. I don't want you to die. Keeping you alive is one of the conditions of our payment, Marta."

The fact he knew her real name was meant to intimidate her, but only served to infuriate Marta further. And it proved nothing, his Listener abilities meaning he could have snatched her identity from her at any time during their travels. His statement did intrigue her somewhat though, and she wanted to know what other stories he intended to spin.

"The Covenant Sons paid you to keep me alive?"

"The Sons, no. It was someone in the Public Safety Department, and it must have been a big bug to afford us."

This statement troubled Marta. The Cildra had long known the Public Safety Department was a front for Newfield's own spy service, the Home

Guard their unwitting subordinates. The Cildra used them when they needed an overt hand, her brother having infiltrated their number before the war to ensure it. And this certainly had Carmichael's stink about it. Only he would have gone to such surreptitious ends in giving the freebooters their cover as members of the Covenant Sons. He would have known she would never willingly accept his help, and the fact he had known where she would depart the train line with Caddie caused her blood to boil. She felt like a chess piece moved against her will. She had thought herself safe as a queen, only to realize too late she was again her brother's pawn.

"Your mission must have been secret. Why tell me now?"

"I've never met our employer, while I know your face well, one I quite like." Luca suddenly appeared quite serious, the look so foreign it was comical. "And haven't we proven ourselves by now?"

"What tribe?"

His eyes flicked to the lockblade and back. "Why do you ask what you already know?"

"Because I want to hear you say it."

She expected his shoulders to slump, to show some sign of shame. Instead Luca straighten, staring back proudly.

"Ikus."

Said to deal in Dead Breath and imbued objects, the Ikus were the least trusted of the Dobra tribes, held at an arm's length by even their own kin. But Dobra of any kind were seldom known to travel away from the rest of the ilk, least of all with a half-Ingios woman.

"How did you become a freebooter?"

"Fell into it bit by bit. Took some odd jobs during the war for the West. We were wandering through the East at the time, which gave them eyes to see what was happening across the Mueller Line. At first it was just gathering information then a small task here and there. Might have been content to quit with the war, but my tribe decided to become Cousins as Gatlin rebuilt. I was just too much a Wanderer at heart to put down roots."

Marta did not care about his life in the least, but the mention of her home was more than she could resist. "Tell me about Gatlin."

Luca's solemn look appeared less comical as his eyes fell. "They razed it to the ground. Buildings, bodies, they all burned the same. Couldn't tell what lit up the night, the fires or the Breath of the dying. They were just beginning to rebuild when I left, Carrion Kind swarming around to work with the Ticks. It's not the same now, no more winding roads and open homes. It's all quite straight and square, no more charm. It was your home?"

His question took Marta off guard. Aware he was a Listener, she should have been able to lock him out of her mind. Luca smiled at her confusion. "I don't need to Listen to know that. I could tell by the look on your face soon as I said its name."

Marta was surprised the effect the invocation of her home still had on her. She had known for over two years Gatlin's fate, a city she had not seen since she was a child. If anything, she should have been glad at the misery there from those who had cast her out. Instead she felt like a wound had been reopened, the pain as familiar as it was pronounced.

"Will you let us accompany you to Ceilminster now or are you still looking for your chance to let out?"

"Still considering," she shot back. Marta disbursed her phantom blade as she did though, turning to see Isabelle lower her own weapon. The younger woman's eyes were still cold though, Marta by no means an ally. Despite herself, Marta felt respect for Isabelle. It was the same look she gave when she considered the two of them.

"That's progress," Luca offered. "If you had said yes, I'd know you were lying. At least now we're all being honest."

Honesty from Luca seemed about as natural as a horse walking on its hinters, but he might still be useful. Marta looked to Caddie, the girl still standing where she had stopped upon exiting the cave, left knee-high in the water.

"What do you hear when you Listen to the girl?"

"It's difficult to explain to someone who's not a Listener." Luca's grin disappeared, the man rubbing the back of his head as he sought his words. "An unguarded mind is like a clear lake, the thoughts a school of fish swimming in it. Strong feelings muddy the waters, but if the mind is calm, you can see the fish. Can't quite count each and every one, but you know how large the school is, what direction they're swimming in. But once they know you're Listening, the fish dive down, start swimming deeper. You know they're still there, can see the water moving, but you can't count them anymore."

Luca turned to Caddie, his eyes narrowing, as if examining a confounding knot. "With the girl the pool's the clearest I've ever seen. Can't explain how strange it is to see someone so untroubled, her mind smooth as glass. But when I look into it, I can find no fish, no school."

"You're saying she doesn't have a thought in her head."

"No, she thinks. She must. How could she move without thought?"

"Dogs move and they don't think. Can perform more tricks than the girl too."

Luca shook his head emphatically, as if offended by her words. "Dogs think, don't let anyone tell you different. And Caddie must have thoughts, but they're swimming deep. Her mind is so clear I should be able to see down to the bottom, but I see no bottom when I look. There's no telling how deep her mind goes."

Marta scowled. His abused metaphor annoyed her as she strode through the water to take the girl's hand roughly. But before she could tell the child to come, Caddie turned at her touch. Marta's words proved unnecessary as she followed the woman back to the others.

***

They decided to camp there until noon since the emet would keep the glassman from using the caverns to reach them. It was possible she could scale the ridge and catch them unaware, but to do so she would have to know where the caves let out.

The presence of the glassman gnawed at Marta. The city-states of Myna to the east were still ruled by these monsters, but the woman they faced did not look to be of Mynian stock. If anything, the glassman looked like she had stepped off a boat straight from the Auld Lands, her skin pale and unlike Marta's mother's darker hue. What she was doing this far out in Ingios territory might prove interesting too. Luca said that Isabelle's tongue was ripped out by a glassman, and although one encounter with a glassman was strange, two instances in Ingios territory was too much of a coincidence to ignore. If he was not already aware of it, this would be information Carmichael would covet. Marta would not willingly deliver it to her brother though, perhaps passing it on to her father if they were reconciled.

But to do so she would have to let Caddie's father live, something Marta did not think she would be capable of. Her father had found it within him to forgive Orthoel Hendrix, but he still believed that through this man the East could rise again and throw off the shackles of the West. Marta did not care who won out since she was hated by both sides equally. Both were no better than dogs fighting over a carcass that bore the name of Newfield. No matter which dog won, Marta would still be an outcast and the nation of Newfield would be no less dead.

Though she had killed husbands and fathers before, Marta had no desire to make a widow or orphan, if she could help it. She was not a monster after all. But Orthoel Hendrix was a monster in every sense of the word, was responsible for the murder of countless women and children, not just in Gatlin, but all across the East. She could not allow the monster to go unpunished. He had to pay for his crime, even if his daughter might have to see his execution at Marta's hands. What Luca had told her of Caddie's mind made this decision easier to stomach. Marta at least now knew that Caddie was mindless, and that meant she would not care if her father died before her blank eyes.

Dead tired herself, Marta looked at the girl, surprised to see Caddie's eyes closed and her breathing even. She was asleep, another of the firsts from the child that night, but this progress was an inconvenience to Marta, now no sentry to shake her awake if her companions turned treacherous.

Marta closed her eyes nonetheless. Caddie's protection had been ultimately pointless, Isabelle's sling or Luca's thrown knives able to reach her even under the girl's watch. She was no safer now than she had ever been, Marta absently pondering this fact for many hours, sleep not coming for her until dawn threatened on the horizon.

***

She awoke midmorning to the smell of sizzling meat, her sleep deeper than she had expected, as she realized Luca and Isabelle had been up long enough to build a fire. Caddie was awake as well, hunkered on the ground on the far side of the campsite.

"Did she move on her own?"

Luca prepared her a plate, the fish fresh-caught and enticing. "She got up when we did. Kept walking and I thought she was going to continue on the path, but she just kept going in circles. It was distracting, so I gave her a toy."

Marta looked closer to see Caddie collect the last of his bix sticks from the ground, and suddenly, her food lost its pleasantness.

"You gave her those? They're profane."

"And you've never had your fortune told by a Dobra," he responded blithely. But as he examined the girl holding his sticks, his face fell. "They're nothing, just tools we use to separate outsiders from their money."

"Then why do you still throw them each morning?"

"Habit."

All the sticks picked up, Caddie again scattered them on the earth. She then carefully collected them in a sequence that made no sense to Marta, the girl eschewing the four primary colors that denoted the suits the Dobra claimed had significance. There was no rhyme or reason she could discern as

Caddie again tossed the sticks upon the dirt.

"How long has she been at this?"

"Hours," he replied with a shrug. "It's good for her though. Keeps her occupied."

Marta occupied the next hour by bathing. The pool provided the water, her haversack the soap. Luca played the gentleman by excusing himself and saying he would scout ahead. Marta still did not trust him, but she also did not care as she stripped down to her undergarments. Her slouch hat remained though, Marta unwilling to bear her brand if she could help it.

Their trek through the caves the night before had washed most of the filth off, but it felt good to be scrubbed with soap. On a whim Marta called to Caddie, the girl leaving her new toys behind to join Marta in the water. But the order to bathe did not seem to register, Marta having to pull the child's dress off over her head and wash her by hand. As she ran her soapy hand down Caddie's arm, she again noticed the strange scars, most of them too small to see at a distance. Though tiny, they were hard to the touch, the lot of them prickling at Marta's soapy hand.

"How did this happen, Caddie?"

At the sound of her name, the child looked up at Marta. Her eyes were still as blank and untroubled as the last time, Marta searching her memory for the shade of Caddie's father's eyes. No answer came, and Marta decided to ask the man about the scars if she had a chance before she silenced him.

They broke camp within the hour, Caddie walking along without being held. The direction they headed was not in question once Marta looked around in the daylight. The Lead Mine Hills loomed in the distance, named not for their actual mines, but for their slate-gray color. They were unmistakable, Marta remembering them well from the war. They marked the edge of West Neider, the Mueller Line not much farther and the East awaiting them on the other side. Upon reaching the Mueller Line, they would be halfway to their goal.

***

Graff arrived at the crag shortly after dusk. He had lost sight of his prey, but his Render's Breath showed him there were two untended horses here, each bearing the brand of Newfield dragoons. Of the horses he paid no mind, instead scanning the surroundings with his good eye. The line of ley he was following had disappeared, but he still sensed something nearby. It was powerful and probably a nodus, but there was something else in it, a scent underneath he found foul.

Dismounting gracelessly, only the steady roar of the waterfall and his heavy steps disturbed the silence. Mouth falling open, his head lolled to the side as he strode haphazardly through the site, never in a straight line, but staggering like a drunkard. His good eye gazed nowhere in particular, seeing all but staying on nothing for more than a moment.

Only when his boot tip touched the edge of the pool did Graff straighten, snapping to attention as his living eye focused on the crag. His voice did not match his pose, slipping between his teeth like sludge through a drain.

"Show yourself, monster."

The bear-like emet appeared as he ordered, the word of a pious Render giving Graff command over the beasts of Breath. If the creature was made of flesh, its hackles would be up, stalking towards him on its hind legs, as if it were human. The presumption of its posture alone, the sheer audacity of the animal to walk like a man, was enough to seal its fate.

It stopped within the pool, its distaste of him almost equaling his of it. Graff's question was civil enough though. "You saw the child?"

=Yes.

No sound issued from the emet, but the air vibrated with its voice, the second Soul Breath in the Render's head allowing him to decipher its words.

"You saw her for what she was?"

=A child of Sol, just as you, Render.

Its impudence amused him again. "Tell me where they went."

But the beast remained silent, ignoring his command. Graff put more force into it the second time. "Tell me where they went, emet."

Still the beast refused to obey, its will creating something approaching admiration in the man. It was almost as much as he would afford a loyal dog defending its dead master.

"No matter. I will find them soon enough."

=There is a sickness to you, Render, a sickness that goes down to your Soul.

Again the amusing creature coaxed a laugh. "I am not the sinner. My Breath follows Sol's flow."

=You know nothing of Sol, would not recognize the presence if it was before you.

Graff glanced up at the sky, considering the stars a long moment. The creature's end was never in question, the ghul's sentencing simply a silly formality.

"You are an abomination against Sol and must be released. Will you do so willingly?"

The imposing emet rose to its full height before rushing through the pool for him as unstoppable as a downpour.

Graff's drawing deflected its momentum with a flick of his wrist. Like a puppet master directing his marionette, Graff made it slow its speed, stopping inches before him. Lowering one hand, he forced it to kneel, its head still hovering high above his own.

=You are cursed, Render. Your Breath is stained darker than—

Graff's glass dagger sliced through its throat before it finished: drawn, driven into its being, and returned to its sheath in an instant. Most Renders carried glass sabers, enjoying the weight of their weapons and pretending they would not shatter against an authentic sword. This was all arrogance though. Graff knew when it came to culling Breath, the dagger cut just as well and was released from its sheath much quicker.

The mysterious bonds that held the beast's Breath were cleaved, allowing them to again join Sol's flow along the ley. Like metal filings rotating towards a magnet, the three released Breaths turned away from Graff to enter the waterfall, the nodus that had created the emet surely within. It was this space behind the falls, more than the emet itself, which interested Graff.

Warmed by his skin and the fourth Breath within, Graff's glass eye was still cooler than the rest of his body. His socket made a sucking sound as he removed the hollow orb. Exposing the hole that had so recently pointed towards his brain, his Blessed Breath within slipped through the opening and rose into the air.

It was an odd sensation to remove an aspect that was so central to his being and willingly let it abandon him. Many Renders could not mentally take this step, could not split themselves into pieces without shattering. But Graff was no ordinary Render, was the youngest to pluck his healthy eye from his skull with his own hands. Sacrifice was a price he was more than willing to pay if it helped him complete his given task. It had been years since he had last been given one, but Graff was sure that the death of this peculiar girl would fulfill his last command well enough.

His amethyst-tinged fourth Breath shot away from him, through the waterfall and out of sight. Graff was glad it was gone, though he was now rendered just a fragment of his normal self. Its absence would lead to its speedy return though, brimming with knowledge that would lead him on to his newest kill to fulfill his grand purpose.

***

The glassman Bernice watched the strange Render from the dark of the nearby woods. She knew with his fourth Breath gone, he was without the drawing abilities he used to defeat the emet and would be no match for her. She could easily feast on his three diminished Breaths without incident, and she was ravenously hungry. Having had to release several of her stolen Breaths to speed her healing, she was weaker than she had been in nearly a decade. She had enough Breath left to remain ageless for another six months at least, but when it came to collecting dying Breaths, one was never enough. For each she consumed and contained within her, she starved for another to join it. More just made the hunger more pronounced.

The Render would make for a sustaining meal, but she turned away. The emet was right: there was a sickness to the man, right down to his very Soul. Bernice was afraid if she consumed such a stained Breath, she too would be unclean. It was therefore best to ignore the man and report the strange occurrences she witnessed tonight to her master.

Chapter 21

Iulius 16, 563 (Four Years Ago)

The Traitors Brigade proved invaluable in the battles of the Drinkwine Branch, Big Lovely Arch, and Forty-eight Mile Creek. Bumgarden modified their original formation, now seven phalanxes instead of the original fourteen. Each still consisted of twenty-four soldiers carrying the shields and a flag-bearer, but now each contained an additional six Shapers ready to claim a shield if one of their comrades fell. They were still afforded no weapons, but with Marta's continued training, they could at least defend themselves when they were breached.

Most peaked in their education with the forming of Shaper swords, but Leon Doyle had actually mastered the phantom blade. This made him useful, but Marta did not trust the cousin of the man she killed in the Pit for a moment. The first time she found Leon before her for instruction, he assured her he cared nothing for revenge, but Marta never turned her back on him. He was one of the few Shapers who reveled in the bloodshed, far different to the rest who were pressed into service. Whenever she looked at Leon, he leered at her with a look that made her skin crawl. But he and his phantom blade proved instrumental when they were breached at Glendalose Draw, so Marta allowed his looks so long as he still proved his worth.

With the Traitors Brigade transporting troops safely through the battles, the tides of war were turning against the Covenant. The Western soldiers considered them allies now too, occasionally sharing their own meals with them—the scraps, at least. They ate best when there were battles, hauling the fallen horses from the field to butcher them. Though each skirmish risked their lives, the members of the Traitors Brigade found themselves looking forward to battle as their stomachs rumbled.

There were casualties as well, both Clinton Sheers and Bruell Leichseuring dying just last week when Bruell stumbled to expose the two to musket fire. The gentle farmer Tollie had also succumbed to battle fugue, nearly costing his entire platoon their lives as he froze during an engagement. Kearney was ready to discard this defective equipment, but Abner interceded, keeping Tollie with him in his own tent. Weeks passed, Tollie not stirring except to eat, the majority of it dribbled down his chin. He could no longer contribute to the communal pot, but Abner insisted he would not starve. Due to Abner's largess, Tollie recovered somewhat. He was no longer useful on the battlefield, but could forage and assist Rupert in cooking their meals. Though the company was diminished by Tollie's mental affliction, their cadre at least ate better.

Reid's prison wife, Ida, also fell to a gauche sword, one less seat now occupied at their nightly meals. Reid never spoke about her, and no one intruded to disturb his uncharacteristic silence. They had all lost friends and knew to let each other mourn however they chose.

No one would mourn Kearney though, a fact Marta savored as she entered the dying man's tent. Hidden far from the fighting, it was no bullet or sword thrust that claimed him. The formerly paunchy man instead fell shamefully to sickness. The disease came on quickly in Kearney, no one else in the company contracting it. In a matter of days, he was on his deathbed, the doctors unable to find a cause. Marta assumed it was weakness of character.

Always at the forefront of the fighting, Marta had not made it out unscathed. The ruined remains of her right ear still stung something fierce from being torn off by musket fire at Bergen Creek. Her uniform bore several scorch marks as well, her skin a patchwork of still-healing scars from stray shrapnel. Every bit of her constantly ached, but Marta embraced the pain as a sign she was still alive. Kearney would soon feel nothing at all.

He was so weak he could not speak, but his mind was still with him, his eyes narrowing at Marta's appearance. She again considered crushing his throat as she had dreamed during training. But to do so would cleanly end his misery, and she wanted him suffering until the bitter end. So she leaned in close, her lips nearly kissing his ear to whisper.

"You are the only traitor here."

With that she wrested the pipe from his frail hands and left him to die entirely alone.

She found the remains of the company waiting for her as she stepped out, down to only 200 soldiers from the over 300 that had originally joined. They were a ragged lot, most having survived only by luck and her training. None of them were natural fighters with the exception of Leon and her. This gave Marta no right to assume Kearney's vacated mantle, but she expected no one would challenge her for it. Though wounded, she had still fared better than most, hungry but not starving due to her friends and their shared pot.

Marta considered this fact as she looked them over with Kearney's pipe gripped in her teeth. When no one stepped up to take it from her, she called out loud as she could through her clenched teeth.

"From now on Rupert Kelly's in charge of food. Anything you forage goes to him. Anyone caught hoarding will be treated as if they had destroyed Newfield property. We all eat from the same pot now."

"While you'll be dining with Bumgarden?" someone called out anonymously from the dark.

"Indeed I will. Training will be expected after supper's done. Everyone will attend."

Marta waited for someone to respond, her eyes sweeping over her potential troops. When they fell upon Reid, he gave her a wink, his hand rising to his brow to give her the scornful salute he had mastered. He was perhaps mocking her, but Abner's appeared authentic. Soon all the others in the Traitors Brigade mirrored the men. Marta snapped off a salute in turn then, hoping he would accept the news as she departed to inform Bumgarden.

She found him in his tent peering over several maps, two dinners steaming on the table. Her stomach instantly rumbled at the ample meal, her mouth salivating so much she could scarcely speak.

"Kearney won't make it through the night. I'm his replacement."

Bumgarden did not look up to acknowledge her and Marta decided to wait, the sight of the food taunting her. Most alluring was the plum, bright violet and inviting her to take a bite. She had not touched a fruit since she had been caught by the Render and had almost forgotten what sweetness tasted like.

Finally, Bumgarden cleared the maps away and gestured for Marta to join him at the table. He dug into his plate in silence, Marta letting hers sit. Bumgarden blinked in surprise at the starving woman and then opened his hands politely.

"Please, eat. No need to stand on ceremony here."

Marta left her dinner untouched, and he considered the woman a long time. She thought he might be offended, but finally, Bumgarden pushed his own plate away. "If you can forego a meal, I expect I can as well. But perhaps we can share a smoke."

Marta accepted his tobacco, Bumgarden first stuffing his own and then Kearney's pipe. She had never smoked one before, but lit it easily enough when he offered her his matches. On her first inhale the smell hit her like a blow to the head, scattering her senses and striking her dumb. It was her father's blend, the smell rekindling memories of being summoned to his study for punishment.

"This was sent by an acquaintance in the Public Safety Department, Philo Frost. Do you know him?"

Her wits jumbled, Marta could only force a shake of her head and hope Bumgarden did not realize how twisted she was. He descended back into silence, puffing away like her father once did. Marta founder herself incapable of bringing Kearney's pipe to her lips.

"You are an innovator, Childress. I respect that, consider myself one as well. As such, I encourage you to think hard on any means that can enhance this company. But any innovations you discover you must bring them to me before enacting them. Is that understood?"

Marta's head had cleared enough to give the illusion of considering his statement before nodding. Bumgarden had all the power here, and she could not say no if she chose to, but the pretense of choice was a nice departure from the last year of her life.

"Where are you from, Childress?"

"Gatlin."

"Ah, Mimas, a beautiful state." Bumgarden blew several smoke rings, the last slowly wafting down to encircle Marta's wrists like manacles. "We'll be in Gatlin soon enough. Will you be welcomed back when we arrive?"

She had never considered that question before, but Marta knew the answer. Her father's blend sent by Carmichael proved her family was still thinking on her. "Of course, they will welcome me with open arms."

Bumgarden nodded sagely, knocking out the remains of his pipe on his plate where the smoldering tobacco ruined the meal. He then pushed the food away and unfolded his maps. Their meeting was apparently over, Bumgarden not even considering her worthy of a formal dismissal.

Marta stood, grabbing the victuals from her plate to stuff it into her pockets. She was just reaching for the plum when Bumgarden spoke.

"Are you stealing from my tent?"

It was a direct challenge, but Marta answered without hesitation. "We in the Traitors Brigade share our meals now. This belongs in the pot so all can share, the first of my innovations."

For a moment Marta thought she saw a faint movement on his face, but perhaps it was her imagination as Bumgarden waited until she realized her mistake. "I do apologize for not bringing it to your attention first though, Colonel. Might it be allowed?"

Bumgarden pondered her a long time before he spoke. "You will make a popular leader, Childress. The only question remaining is if you will prove a good one."

He returned to his maps, Marta snatching the last of the food and departing. Before she was through the flap, he called out after her, still not looking up. "Kearney always favored the plums, something Frost took great pains in noting before he sent these. I've only met the man once, but I find what he takes the attention to notice to be of grave importance."

Stepping out of the tent, Marta examined the plum. It was one of the first from the yearly crop; its supple skin begging to be bitten into. As her fingertip traced the fruit, she found a slight indentation, a mar to its perfect form. It could have been where a bug took a bite, but it could also be the point where it was pierced, a poison deposited within.

Marta flung the fruit away, wondering if Carmichael had been the one responsible for Kearney's sudden misfortune and her abrupt battlefield appointment.

An equally good question was if she could be both a popular and good leader. The former she secured the moment she appeared with the haul from Bumgarden's tent to drop the contents into Rupert's pot in front of her troops. She won the Shapers' loyalty then and there, now considered one of their number in a way Kearney never was.

Bumgarden had supplied the means to her victory, had been polite if a bit dismissive. Now that she mulled it over, perhaps he was not the heartless serpent she first thought him. Given time, she might even grow to respect him.

Marta still intended on killing him though. But at least now she would be merciful about it and end him quickly.

Chapter 22

Winterfylled 23, 567

They made their way on foot, the adults carrying their supplies over their shoulders. Twice Isabelle disappeared into the trees, returning the first time with a dead bird, the second with a handful of tough, edible greens. She had not removed the strings from her ears though, still making her silent intentions known to her invisible people. Yet the Ingios tribes had been conspicuously absent while within their territory, and even when their intentions were given voice as Luca had done the night before, Marta considered them mistruths at best and more likely outright lies.

Setting up camp that evening, Luca climbed high in a tree and announced there was a line of ley not far off. They could reach it the next day, the line strong enough to probably connect up to the Dobra network and provide them information as to their whereabouts. The Ingios territories were vast, taking up much of the interior of the continent of Soltera, and this was the first time Marta had stepped foot within them. Though they were probably more dangerous, she preferred the states she was already familiar with. The Lead Mine Hills proved West Neider was near, East Neider and Nahuat not much farther, but for the time being, Marta would not be able to pick out where they were on a map, which made her beholden to her two companions.

Closing in again on the states, the chance they might run into another squad of dragoons increased, Marta stating they should set guards throughout the night. She took the first watch, chewing her pipe absently. Luca and Isabelle retired to separate bedrolls, Caddie contenting herself with Luca's bix sticks by the light of the dying fire. And there she played, alone and totally engrossed throughout Marta's shift.

She woke Luca for the second watch, the man taking his position without complaint. Setting her head down on her haversack, Marta pulled her greatcoat over herself. Sleep did not come though, and had remained a tentative stranger for the last several nights. Rolling over to find a more comfortable position, Marta only discovered she could find no comfort here. A half hour passed and, though wretchedly tired, Marta could not sleep. She still had the bottle of rot gut Carmichael had gifted to her, and though he had meant it as an insult, Marta thought it might be of use now.

The bottle remained untouched for the time being, Marta deciding she would give a 200 count before she uncorked it. She had made it nearly halfway through when she sensed motion nearby. Fully awake again, the mental plans for her Armor flooded her head only to realize it was Caddie silently stalking up.

Without a word or even a look her direction, the girl lay down next to the woman, turning her back to Marta and curling into a loose ball. Her eyes then closed, Caddie falling into a deep sleep in seconds. Looking at the girl's features softened by her slumber, Caddie reminded Marta of Oleander again. The comparison was tenuous at best, as Caddie's skin was pale as cream and her eyes blue, whereas Oleander's eyes and skin had been dark, like Marta's. Though Caddie was about the same age as Oleander was the last time Marta saw her, that alone was not the source of the similarity. Instead it was the look of peace upon her face, the same she had seen from Oleander as a toddler when she would invade her older sister's room to escape a nightmare. Oleander would climb into Marta's bed, never their parents', and immediately dissolve into an untroubled sleep. The looks on their faces were the same, both comforted by her presence.

Marta knew she should not allow this instance to become a habit—should not let the girl attach herself to her. Soon she would kill the girl's father, and allowing Caddie close now would only make the act all the more difficult. She should shove the girl away and make her find her own sleeping spot. But the girl was not worth the trouble, her mind clear and empty according to Luca, and so Marta simply turned her back upon her as sleep soon took her.

She realized she made the wrong decision when she awoke in the morning to find her arm around the girl, the two of them sharing the blanket of her greatcoat. Curled up next to Caddie, Marta reconsidered her father's words: *Families did indeed belong together*, she thought, the girl reaching out to Marta for succor when her own family was unavailable. She had not given comfort to another in years, the idea that someone would turn to her for it nearly breaking the remains of her heart. And in that moment Marta decided her father was correct in his forgiveness. She would turn her back on her brother's mission and make sure the girl was reunited with her father, even if it meant the nation of Newfield would again go to war.

***

They reached the ley before noon, their headaches alerting them to its presence despite it being nearly invisible in the daylight. Luca strode straight to it, placing his hand within the flow and connecting to the Dobra network. Marta knew the basics of how their network functioned, but only the Dobra knew how to pluck these strings of ley and make them sing. And even if another Listener discovered how to hear their messages, they could not decipher them since they were transmitted in the Dobra's own secret language. For a Dobra to intercept a message and use it for his own benefit was an instant death sentence. Everyone knew this and none dared to defy it, which made Luca's willingness to do this so readily troubling to Marta.

He remained in the ley for nearly twenty minutes before his eyes began to flutter. Due to the ley headaches, the Dobra usually only sent their missives once an hour, a quick flurry of messages before the pain set in. Only in the largest cities did the Cousins keep a Listener at the station at all times, rotating them in and out when the pain began. Luca Listened a long while, finally removing his hand and returning to them.

"What did you learn?"

"That it's noon," he offered blithely. Before Marta's anger could get the better of her, he went on. "They're all searching for you. Or, more accurately, a woman who was in the Traitors Brigade named May Oles in the company of a blue-eyed girl. No mention about Isabelle or me, so we're lucky in that regard, at least."

The confusion as to her name was cold comfort to Marta, the brand on her forehead and the blue-eyed Caddie more than enough to warrant capture no matter what they believed her identity was.

"The message came on the hour," he continued, "which means it's a general alert sent out through all the ley. Anywhere we go, so long as there's a line nearby and someone to read it, they'll know you. But there's good news as well. Most of the messages on this line were addressed to Colonel Davis Underhill. Seems he's in charge of the military outpost here."

That actually was good news, Underhill's mismanagement of the Western war effort so egregious he earned himself a demotion and was relegated to a forgotten outpost far on the edge of Ingios territory. With Underhill mishandling his troops here as well, they had a much better chance of slipping by.

"And, most important, I know where we are. There's a road not far from here that will make travel much easier."

She believed him in this, at least, since Dobra Listeners memorize all the lines of ley connecting the land. Few knew the layout of the nation better than a Wandering Dobra. Fewer still would know how to navigate the territories unseen better than a Dobra with a death sentence hanging over his head. Luca's status as a freebooter would play to their advantage.

Marta mulled this over, finally coming to her decision. "We'll walk the road in pairs—Isabelle and me together and Luca ahead of us with Caddie. They're searching for a woman with a blue-eyed girl, so hopefully no one will look too closely at a man traveling with one. We'll take the road far as we can, meeting up again at night."

It was a bit of a gamble letting Caddie out of her sight with Luca, but with her rabbit legs, Marta was sure she could cover the ground faster than he if he attempted anything. Isabelle would also function as her hostage, Luca sure to know Marta would kill her without hesitation if she sensed any treachery. The only question was how much he cared for his mute cohort.

Caddie's hand in his, Luca immediately shattered the silence with his constant flow of trivial words. Marta listened as his babble finally receded into silence before she and Isabelle set out. Isabelle had removed the colored strings from her ears, letting her hair and false skirt down to now appear more Mynian than Ingios.

Their footfalls and occasional snippets of Luca's one-sided conversation floating by on the wind were the only noise on the road, and Marta wondered again about this woman. Isabelle seemed far more capable than her companion, had already proved she could easily live off the land and did not seem to care for money or possessions. So why tie herself to him?

Marta had caught the woman gazing at Luca with outright disdain when she thought neither of them was looking. Other times she stared at him with something approaching sorrow, pain etched across her usually unreadable face. Why she kept these looks hidden also confounded Marta. As a Listener Luca was sure to know what was on her mind. So why keep her sentiments hidden from her partner?

Four times they encountered travelers along the road, Luca's steady stream of words alerting them well in advance to their presence and allowing Marta and Isabelle time to flee the path and conceal themselves. His conversations with the strangers took an interminable amount of time to Marta. The man was able to talk about anything to anyone, conversation coming quite naturally to him, but each time the chat would come to an abrupt end, Luca bidding his new friends well before departing.

It was not until the third interlude that Marta realized the conversations served two purposes: to allow her and Isabelle a chance to hide as well as to create an opportunity for Luca to Listen to their minds. Without his required pin to warn them, their minds would be unguarded and their thoughts easy to ascertain.

It was a big risk to flaunt the laws that required all Listeners to openly declare their abilities. Picking the Dobra network was a death sentence, but the Dobra would be the ones to carry out the act. But defying the laws of Newfield meant that he would not be safe anywhere except the Ingios territories they had departed. The Cildra also disobeyed these laws, but they were practiced and careful in their deceit, whereas this flamboyant man demanded attention.

Luca seemed to have no fear of death though, even when he had faced Marta with murder on her mind. Perhaps he actually believed that his imbued lockblade would ensure him his victory. Or perhaps that had just been a bluff to keep from fighting her, his confidence actually fear dressed up in another lie. Marta did not believe it was an excuse though, instead that he firmly clung to the illusion that his weapon would defend him. He seemed utterly and unshakably sure in both his abilities and the blade, and it was only a matter of time before those illusions would be horribly shattered, perhaps by Marta's own hand.

***

They were in the shadow of the Lead Mine Hills when they met up again at dark. Luca already had a fire going, Caddie tossing his bix sticks by its light when Marta and Isabelle arrived. Whittling away, Luca's smile was warm, though the information he imparted sent a chill down Marta's spine.

"Underhill's dragoons are patrolling around the hills, but we should be safe here tonight." With that he turned back to Caddie. "Though Gerjet had been caught, she knew that Baas was still free since no one expected much from a dog. Her hands were bound behind her back, you see. So while everyone else in the tent was asleep, she pressed her hands under the sides and Baas chewed through her bindings."

The story he was telling the girl was "Gerjet and the Thirty Turgs," a favorite of children everywhere. The hero was the ancient Shaper Gerjet, her constant companion the dog Baas, who was said to be Blessed with a Soul Breath, even though an animal. This extra Breath made the dog intelligent as a human and loyal to Gerjet for having saved his life as a puppy. Although a Shaper and capable of great feats of strength, Gerjet prided herself on her cleverness and always outsmarted her enemies, her adventures spanning volumes.

As a child Marta loved the stories of Gerjet. Every time one of her father's dogs whelped, Marta would pick through the litter, eager to find a Blessed dog, like Baas, the two sure to forge a bond and go out on all sorts of grand adventures. Those dreams were the heartfelt hopes of a child, but now that Marta was an adult, stories of Gerjet and Baas rankled her.

Luca reached the climax where Baas lured the thirty Turgs into a cave, Gerjet sealing them in when Marta interrupted. "Don't go filling the girl's head with that nonsense."

"It's just a silly story."

"It's horrific is what it is."

Luca stared at her like she had suddenly sprouted a second head, forcing her to explain herself. "The dog Baas was said to be Blessed, possessing a third Breath that made him aware like humans. That means animals can be Blessed and equal to us. But if one in twenty humans is Blessed, it would stand to reason that the same number of animals would be as well. If that's the case, then every twenty times you've eaten meat, you've eaten something with a Soul and been a cannibal."

She could see that he understood her argument, but did not agree with her bringing it up now. "It was only meant to pass the time. You have no way with children, no Soul within you."

Marta had been called worse than soulless on more occasions than she could count, but his slur still got her back up for some reason. Her anger flared, and with the lucidity it provided, she saw how she could cut him deeper than any knife. She smiled brightly as she approached Caddie, malevolence flickering in her eyes.

"Have you ever heard the story of Dobradab?"

Marta could hear Luca's jaw click shut and knew her blow had landed. Caddie's head turned to behold Marta, and though there was still no spark to her eyes to indicate any intelligence, Marta at least had the girl's undivided attention.

"Long ago, in the time before glass, there was a very good man named Abet. And because Abet followed the will of Sol in all things, he was blessed with a good life, with herds that spread further than the eye could see, a loyal wife, and six healthy children. His children were like him, upright and obedient to the will of Sol.

"Now, Abet and his family lived near a huge nodus known as the Nine Lines. And one night the lights of the nodus flared, expanding until they engulfed their camp. Awakened by the surge of ley, Abet roused his wife and together they watched the strange lights. But their youngest son, Dobradab, heard them stir and sat beside them through the night. Though Abet knew he should send his youngest to bed, he let him remain because Dobradab was Abet's favorite child.

"And when the sleeping children awoke the next morning, they found they were different than they had been when they went to bed—they were now Blessed. The oldest son, named Abad, after his father, became the first Render, his sister Ceil, the first Weaver. The next two children were twins—Blania, who became the first Whisperer, and her brother Balat a Listener. And their younger brother Emil awoke to find himself the first Shaper. Only Dobradab, who had been awake with his parents, was not Blessed, like the rest of them.

"Discovering their new abilities, the children of Abet went to the nearby town and word of their powers quickly spread. The tales soon reached the greedy ears of Waer, who heard of humans with the abilities that had hitherto been hers alone. So Waer sought their camp that night, doing battle with the children of Abet.

"Waer was a terrible thing to behold, tall as a mountain and with sixteen heads shaped like snakes. But the children of Abet easily defeated her, not because of their Blessed abilities, but because they were doing the will of Sol."

To Marta's surprise Caddie did not turn away and return to her bix sticks as she had done during Luca's tale. He was by far the more gifted storyteller, but as she went on with her story, Marta felt her cadence changing, her voice shifting to match the ebb and flow of the tale. If she so desired, Marta could have quoted the scriptures verbatim from the Biba Sacara. All Cildra children were required to memorize the texts, the clan using specific quotes from the Biba Sacara for when general missives needed to be broadcast widely on the Dobra network. Though she could have recited the texts word for word, Marta instead added her own take to the tale meant for Luca.

"The evil Waer driven off, Abet realized the good his Blessed children were capable of and therefore sent them out to make the world a better place. Only Dobradab was ordered to remain, his father telling him that it was because he loved him dearest of all. But Dobradab knew in his heart of hearts the real reason was because he was the weakest.

"And though Dobradab was meant to inherit his father's lands and herds, he coveted his siblings' powers. So that night he went out to the nodus of the Nine Lines and summoned Waer. She answered his call, not as the serpent, but as the beguiler, and Dobradab begged her to make him Blessed, like his brothers and sisters. Knowing that Dobradab was not made Blessed because he had stayed up that night while his siblings slept, but that his eyes were already too opened to do the will of Sol, Waer granted his request, bestowing a fourth Breath in his Mind.

"Suddenly Dobradab found himself a Listener, able to hear the thoughts of others. But what's more, he realized he could hear the thoughts of anyone on the lines of ley that he touched. He was like a spider, the lines of ley the strands of a web in which he sat at the center.

"Reveling in his newfound powers, Dobradab hurried to show them to his father. But when the righteous Abet heard that his son's powers came from Waer, he knew no good could come of them and threw Dobradab out. Enraged by this, Dobradab killed his father, Abet's dying words a curse that Dobradab would find no peace so long as Waer's stain remained within him.

"Hearing of their father's murder, the Blessed children of Abet returned to do battle with Dobradab. And together they easily defeated him, not because they were more powerful, but because they were doing the will of Sol. But despite the murder of their father, the Blessed children of Abet could not find it within themselves to kill their brother, would not harm a member of their own family as he had done. Instead they cast him out. And so Dobradab was exiled to forever wander the wild lands where the ley flow, his father's curse eternally upon him.

"And so Dobradab wandered all of Ayr, bringing misery with him wherever he went. His descendants also bear his stain, bringing misery with them wherever they go."

Marta suddenly felt lightheaded, as if she had drank too deep from some heady draught. Though Luca paced back and forth, Caddie had not stirred throughout her story. Marta expected her to now return to her bix sticks, but Caddie kept staring at her, face blank and without any sense of recognition.

"That's an unkind story," Luca spit. "It's stupid, with a cruel moral."

"You're right, the moral is stupid, but no more than any other story. There is no Waer any more than there is a Sol. The story's just a way simpletons explain away the past and try to make sense of the Blessed. Everything that happens in life, it's all by happenstance. There's no order to it, no plan, no Sol guiding it."

"That's your moral? That life has no meaning, no purpose?"

"No." Marta rolled her eyes at the uncomprehending man. "The moral is beware of what you wish for. For instance, Davis Dunderhill is seeking us out, and tomorrow he will find us. But when he does, he will wish he never did."

Chapter 23

Blotmonad 18, 563 (Four Years Ago)

Marta hated the city of Sinton with her whole heart. When she visited it as a child, she found pleasure there, but now she wished the place was a man so she could slide her Shaper blade slowly across his throat. She dreamed she had a bowl big enough to pour poison upon the entire city and drown it in horror. Marta would save the coronet player though; he had earned his life with his skill, but no one else in that Sol-forsaken place would survive if she had her druthers.

Called the Jewel of the East, Sinton was the center of industry for the state of Nahuat and the Covenant as a whole. Perched high on a cliff behind its high walls, it was said it could never be overrun by the West.

So far that claim had proven correct, the city buried deep enough into the Eastern territory that they had time to fortify before Underhill reached it. In addition to its high walls, miles of trenches and tunnels now spread out around it, all occupied by Eastern forces. Their sappers also left thousands of traps and pits hidden for their enemies, cutting the first wave of Western attackers to ribbons without having to fire a single shot.

Encountering Sinton, Underhill blundered yet again by choosing to lay siege to the city rather than bypass it as he cut to the heart of the Covenant. He claimed his choice was a victory for the West: though the Sinton factories might still be running, they could not deliver their sorely needed munitions to the Eastern troops. He believed a strategy of economic attack would prove more useful than the symbolic victory of capturing the Covenant capital of Oreana.

Underhill compounded his mistake when he called the Traitors Brigade away from their successes on the southern front to join his pointless cordon. Here the Traitors Brigade waited for two months, the siege having gone on another four before that. Having stymied the Western advance, the city of Sinton became another rallying cry for the Eastern troops, who believed that so long as the city could not be felled, the Covenant armies could not be beaten.

It was, of course, not true. Cut off from supplies by the Western armies, the people of Sinton would eventually be starved into submission, but until that time the Traitors Brigade paid the price for Underhill's latest blunder.

The land had already been picked over twice by the time they arrived, Rupert's usual skill in foraging reduced to almost nothing. So he instructed them to tear through any rotten wood they found for bugs, showed them how to dig for wild tubers before the ground froze. Rupert also began unloading the herbs he collected over the last year. Carefully set in the sun to dry when not deployed, Rupert had amassed quite a collection of flavorful seasonings. Marta initially wondered why he did not use these herbs when preparing the tasteless Shapers' meals, but now she understood, as Rupert traded his flavor to the other troops for food. Outfitted by the quartermasters' stores, the Western soldiers were well-fed enough to value seasoning over sustenance, making Marta hate them just a bit more.

Marta originally tried to keep order among her Shapers by continuing their training each night. But soon her soldiers were too tired, too weak for any unnecessary exertion, and so she had suspended any activities that did not pertain to finding food. Soon they would be too weak to fight, Marta again angrily explaining this to Bumgarden as she met with him over dinner.

Bumgarden took her outburst well, again reminding her that his hands were tied. General Underhill had left explicit instructions that the Traitors Brigade was to remain unsupplied from the quartermasters' wagons.

"Dunderhill's going to lose the war that way," Marta cried. "He's weakening the one force that's proved successful!"

Bumgarden did not dispute this, instead giving Marta half his own rations despite the edict against it. It did little to sate the hunger of her troops, the nourishment spread too thin among the remaining 187. They would be reduced to boiling bark and dried leaves soon.

Their weakness did not stop Underhill from occasionally flinging his forces against the city, the Traitors Brigade always at the forefront of his charges. But the Eastern pits and trenches were treacherous, as proven that day when Domingo Bousall stumbled to expose their flank to a barrage of grapeshot. Her platoons were cut to ribbons, Marta watching as Collins Mahon, Fernando Pardue, Andrea Farley, and Orson Lackie fell along with nearly the entirety of the musketeers they were transporting.

Their corpses littered the ground around her, the carcass of her mobile fortress butchered and left on the battlefield to decay along with the men and women inside. The bodies trailed all the way back to the Western line, no one able to retrieve them under the heavy fire from the Eastern trenches. Though the citizens might be starving, Sinton still could produce munitions to defend itself. It seemed that if the Covenant army could feed off of musket balls, they would live forever, and the Eastern soldiers sought to share their bounty with their enemies, delivering the bullets one at a time through a constant hail of fire.

The Traitors Brigade remained trapped in the no-man's land throughout the day, pinned down as the winter winds ripped down upon them. So they hunkered behind their fallen shields, digging themselves deep as they could in the frozen dirt as they waited for rescue.

Night had been upon them for several hours now, the darkness allowing the Breath of the dying to illuminate the ground as it departed now-hollow bodies. Marta watched as four arose into the air, the Breaths hovering there a moment like disoriented bumblebees before disbursing and floating slowly away. The four fragments meant the newly deceased was Blessed, probably a Shaper and one of Marta's own.

The dark hid the identity of the corpse, and Marta realized she did not care who it was. She would gladly sacrifice five of her own if it meant she could steal a moment of warmth. The wind was brutal, and as she shivered Marta found herself wondering what else she would give up for just a second of succor. Strangely enough, she found herself missing those nights in the Pit when she had Abner to keep her warm. She had thought that place a nightmare, but it seemed a sweet dream when compared to the ground surrounding Sinton.

The bloodthirsty Leon was not far off on the field, Marta having transferred him to her platoon to keep an eye on him. His eyes had wandered all over her in that time, the man now calling out from his cover.

"If you want some company, I'll gladly keep you warm."

Marta would willingly sacrifice him and considered taking him up on his offer, though not to share his body heat. Alone and unseen in the dark, she could finally put the mad dog down. But he was an adept fighter, and Marta decided he would live for now because he was still useful.

The dead were useful as well, Marta realized as she reached over to snag the shirt of Collins Mahon. The cloth gave way on her third tug, but Marta stretched herself farther until she finally caught his cold hand and hauled his corpse to join her behind her overturned shield.

Marta risked crawling out from behind her cover to acquire Andrea Farley, dragging her dead body back to her shelter inch by inch. With the two cold forms of her former comrades, Marta fashioned a screen against the chill, their bodies providing a bulwark against the wind's bursts. She cuddled against their corpses, their cold forms providing her a bit of comfort.

In that moment Marta understood misery in its entirety. Most believed misery had a purpose, its existence to make joy seem all the sweeter in contrast, but they were all fools. There was no real comfort, no joy or ease in life. Moments of joy just existed to make the pain of every day more pronounced since one could not understand the true depths of suffering without the dizzying heights of joy. Those brief moments were nothing but the carrot held before the plodding beasts known as humans, a goal they could never reach as they slouched stupidly on towards their inevitable deaths.

She could give it up, turn her back upon the carrot and walk slowly towards the city of Sinton until some musket ball took away her misery. By midnight Marta was genuinely considering this possibility when the coronet player finally set his instrument to his lips. Hidden away next to their crimson Covenant flag on the highest tower in Sinton, his first plaintive notes reached her despite the distance.

They were told his song was a tradition throughout the siege from the very beginning, and this same coronet player performed "The Sun Rises in the East" each night at midnight. It had to be the same musician because Marta had never heard the song delivered so beautifully before.

The melody was usually played with the harsher tones of the trumpet, but this musician used the warmer coronet, if by choice or the necessity of scarcity, Marta was unsure. Although traditionally a lively march to inspire the Easterners, the coronet player slowed it down until it was almost a dirge, each note a stab to Marta's heart by conjuring memories of Gatlin. It was more effective than any weapon they had thrown at the Traitors Brigade thus far by reminding them of the home they now fought against.

Marta knew it was a trap, but she still stayed up each night to listen along with the rest of her troops. It was so beautiful she could not help herself, the song a slow poison that stole her heart away, a venom that sapped her will to fight more effectively than their lack of food. But the best traps were the ones their prey walked into willingly, and Marta was yet another eager victim.

From nearby Marta heard the voice of a dying man sing along with the tune. His position on the battlefield ensured he was one of Marta's men, but she did not risk raising her head up to discover his identity. Instead she cuddled closer to the corpses beside her.

He sang for the entirety of the song, each word more ragged than the last. And as the final strain of the song died, so did the Shaper, his four Breaths rising into the air and scattering. Though no longer bound by his life, they still traveled together towards the city of Sinton and the nodus hidden within. The man was lucky, she decided. He had died in the East, his misery at an end, and some part of her envied him.

Marta truly hated the city of Sinton with her whole, withered heart.

Chapter 24

Winterfylled 24, 567

They broke camp before dawn, Caddie quietly playing with Luca's bix sticks as he shaved with his straight blade. He was about to reclaim them from the child when he stopped dead, peering at how they had fallen.

"What did you see?" Marta inquired.

"It's nothing." Luca still watched Caddie carefully as she picked them up in her indecipherable order. "Throw them again."

Caddie did as he bid and again Luca did not seemed pleased. Not waiting for the girl to perform a third throw, he scooped the bix sticks up and grinned at Marta.

"It's just a stupid toy."

But there was now a strain to his smile Marta could not ignore.

***

They swiftly hiked over the nearest hill through the predawn, their target the trace of smoke wafting into the air to show them the way to Underhill's dragoons. Leaving Caddie with their supplies, they stalked the last hundred yards through the trees to find the patrol still hunkered over their breakfast. The Western forces had left no picket line, allowing the three to slip up unseen. Their targets wore the insignia of the Arcus 2nd Dragoon Company, men Marta had fought with at Watkins Run not far from here.

Though they bore the same style of uniform and insignia, these were not the men Marta had fought beside. Just looking at them she saw they were nothing but six youths untested by the war. Only their sergeant appeared to have seen any action, his skin like leather. Again Marta could recognize her own as she kept an eye on the dangerous man. The rest of his platoon would prove easy pickings for the three as they fanned out through the trees.

Marta expected she would feel some excitement as she was again about to enter into battle. Instead she only felt annoyance, these troops just another inconvenience on her path to Ceilminster. Any fear or anxiety that used to precede a battle had been burned out of her from the Grand War, her formerly constant companion in her anger barely bothering to stir its sleepy head at the appearance of these boys.

She did not hear Isabelle's first shot with the sling, but watched as one of the soldiers in the back fell. The second joined him on the ground before their victims knew they were even under attack, Isabelle's third steel bearing striking the sergeant as he reached for his scattershot musket.

Marta was in motion at once, her rabbit legs covering the ground to crash into a knot of three before they could disperse for their weapons. The first she caught in the chest with her gauntlet, feeling his ribs give way through her exuded Breath. She had just belted the second in the head when Luca engaged the last straggler she could not reach.

The dragoon drew his long saber, Luca armed with his significantly shorter lockblade, but the man showed no fear as he regarded his foe. "Put that down, boy. It's already over. No need to get yourself hurt."

Marta's final victim surrendered without further violence, his arms high above his head when the dragoon with the saber foolishly reared back to swing the thing at Luca.

The attack was a clumsy attempt, its inelegance made more evident as the man stepped in on the swing. The saber never had a chance to cut him, Luca far inside its arc and now close enough to smell the boy's breakfast on his breath. Luca could have ended his life then and there with his lockblade. Instead Luca's left hand flew back to land a stinging slap to the boy's face.

Though the blow was more surprising than damaging, the boy stumbled upon the ground. Luca towered over his foe, the boy still clinging to the ineffectual cutlass as Luca reached down to help him up with the same hand that dropped him.

"Leave the pig-sticker. There's no shame in surrendering."

Marta disarmed her own adversary, the dragoon's arms above his head as she grabbed his saber and knife and hurled them away. Unlike his companion, he had resigned himself to his defeat and seemed more interested in his fellow soldier facing Luca than the indignity of his own surrender.

The boy on the ground swung his saber towards Luca, keeping the blade low as he flailed about. The awkward attack was meant to drive Luca back as he regained his footing, but Luca simply hopped over the blow, bringing the hilt of his knife down on the boy's head as he tried to stand. The blow was heavier than his last, the boy's eyes swimming as he plopped back to the earth.

"That's your last warning. Stand down while you still have the chance."

For a moment Marta thought the soldier would indeed yield as his grip on his saber slackened. Then the dragoon who surrendered to her called out.

"Don't give them the pleasure, Jackson!"

Marta could not decide if the fallen Jackson was not meant to give them the pleasure by standing down or by continuing his embarrassing assault. Either way, the boy leapt to his feet, the sword held at the ready. He brandished it defensively, the blade close to his body so as to ward off Luca's impending attack. Luca did not attack though, his mouth drawn tight and making his words clipped.

"I'm sorry."

Jackson's end came quickly, the boy tentatively jabbing with his saber. Luca easily sidestepped the lunge, catching Jackson's wrist with his free hand to drive the point of his lockblade into the attacking appendage until it pierced its way through to the other side. Blood bloomed bright red as Luca withdrew his knife, the boy dropping his saber and crumpling to join the discarded weapon on the ground.

Luca kicked the saber away, flicking the boy's blood off his blade before closing it. The act of kicking the weapon was purely perfunctory though. The injured boy was no more a threat to him now than when he held the saber. But although Jackson had held his tongue during the short battle, he now screamed bloody murder. His cries had a keening edge to them Marta usually associated with newborns. It was equal parts piteous and humiliating, and Marta felt shamed for having to bear witness to it. Her eyes sought out her latest victim, the one who told his companion to not give them the pleasure.

"Care for him."

"Care for him how?" he asked, his eyes horrified. He had not seen a punctured artery before, and Marta did not have the time or interest to explain how to fashion a tourniquet from his belt. Not that it would have done the wounded Jackson much good.

"Keep him quiet. If you don't, I will."

He hurried away to hunker next to Jackson, Luca watching over the two as Marta collected all the discarded weapons. The muskets she tossed into a pile beside the fire. She claimed the sergeant's scattergun though, tucking it into her belt as she made her way to the horses. She cared more for the beasts than she did for the men they usually carried or the weapons the men carried in turn.

Only when four horses were saddled did Marta realize the wounded Jackson was not screaming anymore. Walking over, she saw the grass stained crimson, the boy's life spilled away in a matter of moments, though he still clung to it. The other soldier tried desperately to comfort his dying companion, whispering over him, "You did good, made your father proud. You fought bravely and fell honorably."

It was the same silly refrain Marta had heard a hundred times before during the Grand War, but hearing it now raised her pique. What raised it even more was the look she received from Jackson. Though his gasps came in diminishing huffs, his eyes still had the strength to lock onto hers. Although he was weakening by the moment, his eyes still held a want, a need. He demanded something of her—seeking succor from her. He stared at her as if she could be his salvation, as if she could somehow deliver that spilled blood back within his dying veins.

Scant moments ago she might have been able to save his life, to secure the tourniquet to staunch the blood flow. Instead she saw to the horses, and due to this decision, his life was forfeit. He did not understand her choice, could not comprehend how those animals mattered more to her than his life, and this lack of understanding riled her all the more under his stare.

It was not her voice that broke the silence, rather Luca stating her thoughts. "There was no bravery on either side of this, no honor at all. To call it anything else is to lie."

Marta regarded the man invading her mind with his Listener abilities. Her companion was challenging her, Luca daring Marta to take action and end the situation he allowed to come to a head. So she extended her phantom blade.

The soldier caring for him did not notice, but Jackson's eyes went wide at its appearance. His eyes silently screamed for life, but Marta instead fed him death as she slid the blade across the dragoon's throat to speed his end. It was the only merciful thing she could do.

Luca shook his head as the last of Jackson's blood spurted out his throat. A sucking sound came from the wound as he gasped, but his final flailing at life ended quickly. His grin long gone, Luca offered the only benediction the dead soldier would receive.

"May your Breath's next turn on the wheel of life be better than this one."

His hands still on his dead companion, the remaining dragoon stared fixedly at Marta. She could tell this was his first encounter with death—the first time he was wetted by blood. How he responded would decide his fate and prove if he could accept the inevitability of death or not. It was a harsh lesson, but one the boy needed to learn if he would become a man.

Unfortunately, he did not heed her instruction, as he launched himself at Marta with murder on his mind.

She thrust her blade deep into his chest without a second thought, her face suddenly pressed to his as he went slack in her arms. She could see his shock firsthand, the look of surprise almost comical. He did not understand and now never would as she let him fall beside his comrade. The two dragoons' Breath joined Sol's flow within seconds of each other, now brothers in life and death. When the rest of their regiment found their remains, they might also share the same grave.

"That was unnecessary," said Luca, his voice barely above a whisper. "You didn't need to kill the boy."

"You were the one who killed him. I just sped what your damn lockblade started."

"I didn't mean the poor wretch with the saber. Him I gave two chances to walk away, so he earned his end. I mean the other one, the one overcome with grief. What did you accomplish by killing him?"

"I taught him the world's an unpleasant place," Marta answered evenly. "He had to learn that if he was to survive. He didn't."

Only then did Marta notice Caddie watching from the edge of the woods. The child may not have seen it all, but was sure to have witnessed Marta killing the two boys without hesitation. From another child Marta might have expected hurt or fear from this, but there was no judgment in the girl's blue eyes, only something close to curiosity. And that look irked Marta more than the want or confusion she had seen in the dead dragoons.

Marta grabbed two of the horses, pulling them to Caddie. Grasping the girl under the arms, Marta hefted her onto a horse as she called out to the others. "Truss up the survivors then take all the horses and supplies. We need to hie out quick."

Luca and Isabelle obeyed without comment, Marta about to mount up when Caddie slid off her horse. She said nothing, did not move, but her intention was obvious enough. Caddie wanted to ride with Marta rather than on her own. It was the actions of a coddled child, and Marta had no time for it as anger infected her voice. "Get on your horse, now."

"She can ride with me if—" Luca began, Marta cutting him off.

"This is not a discussion. She will do as she's told."

Caddie made no motion to obey, her blank eyes meeting Marta's dead ones. It was a stupid game of wait-and-see, and Marta had no time for games. So she grabbed the girl by the wrist, painfully hoisting her up and unkindly depositing her onto the horse.

The girl did not cry out at her rough handling as Marta mounted the beast behind her. Instead her hand reached down to cover Marta's, Caddie's finger fiddling with Marta's woven ring. Yanking her hand away, Marta kicked her horse's flanks, leading the way back to reclaim her haversack without a word.

***

Graff emerged from the cave and set out towards the Lead Mine Hills. As he walked he removed his glass eye to release the Breath within. While contained within the caves, he needed its knowledge to navigate the labyrinth, but now his need was again calling to him, its voice hard and demanding. He had no idea where his prey had fled to, but he was not worried as he continued at his unhurried pace. Something seemed to be drawing him as surely as the eternal flow of Sol. Both he and his quarry were like individual Breaths on the flow, moving on until they joined a ley. They might be on separate lines for now, but soon they would connect at a nodus, and when they did finally converge, nothing would stop him from carrying out his appointed task.

***

The stolen dragoon mounts were well-rested and fed, allowing the four fugitives to make good time even with the extra three horses in tow. Marta spotted the other half-dozen campfires from afar, most likely more of Underhill's patrols. She gave the campfires a wide berth, heading south rather than east and leaving the extra horses along the way until only the three they rode remained.

As they hurried through the woods, Marta's memory of the place came into clearer focus. Years ago the Traitors Brigade had fought in the battle of Watkins Run as a part of Underhill's command. It was this knowledge that she used to convince Luca and Isabelle of her plan the night before. She knew the land well, the city of Point Place and its nodus not far off, so Marta turned the horses to avoid it and the colonel stationed there.

Davis Underhill was a man she detested, not just personally from her suffering at his command, but on principle. He came from a long line of military men, his ancestry dating back even before the war for independence from Acweald. The name of Underhill was intimately entwined with the history of Newfield, his father's last command proving instrumental in the Newfield defeat of the Mynian forces to claim the state of Lacus. Like his father, Davis Underhill attended the prestigious New Spring Military Academy. Unlike his father's innate military acumen, Davis constantly demonstrated he was a middling student. His pedigree still proved enough to overcome his shortcomings, landing him a starring role in the Grand War, but upon his appointment Underhill seemed to be doing his damndest to ensure his surname would not withstand his blunders.

In the battle of Watkins Run, Underhill had been outmaneuvered yet again, Loree using the land to his advantage as he outflanked his enemy. Underhill never understood how to use terrain properly, and Marta was sure that with her knowledge of this area, they could slip away before he even knew they were near. If they were lucky, the bodies they left behind would be the only evidence of their passing. If her plan held, they would be across the Mueller Line and out of Underhill's grasp by nightfall.

All this in mind, the sound of the dragoons' bugles took Marta by surprise. Luca also appeared taken aback as he hurried his horse to come up alongside her.

"How did they sniff us out so quick?"

"Doesn't matter," she answered as she shifted their course eastwardly. "And even if they have come across our trail, they can't follow our tracks at a gallop. We just need to stay ahead of them and ford the Limestone River. There's a crossing we used during the war, and these greenhorns won't know it. So long as they don't see us cross, we'll have a river between us and them. We'll be home free."

Luca nodded his assent, Marta keeping one aspect of her plan hidden from his Listener talents. This maneuver would be risky since there was a large stretch of dangerous open ground between them and the bend. Speed was now of the essence as Marta urged her horse on.

The bugles edging ever closer, they galloped at a breakneck pace for the open ground. As the trees began to thin, Marta breathed a sigh of relief. Once they made it across the river, they would be safe.

The lake they found when they broke through the woods took Marta entirely aback, the dam in the bend not having existed when she was there last. They were suddenly caught on open ground, the body of water too vast to cross and the dragoons closing in on either side of its shore.

"What is this?" Luca howled. "Where's your bend?"

Marta was too caught off guard, too dumbfounded by this inexplicable lake to respond. Her eyes traced the edges of it, realizing she had no idea where they led or what to do now.

"Marta? Marta!"

His cry jolted her out of her torpor, but Marta's thoughts were still scattered. "This lake wasn't here before. I didn't know. The bend must be..." Marta trailed off as she realized that Underhill had finally learned how to turn the terrain to his advantage.

Her horse paced as Marta's mind whirled. She had been outsmarted by the ineffectual former general who could not have won a battle during the Grand War if his life depended upon it. Her anger flared at the insult of it even as their enemies encircled them. But with its clarity she realized there would be no escape this time. They had been outflanked and utterly outmaneuvered.

"What now?" Luca demanded.

Her Breath and her rage begged to go out gloriously, killing as many as she could before finally being shot down. Suicide by musket fire would at least be a quick end to her miserable existence. But there was an even greater leviathan swimming in the depths of Marta's mind that dwarfed her anger, a survival instinct that reared its head now. She had somehow survived the Pit and the Grand War, and she had no intention of being brought down now for some simpleminded little girl.

She had failed, but the situation was not untenable. Carmichael might still be able to salvage it, though he would no doubt make her pay for forcing him take a more active hand in the matter. Although both he and their father did not mind letting her suffer, neither had shown any predilection for letting her be executed outright. As she removed the stolen dragoon scattergun from her belt and dropped it upon the ground, she decided her and Caddie would be safe if they surrendered.

"Go if you want. I'm done running."

"But the girl? We need the girl!"

"You'll have to take her from me."

Marta did not bother to extend her blade during her challenge to the man. The thunder of the oncoming dragoons' hooves was enough to make Luca choose escape rather than claiming the child by force. Muttering several swears in the Dobra language, he galloped pell-mell for cover with Isabelle.

Only Marta and Caddie remained on the open ground when the dragoons broke through the trees. To Marta's surprise, Underhill rode at the head of the platoon, the man even more corpulent than when she had seen him last. They stormed towards the two, Marta noticing that Caddie was again toying with her woven ring.

"Enjoy it while you can. It will be the last time you see it."

It might well be the last time Marta would as well, the woman memorizing its feel on her finger as the horsemen surrounded them with their muskets aimed at her. Disentangling her hand from Caddie's, Marta deposited her on the ground and kept her surrender short.

"Here."

Underhill stared at Marta a long time as if he might recollect her. She had spent seven months in the same camp with him and knew him by sight quite well, but he did not recognize his former soldier in the least as he turned to Caddie.

"Come here, girl."

Caddie remained where she stood, her eyes on Marta.

"Go on. You'll be safe with him."

It was not an outright lie, but Marta felt there was some untruth there when she saw the gleam in Underhill's eyes as Caddie approached. He dismounted to help her up to his own saddle, Marta beginning to climb out of hers when the surrounding dragoons began to holler at her from behind their readied muskets.

Marta could not help but feel some degree of pride at their fear of this former Fury. Their wariness made them much more dangerous than the arrogant Render, their preparedness surprising her even more when Underhill tossed her a vial. Marta caught it, the weight of the thing horrifying, though she kept the disgust from her face.

"Drink it down before you dismount."

Marta did not need to look at the contents to know it was ekesh, the taste as revolting as she remembered. The effects were immediate, Marta not so much dismounting as tottering from her horse like a drunk. She was defeated, her head swimming as she realized that Caddie's dire premonition with the bix sticks that morning had proven correct. But one question still haunted her, Marta wanting to get it out before the ekesh consumed her entirely.

"What's the name of the lake?"

If they gave an answer, Marta never heard it, collapsing face first into the dirt as the drug divorced her from her consciousness.

Chapter 25

Solmonad 13, 564 (Three Years Ago)

Bumgarden saved Marta after the failed charge by sending Abner slowly picking his way through the battlefield in his phalanx the next morning. They left the interior empty of fighting men, instead filling it with Shapers and sleighs to collect both the living and the dead.

There were too many casualties to bury in the frozen ground, the Traitors Brigade's Shaper strength having been utterly depleted that day in Blotmonad. Marta could not remember the names of all who died on the wrong side of the Grand War, but through their sacrifice they allowed the survivors to continue slogging on a little longer. And soon the dead served as bait.

"So the Ellian crows ate," Reid quoted from the poem. The saying meant only crows feasted well during battle, but to Marta and her starving forces, it was an epiphany.

Upon hearing Reid's quote Rupert instantly sprang into action, setting up thin wires above the dead bodies of their comrades to catch the crows' wings when they descended to eat. The Shapers devoured the carrion crows in turn, feasting on the eaters of the dead. And they ate well a few days until the murder of crows dwindled down to nothing. The bodies of their fallen friends still acted as bait, but now there were only people left to be tempted.

Stacked into small piles like logs, the corpses taunted the starving Shapers, Marta overhearing whispers from some of her men that their fallen comrades might still be of use as meat. It was a horrible jest, but Marta suddenly found her mouth watering as she imagined how good Andrea Farley might taste.

It was this desperation that made her turn to Bumgarden with her plan. She had traveled to Sinton as a child, as had Reid. Better yet, Taylor Keeting, one of her Shapers, had grown up in the city and knew its layout well. She believed a small force of her Traitors Brigade could steal inside to open the gates and replace the Covenant banner with the Newfield flag. This would be a sign to the Eastern soldiers outside the walls that Sinton had finally surrendered, and with any luck, they could take the entire city with their deceit.

Bumgarden agreed it was a sound plan, but General Underhill still commanded the Western siege personally, and he would never entertain such a daring gambit. It would be treason for Bumgarden to ignore the chain of command and earn him a date at the end of a rope. Marta was crestfallen, but not surprised, gathering her meager meal to share when Bumgarden spoke.

"Which is why I will dine with Underhill tonight and will be utterly unaware of anything you and your men get up to. I have a lovely bottle of rye that's just arrived, Underhill with a particular weakness for that draught. I'm sure he'll miss morning reveille again, and I'll be forced to lead the morning maneuvers myself."

He regarded her closer, assessing the gaunt woman, who looked no more than a bundle of sticks bound up in a bag of parched flesh. Finally, he pushed his own untouched plate to her.

"If the gates go down, I will lead the 1st Shapers across the field personally."

***

Marta dutifully dropped her doubled stores into Rupert's pot, calling Reid, Abner, Leon, Taylor Keeting, and another six Shapers to join them. Soon as she did the whispers started, flicking through the ranks like the lightning from a summer storm. The plan was no secret among her men, and they knew it was about to finally be put to action.

To her surprise, Tollie retrieved her food and moved it to a much smaller pot. She eyed the weak-willed farmer unkindly, but he held her gaze. "It's not enough for everyone," he said. "We need you to be strong, or else the rest of us won't ever eat again."

Her troops had decided without Marta's knowledge, the lot of them choosing to forgo the shared pot so those on the mission could take it all. It was a dear sacrifice, but Marta remained unmoved as she gobbled down her share. Though her teeth were loose as she chewed, she knew they had made the right decision. She also knew her squad would be the lucky ones if they were caught and executed. The death of the rest of the Traitors Brigade would be a slow and more painful ordeal if they failed.

***

They set out soon as it was dark, skirting the city until they reached the sludge. Sinton's sewage exited the city from high on the craggy hill it was built upon. The grate it sluiced through was well-guarded, as the Westerners learned when they tried to send their own sappers through it into the heart—or, more accurately, the gut of the city.

Not a single soul returned.

But the grate was not the Traitors Brigade's target, rather the sludge it produced. Constantly flowing, it had never frozen during the winter, providing them a hidden path to reach the walls of Sinton. Reid and Rupert fashioned long tubes they clasped in their mouths, the tops reaching above the sewage and allowing them air beneath the waste while not giving their position away. Again the inspiration came from one of Reid's remembered legends, and Marta hoped the Covenant defenders were not as intimately familiar with the story. It was slow going as they tread the clinging silt of the river of sewage, the twelve of them blind to the world around them and aware only that they must continue onward.

Reaching the base of the hill, they chanced raising their heads above the slime and heard no cries of alarm when they emerged. So they waited, shivering in cold shit until midnight when the coronet player sounded his mournful song. It was as beautiful as ever, but no one in her squad sang along. They knew if they succeeded this night, the Traitors Brigade would soon tear the heart out of the East.

They waited another three hours after the melody before they made their ascent. The men Marta had chosen were those with the greatest understanding of her Cildra training, each able to fashion both the rabbit legs and gauntlets that aided their climb. It was hard going first up the side of the hill then the sheerer stone wall as the spring winds attempted to tear them free. Marta briefly wondered if the weather was conspiring against them, trying to defend the city and the Covenant, but then they finally reached the summit of Sinton's walls and such flights of fancy were driven from her mind.

They divided into two groups: Taylor Keeting leading Abner, Reid, Rupert, and the other six men to take the gatehouse. The Covenant flag, crimson field with its single silver circle in the center, flying atop the tower belonged to Marta and Leon. Abner was about to depart with his troops when Marta caught his shoulder. It was still slick from the sludge, but quickly freezing again as she spoke.

"There's more ways than one to top the mountain."

He smiled wryly, pressing his cheek to her soiled hand. "By grace or grave."

He then disappeared with his men, leaving Marta alone with Leon. The bulk of the mission resided in opening the gates, which was why she gave the majority of her troops to Abner. Capturing the flag was important, though not crucial, which was why Marta selected only the two of them for the task. She was also still unwilling to let Leon out of her sight and was not pleased at all when he chose to skulk behind her as she led the way through the city.

Darting from alley to alley, they quickly arrived at the watchtower. Marta suspected they might have to dodge sentries on their path, but no patrols awaited them, the citizens of Sinton too assured by their high walls and the army outside to set watch within the city. Or perhaps they were too tired, starved into submission like the Traitors Brigade.

Being the highest point in the city and a perfect vantage point to watch the movement of Newfield troops, the tower would surely be manned. Marta considered pressing through the front door in a vicious rush, but decided if any guards sounded the alarm, it might spread through the city and end their plan before it truly began. So she opted to assault them from above, bidding Leon to follow her as she scaled the wall to the second story.

The window was barred from the inside, but Marta set her hand to it and summoned her open palm. She then pressed her Breath between the cracks, sliding it along until it found and opened the latch. Even in the dark she saw Leon's eyes gleam. She had never demonstrated this technique to any of the Traitors Brigade, Leon's obvious hunger at witnessing it proof she made the right decision. The idea of this horrid man being able to enter any home was almost more than she could bear. She was glad of his bloodthirsty nature now though, as they descended upon the unaware guards, Leon silencing four to her two.

They added barricades to the front door before beginning their ascent to the top. At each floor they paused to search for more guards and found none. They encountered no one but the guards on the ground floor, and by the time they neared the top, Marta allowed herself to believe they might succeed. It was then that Leon whispered to her.

"It was the Renders who caught me, but it was the will of Sol that put me in the Pit. He had a purpose—so I might meet you. Your beauty belongs to me, Marta."

The hairs on the back of her neck stood up at the touch of his voice. It was unclean, far worse than the river of waste they had just bathed in, and

Marta realized now was the perfect time to put him down for good. No one would mind the loss of Leon, her men sensing as she did that there was something off in his head. Using her body to screen her actions from Leon, Marta extended her phantom blade.

Suddenly, she heard a body drop, whirling to find Leon's own blade extended and a corpse at his feet. In her disgust Marta had unknowingly walked right past the hidden defender. Leon had saved her life, and in that moment kept his own, though Marta swore to herself that Leon Doyle would not live to see the end of the Grand War.

High above the city the wind buffeted them with all its fury, the Covenant flag snapping with each gust. The air was frigid, but neither felt it as they looked down to see the world spread out before them. Though still covered in the quickly freezing mire, they were suddenly above it all, seeing the sleeping world as Sol must have when he discovered Ayr. Marta could not comprehend happiness anymore, so it was not that she felt, but rather a sense of knowing that if she died then, she would at least be content. She may still smell of shit, but at least she had reached the top of the world as she summoned all her salvia to spit her hate down upon it.

Shortly before dawn the Newfield forces awoke, marshaling and turning towards the field. *At least Bumgarden was as good as his word*, Marta thought absently. It would be a cruel jest if they had performed their mission perfectly only for the Western army to abandon them there in Sinton. The Eastern ranks soon rose as well, checking their weapons as they prepared to meet another foolish Western charge. The slaughter would be terrible unless Abner succeeded, and each moment Marta waited seemed like an hour.

Just as dawn broke, the gates of Sinton began to ratchet their way up, the clamor of the protesting gears loud enough to turn the Eastern soldiers around to ascertain the source. From her height Marta could not make out their individual faces, but she was sure they must be full of both defeat and relief in equal measure.

Seven mobile fortresses began their ponderous march from the Newfield line, aimed for the open gates of Sinton. It was Marta's cue and she lowered the Covenant flag to replace it with the Newfield banner they brought with them. The Western flag was stained from their trip through the sludge, but Marta thought only she and Leon would notice as it unfurled in the wind. It appeared to all that the city of Sinton had surrendered, but the question remained if its defenders would accept their defeat.

The Western phalanxes continued their slow, steady march, reaching the first line of the defenders without a shot fired as the Covenant men laid their weapons down. Halfway through the Eastern rank, the foremost phalanx opened, Bumgarden emerging on his horse to lead the procession regally on. Marta's breath caught, not exhaling until he reached the gates. There, the mobile fortress opened entirely, spilling the Western army into the city to end the endless siege. Assured her plan had succeeded, Marta awkwardly folded the crimson Covenant flag before trudging down the stairs.

Dawn's light streaming through the windows allowed them to see the identity of the dead man Leon had saved her from hours before. He was more of a boy, really, judging by the fuzz that he had attempted to fashion into a beard. Thin and malnourished, the undignified pose he fell into during death made him appear all the more pathetic. He had been the last of Sinton's defenders, losing his short life in the attempt.

Despite her weariness, Marta's eyes were still sharp enough to catch the glint reflecting daylight from his pack. Shoving his corpse aside, she uncovered the boy's coronet.

"Shame," said Leon without much emotion. "He played beautifully."

"There's no beauty left anymore," Marta answered, her affect as flat as his. Throwing open the nearest window, she tossed the instrument out and continued on without a look back.

***

Her and Bumgarden's trickery was not revealed until the Western army was within the city walls, the Easterners outside suddenly caught between two enemy forces at either end. The Covenant army wisely surrendered officially not an hour later, the siege of Sinton broken before the hung-over Underhill even awoke. They had succeeded in breaking the back of the East; Ceilminster, Gatlin and Oreana the only major cities remaining to conquer. Glories would surely be heaped upon the man who rode at the head of the Western army, Bumgarden summoning Marta to his new headquarters situated in the mayor's office in City Hall.

Many adjuncts were at his side as she entered, Bumgarden dismissing them all at once to leave just the two of them. They had been alone together hundreds of times before, but outside his tent it felt different as Marta presented him the captured Covenant flag. He tossed the bundle to the table without a second thought, instead focusing his green eyes intently on Marta.

"I will not forget who really provided this victory and will ensure those miserly quartermasters open their wagons to the 1st Shapers. After today I should have enough pull to accomplish that at least. You deserve your fair share in the army that you've served so well."

Marta dully nodded at the promise of food as she watched a bit of sludge drip off her sleeve to mar the floor. The room was warm enough that the frozen filth covering her began to thaw, her stench in stark contrast to the fastidious man opposite her.

"Casualties?" she asked as if inquiring about the weather.

"Taylor Keeting both started and ended his life within Sinton. Other than that, only Rupert Kelly."

Marta knew she should feel something at Rupert's death, but all she could force was relief that they were promised a new source of food. She also wondered if Rupert would appreciate that it was his death that helped earn them their sustenance after singlehandedly supplying it for so long.

Bumgarden was staring at her again, and Marta realized she had not responded. Etiquette dictated she say something clever to commemorate the momentous event, but all Marta could muster was, "I'm sure you'll earn an engraved pistol now."

He nodded, but with the same patronizing look Mitchell gave when she did not comprehend some math lesson. "Yes, today was a career-making victory, but I plan on forging a new career now. I've outgrown the military and believe I'll try my hand at politics. Ruhl is up for reelection in Weodmonad, the fool still stumbling from his promise of a short war. He still craves peace, but peace is an old and outdated understanding. This is a new age, demanding a new form of peace. The nation of Newfield has gone too far now, the only victory possible an absolute one. The other generals don't understand this, and I'm afraid I cannot open their eyes by serving as one of their number. No, the only way I can save this nation is by becoming the Commander-in-Chief."

He extended his hand and Marta absently took it. It was the first time the two made physical contact, his hand dry and soft, whereas hers was rough and still dripping the melting sludge. As they connected Marta remembered of the first time she had seen him and how she had sworn she would end his and Kearney's lives. She had allowed fate to claim Kearney, and believed if she would ever make good on her promise of killing Bumgarden, now would be her last chance. But she was too tired for vengeance, too weary to care anymore.

"Will I have your vote, Childress?"

"I can vote?"

Bumgarden laughed long and hard before he removed his hand, a stain from touching Marta oily on his palm. He tried to wipe it away on his trousers, but only succeeded in smearing the shit deeper in.

"The army will be in Gatlin in a matter of months," he said. "Are you still sure your family will welcome you with open arms?"

Marta had not thought about her family in months—was too tired to think on anything but surviving until the next day. She tried to remember them then, but could only conjure the image of Oleander's brown eyes. The rest of her face remained a mystery, and Marta realized even if she could recollect the image of her sister, it would be too old to be accurate. It had been nearly six years since she last saw Oleander, the girl sure to have outgrown Marta's memory in the intervening years.

She finally felt something as she departed Bumgarden's presence without a word. It was loss for something precious, though Marta could not decide if it was the last scrap of her tattered innocence or an important opportunity that she had let slip away.

Chapter 26

Winterfylled 24, 567

Ekesh might taste far worse than the bark juice Marta was accustomed to, but the effects were far more pleasant. Her mind swimming, her senses numb, Marta did not have a care in the world when they tossed her into the cell in Point Place. The room was dry and warm, the stone floor surprisingly comfortable. So Marta remained there with her cheek pressed against the stone and eyes gazing fixedly upon her hand. It was a long while before she realized they let her keep her woven ring, its appearance confounding her. She knew it was missing and taken from her, but here it was on her hand.

Simply staring straight ahead as blankly as the kidnapped girl had, her thoughts never turned to Caddie or her mission. She did not realize Underhill had commandeered the town sheriff's cells, and neither did she notice the two soldiers checking in on her every hour before retreating back to their chairs in the lobby. Nor did she notice that there were nearly a score of other prisoners interred there in the building, though she was the only one in a cell alone. It was a long while before she realized they let her keep her woven ring, its appearance confounding her. She knew it was missing and taken from her, but here it was on her hand.

After the first hour the town's Dobra Cousins Listener burst in saying he had a message for the prisoner. It was sent from one Philo Frost, but Marta did not recognize the name and refused to rise as he recited it. Her eyes never flicked up at either his appearance or departure, instead focusing on her hand. It was a long while before she realized they let her keep her woven ring, its appearance confounding her. She knew it was missing and taken from her, but here it was on her hand.

***

Luca and Isabelle escaped because Underhill proved as much a dunder as the papers had dubbed him during the war. Not a few hundred yards within the cover of the trees, the two ditched their horses, slapping their flanks and letting them ride away wherever they chose. Disappearing into the wilderness was a tactic they were very familiar with as they scurried away before finally burying themselves under the fallen autumn leaves. In the confusion of the chase, their tracks would certainly be obscured by the dragoons' own—meaning they just had to elude capture until nightfall to make good their escape. The next few hours would be nerve-wracking as they waited for the horsemen to stumble upon them.

But after a half hour, they did not hear any hooves, Luca finally entertaining the idea that Underhill had not sent out additional pursuers after he sprang his trap. He might not even know about the two of them, their anonymity keeping them safe. They were small fish, and once Underhill had landed his big catch, it had not occurred to him to throw his line in again.

Luca chanced a glance up from the leaves, the woods still silent and with no sign of the soldiers. They could escape easily, but to do so they would have to return empty-handed and he had no intention of failing at his mission. Isabelle shot him a look from her camouflage as he stood, her thoughts clear in his Listening mind.

"No, we can still salvage this. They'll probably take the girl to the city."

Isabelle still did not move, Luca waiting until she silently said her fill. It ended with a string of curses aimed at Marta that were so inventive Luca could not help but chuckle.

"Wouldn't dare to argue with you there. She's probably already rotting in the ground, but if we're lucky, they'll horsewhip her with salted leather first. We can find out for ourselves in town. There will be a ley there, so we can find out what Simza wants done, at least."

He departed before she could respond, disappearing back the way they came. Isabelle remained under her cover until she could not hear him anymore, finally bursting from the leaves to sullenly catch up.

***

Graff's Breath watched his prey's capture from afar, returning to him once the girl was led away towards the city. He was still many miles away when it returned, but his Blessed Breath provided him more than just his destination:

it also provided him transportation.

The Render shifted course, turning from his straight path aimed at Point Place and crashing through the woods until he found the road. There, he waited, the family his Breath had spotted arriving within the hour. The draft horse pulling their wagon was not much to look at, but Graff smiled at their appearance. Sol had provided for His soldier yet again.

***

Dusk descended upon Underhill's house, the servants laying out a bountiful spread. Only two places were set, the host seating the much-sought-after daughter of Orthoel Hendrix across the long table from him. The portions were ample, the dishes divine, but the blue-eyed girl refused to eat, ignoring the appetizers, whereas Underhill had two helpings. She only stared straight across the table, not at, but through him as if he were not even there. Underhill had been the subject of quite a bit of bad press over the years, realizing only now that the only thing worse than scorn was to be ignored. Hate he could handle, but indifference was intensely irritating.

"You've certainly stirred up quite the hornet's nest," he boomed, the girl not flinching at his outburst, though several of the servers did. "Already got two messages from the big bug himself. He said to release you and the traitor, even though she killed two of my men."

Still, Caddie stared through him, Underhill waving for the servants to bring the next course as he met her gaze. Falling silent, he stiffened at her look.

"I may not have known their names, but they were still in my care!"

He attacked the next plate with redoubled gusto, Caddie's remaining untouched as he continued under his breath, "Never trusted that Frost, he's of no account. Well, go on. Eat!"

Spittle and specks of potato splattered the table with his eruption, the girl's composed indifference vexing him further. He set his fork down, announcing, "This tastes like ash."

The servants snapped to, ready to replace the dishes with the next course when he ordered them out. As the door shut behind them, the gleam that Marta had seen returned to Underhill's eyes at finally finding himself alone with Caddie Hendrix.

***

Luca and Isabelle stuck to the outskirts of Point Place, traveling through the woods to arrive at the ley. It was the Akoka line, one large enough to support a train and connecting up with the Cache line in East Neider before it continued its path on to Brimstone. The fact it was so large was good in that Luca's message would reach Simza sooner. It had its drawbacks as well—drawbacks Isabelle reminded him of with her look. Luca had no need to Listen to her mind to register her disapproval.

"Even if the Hammat do recognize me, they still have to raise the Cousins here first. And the Naphat tribe is not exactly known for their warlike ways. And even if they were," Luca teased, "they'd still have to deal with you, wouldn't they?"

Luca formed his mental message before Isabelle could object, his concentration on the act keeping him from hearing inside her head. The note was simple enough: just an order from one Millie Knowles for more flour from a mill run by Dora Carmody in Gatlin. Mrs. Carmody and her shop did not exist anymore than Millie Knowles did, and none except the Ikus Listeners in Gatlin would understand whom the transmission was meant for.

His message complete, Luca mentally sealed it up. When Simza taught him this trick, she instructed him to visualize the contents as a parchment contained in a glass luz jar. Only once the message was entirely secure could it be deposited into the stream of the ley without getting lost. Then the flow would do the rest, its current pulling the bottle down the line. Luca exhaled heavily as he released the message, the sense of water washing over him almost physical as the ley sucked his message away. Even by the time he blinked, it was already received at the next nodus, soon to be sent on down the proper line until it reached Simza. Now it was only a matter of waiting until she responded, Luca giving Isabelle his most reassuring of smiles as he removed his straight blade and the half-carved piece of wood.

Luca got to work whittling as Isabelle disappeared into the darkness outside the range of the ley. Though her father hailed from Newfield and Isabelle had spent nearly as much time away from her mother's people as with them, she still carried the Ingios mistrust of the ley. Luca had never been able to pry the why of it from her mind, Isabelle always switching to the indecipherable language of the Nahu tribe whenever she tried to explain it to him.

Isabelle hated Marta though, and was glad to be rid of her. That much she had made abundantly clear. Luca did not share his comrade's prejudices, either towards the ley or their former traveling companion. Marta had been by far the most mistrustful person Luca had ever met. She outshined even

Isabelle in that regard, a fact Luca was sure would irk Isabelle to no end if he gave voice to it. Marta was wise not to trust the two of them, though they meant her no physical harm and never had. If they had met by him buying her a drink rather than in that alley, Luca was sure Marta would have been more than happy to pick up the second round. More than just an outgrowth of his Listener talents, Luca knew he was awfully adept at collecting companions. He was innately able to put people at ease, and the fact that Marta was one of the few holdouts made him like the woman all the more. He heard ranchers felt the same about the colts they broke, valuing the spirited ones over the docile beasts that easily submitted to their will. But Marta was no colt to be broken. No, she was more of a frightened dog.

There was an old man named Onas in Luca's tribe growing up, a dried-up relic who barely spoke to anyone. Though no one knew how, Onas was wealthy with two horses and a wagon utterly to himself. Luca's sister, Esme, had yet to be born, so it was still just the four of them crammed into the same space Onas enjoyed alone. Onas ensured his solitude with his brute, a nameless mutt that was as mean as it was ugly. Luca would have sworn the animal was ancient when he was yet a toddler, but the dog still terrified the children of the camp even when he had reached the age of nine. The mutt seemed immortal, many of the adults telling the children that the dog would not die until Waer called her servant home. It never slowed as the years passed and only seemed to grow cleverer in its eternal war against the children.

So the children of the camp turned it into a game, seeing who could sneak up and touch the old man's wagon. It was a rite of passage that separated the brave from the boastful. Almost all tried, first reconnoitering the area to make sure Onas' dog was nowhere nearby. But if by magic or Waer's guidance, the mutt would always appear as if from the empty air in a froth of teeth and jowls to drive the child away. Some of the crueler boys chose not to wait until Waer called her servant home by slipping nails into scraps of meat and tossing them by Onas' wagon, but it never worked. Some suspected that the dog was simply too smart to eat the deadly meat, whereas others believed that it devoured all the scraps, but was just too mean to die.

Luca was not the first to touch Onas' wagon, but his feat was still talked about. This was not because he was braver than the other boys or even cleverer. It was because Luca was the only one to bother Listening to the dog, even though there were many other Listeners in the camp. He was the only one to spend the time to learn that, despite its gnashing jaws and rabid snarls, the animal was afraid. Luca could not see the cause in the mutt's muddy mind, but it feared everything in the camp, its master, Onas, most of all. So it aimed its wrath at everything around it, the mutt making itself seem terrible because it was terrified.

Armed with this knowledge, Luca invited all the boys and girls in the camp. His audience in place, Luca made his way to the wagon. But while others slunk to it on bare feet so as not to alert the dog with their footfalls, Luca instead marched on as if he owned the wagon.

The dog did not strike until Luca was only a few feet away. Luca had been watching for it, but did not spot the beast until its jaws tore through the air inches from his belly, its slaver splattering his shirt. It must have weighed more than he did, its barks so deep that Luca could feel them reverberating the earth beneath his feet.

Luca forced himself to stand his ground, to match the brute's eyes. The dog seemed to swell under his gaze, its maw moving up until it was snapping just shy of his neck. Others may have run before the aural onslaught of the beast, but Luca took a step forward.

The act was a gamble, a roll of the dice that paid off when the dog took a step backwards even as it redoubled its racket. So Luca took another step, the dog retreating at his advance until it was pressed up against Onas' home. Only when the beast's back hit the wooden wagon did it silence, its head sinking in submission.

Luca claimed his victory by lingering a long moment before touching the wagon at his leisure. Gazing back at his audience, he could see they were impressed, but he wanted to forge a legend that day. So Luca patted the dog's head. It could have crippled his hand, claiming a finger at least, but the terrified dog ultimately submitted to his touch because Luca was unafraid.

Actually, he had been nearly as terrified as Onas' dog. But in Luca's heart he knew he was capable of this task, and that knowledge was enough to tamp down his fear enough to face the beast. It was the first time Luca took part in this balancing act, to feel the exquisite torture of teetering between success and failure. In time he would find this feeling the most intoxicating emotion in existence, drinking deep through greater and greater tests of his ability.

Facing Marta was like his experience with the dog, the difference being he was quite sure Marta was not afraid to do more than bark; one misstep and he would lose much more than a finger. Getting close to her was therefore a much greater accomplishment. It was a shame they would not see Marta again, the two of them absconding with Caddie and leaving the woman to whatever hole she had dug for herself. But that eventuality still hinged on what Simza had to say.

Luca had decided to whittle away until his headache began. When it did, he intended to retire with Isabelle out of range of the ley and pick up Simza'a message in the morning from the Cousin Listener in Point Place. He need not have worried about the pain though, as his answer arrived in moments.

But it was not from Simza.

It was a general broadcast, sent through the entire line and addressed to Millie Knowles. The fact it was dispatched to his false name caused Luca concern, but it paled in comparison to the fear he felt at the fact it was a general missive. It would have had to come from one of the largest nodi in Newfield to have flooded the network so quickly: either Brimstone, Ceilminster, Polis, or, most worrisome, the home of the Public Safety Department in Vrendenburg.

But most frightening was the message itself, to be delivered "To the Traitor." The demand of the message was implicit, as was the threat of death if he refused.

Luca considered himself a cat, a sleek hunter making his meals of the mice that were the people of Newfield. The clueless citizens had no idea that a predator stalked among them, Luca's invisibility allowing him easy access to his prey. But now a dangerous new set of eyes had caught sight of him from on high. The originator of the message was a hawk circling far above, and to its indifferent gaze he would prove indistinguishable from the mice scurrying around him. Luca suddenly felt exposed on open ground. His first instinct was to disappear, to flee until he found a safe hole to hide in. But he also had the impression that he would neither be able to run fast enough so this new set of eyes would lose sight of him nor be able to find a hole deep enough where its talons could not reach.

His face must not have been able to hide his horror as Isabelle appeared beside him, her hatchet in hand as she peered about the darkness. Luca knew her preparedness would prove futile, and that the two of them and their pair of sharp eyes would never be able to spot this new threat until it descended upon them and silenced them for good.

Closing his eyes, Luca mentally thumbed through the message, but could find no meaning in it except for whom it was meant to be delivered to. The message itself was as good as garbage and made his head hurt worse than any ley headache as he sought to decipher it. All he knew was that he had to deliver it that night.

Luca's smile bloomed as he opened his eyes, bestowing both upon the skittish Isabelle. He only hoped his companion would believe his lie.

"Simza has spoken, and it seems we're not through with Marta Childress quite yet."

Chapter 27

Marz 21, 565 (Two Years Ago)

Bumgarden proved good to his word by soundly defeating Ruhl in the presidential election. He never seemed charismatic, had never raised his voice in Marta's presence, but the papers declared him a fiery speaker that drew crowds by the thousands. He beat Ruhl by a landslide, the vote count halted in a matter of hours. As soon as Bumgarden took office, his first act was to thankfully dismiss Underhill and take control of the Western armies himself.

He remembered the Traitors Brigade as well. *No, they were now the Furies*, Marta reminded herself. Not only securing them access to supplies, Bumgarden swelled their ranks with Western Shapers and renamed the company yet again. He had removed the moniker Traitor from their name and much of the stigma that came with it, but even with his newfound power, Bumgarden could not remove their physical scars. Marta oversaw the training of these new recruits in her Cildra techniques the same as she had with the Traitors Brigade, but only those that bore the brand did she consider her brothers and sisters in arms.

The Furies became victims of their own success, now at the forefront of every battle. But between Bumgarden's brilliant deployments and their perfected techniques, they were winning the war by pressing deep into Eastern territory with minimal casualties. The Furies leading the charge, the end of the Grand War was finally in sight.

But then the daemons appeared.

The monsters were one last desperate strategy by the Covenant government, now in exile in Ceilminster. Terrified of their impending defeat, their fear was the only possible impetus to create such abhorrent creatures under the tutelage of their resident emet Greybone at the Weaver university. Marta had heard rumors of the beasts skittering amongst the soldiers over the last few days, but dismissed them as simply battlefield gossip until she saw the daemon at the battle of Sherman Pass.

The encounter had been going well up until that point, the Western army pushing the Eastern forces through the pass in what would be yet another quick victory. Then the daemon arrived and ruined it all.

The monster was unlike anything Marta had seen before, made entirely of Breath like an emet, but nearly four stories tall and formed from the Weaving of at least two dozen Breaths. It was a glimmering colossus striding among men like a child among dolls. It tore through the Newfield ranks in moments, immune to their weapons and dealing out death in droves as it smashed men to nothing but vague smudges on the ground. It smashed through their phalanx as well, sending several one-ton shields sailing with an offhand swing of its massive arm. Many of her Shapers, born in the East and West both, died instantly as they were crushed beneath the shields designed to protect them. And still the daemon advanced, its assault hardly paused by their decimation.

Although formidable in size and strength, the daemon should have proven no more effective than the manifestations had at the beginning of the war when facing Renders with their glass blades, and so the contingent of Renders soon arrived to do battle with the beast. But their Blessed drawing proved futile against the daemon, their glass sabers shattered along with their bones by the titan. The Weavers had finally discovered an answer to the Render's drawing, the scholars in Ceilminster demonstrating their new superiority on the battlefield to their enemies who shared their fourth Breath in the Soul.

The solitary daemon collapsed the Western ranks, singlehandedly shattering their lines and sending the army into a full retreat. Though snatching victory from their hands, the daemon did not follow them on their flight. The dismantling of their fighting force had been too swift, their destruction too abrupt for the Weavers controlling the beast at a distance to catch up. But aided by their abomination, the Eastern forces secured the Sherman Pass and sent the Western armies reeling.

It was nearly twenty miles before the Newfield forces regrouped. Hurrying through the bivouac, Hugo Propst, Bumgarden's replacement for commanding the Furies, took Marta to meet with their new general, Erla Grubb. Bumgarden never bothered to bring Marta with him to meet his superiors, viewing her as a subordinate at best and, more likely, nothing more than a clever pet. Although he was more than happy to consider her innovations in private, the two of them arguing in his tent as if they were equals, she was never treated as such in front of anyone else.

Propst proved much kinder, giving Marta free rein in the administration of her troops and attesting to the fact he was just a rubber stamp to give her commands the illusion of authenticity. He never had any illusions as to who ran the outfit, often deferring to Marta when in the presence of his superiors. Although she had never cared for Bumgarden, Marta at least respected the man. Propst treated her better, like a fellow human being, and for that she detested him.

Though General Grubb was a woman, Marta received no sisterly kindness from her since Grubb despised all things Eastern and Marta in particular. Another of Bumgarden's recent appointments, Grubb was incredibly effective, and for that reason Marta endured her disdain without complaint. In Grubb's tent they learned that not one, but four daemons had been deployed that fateful day along several battle lines, all the Renders and Western forces suffering heavy casualties. The Newfield army was on the run, and Grubb demanded that they halt the rapid Eastern advance.

That night Abner asked Marta about Grubb's decision to face the daemons. When she told him, he fell silent a long time, finally taking her hand and saying, "I have a wife—Della in Meome, Aiou. If I fall, will you write them and say I died bravely?"

Marta nodded, not willing to break the pall smothering the Western encampment. It was Abner who finally did.

"And if you die, where should I address my letter?"

She pulled her hand away, walking off without a word. There would be no need to tell the Childress family if their middle daughter had died. Marta was sure they would already know.

***

The next engagement two days later proved just as deadly for the West, another squad of Renders massacred when they tried to face a daemon on its own terms. The Furies had transported them, Marta watching their swift slaughter from the slit in the shield Gonzalo carried. The Furies did not have a chance to retreat before the daemon turned its wrath upon them, scattering their phalanx as easily as the last one had.

It was Gonzalo who saved both her life and the Western war effort as he snatched up one of the fallen Renders' glass blades, racing at the daemon as it turned toward the dazed Marta.

She thought his sacrifice would prove as pointless as the dead Render's whose saber he carried, but when Gonzalo swung his blade, it miraculously bit deep into the creature's leg. To their amazement, the creature stumbled as its wounded Breath retracted into its body, Gonzalo's second blow severing the leg entirely. The daemon made no sound as it fell, but the realization that hit Marta was thunderous.

"The sabers," she cried, her voice carrying above the din. "Cut it down with glass!"

Marta did not look back to see if her troops obeyed as she leapt with her rabbit legs to claim one of the discarded glass blades. With the fragile yet strangely heavy weapon in hand, she rushed to Gonzalo's side, slashing the toppled daemon with all her might.

Leon joined them an instant later, the three swarming over the downed daemon like ants picking apart a dying bird. Those were the only three weapons her platoon could claim, the one Leon swung already shattered and nothing but a short stalk of glass wound round the steel core, but with them they hacked the daemon until it finally was no more. With each slice the creature's Breath retreated, retracting back into its body until they found the daemon's heart.

The device was no natural thing, rather a ticking engine of Tinker design with a glass center containing the daemon's writhing Breath. Leon unceremoniously smashed the meticulous machine with his boot, releasing the last of its abominable Breath and distinguishing him as the first to destroy one of the monsters.

Silence descended upon the field with the destruction of the daemon. Like the tale in the scriptures of Ezria and Giant, they felled the monster by cutting out its legs so they could dispatch the giant as it lay helplessly on the ground. Marta could already imagine Reid's quip alluding to this when the bark of musket fire began anew, the three carrying their glass blades with them as they retreated back behind the cover of their steel shields.

***

The Western forces were not victorious that day though, the oncoming Eastern troops still pushing them from the field, but they had earned a moral victory, at least, one that came at a high cost with the loss of five of Marta's men as well as the entire squad of Renders.

Yet it was the uncompromising Renders that nearly lost the survivors their lives back in the Newfield camp. There, the Renders' commander demanded the deaths of Marta, Gonzalo, and Leon for having dared touch a glass blade. Only Renders were allowed this distinction, any who defied their edict executed on the spot. The Render commander was ready to put them down then and there, his wrath compounded further when Marta turned her back upon him. Departing the meeting without being given leave, she hurled her final insult over her shoulder.

"You can go ahead and carry out your Sol-forsaken sentence once you've won this war. Until then, let us work."

Propst had to plead with Grubb then to President Bumgarden himself to intercede on their behalf after that. Grubb's rank of general was able to at least keep the Renders from executing them until Bumgarden gave his answer.

Their former commander and current president responded by sending a shipment of glass blades addressed to the Furies on the first supply train in the morning. As always he looked after his tools, making sure they were able to carry out their task in the most efficient means possible.

Armed with their glass weapons, the Furies proved to be the only force capable of dealing with the daemons by darting around them on their rabbit legs and cutting them to ribbons. But it was not true victories they earned, their numbers too low to do more than slow the advance of the Eastern armies. The Furies did not fight to win though, but rather to leave a mark upon their unstoppable enemies, to ensure they did not escape the conflict entirely unscarred. The Furies lost valuable men and women in each encounter, their deaths doing no more than providing cover for the Newfield army's retreat, first across the Mueller Line and out of the East, then deep into Western territory.

With at least a dozen confirmed daemons at his disposal, the Eastern general, Loree, made a mad push for the heart of Newfield with the intention of taking Vrendenburg. If he could capture the capital and Bumgarden within, Loree could end the war in one fatal stroke.

After another encounter with a daemon—the creature destroyed, but Marta losing Austin McMillen, Noys McCarty, and Delia Sumny in the fray—she decided their sacrifice was ultimately in vain. By chance and one horrible choice, the Traitors Brigade had ended up on the wrong side of this war, but she was too ground down now to care about their plight anymore. She and her troops would keep fighting, not because they were fighters, but because they were killers. The Grand War had made this of them and they could not deny their true natures any longer. They would fight and they would die, but she hoped they would take more lives than they lost.

If killing was what was called for, they would answer their calling without question.

Chapter 28

Winterfylled 24, 567

Ascertaining the jail's location was a bit of a gamble as Luca spotted a uniformed dragoon on the street of Point Place and marched right to him. Inquiring after an affordable saloon, he ignored the dragoon's words and instead Listened to the man's mind. Luca had stolen thoughts in this manner countless times before, but never from someone who may have been hunting him not a few hours earlier. The soldier was indeed a part of their pursuit, but had seen neither hide nor hair of Luca and Isabelle. As far as he was aware, they were only after the woman May Oles and the girl with her. Once their prey had been caught, the dragoons were given leave to celebrate their success, Underhill taking possession of the girl while the Traitor was sent to a cell in the sheriff's station.

Finding Marta proved no more difficult, the two freebooters slinking around the edge of the station and Luca hoisting himself up to peer through the barred windows until he spotted her. What was difficult was to behold Marta in her state, the woman not stirring when Luca whispered her name as loudly as he dared. She seemed to hear him, but could not force herself to even sit up.

"Ekesh," he whispered.

Isabelle pressed the bundle of herbs into his hand and he tossed them to Marta. They were only inches from her, Marta's face laboriously turning to look at them before she returned to her hands. Luca called her name again, but Marta did not look his direction.

***

Underhill strode to Caddie, the girl not even deigning to look his direction. The former general was used to men snapping respectfully to attention at his approach, her continued apathy infuriating him to no end. He wanted to slap her with all his considerable might, but she was only a slip of a girl and he thought perhaps the carrot might work before he brought out the stick.

"Have a bite, it's delicious."

The girl did not stir, Underhill suddenly snatching up a handful as he grabbed her head with his other meaty paw. Forcing her mouth open, he crammed the food in hard as he could. And there the food remained until her mouth opened slightly, the victuals dribbling down her chin to plop on the table. Again he wanted to hit her, but his voice softened instead.

"It's not poisoned, see?"

He took another handful and chewed it to show her. Still she did not move and he finally had enough. Levering her jaw open, he drew the masticated mess from his own mouth and shoved it into hers. His hand then covered her face, particularly her nose as he waited.

It took longer than he expected, but finally the girl swallowed, Underhill beaming at his victory. "So you do understand. Now, will you eat the rest yourself or will I have to help you some more?"

The girl remained motionless, so Underhill seized another handful and began to chew.

***

Marta was vaguely aware that something significant was occurring around her, but the what of it still eluded her. She tried to concentrate on the situation, but the only image she could manage was the pair of blue eyes. They were indelibly tied to her somehow, but they did not make any more sense than the ring on her finger. Had not the Home Guard taken it from her just that night in Vrendenburg? How was it then that it was returned to her now?

Isabelle finally shoved Luca aside to hoist herself up and peer inside. One look at the woman within and she spat contemptuously upon the ground, letting herself down and stalking away. Yet Luca returned to the window, his voice even louder as he called, "Marta."

To his surprise she finally stirred, calling out, "Carmichael?"

Confusion swept over Luca at the name. He had never heard Marta speak it before, had never caught it when he had brushed her mind. The woman had been quite adept at keeping her thoughts hidden from him on their journey, but under the effects of ekesh, her will was gone and allowed him easy access as he Listened in.

Her thoughts were scattered like debris after a hurricane, the school of fish that usually made up a notion ignoring each other and swimming individually on indiscriminate loop-de-loops. But one was close to the surface of her mind, Luca able to spot it at once. It was her brother, Carmichael Childress, now head of the Public Safety Department.

Luca's air departed his lungs at the realization. If this was true, then her brother headed both the Home Guard and the Newfield spies. He was most likely the man who sent Luca the message to deliver to Marta, which meant he was in greater trouble than he had previously imagined. Luca considered making a run for it then and there when Marta cried out again.

"Carmichael!"

***

Chewed food covered both Underhill and Caddie's faces as the man basked in his total triumph over the girl. She ate the entire plate just as he had ordered. His hand still slick with saliva, he held her chin and turned her head back and forth as he examined her face.

"I know what you are. You're not ripe yet, not ready to be plucked, but even green fruit can make a sustaining meal if prepared properly."

***

Marta cried her brother's name louder the third time, Luca sure if she continued at this rate, she would soon summon the guards. So he answered.

"I'm here, Marta, and I have a message. Are you listening?"

An inarticulate grunt escaped Marta's mouth as she swung her head like a lowing cow. Luca could not decide if this was meant as a yes, but passed his message on nonetheless.

"And I looked to behold the nodus split, Sol the Father stepping from the ruins, the light of truth in one hand, a sickle in the other. And Sol looked over the multitudes, the wicked and righteous alike and He spoke. 'The Harvest has come.'"

Luca was no scholar and disdained the Biba Sacara, like most Dobra, for how it portrayed Dobradab. He did not understand the significance of this scripture, but the message had an effect on Marta, the woman attempting to stand, but only able to rise to her elbow.

Marta closed her eyes to concentrate. It was hard, her thoughts hardly hers to control anymore. There was a message she was meant to understand in the Cildra code, but the crux of it eluded her. All she could see in the dark behind her eyelids were two blue orbs.

"Again," she slurred.

Luca repeated the message, and upon hearing it Marta claimed the bundle of herbs to place them in her mouth. The medicine cleared her head somewhat, but it was the image of the blue eyes that prompted Marta to her unsteady feet. They, coupled with Carmichael's message, meant she had to move.

"He's going to kill her. Underhill, he's going to kill Caddie."

Her rage was there fueling her movements, but for once the clarity did not come with it, the effects of the ekesh too strong to simply shake off. The drug had unmoored her from herself, made her unable to connect with her Blessed nature. It was still there, Marta was sure of it, but she could not uncover it.

Marta inhaled deep, closing her eyes again as she searched herself. Soon she found it, her Blessed Breath nestled deep in her chest next to the Body. It was feral and thrashing, riotous as a wild stallion. Marta set her will after it, struggling for control until a single pinprick of Breath escaped her fingertip. It was not much, but it was a start.

"Just use your Armor to come through the wall," the exasperated Luca called.

"Too many moving parts," she shot back before examining the lock to her cell. It was a simple one, but the open palm she required was a complex technique. Given enough time she should be able to spring it, but time was in short supply. "If I'm not out by a 500 count, you have to rescue Caddie on your own. Promise me you will."

Luca considered. Rescuing the girl had always been his goal, with or without Marta. He and Isabelle could probably accomplish it alone, but Marta's brother would not appreciate them leaving his sister to rot. Marta was the key to their success, but she would not be able to escape without a dear sacrifice on his part. So Luca snapped open his lockblade and shoved it through the bars. And there it remained, Marta unwilling to take it.

"What good's a knife now?"

"It's not the blade that's important. Just keep it open and you cannot be defeated."

He seemed so sure of himself that Marta was nearly swept up in his confidence as she took it. "This is quite a gift."

"More a loan," he said quite sincerely. "I expect it back in less than a 500 count."

For once it was Marta who grinned. “But how are you going to take it from me if I cannot be defeated?”

***

“Look at me,” Underhill demanded as he plucked a knife from the table, its edge sharp and serrated. The girl did not, and so he twisted her neck until she faced him. She peered straight ahead, straight through him, and his resentment rose again as he picked his teeth with the blade.

“I’m tired of being the low rung, sick of the others simply stepping on me as they climb higher up. They would not be where they are if not for me. Loree only appeared a genius because he had a good partner who knew all the steps. It’s a hard thing to lead the dance without anyone the wiser, to make your partner seem gifted through your stumbles.”

Hunting after a speck of food stuck between his teeth, Underhill dug too deep and sliced his gums. It was only a slight cut, but the coppery taste of blood flooded his mouth. It meant he had made yet another mistake, but he savored the taste nonetheless.

“In the scriptures when people turned away from the will of Sol and sought to summon Waer, they needed to sacrifice something. It’s the mix of blood and Breath that brings her for a bargain, they say. If that were true, she was forever at my side during the Grand War. Thousands died for me, thousands and thousands again. It was so easy in the beginning. Everything was so clear, so obvious. Inspiration was just below the surface, willing to come forth with just the slightest nudge. But now it’s burrowed deep, and no matter how I dig, I can’t find it anymore, can’t hear her voice. I know it’s still there, yet I just can’t find it. But you, you’re obvious and gleaming like a nodus in the dead of night.”

Wiping his blood and the bit of offending food away on his sleeve, he set the knife down to unholster the silver pistol from his waist. Since his demotion he was not allowed to wear it outside his home, but he was home now as he considered Caddie again.

“Why don’t we see if together we can summon Waer here tonight?”

Chapter 29

Septembris 14, 565 (Two Years Ago)

They retreated until they could not retreat any farther, finally setting up their fortifications at Fieldhollow, a city only twenty miles from the Western heart of Vrendenburg. Nothing stood between the raging Eastern forces and the capital but the scattered remains of the once-mighty Newfield army, now not numbering more than two regiments in size. The troops were a motley gathering at best, only fragments of once proud divisions: the remains of some sabermen here, a squad of musketeers there, and the untested reserves making up the rest. The Furies were the most useful unit, but they were only a fraction of their former strength, their numbers, even swelled by the new Western recruits, down to less than half of what they had marched off of Mitkof Island with.

Despite their shoddy state, the Grand War would be decided in Fieldhollow. President Bumgarden's personal note to Marta said as much when he ordered her to hold the line for three days. He had not disbanded the government, had not retreated, instead remaining in Vrendenburg to stake his life on Marta and her Furies. It did not ultimately matter to Marta who won the Grand War. Newfield was too far gone to save now. She only hoped this battle would do the merciful thing and finally let the nation die.

Marta had every intention on holding the line though. She would not do this for Bumgarden, for Newfield, or the Covenant, her father, or even herself. She would hold the line because she had been hollowed out by the war, all her humanity spent and leaving nothing but a shell. She was a far better killer now than she had ever been a Cildra spy, so kill she would until the grave; no grace left in the world for such as she.

And hold the line the Furies did the first day of fighting in that blustery Septembris, setting up their phalanxes between the Browns River crossing and the Kuk line of ley that ran alongside it. There, they met the vanguard of daemons preceding the human Covenant troops alone on the field, waging war against four and smashing each of their glass hearts.

Their victory came at a cost though, nearly two dozen soldiers dying including Gonzalo. Marta was unable to say goodbye as his life bled out of him. She instead continued the fight knowing he would understand, knowing that he fully realized the harsh realities he hinted at with his stargazing. She had no comfort to give him because there was no comfort left in all of Ayr, only bloodshed that she perpetuated. He died looking ever up at the sky, though his precious stars were not out in the daylight to greet him. At least he died looking up. His body might not be anything but an empty husk now, his Breath scattered to the winds, but at least he would be bathed in starlight when night descended.

***

The next morning as the Covenant forces continued to gather along the Eastern bank, six daemons approached, Marta aware her depleted Furies would have no chance against their number. So she took the remains of her troops through the woods on horseback, the Eastern army having established no flank across the Browns River. So while the daemons battered the Western forces, Marta and her men struck at the Weavers controlling the monsters, catching them unaware and slaughtering them to the man.

At the death of their Weaver masters, the daemons disengaged, not turning for home, but crashing mindlessly through the woods surrounding Fieldhollow. The devastation they wrought wherever they trod was truly horrible, but at least they were not aimed at Vrendenburg any longer. The countryside could absorb the damage, whereas the fragile capital could not.

The death of the Weavers bought the Western forces time, but not much, as the human troops on the eastern bank of the river formed up to make the final press on the morrow. Against their superior numbers even the Furies clearly could not hold. The Easterners were not content with just their living forces, but also added more daemons to their ranks, the light of their Breath moving through the night on the opposite bank like living nodi.

Watching their former countrymen from the western bank, the Newfield army was clearly spent. The third day outside Fieldhollow would be their last, as they ate what they expected would be their final meal together. Despite the sword dangling above their heads by the thinnest of threads, Reid seemed to be in fine spirits as he joked with the sullen Furies. But his usually jovial riddles took on a darker edge as Reid inquired to each as to the most pleasant way to die.

Initially the remains of the Furies refused to take Reid up on his topic, but finally Presley Biddox curtly replied, "The answer's obvious, ain't it? Not to die at all."

"Well-reasoned," Reid responded. "But, unfortunately, death cannot be avoided. We all get but one turn on the wheel of life, death the outcome that cannot be denied. So we should think on it well since it is the one thing every man, woman, and child on Ayr has in common."

"Then I'd like to find my death at the bottom of a bottle of whiskey," Biddox intoned.

"Ah, poison." Reid nodded sagely, as if this might be the true answer. Then a theatrical frown replaced his artificial agreement. "You know, every drunk I've ever seen dead in the street did not look happy. In fact, I'd say there's nothing sadder than a dead drunk. So I'm afraid that's not the answer. Abner?"

Abner picked at his meal, unwilling to look at Reid directly. "At home, in my bed beside my beautiful wife, many years from now."

A smattering of sighs filled the air, Marta unable to tell if her men were agreeing with Abner's assessment or just missing their own families. Reid did not even maintain the pretense of consideration before he answered, "But what about your lovely wife? Would she not awaken to a darker day upon finding her husband dead beside her?"

Abner flinched at Reid's words, the prankster turning his attention to Marta. "What about you, Commander Childress?"

Marta did not bother to answer, only giving him a look so cold flowers would wither. Reid incongruously brightened under her stare, his eyes crinkling with his smile. "Your eyes say you're dead already. An interesting argument, but unfortunately, incorrect. Since no one can answer my question, I shall play the gentleman and enlighten you all. The best way to die is not by saber stroke, musket ball, age, or infirmity. The best way is to be crushed like a bug swatted by Sol Himself. There is no pain in that end, only immediate oblivion."

Despite all his clever words, Marta found Reid supremely stupid in his statement. Pain was the only proof of existence, hurt the only sure sign they were even still alive. Life was cruel, but Marta intended on holding on to every last raw and aching moment of hers.

Reid's analogy to a bug was apt though. To call someone a bug was to invite them to a duel, since insects were deficient. Though they moved like animals, insects only had one Breath, like plants. They had no Mind to guide them with intent, only a Body Breath. Insects were the lowest of the animal kingdom and a good comparison for the Eastern Shapers though. Marta felt like several of her legs had been torn off, but she would still keep crawling mindlessly on with her remaining limbs until the final blow fell.

As she trudged to her tent, she realized there was nothing holding her there any longer. No more chain of command existed. The Western ranks were scattered, confused, and working singularly rather than as a whole to hold the line. She was certain she could slip unseen through their midst and leave all the bloodshed behind. The Traitors Brigade she would desert to ensure her escape, her brothers and sisters' sacrifice a means to buy her more time to flee.

Marta considered this potentiality, already mentally penning the letter she would send to Abner's wife, Della, as she collapsed upon her cot. But she was simply too tired to act now, promising herself she would escape on the morrow.

***

On the third day of the battle for Fieldhollow, Marta strode to the head of the Furies, ordering them to carry their shields to the front of the Western defense even as the Eastern forces began their charge across the Browns River.

The Western hail of musket fire was a dense rain striking the Eastern forces with its deadly drops. Hundreds fell, but still the Eastern armies advanced through the river, now choked with their dead and dying. The Westerners would eventually run out of musket balls, whereas the Eastern army seemed endless, surging forward like a wave of flesh destined to crash against the Furies' shields. There would be no stopping them, either from taking Vrendenburg or slaughtering the defenders, and Marta was just turning to make good her escape when the airships arrived.

The sight stole her senses as an even dozen of the imposing vessels swiftly sped in formation through the air above the Kuk ley. Each ship was half the size of the massive Sanct Rosario that had taken her across the Saulshish Ocean all those years ago, their propellers tearing violently through the air. Bulbous balloons held them aloft, the ships' bottoms made of thick steel capable of repelling the heaviest of musket fire. As they flew towards the fray, Marta could see the cannons poking out their sides, aimed downwards to rain destruction upon their enemies.

The ceaseless rush of Eastern forces finally broke at the arrival of the airships, the dirigibles' shadows distributing despair among the Eastern ranks as they slid across them. The airships would turn the tide, would win the West the battle of Fieldhollow, and the remains of the Newfield army rallied at their appearance to lead a new charge against the invading Easterners.

They were already halfway across the field towards the Browns River, Marta and her Furies at the head of the charge, when they realized the airships were not stopping. Instead they continued hurtling down the Kuk line and on towards the East, gone as swiftly as they had appeared.

Out in the no-man's land and out of formation, the Western forces were in tatters as the Eastern army rallied. The swelling boom of Eastern cannons and musket shots assailed Marta's ears, but over the din she caught what she believed would be the last words she would ever hear.

"Remember Creightonville!"

Chapter 30

Winterfylled 24, 567

Her instructor, Cyrus, would be appalled to see how long it took Marta to spring the lock, nearly the entirety of her allotted time. The other prisoners ignored her, she not the first captive to fiddle with a lock when boredom took hold. But judging by the looks on their faces, she certainly was the first to step out of her cell holding an open lockblade. Her escape now hinged on them keeping their mouths shut, and Marta gave them a hard stare that she hoped inspired fear rather than revealing the anguish she actually felt as she passed.

Isabelle's herbs certainly helped, Marta's heart beating fit to burst as it burned off the poison. Her thoughts sped up as well, no longer flowing like molasses in winter as they had under the ekesh's effects. But it was almost too much now, her thoughts rushing about her head so rapidly it was all she could do to concentrate on putting one foot in front of the other.

Overcoming her guards was easier than she had expected, the men poised from an attack aimed from without and not within, and certainly not from a supposedly unconscious Shaper. The younger one tried to draw his saber before she left him crumpled on the ground. The older one made no motion to resist, readily offering up directions to Underhill's house before Marta knocked him silly. He might have lied, but Marta had no time to dwell as she collected her hat and haversack.

The keys she grabbed as an afterthought, tossing them to the prisoners whose silence secured her escape. They were most likely bad people, like herself—people that deserved to be locked up as she did—but Marta had a soft spot for those left languishing in cages.

Outside she found Luca waiting, closing his precious lockblade and handing it over without hesitation. It was only then that Isabelle materialized in the darkness behind her, her appearance making Marta smile. Luca had hoped for the best, but Isabelle bet against her better nature all the same. Perhaps they could be trusted after all—if not entirely in their intentions, then at least in their ability. Not trusting her made them smart, and Marta would rather work with smart people than those with good intentions. There was killing to be done if they were going to save the girl, and she wanted killers by her side.

The released prisoners spilled out into the street, Marta hoping they would provide a distraction as she led the way to Underhill's mansion. She was glad it was Underhill they would deal with. Countless needless deaths were on his hands because of his mishandling of the war. And perhaps the girl as well if they were not swift enough.

Caddie, Marta reminded herself. The girl with the blue eyes was named Caddie Hendrix, and she would die if they did not act swiftly.

Marta's rage provided the fire that fueled her now, but it was fading. She was still not what she needed to be, a fact she was reminded of as she turned a corner to run into a squad of soldiers. The two sides stared at each other a moment, both equally dumbfounded as Marta tried to recall the plans for her rabbit legs to leap away.

Luca and Isabelle saved her yet again, the woman's sling whistling as he leapt into the fray. The soldiers were not prepared for the man and his lockblade, Luca slashing with abandon and leaving them bloody in the street as Isabelle hauled Marta along. But each step became harder than the one before, Marta's mind slowing down as they advanced.

She tried to make her comrades understand, but all that came out was, "Not right."

Luca seemed to understand her slur though. "That weed burns faster than ekesh."

"More," Marta mumbled.

"Can't, too much is poisonous."

Marta's heart fell as she stumbled on. She tried to push away from the assisting Isabelle to save herself some dignity, but found she did not have the strength. She attempted to summon her old friend in her rage, but even it deserted her, too tired to raise its sleepy head.

There were guards posted outside the Underhill estate, but Isabelle's sling took one as Luca slipped behind the other with his blade. The door was unlocked, the three slinking inside. Marta was just motioning for them to separate when Underhill bellowed from the next room.

"I always pride myself on being a good host. Come and say hello."

His words were polite, but there was a hard edge to his voice Marta did not like. For the first time she willingly opened her mind to Luca, hoping he was Listening and would find a way to flank their foe as she stepped around the corner.

The behemoth that was Underhill waited for her with his back to the huge table, Caddie standing between him and the door, an engraved pistol to her head. The man's eyes flashed as if consumed by a fever, and Marta wondered if he were in his right mind when he spoke. "We were just discussing summoning Waer, and here you are. Was it that you heard your name?"

"I am not Waer," she responded flatly. What she said made no matter, only that she keep Underhill's attention occupied as Luca and Isabelle slunk up on him. "There is no Waer, no monster that makes us turn away from the will of Sol. Mankind—we are the only monsters on Ayr."

His laughter took Marta aback, the man needing several moments before he got himself back under control. Marta was happy at his distraction, happy for the time it bought her until he spoke. "Perhaps you're right and we are the only monsters here tonight. Us and the other two. Don't think I don't know about your friends. I'm not a fool no matter the role I've been cast. Have them come out or the child dies before your eyes."

Luca and Isabelle soon joined her. It was all Marta could do to remain upright and focused on her target. Caddie seemed as serene as ever and utterly oblivious to her plight. Underhill kept his pistol pressed to the child's temple as he nodded to Marta. "You're more right than you know. You need to take her from me before I do something terrible."

He seemed sincere, and Marta forced herself to take a step forward only to find the pistol leveled at her. "Don't come near me, Traitor!"

Marta froze as tears threatened in Underhill's eyes. His face twisted, the pistol turning from her to Caddie and back again as his voice became plaintive. "I try to be a good man. I want more than anything to do the right thing."

Opening her mouth to try and talk some sense into the madman, Marta never got the chance as he turned his sudden furor towards Caddie.

"Shut up!" The man was clearly insane as he continued screaming at Caddie. "I can make my name off of you, make my name ring from shore to shore!"

"As a murderer of children?"

She wanted his attention back on her, and Marta got her wish as the pistol again turned towards her. But Underhill seemed confused by her suggestion, his mind unable to process the act he threatened. "Can't you see?

Can't you? Look at her. Look!"

Marta was doing her damndest to summon something: her rabbit legs to flee if his finger flinched on the trigger or her sword so she would at least not die unarmed. But the plans refused to come, as did her anger when she demanded it to rise and bring with it the clarity she so sorely needed. Her anger refused to stir. It was burned out and worn away, finally abandoning her entirely in her time of need.

She looked into Caddie's blue eyes as Underhill had commanded and, for the first time, saw something within: there was fear; there was longing; there was need as Caddie opened her mouth and spoke.

"Mother."

The word cut Marta to the quick and nearly tore out her withered innards, though her voice remained calm.

"Kill him as he reloads."

Her rage was too tired to stir, but her clarity was suddenly there and burning brighter than ever before. The room seemed to suspend around her as plans for Armor inundating her head in intricate detail. They were neither what Cyrus had instructed her in nor the childish plans that Abner had taught her, but something grander as she inhaled.

Marta exhaled her Breath even as Underhill's finger constricted on the trigger, feeling her Breath flow through her pores as it erected itself around her. Through her exposed essence she felt the world in a new way, the air passing through the tangled latticework she wrought. Like veins in some massive circulatory system, they enveloped her entirely to expand her senses.

She felt it all.

Including the bullet lodged deep in her Armor as she took her first step. There was blinding pain that came with its impact, the exuded Breath another sensory organ that suffered the shock of the bullet as surely as her skin would. But this was no rigid and brittle form Marta summoned, her Breath instead flexing with the projectile's force, absorbing and ingesting its deadly momentum.

Marta had no time to reflect on this inexplicable occurrence as she covered the ground, slamming into the massive Underhill and continuing on without pause. Through her Armor she felt the table give way, splintering under her power as she barreled onward. His skull gave way too, Marta experiencing each crack in exquisite detail through her second skin.

His shattered bones did not stop her from slamming him against the far wall again and again until his enormous body flapped in her grip like a ragdoll. She could still feel his pulse through her Armor; she could feel it flickering then finally sputtering out. So she dropped his remains like the disgusting thing they were: something that would dare to threaten her daughter.

The thought was not right, was not hers. Caddie was no kin to her, and the strangeness of the incongruous impulse brought Marta back to the moment. Though the new Armor had been a part of her scant seconds before, Marta wearing it as if it were her own familiar flesh, she examined the thing encircling her with new eyes after her mind returned to her.

It was like nothing she had seen before, as most Shaper Armor scarcely covered the human form with simple thin lines that traced the major bones of the body like a child's stick-figure drawing. The Breath could only be stretched so far, so to build the full Armor, the Shaper had to draw it out until it was no thicker than a hair's breadth.

Yet this construct enfolded her entirely, the strange and intricate latticework covering every inch of her like skin. There were gaps between the bundles of Breath, but it was a far cry from the usual slender extensions Shapers employed. But even more than that, the Breath moved and was not static like the childish Armor Abner had taught her or the more complex Armor he preferred. No, in this living form her Breath seemed to breathe its own, steadily in and out. It was truly unsettling in its uniqueness.

As was the bullet hovering inches before her heart, still contained in the animated web that wrapped round her.

Marta forced her attention away from the wonder to the other three. Luca and Isabelle gawked back with astonishment, but Caddie focused on her with a look that was harder to gauge. She looked to Marta like an infant who had fallen and could not decide if she was injured or not. The right word from her mother would decide if the outcome was either laughter or tears, so Marta released her Armor. It was a jolt like the sudden loss of a limb to dismiss it, this loss nearly costing Marta her consciousness. But she held on to the tenuous thread for all she was worth.

"Come here, Caddie."

Caddie came running through the remnants of the shattered table, Marta engulfing her in her embrace. Holding the child, Marta realized Caddie was not the only one who had been shocked and teetering on the edge of either laughter or tears. Marta too had been on the precipice and might have fallen if the girl had not come to comfort her. It felt good to hold someone close again. It felt right.

It felt like home.

The sound came from behind them, one Marta knew quite well. It was Underhill's death rattle, and she pulled Caddie away so the child would be spared the sight. But Caddie turned with Marta, twisting them insistently around until they were both facing the dying man. The girl never flinched, even as he gurgled out his final note. Despite the light of the room, they could see the three smudges that were Underhill's Breath rise from his body and join Sol's flow.

It was time the four fugitives were through with the place, but before they could depart, Underhill's body stirred. Marta thought for a moment he might somehow still be alive, though she had seen with her own eyes as his Breath left his body.

But the movement did not come from his body, rather from within it.

The black Breath did not pass through his skin as Underhill's natural Breaths had. Instead it pushed through his throat, the skin engorging, his mouth opening through no motion of his own to reveal the thing extricating itself from his body like a burrowing black maggot.

Horror took hold of Marta as she beheld the abomination, the wretched thing slowly rising from Underhill's corpse to hover above his dead lips like an indecisive wasp. There, it halted and made no motion as Marta felt malevolence fanning from it in waves. Unlike the natural Breath she had seen all her life, it did not depart, did not join Sol's flow.

"Get back!"

Marta readily obeyed Luca, keeping herself between Caddie and the monster. Luca strode forward with his lockblade brandished as he spoke rapidly in the Dobra language. She could not understand him, but Marta caught the words "ix" and "Waer" several times. It sounded like he was ordering the Breath, demanding its obedience, and Marta found herself wondering if it was true that the Ikus tribe could indeed control Dead Breath, as the rumors claimed.

It was not until he was beside them that Luca revealed all his calm words were just an attempt to get close, as he lunged at the black Breath with his weapon.

Swift as he was, Luca never came close, the black Breath disappearing through the ceiling instantly. It was almost as if it were never there, it easier for Marta's mind to accept that it had never existed rather than grapple with what she could not explain.

"What was that?"

Luca's face bore no grin as he pronounced, "The Black Breath of Waer herself."

Waer was just a myth, so all the great scholars said, Marta having agreed with them for most of her life. But upon witnessing this apparition, she was certainly considering the possibility that all those learned scholars might be wrong. Between the black Breath and her new Armor, she felt like someone who had lived on a little island all her life. She had thought its shores encompassed the whole world only to be plucked by some gargantuan hand to be deposited upon a new and immense landmass. She had no map and could not even comprehend the edges of this new, inhospitable continent.

But the existence of Waer would have to wait, as Isabelle pointed towards the corner of the room, drawing their attention to the amethyst-tinged Breath hovering there. They had seen it before and it heralded peril, especially when it shot away before they could act.

"We need to get out of the city," Marta said as she took a step.

The strain finally proved too much: the week of running; exertion of the odd, new Armor; and the daze of ekesh finally overcoming her. Marta's body gave up as she collapsed into Caddie's arms, the girl supporting her now.

"And how are we escaping when you can't even walk?" Luca asked.

"By taking a train."

Luca threw up his arms in exasperation. "You're a wanted fugitive! There's no way we can slip aboard a train unseen!"

"You misunderstand," Marta replied with the barest hint of a grin. "We're going to take the train."

Chapter 31

Septembris 17, 565 (Two Years Ago)

Caught away from cover on their foolish charge, the Western forces were mowed down by the Easterners, musket balls dropping all but those huddled behind the Shapers' shields. The few troops who remained were now in full retreat, breaking any semblance of formation as they fled into the woods, their weapons heedlessly discarded as they ran.

"Abandon the shields!" Marta cried. "Into the town!"

"And what salvation do you expect—"

The bullet cut Reid off, snapping his head back as a plume of red exited his temple.

Marta did not pause to watch him fall as she leapt away on her rabbit legs to abandon Reid on the field. Marta assured herself he would understand her decision if the musket ball left any remnants of his mind. Reid had not been squashed like a bug as he had hoped, but his suffering was at least at an end.

Only her brothers and sisters of the Traitors Brigade obeyed her order, the new recruits that made them the Furies deserting with the rest of the Newfield troops. Those that had served by her side from the beginning were the only ones who understood this would be their last stand, that there would be no quarter offered from the East. It was now no longer a battle for victory or even survival, but only to take as many bastards with them as they could before breathing their last. They were going to fall, but they were going to make the East pay dearly for each inch they took.

For once securing weapons was not difficult, her troops scooping up discarded muskets as they ran. With them Marta set up ambushes in the empty building, dropping any Eastern pursuers that dared enter the city. She then split the Traitors Brigade into squads of four, each cell independently fortifying its own building and moving on before the Eastern forces could discover where they hid. The Easterners never knew from where the next terrible blow would come, hundreds dying while only claiming a few blocks on the outskirts of the city.

Miraculously Marta and her men held Fieldhollow for the third day, the Covenant armies finally falling back at nightfall to the Browns River that was now stained red. If they were wise, they would skirt the city and make the final press on to Vrendenburg.

Instead they sent the daemons in after them.

Perhaps they were afraid a larger Western contingent awaited them in Fieldhollow. Or perhaps they were just tired of the loss of human life, but the nine daemons stormed the city no matter the Eastern rational. At their appearance, the buildings the Traitors Brigade held so well against the human forces became a liability as the daemons toppled them upon their inhabitants.

Marta was just ordering her squad's retreat when their building came crashing down, the rubble rumbling towards her. It was Abner who pushed her to safety, the crushing weight claiming him instead. Her anger flared as she stared at the wreckage, Abner surely dead at its core. But her anger was not aimed at the daemon that took his life or the Eastern Weavers who controlled it; rather, it was aimed at Abner for not letting her die.

She unleashed her rage on the daemon though. Her glass saber was shattered with just a few shards left around the hilt, but it was enough, as Marta hacked the daemon down to nothing with the remains, finally smashing its glass heart with the steel hilt before retreating farther.

***

It was a long night of brutal fighting block by bloody block. Skill and desperation saved some of the Traitors Brigade along with a healthy dose of luck, but the last of their luck had finally run out, Marta cornered with Leon, Tollie, and a few others in the rubble of a building as two daemons raged outside. Their glass blades were now entirely gone, the five muskets between them no use against the monsters. Gazing at the cowering Tollie, Marta realized he was the only one who remained of Abner's cadre from the Pit. Abner, Reid, Ida, Rupert, and Gonzalo were all gone now. She did not mind dying beside the gentle Tollie, but Leon's presence irked her. She hated the idea that their bodies might share the same mass grave, their Breath the same air as they entered Sol's flow.

They were expecting their end at any moment when the daemons suddenly withdrew, a ghastly silence filling the ruins of Fieldhollow. Her soldiers fell silent as well, afraid to jinx their reprieve by giving voice to it.

The silence was finally broken by the slap of feet running through the city, the man's hair that disturbed the somber scene nearly as white as the flag he carried. "Where's your commander? We must have terms!"

"They'll allow us to surrender?" Tollie asked, hope climbing into his voice.

"No surrender," Marta answered with a voice as flat and lifeless as her eyes. "Put him down."

Leon was still setting the musket to his shoulder when Marta recognized the Eastern soldier in his decorated uniform. His white hair was what had confused her, it being quite dark in all of the photographs from before the war. The Eastern General Loree had aged badly in the last four years, no longer hale and hearty, but teetering on the edge of elderly.

She caught Leon's hand before he pulled the trigger as Loree cried out in the empty street, his voice tremulous. "Send out your commander so we can surrender properly!"

It looked like a trap, but Loree was known for being honorable and Marta had no other available option as she stepped out of their crumbling shelter. As she approached, Loree stripped out of his uniform and threw it to the ground.

"Stop it. Please tell them to stop the devastation," he begged, punctuating his plea by spitting upon his discarded insignia. "Please, for the love of Sol, call a stop to them."

"To what?"

"The airships!"

***

And so the Grand War was won by the West, Loree's surrender officially taken by Grubb for the history books, though she had fled earlier that day. It was only symbolic though, the Covenant President Langdon having surrendered unconditionally to Bumgarden via the Dobra network over an hour before. Ever eloquent, the papers later quoted him as saying he accepted the West's dominion "until the end of Ayr and Sol's merciful return," leaving no doubt as to who the victor was.

At least that was what Marta pieced together after Grubb's reformed ranks swept through the remains of Fieldhollow to quickly usher the remnants of the Traitors Brigade onto trains. The soldiers of the Traitors Brigade could have resisted, could have fought their way free rather than being led away like prisoners. They might not have even had to fight since many of Grubb's troops understood they were alive today because of the Eastern Shapers' sacrifice. They might have willingly let them escape, but the survivors of the Traitors Brigade knew they had nowhere left to go and marched to the awaiting trains meekly as sheep to the slaughter.

They were shipped back to their training grounds of Mitkof Island, again imprisoned by the vast Arrowhead Lake. On their route the name Orthoel Hendrix was on everyone's lips, the airships that ended the war apparently his invention. Marta remembered the oddly manic and mechanical man that unsettled her at the start of the war and wondered if she would still be alive now if his life had ended long ago, like she had insisted at the time.

Though the newspapers they were provided on Mitkof never explicitly stated it, the Shapers knew the devastation wrought by the airships was horrendous. How else would such a titan like Loree be reduced to whimpering, the proud Langdon debasing himself and his Covenant with his unconditional terms? Each morning when the news arrived, the Traitors Brigade flocked around, pouring through the papers to see if their homes had been spared. Marta did not join them, not since the first day when she discovered Gatlin was one of the first neutralized cities.

The papers made no mention of the Traitors Brigade at Fieldhollow, not one word of their sacrifice that had helped secure the West's victory. Nor was there any information on their men and women who had fallen there, no indication as to who was dead or wounded. Those who could still walk were herded onto the trains to Mitkof. There, they were fed well enough, but their hunger now ran deeper than their bellies. It had invaded their bones as they yearned for home.

Marta wrote her letter to Abner's wife in Meome, handing it to their captors without postage and only the faintest prayer that they would mail it for her. She tried to get word to Bumgarden as well, imploring him to remember his tools that had earned him his victory.

She received no reply from the president she had not voted for, but had helped elect.

***

It was near the end of the first month when Leon finally approached her. Somehow he made it through the entire war scarcely scathed; the only mark blemishing his face the brand they both bore. Although all the others in their company had visibly diminished during the Grand War, Leon seemed to swell from the bloodshed, seemed to grow stronger with each life he took. Marta had sworn he would not see the end of the war, but it was just another promise she had been unable to fulfill as he spoke.

"I have waited for you each night, but still you have not come. Why? Don't you realize we are meant for one another, that no one can love you but me?"

At first Marta could not comprehend his twisted mind and how it was he thought she belonged to him. She may have been a sought-after beauty in her prime, but she was monstrous now. How could he desire her?

Then she realized it was this new aspect that he craved. He saw the killer in her better than any of the others and thought that her bloody nature reflected his own.

Marta acted before she was even aware the anger was there, cracking him in the mouth with her gauntlet hard enough to shatter his teeth as her phantom blade slid unbidden into her hand. Leon fell, her weapon rising as the clarity hit her and saved his life yet again.

She would be hanged if she killed him, but it was not that which stayed her hand. It was the fact Leon was still grinning at her through the fragments of his teeth, the full fury of her rage exciting him. If she killed him, she would prove that he was right; she would become a monster in that moment and confirm his conception of her was correct.

Marta decided then and there she would not let Leon be right about her, so she stalked away to reclaim her humanity. The Grand War had made her a monster, but she would not embrace her state any more than she would Leon.

Chapter 32

Winterfylled 24, 567

The plan was sound, but Marta's mind hardly was. An eastbound train would arrive any time now, stopping in the city long enough to exchange its passengers and cargo. Marta would simply open the gate that kept the train in place while Luca and Isabelle collected the engineer to man the throttle and set the lodestone for their departure ahead of schedule.

It was a simple plan, just as the plans for Cildra Armor were. But despite their simplicity, both had several moving parts, and Marta was hardly capable of movement anymore. The remains of the ekesh still swam through her veins and Isabelle's drugs wore off long ago. It was force of will alone that kept Marta awake, and it was a dwindling resource.

It was the longest hour of Marta's life as they hid below the train's platform and waited for someone, anyone, to give the cry of alarm when they were spotted. They peered about for the Render Graff's Blessed Breath, but the flickering lights of the constantly flowing ley buried any hopes of finding a single one amidst the myriad. Marta's headache was already thunderous, though Luca seemed unaffected, she desiring nothing more than to retreat into unconsciousness to avoid the agony.

Finally the train arrived, slowing to a stop as it reached the giant gate to keep it in place. As the turbines above the engine came to a rest, the fugitives kept watch through the slats of the platform for the engineer. She departed with the rest of the emerging crowd to head for the first class lounge. It was a high honor to hobnob with the pilot of the contraption, one they intended to avail themselves of shortly. So they waited until the train was empty before Luca and Isabelle headed away with the rope Marta provided from her haversack.

"By grace or grave," Marta called out after them. Luca did not quite hear her words, but grinned back nonetheless.

The two arrived at the lounge and halted at the door. There, Luca pulled his kerchief up to cover his nose and mouth, Isabelle tearing a strand from her skirt to do the same. Luca gave his companion one last wink before they shoved the door open.

Decorum usually kept the riffraff out, but it did nothing to stop the two freebooters as they barreled through the unlocked door. Inside, the engineer awaited them along with a dozen well-dressed guests, including the Home Guardsman, his bear-headed silver pin shining. He did not need to Listen to know their intent as his hand reached for the pistol at his waist.

"Brigands!"

Luca was on him instantly, his lockblade pressed against the man's neck with just enough force to leave a thin trickle of blood. The rest of the startled crowd cowered as Luca wrested the pistol away and turned it upon them.

"Pull that trigger and you'll swing. Thievery is one thing, but murder..." the guardsman intoned.

They were there for kidnapping actually, the idea of theft not having entered Luca's mind until that moment. But if it was expected of him, he figured he might as well oblige. One could only swing once after all.

"You," he nodded to the engineer, "collect their lucre."

Isabelle mentally screamed at him for this deviation from their plan, Luca's placating smile hidden beneath his kerchief. He cared nothing for the money, only the cover it would afford them as Isabelle began binding the frightened passengers with rope, the guardsman first.

The engineer was dutifully collecting their billfolds when Luca spied the real prize in its case against the wall. It was no mandolin, but it would have to do as he called out, "Leave the rest and grab the fiddle. Step quick, you're coming with us."

***

Marta struggled with the gate, its massive weight usually requiring the pulleys that resided on the platform. She was walking through the ley beneath the platform though, and did not have the time to muddle through the machinery. The strange new Armor she recently wore would make short work of the gate, but when she searched her mind for the plans, they remained elusive. So she summoned her childish Armor, the last of her reserves spent as she pressed the gate upwards and slogged back to Caddie.

***

The engineer before them, Luca and Isabelle had almost reached the train when they recognized the familiar figure. It was his bummers cap that gave him away, the musket ball hole torn straight through the center.

The hat's owner did not seem to see them though, his back turned and face pointed up at the sky as if searching the stars. The man never turned their way as they passed behind him, but they were not three feet farther when his heavy footfalls fell into step behind them.

Isabelle continued on as Luca whirled to face the Render with his open lockblade. But beholding the man up close, Luca was sure there was some terrible mistake. The Render had the countenance of a child, his eyes unfocused and vacant. There was no recognition in the Render's face, and suddenly the Dobra found himself feeling sorry for the man who was about to die.

Luca would not be his killer though. He was only the distraction.

Isabelle's steel bearing tore through the air, her aim a deadly thing that never faltered.

Yet somehow she missed, the missile simply knocking Graff's cap off rather than aerating his skull. Luca had never seen her miss before and found this sudden shortcoming in his constant companion startling. It would be up to him to kill the Render, then, and he best end the man quickly before the Render killed him in turn.

Before Luca could act Graff fell to his knees and began searching the platform for his lost hat, as if the two of them were not there. It was only a few feet from him, but the Render seemed blind as his hands reached pitifully about. In that moment he reminded Luca of the doddering Onas he knew growing up rather than the terrifying fiend they had been fleeing all this time.

Watching the woeful man, Luca concluded it was quite possible that Marta had lost her mind. There was no way this bottom pull of a bug could be as frightening as she claimed. Luca could easily finish him off, could kill the killer of Stone Cleaver, but Luca instead chose mercy. Killing to survive was one thing; there was a purity in that, but slaughtering a simpleton was entirely another as he retreated to the train.

The others were already aboard the floating locomotive, the engineer bringing the huge turbines to life. The train lurched forward as Luca leapt inside the engine car, its momentum increasing as it pulled away from the platform. It left surprised shouts in its wake, the passengers crying out for their belongings still aboard. Looking back at the quickly fading platform, they saw no sign of the Render.

The last car was just pulling away when the pudgy man made the leap with an agility that belied his girth. The train still gathered speed as they made their escape, but Marta shook her head.

"It's no use. Graff has us. It's only a matter of time before he finishes us off."

"Then we jump," Luca replied.

"And so does he. Then he'll be ahead of us, the army behind. I'd rather face the army, but it will be Graff that finds us first."

Luca was shocked to see the defeat in Marta's tired eyes, her jaw set grimly. "He still has ten cars to go before he reaches us. So we detach them," he said.

A spark of hope returned to Marta's face, their gazes turning to the engineer. But the woman shook her head. "They have to be released manually from underneath the train."

Yet another avenue of escape closed for them, Luca brandished his stolen pistol. "We wait until he's close enough and bury a bullet in him."

"And do with one shot what the entire Eastern army couldn't during the war?" Marta would have been furious, at the man who could not give up even in the face of defeat, of the Render who would show them no mercy; at the simple plan they had almost pulled off were it not for the fickleness of fate. But she was too tired for anger and did not have time to rage.

"I'll detach the cars."

She doffed her hat before anyone could argue, Marta unsure what to do with it before finally placing it on Caddie's head. Graff drawing ceaselessly nearer, she had no more time to waste as she threw open the door leading to the rest of the train. The air rushing around her, she unbolted the door to the next car as well to keep the way clear for their single shot if it came down to that.

Matching eyes with Luca, she held them with all the intensity she could muster. "If I don't make it back, make sure she gets to her father. Swear on your life."

Without waiting for an answer, Marta climbed down the terrace to reach the glass-covered underside of the train. As she descended, the last thing she saw was Caddie staring out from under her own slouch hat, something approaching interest in the child's eyes that caused Marta to wonder again what was really swimming in the depths of that girl's indecipherable mind.

Marta pushed those thoughts from her head as she made her way. The design of the trains quickly made sense as she surveyed them, the cars connected by two points: one from platform to platform by chains where the cars came together, whereas the second had a long, stiff cable that ran from the center of each car to the other. Again the plan was simple, the execution exceptionally difficult. To disconnect the cable she would have to climb along it until she reached its connection point at the next car. There were steel handholds driven into the thing at regular intervals, but Marta ignored them as the winds from the turbines assaulted her. The roar from the force propelling the several-ton train along at its breakneck pace was deafening, but she had no more time to dither.

Hanging upside down, her legs wrapped round the cable, Marta made the climb one hand at a time as fast as she dared. She tried her best to ignore the drop below, the ground surging past and getting faster every mile they went. She slipped only once, dangling by her legs to watch the ground scream past before finally reaching the cable's connection. Its mechanics were easy enough to surmise, a giant cross bolt holding the cable in place. She just needed to pull the bolt and they would be free, Marta summoning her gauntlet to give her strength.

Although strength she had in abundance, she had no leverage and could not get enough distance from the bolt to give it a proper yank. She still tried with all her might, finally giving up when she realized she was just squandering more of her diminishing time.

So she attacked the glass surface surrounding metal connector, shattering it to reveal wood underneath. The bolt might be metal and more than she could manage, but it connected to weak wood, Marta bashing her gauntlet around it until it finally tore free. The cable she had clung to fell away immediately, Marta barely fast enough to catch one of the handholds. The car above her swayed and rolled, the loss of the glass keeping them aloft along the ley dropping it down several feet. The cable she clung to dropped even farther to drag on the ground in a series of angry sparks. She was halfway home, but Marta did not allow herself to dwell as she began the long climb back via the steel handholds.

Released of the cable, the car was only attached by the significantly thinner chains between the platforms, the loss of the stabilizing cable causing the car to shimmy back and forth nauseatingly. The roar of the turbines again greeted Marta as she reached the head of the car, ready to pull herself up to join her companions before separating them from Graff for good. Gambling a glance into the engine, she expected to see their looks of relief at her return.

Instead she saw Luca throw Caddie behind the door jamb, he and Isabelle joining the girl immediately. The pilfered pistol peeked round the door, though no head joined it to aim, all Marta could see now being the back of the engineer.

Marta could not see Graff directly above her in the train car, but Graff spotted the engineer well enough. The unfortunate woman's Breath suddenly fled from her body to enter the next car only to dissipate into the air a moment later. The engineer fell dead at the touch of his glass blade, the woman never even having seen her killer.

The others were pinned down in the engine car, afraid to show themselves and become a victim of Graff's drawing and glass dagger. They could not separate the cars, so Marta did it herself. Her gauntlet ripped through the wood of the terrace, tearing through the supports connecting it to the engine car. Marta made a grab for the disappearing chains, but she was too slow, her hands only brushing them as they slipped through her grasp.

Marta grinned nevertheless as the engine pulled away, the momentum of the now-leaderless passenger cars still keeping a slackening pace. But detached from the turbines, they began to slow, the engine car widening the gap between them. She still could not see her companions, but Marta knew they were safe. She would surely die for her sacrifice, but at least she had won.

Graff's face appeared over the edge of the platform to spy Marta clinging to the handholds, the Render gesturing as he drew her Breath. Firmly in his Blessed grasp, Marta's Breath jettisoning her body against her will to be jerked up into the car where his glass blade waited. Not wanting his face to be the last thing she saw, Marta gazed at the retreating engine for solace.

But Graff did not sever her Breath, instead drawing it all the harder. Her Breath stretched to the breaking point as he yanked at Marta's being; the pain was excruciating. It was if he was trying to rip her Soul in two, Marta with no choice but to pull herself up and physically enter the car to join her violated Breath before he tore it from her by the root.

Soon as she was over, the side Graff manipulated her Breath again, making her move like a marionette. First, he forced her to approach before holding her in place. She was paralyzed in his grasp as he looked her over. His good eye focused on her brand, the scar seeming to spark something in the man.

"Do I know you, Traitor?"

The seat beside Graff suddenly exploded into splinters from Luca's pistol shot. The Render did not even flinch as he took another step towards Marta, his face hovering inches from hers. It would be her last chance to put an end to him before he severed her tether to the world of the living, and so Marta took full advantage of the moment.

"You saved my life," she said before sending her snake tongue shooting at his good eye.

Her Breath should have hurtled into his brain with the speed of a bullet, but Graff somehow caught her Breath in his hand even as he gestured simultaneously with the other. He shoved the Breath left within her body away and flung Marta to the ground. There, he pressed her hard into the floor, Marta barely able to turn her head. The exertion was worth the effort though, as Marta watched the engine pull even farther to safety, now twenty yards away and out of the reach of his drawing.

"Pointless," Graff said. "It's all pointless. Just postponing what is meant to be."

Marta did not listen to the man. Instead she retreated into her mind to make her peace. For a moment she remembered Tollie and how he had succumbed to battle fugue. Caddie had retreated into her head as well, Marta absently wondering if they had weighed their lives in their mental havens as she was now.

She had led a cruel and bloody life, sure to stain her Soul when that Breath joined a new set on the next turn on the wheel of life. But she had done one good deed, at least, in ensuring Caddie's survival, and for that she would embrace oblivion as an old friend. She was ready for Graff's glass dagger to swing and take away her pain when Caddie stepped to the door in the disappearing engine.

Terror took hold of Marta at the sight of the girl. She feared Caddie might still be within the range of Graff's drawing, that even at a distance he could still prove deadly to her child. He would never stop, never hesitate, and her daughter would never be safe so long as he still stalked her. She could not survive if Marta was dead.

Caddie needed to be protected.

No rage touched Marta, but again the clarity was there and brought with it the plans for the Armor she used on Underhill. She summoned the impossible Armor immediately, Graff's drawing suddenly unable to restrain her as she swiped his feet out from under him. He was taken entirely off guard, flailing to the floor as Marta stood. Encased in her Armor, Marta's fist was the size of a mallet, Marta ready to put it to use when she caught Caddie's call.

=Mother.

In her rational mind Marta knew it was impossible what she heard, the distance and roar of the turbines swallowing any chance of communication. But she still heard Caddie's voice clear as day. She was being summoned, sure as she did with her own Blessed Breath, and just like her Breath, Marta could not deny the call. Turning her back upon Graff, she raced for the door in fast, fluid steps. With the impossible Armor she was suddenly so much more than she had ever been before: stronger, swifter, a powerful and hitherto unknown creature on Ayr.

The distance was nearly thirty yards, but Marta made the leap with ease. Landing lightly in the engine car, she engulfed Caddie in her embrace, her new Armor still a barrier between them. Seconds ago it had been a weapon capable of annihilating Graff entirely, but now it delicately held the girl as if she were a fledgling bird having pecked its way through its shell. Through the Armor Marta could feel the child's breathing more vividly than she could in her own skin.

As she held the girl, the plans that had been so clear before began to fade, Marta's Breath diminishing as it retreated back within her body until she and Caddie were finally pressed together flesh to flesh as mother and child.

Chapter 33

Decembris 21, 565 (Two Years Ago)

They had been sequestered at Mitkof for three months, Yuletide only a few days off and bringing the Traitors Brigade no joy or ease when Marta was finally summoned to the offices. Carmichael awaited her, sporting the same false glasses and beard she had seen him in last. This time he did not even offer her his hand as the guards left them utterly alone.

"Philo Frost again?" Marta asked with all the politeness she could scrounge.

"No, today I come to you as Carmichael Childress. The identity of Philo Frost has inadvertently taken over my life, and I now have to go out in disguise when I wish to be myself. It is... comical, I guess, in the way a farce is humorous as it yet reveals harsh truths through jests. But it is somehow fitting, I feel."

Despite her ongoing attempt at regaining her humanity, Marta's anger sparked to life at his dethatched discussion of his current choice of names while she had been suffering for the last four years. But she kept the anger contained, one of her first Cildra lessons being not to harm another of the clan. So she kept her voice composed as she asked, "Are they alive?"

"Mother and Father are well, having evacuated Gatlin long before the airships reached them. Hillbrook Manor was unfortunately destroyed along with the kennels, the government claiming much of the plantation and divvying it up—"

"What about Oleander?"

"She did not make it out of Kekoskee in time," he answered without emotion. "The reports say she died bravely."

Marta felt nothing at first, the abruptness of his announcement too much for either her heart or head to comprehend. But then she felt the pain in excruciating detail at the loss of the one good and pure part of the

Childress family. She would never see her sister again, had spent her last moments with Oleander already almost eight years ago, and had not been aware of it until now. Marta crumbled under the weight of the realization, all her strength deserting her and dropping her into a heap. She had seen hundreds die, dozens by her hand; enemies, comrades, and friends in equal measure, yet she had never felt hurt such as this. She wanted to cry, but her body seemed unable to remember how to anymore.

Again Carmichael made no effort to comfort her, leaving her in anguish on the floor. She was glad he did not attempt to give her succor, sure she would blindly lash out if he tried to soothe even an ounce of her hurt. Oleander had never meant anything to him and to pretend otherwise would blaspheme her memory.

Not bothering to rise from the floor, finally Marta recovered enough for her tongue to form words. "We failed. It was all for nothing."

"Was it? Our home may have been destroyed, but Newfield is again whole and my sway in the Public Safety Department has become total. It did not go entirely as planned, but Father's result was reached nonetheless."

Marta could not comprehend his words. Finally providing elucidation, Carmichael said, "Father hedged his bets, could not decide which side would win in the Grand War. So he placed agents on both sides of the conflict. In a way it was the wisest of decisions. Either way he would lose, but either way he would win."

It was chance, Marta realized, only chance that left her horribly scarred and Carmichael at the pinnacle of power. Had events unfolded slightly differently, their places might be reversed and Oleander might still be alive. Faced with the horror of the Grand War, their father had made the rational decision in ensuring at least one of his bets paid off. He had not played to win, rather to break even no matter the cost. It was the right choice, but it was cynical—a heartless decision that had caused both her suffering and her sister's death.

She had played her role well though, as had Carmichael and Oleander. They had followed the first Cildra tenant of being obedient to the clan and complying without question. It was a bitter draught she had been forced to drink, but she had done her duty; something she was sure her father would assure her of when she returned.

"When can I come home?"

"I already told you Hillbrook Manor was destroyed. You have no home now. Father can't be seen consorting with a known traitor, especially one so infamous. He's already lost much of his influence from even being associated with you. It would be best if you disappeared."

The shock of Carmichael's previous announcement about Oleander and his mission during the Grand War deadened this blow's pain. She could not hurt anymore, leaving only confusion as Marta touched the scar on her forehead.

"Why? I did everything Father demanded. I sacrificed everything for him."

"Did you? Father told you to hold the line at Fieldhollow long enough for the airships to destroy Gatlin and Kekoskee? It was Father who told you to teach Cildra techniques to outsiders? Father who told you to become a traitor for the West when you were sent to spy for the East?"

"Yes!" Marta bawled. She meant to go on, but her cry cut off as she made the realization.

Carmichael had lied to her. Again.

"You should have remembered your training, should have only followed Father's orders when verified by your codex. And you should have kept Father's most important lesson closer to your heart." Carmichael was completely calm as he spoke, as if explaining an obvious lesson to a dull student. "Never provoke someone more powerful than yourself."

Marta's mind reeled, her thoughts jumbled and unable to grasp how her brother could betray her like this, how he could force her to become the monster crumpled before him. He had never cared for her or Oleander in the slightest, but was he truly capable of something as evil as this? Yet his repetition of their father's lesson from nearly twenty years past echoed through her head. Could he have done all this simply because she broke his nose all those years ago? Was he really that petty and cruel?

Suddenly her anger was there, terrible and roaring and outstripping anything she felt before. Carmichael's life would be forfeit for his treachery, his limbs slowly plucked from his body like petals by her hand. He would finally understand not to provoke someone more powerful than he, this the last lesson he would learn before she snuffed out the light behind his eyes. The plans for her gauntlets were fully formed in Marta's mind, her Breath howling to be released as she rose.

"Stop," Carmichael said as casually as if he were informing a carriage driver he had reached his destination.

And, to her horror, Marta froze in place.

She had been the subject of both her brother and mother's Whispering talents before as a child, this Cildra training allowing her to realize when she had been manipulated by being familiar with the sensation. They were always gentle mental nudges, as if brushing against someone in a crowd and shifting your gait because of the bump. It was like picking a pocket: the touch light lest the victim realize the violation.

Those times before were nothing like this; Carmichael was not Whispering, but Bellowing. There was no guile or gentleness to it, just the brutal slamming of his will upon and over hers to nearly crush her consciousness with the force of it. Marta tried to open her mouth to ask how he was capable of such force, but he simply told her to hush and her tongue suddenly became a dead thing in her mouth.

Utterly mute and frozen where she stood, Marta could do nothing as Carmichael examined her. He peered into her eyes a long time, clinically measuring the hate there before finally brushing the dull hair back from her forehead to inspect her puckered scar. He traced the outline with his finger, her skin wanting to recoil at the vileness of his touch, but her muscles no longer hers to command. She was a prisoner within her own body until he said otherwise.

He no longer met her eyes, instead staring at her brand. When he finally spoke, his voice did not seem his own as real emotion tainted it. "I've taken to breeding mudbirds, just like father did with his hounds. The ugliest ones sing the most lovely, those bred to shed their ugliness losing their sad songs along with it. They say it's impossible to raise a beautiful mudbird, but I don't think they truly understand what it takes to make change. They do not have the patience. The Grand War has made Newfield ugly, but I believe there's still something worthwhile left in the husk. Ugly things always have the most beautiful stories to tell."

Carmichael dropped her hair to again cover her scar as his daydream broke, his voice again the same calm insisting one she had grown up with. "You will seek no vengeance against me; will not raise your hand or Breath against me ever."

His pronouncement instantly became the word of Sol in Marta's mind, she suddenly knowing with full certainty she would not be able to harm him. It was as sure as her given name, sure as the scar on her forehead, or that the sun rose in the east.

"The Traitors Brigade will be disbanded tomorrow. You are all free to go where you wish, all now full citizens of Newfield, as we promised. But I would not suggest returning east. The only people hated as much as Hendrix and your friend Bumgarden there are you lot. You will die if you ever cross the Mueller Line. You are an enemy now, Marta, a Westerner, no longer Father's favorite."

He left her frozen there, his fingers alighting on the door as Marta silently wondered why he did not just kill her now and be done with it. Her brother was no Listener, even though his silver pin denoted otherwise, but he paused at the threshold nonetheless.

"Because you may still have a song to sing, Sister. Because hate is easy, love is hard, and indifference the most difficult. And despite all my power, I am still not strong enough to be indifferent towards you."

The door shut softly behind him, her brother gone and Marta released from his mental grip. She collapsed back upon the ground, the weight of her state crushing her. Oleander was dead and her home lost. She had no family, no future anymore.

Finally, Marta cried, racking sobs that came from down in her core, her soul sick and trying desperately to expel the poison. And with her tears the last tatters of her tenderness and sympathy left her body; the last of her remaining humanity evaporating there on her cheeks.

She cried until she finally went dry.

Chapter 34

Winterfylled 25, 567

Though the ley headache pounded through her brain like a rockslide, Marta did not care as she clutched Caddie close. Luca said the line was nearly 200 miles long, so they prolonged their journey by adjusting the throttle and cutting their speed to a third. They knew they could not remain on the train when it reached its terminus at the Taloapus nodus where it connected up to the Cache line. Messages along the Dobra network traveled faster than their train, and Newfield troops would certainly be waiting for them there, but until they disembarked they could at least enjoy the ride despite the headaches.

Luca and Isabelle initially stared at Marta when she arrived in the inhuman Armor. Luca held his tongue at first, but eventually the silence was too much for the man. "We are truly blessed by Sol! That was like the fables of old. Gerjet, you were like Gerjet then!"

"Then does that make you my faithful dog, Baas?"

Marta aimed for a laugh with her retort, but found nothing humorous about her strange Armor. Luca's thoughts may have turned to the heroic Gerjet, but Marta's mind sought the stories of the Shaper Ernot. He was a terrible tyrant, said to be the consort of the fiendish Waer, whom he derived his unnatural Shaper abilities from. Ernot's Armor was no slow and ponderous thing like most Shapers, rather swift and vicious while protecting him from sword thrusts the same as any knight's metal armor would. The day before this Marta would have chided herself for having even entertained a children's tale like that, would have scowled at Luca's talk of Sol taking a hand in their fate.

She had seen the Black Breath with her own eyes though, and had watched it emerge from Underhill's body like some awful moth shedding its cocoon. The memory of it still sent shivers down her spine, and she clutched Caddie closer as if she could somehow protect the child from horrors such as these.

Marta must not have been minding her thoughts, because Luca said, "Ernot was a vile man, one of Waer's willing lovers. You may have darkness in you, Marta Childress, but there is some light as well, no matter how you try and hide it."

He again fell silent, only the whoosh of the turbines disturbing the stillness as they rode the next hour. Graff could still be watching them through his Blessed Breath, but it did not matter. They would jump from the train soon, far from his reach to continue their march east. The only question was where to disembark.

Their answer came around midnight in the form of the Old Channel Lake. Though they had no clock by which to mark the hour, it felt like a new day when they reached the boundary between West and East Neider. Somewhere below resided the invisible Mueller Line separating the West from East, and they passed over it without ever knowing when exactly.

Marta slowed the train again until it was scarcely crawling, waiting until they were almost to the Eastern edge of the lake before she scooped Caddie into her arms and jumped. The cold of the water washed the last remains of the ley headache away as she reached the shore. The last of the West was washed away as well when Marta stepped upon Eastern soil, Caddie's hand still in hers. Marta felt strange holding her such. Though she had often grasped the girl to direct her, this was the first time she did not believe she needed to just to make the girl move.

As they cleared the water, Luca and Isabelle not far behind them, Marta realized she had never told Caddie her name. The girl might have heard it from Luca's lips, but Marta could not be sure, so she decided it was time for a proper introduction. Hunkering down beside the sopping child, Marta took her hand again.

"I'm Marta Childress, and I'm going to take you to see your father."

Caddie stared back as dumbly as Marta had expected, but she also thought the girl grasped her hand a bit tighter. It was a step, but it was not yet quite enough for the woman.

"Now you need to introduce yourself to me. Go on, Caddie."

For a moment it looked like the girl would react, her mouth twitching as if to speak, but it faded as quickly as it began. Marta was not upset since what she had seen already was more progress from the child than she had ever expected. She was ready to straighten back up when she noticed Luca's bewildered stare.

"Ask her this time."

Marta thought the moment had already passed, Caddie only peeking her head out of her shell before retreating again, but Luca had earned her trust this night, and so she did as he said.

"Will you say hello, Caddie?"

"Caddie," the girl chirped, Marta unsure if she was answering her question or simply echoing the last word she heard. But it still felt momentous as the three surrounded her solemnly.

Marta decided such a big step deserved something to commemorate it, her thumb rubbing at her woven ring. It would be a dear gift to give up, but Marta had already parted with it twice before as she slipped the ring from her finger to place it on Caddie's.

"I'm very proud of you, Caddie, very pleased that you are here with me. You are a single gleaming gold strand in a world of dull silver."

If the girl treasured the gift, her face showed no sign, but she did not take her eyes from it as she slowly walked away. No one had told her where Ceilminster and her father resided, but Caddie plotted a path for the city sure as any compass.

Luca shot Marta a strange look before falling into step behind Caddie, Isabelle beside him as silent as a shadow. Alone, Marta watched them go, wondering if all four of them would be lucky enough reach their destination.

They were more than halfway there, Marta realized, Ceilminster only a few weeks away even on foot. Unfortunately, this half was made up of Covenant sympathizers who would happily slit her throat if they spied her traitor's brand, but that would not stop her as she hurried to catch up to the other three.

She had commemorated the child's progress with her own cherished ring, and so Marta reckoned her adult companions deserved something to mark the moment as well. Their reward came in the bottle Carmichael had gifted her with. It was originally meant as an insult, so she could not think of something more fitting to share with the agents he sent to aid her on her quest. Marta took the first swig of harsh whiskey before handing it on to Luca. The man delighted in the drink, taking a big swallow before handing it on to Isabelle. The half-Ingios woman took two pulls to his one before passing it back to Marta. And so they shared Carmichael's bounty between them.

As they headed on Luca examined his stolen fiddle. In time the wood might still warp from being dunked in the lake, but for now it was a fine instrument, especially considering what he had paid for it. He ignored the bow, instead plucking the strings with his fingertips. His first cord was the opening to "Joy and Ease," but he did not reach the second stanza before

Marta cut him off.

"Not that one. Play us something more fitting."

"Like what?"

The first strains of "The Sun Rises in the East" escaped Marta's lips before she was aware they were there. She had not sung since her capture, her voice as unfamiliar as a stranger's. Soon Luca joined in with his makeshift mandolin, Marta's tune strained, but serviceable. She might not sing like a mudbird anymore, but she certainly resembled one in her shabby state.

Families belong together," her father said at the start. She had not seen her family in over nine years, nine years of no one except for her hateful brother. Their family was no healthy thing, but it did not make her father any less right in his assessment.

Her thumb rubbed the space on her finger where her ring recently resided, and Marta decided it would have a happier home on Caddie's hand. In a way the girl reminded her of the damaged nation of Newfield. Both had gone through terrible trials, each left savaged and nearly crippled by their ordeals. The damage left deep scars, but if Caddie could make progress, perhaps there was hope for Newfield as well. Not long ago Marta had thought the nation a dying beast not long for the world, but perhaps it too could heal from its wounds and make its way whole again.

There would be no hope for Newfield if the Covenant Sons had their way though. Working with Orthoel Hendrix, they would usher a second Grand War, and such an outcome would be the death knell of the nation, no chance remaining for it after that. So to ensure its safety, Orthoel Hendrix would have to die by Marta's hands.

It was true she now cared for Caddie, the girl's improvement in their short time together inspiring her hope for the nation of Newfield again. And for that reason Marta would soon have to shatter all that headway by killing the girl's father. Peace could not be sustained while Orthoel Hendrix lived, Marta decided. She also swore she would do her best to ensure Caddie did not witness the murder of her father by the woman she had chosen as her protector. Marta would be quick and merciful about his assassination for the girl's sake.

She was not a monster after all.

Acknowledgments

To my family and friends, whose personalities I plundered mercilessly as I created my characters. To Sotiris, who offered some early encouragement, and to Will, who refused to tell me what I wanted to hear. To Ashish, whose notes and advice proved invaluable. And finally to my grammar guru Chris, whom will discover firsthand what an aneurism feels like when I say he made all my words sound real good.

About the Author

Never passing up the opportunity to speak about himself in the third person, M.D. Presley is not nearly as clever as he thinks he is. Born and raised in Texas, he spent several years on the East Coast and now waits for the West Coast to shake him loose. His favorite words include defenestrate, callipygian, and Algonquin. The fact that monosyllabic is such a long word keeps him up at night.

For more stories within the world of Ayr, please visit his website: www.mdpresley.com

16375125R00155

Printed in Great Britain
by Amazon